"A provocative, poignant look at marriage, money and the things that matter most."
—Beth Kendrick, author of *The Pre-nup*

JULIA DUNHILL, A THIRTYSOMETHING PARTY PLANNER, seems to have it all: Married to her high school sweetheart and living in a gorgeous home in Washington, D.C., she imagines her future unfolding very much as it has for the past few years, since she and her husband, Michael, successfully launched their companies. There will be dinner parties to attend, operas to dress up for, and weddings and benefits to organize for her growing list of clients. There will be shopping sprees with her best friend, Isabelle, and inevitably those last five pounds to shed. In her darker moments, she worries that her marriage has dissolved from a true partnership into a façade, but she convinces herself it's due to the intensity of their careers and fast-paced lifestyle.

So as she arranges the molten chocolate cupcakes for the annual opera benefit, how can she know that her carefully constructed world is about to fall apart? That her husband will stand up from the head of the table in his company's boardroom, open his mouth to speak, and crash to the carpeted floor . . . all in the amount of time it will take her to walk across a ballroom floor just a few miles away. Four minutes and eight seconds after his cardiac arrest, a portable defibrillator jump-starts Michael's heart. But in those lost minutes he becomes a different man, with an altered perspective on the rarefied life they've been living and a determination to regain the true intimacy they once shared. Now it is up to Julia to decide: Is it worth upending her comfortable world to try to find her way back to the husband she once adored, or should she walk away from this new Michael, who truthfully became a stranger to her long before his change of heart?

Also by Sarah Pekkanen

The Opposite of Me

Skipping
a
Beat

a novel

SARAH PEKKANEN

WASHINGTON SQUARE PRESS

New York London Toronto Sydney

WASHINGTON SQUARE PRESS
A Division of Simon & Schuster, Inc.
1230 Avenue of the Americas
New York, NY 10020

First Washington Square Press trade paperback edition February 2011

WASHINGTON SQUARE PRESS and colophon are registered trademarks
of Simon & Schuster, Inc.

For information about special discounts for bulk purchases,
please contact Simon & Schuster Special Sales at 1-866-506-1949
or business@simonandschuster.com.

The Simon & Schuster Speakers Bureau can bring authors to your
live event. For more information or to book an event contact the
Simon & Schuster Speakers Bureau at 1-866-248-3049 or visit
our website at www.simonspeakers.com.

Designed by Jill Putorti

Manufactured in the United States of America

10 9 8 7 6 5 4 3 2 1

Library of Congress Cataloging-in-Publication Data

Pekkanen, Sarah.
   Skipping a beat : a novel / Sarah Pekkanen. — 1st Washington Square Press
trade pbk. ed.
      p. cm.
   1. Spouses—Fiction. 2. Successful people—Fiction. 3. Life change events—
Fiction. 4. Downward mobility (Social sciences)—Fiction. 5. Marital conflict—
Fiction. 6. Quality of life—Fiction. 7. Washington (D.C.)—Fiction. I. Title.
   PS3616.E358S55 2011
   813'.6—dc22   2010026714

ISBN 978-1-4516-0982-0
ISBN 978-1-4516-0983-7 (ebook)

For my wonderful parents,
John and Lynn Pekkanen

Part One

One

WHEN MY HUSBAND, MICHAEL, died for the first time, I was walking across a freshly waxed marble floor in three-inch Stuart Weitzman heels, balancing a tray of cupcakes in my shaking hands.

Shaking because I'd overdosed on sugar—someone had to heroically step up and taste-test the cupcakes, after all—and not because I was worried about slipping and dropping the tray, even though these weren't your run-of-the-mill Betty Crockers. These were molten chocolate and cayenne-pepper masterpieces, and each one was topped with a name scripted in edible gold leaf.

Decadent cupcakes as place cards for the round tables encircling the ballroom—it was the kind of touch that kept me in brisk business as a party planner. Tonight, we'd raise half a million for the Washington, D.C., Opera Company. Maybe more, if the waiters kept topping off those wine and champagne glasses like I'd instructed them.

"Julia!"

I carefully set down the tray, then spun around to see the fretful face of the assistant florist who'd called my name.

"The caterer wants to lower our centerpieces," he wailed, agony practically oozing from his pores. I didn't blame him. His boss, the head florist—a gruff little woman with more than a hint of a mustache—secretly scared me, too.

"No one touches the flowers," I said, trying to sound as tough as Clint Eastwood would, should he ever become ensconced in a brawl over the proper length of calla lilies.

My cell phone rang and I reached for it, absently glancing at the caller ID. It was my husband, Michael. He'd texted me earlier to announce he was going on a business trip and would miss the birthday dinner my best friend was throwing for me later in the month. If Michael had a long-term mistress, it might be easier to compete, but his company gyrated and beckoned in his mind more enticingly than any strategically oiled Victoria's Secret model. I'd long ago resigned myself to the fact that work had replaced me as Michael's true love. I ignored the call and dropped the phone back into my pocket.

Later, of course, I'd realize it wasn't Michael phoning but his personal assistant, Kate. By then, my husband had stood up from the head of the table in his company's boardroom, opened his mouth to speak, and crashed to the carpeted floor. All in the same amount of time it took me to walk across a ballroom floor just a few miles away.

The assistant florist raced off and was instantly replaced by a white-haired, grandfatherly looking security guard from the Little Jewelry Box.

"Miss?" he said politely.

I silently thanked my oxygen facials and caramel highlights for his decision not to call me ma'am. I was about to turn thirty-five, which meant I wouldn't be able to hide from the liver-spotted hands of ma'am-dom forever, but I'd valiantly dodge their bony grasp for as long as possible.

"Where would you like these?" the guard asked, indicating the dozen or so rectangular boxes he was carrying on a tray draped in black velvet. The boxes were wrapped in a shade of silver that exactly matched the gun nestled against his ample hip.

"On the display table just inside the front door, please," I instructed him. "People need to see them as soon as they walk in." People would bid tens of thousands of dollars to win a surprise bauble, if only to show everyone else that they could. The guard was probably a retired policeman, trying to earn money to supplement his pension, and I knew he'd been ordered to keep those boxes in his sight all night long.

"Can I get you anything? Maybe some coffee?" I offered.

"Better not," he said with a wry smile. The poor guy probably wasn't drinking anything because the jewelry store wouldn't even let him take a bathroom break. I made a mental note to pack up a few dinners for him to bring home.

My BlackBerry vibrated just as I began placing the cupcakes around the head table and mentally debating the sticky problem of the video game guru who looked and acted like a thirteen-year-old overdue for his next dose of Ritalin. I'd sandwich him between a female U.S. senator and a co-owner of the Washington Blazes professional basketball team, I decided. They were both tall; they could talk over the techie's head.

At that moment, a dozen executives were leaping up from their leather chairs to cluster around Michael's limp body. They were all shouting at each other to call 911—this crowd was used to giving orders, not taking them—and demanding that someone perform CPR.

As I stood in the middle of the ballroom, smoothing out a crease on a white linen napkin and inhaling the sweet scent of lilies, the worst news I could possibly imagine was being delivered by a baby-faced representative from the D.C. Opera Company.

"Melanie has a sore throat," he announced somberly.

I sank into a chair with a sigh and wiggled my tired feet out of my shoes. Perfect. Melanie was the star soprano who was scheduled to sing a selection from *Orfeo ed Euridice* tonight. If those overflowing wineglasses didn't get checkbooks whipped out of pockets, Melanie's soaring, lyrical voice definitely would. I desperately needed Melanie tonight.

"Where is she?" I demanded.

"In a room at the Mayflower Hotel," the opera rep said.

"Oh, crap! Who booked her a room?"

"Um . . . me," he said. "Is that a prob—"

"Get her a suite," I interrupted. "The biggest one they have."

"Why?" he asked, his snub nose wrinkling in confusion. "How will that help her get better?"

"What was your name again?" I asked.

"Patrick Riley."

Figures; put a four-leaf clover in his lapel and he could've been the poster boy for *Welcome to Ireland*!

"And Patrick, how long have you been working for the opera company?" I asked gently.

"Three weeks," he admitted.

"Just trust me on this." Melanie required drama the way the rest of us needed water. If I hydrated her with a big scene now, Melanie might miraculously rally and forgo a big scene tonight.

"Send over a warm-mist humidifier," I continued as Patrick whipped out a notebook and scribbled away, diligent as a cub reporter chasing his big break. "No, two! Get her lozenges, chamomile tea with honey, whatever you can think of. Buy out CVS. If Melanie wants a lymphatic massage, have the hotel concierge arrange it immediately. Here—" I pulled out my BlackBerry and scrolled down to the name of my private doctor.

"Call Dr. Rushman. If he can't make it over there, have him send someone who can."

Dr. Rushman would make it, I was sure. He'd drop whatever he was doing if he knew I needed him. He was the personal physician for the Washington Blazes basketball team.

My husband, Michael, was another one of the team's co-owners.

"Got it," Patrick said. He glanced down at my feet, turned bright red, and scampered away. Must've been my toe cleavage; it tends to have that effect on men.

I finished placing the final cupcake before checking my messages. By the time I read the frantic e-mails from Kate, who was trying to find out if Michael had any recently diagnosed illnesses like epilepsy or diabetes that we'd been keeping secret, it was already over.

While Armani-clad executives clustered around my husband, Bob the mail-room guy took one look at the scene and sped down the hallway, white envelopes scattering like confetti behind him. He sprinted to the receptionist's desk and found the portable defibrillator my husband's company had purchased just six months earlier. Then he raced back, ripped open Michael's shirt, put his ear to Michael's chest to confirm that my husband's heart had stopped beating, and applied the sticky patches to Michael's chest. "Analyzing . . . ," said the machine's electronic voice. "Shock advisable."

The Italian opera *Orfeo ed Euridice* is a love story. In it, Euridice dies and her grieving husband travels to the Underworld to try to bring her back to life. Melanie the soprano was scheduled to sing the heartbreaking aria that comes as Euridice is suspended between the twin worlds of Death and Life.

Maybe it shouldn't have surprised me that Euridice's aria was playing in my head as Bob the mail-room guy bent over my husband's body, shocking Michael's heart until it finally began beating again. Because sometimes, it seems to me as if all of the big moments in my life can be traced back to the gorgeous, timeworn stories of opera.

Four minutes and eight seconds. That's how long my husband, Michael Dunhill, was dead.

Four minutes and eight seconds. That's how long it took for my husband to become a complete stranger to me.

Two

MICHAEL AND I PROBABLY wouldn't ever have fallen in love if it hadn't been for a violent man who'd just been released from prison, a little girl in a wheelchair, and the fact that Michael was constantly—almost savagely—hungry.

As a teenager, Michael could wolf down a gallon of ice cream like a pre-dinner hors d'oeuvre, and his slim-cut Lee jeans *still* bagged around his waist. I know a lot of women in D.C. who'd trade their summer homes for a chance to revel in that spectacular metabolism.

I'd always known who Michael was, of course. In the small town in West Virginia where we both grew up, it was impossible for anyone to be a stranger. By the way, my husband and I aren't first cousins, and we've both got full sets of teeth. I've heard all the West Virginia jokes by now, but I still toss back my head and laugh harder than anyone else at them. If I don't, people think I'm grumpy *and* a hick, even if I'm draped from head to toe in Chanel and I've just had my eyebrows professionally shaped. Which I now do, every three weeks, even though I can't believe I'm spending as much to bully a few hairs into submission as my mother used to for an entire year's worth of perms and trims at Brenda's Cut and Curl.

We were Mike and Julie back then—by now we've upgraded our names along with everything else about us—and although our paths crossed almost daily, we never really spoke until that spring afternoon. I was sixteen years old, and I was walking along the railroad tracks to my after-school job as a babysitter for sweet Becky Hendrickson, who'd been paralyzed from the waist down in a car accident a few years earlier. It was warm and sunny, the kind of afternoon that arrives like a surprise gift after winter's dark shadows and icy toes. I walked quickly, swinging a plastic bag in my right hand, hoping the two half gallons of strawberry and chocolate wouldn't melt before I reached Becky. That eleven-year-old kid liked ice cream more than anyone I'd ever met.

"What's the rush, sweetheart?"

The man seemed to materialize from out of nowhere, like a ghost. One minute I was looking down at the parallel wooden tracks stretching in front of me; the next, I was staring at a pair of scuffed yellow work boots planted in my path. I raised my eyes to see the man's face.

I was wrong; there was a stranger in my little town, after all.

He appeared to be in his early twenties. His long-sleeved shirt was hiked up to reveal strong-looking biceps, and his blond hair was cut so short I could see the white of his scalp shining through. Some girls might've found him good-looking, might've even mistaken the coldness in his face for strength, if they'd met him in the safety of a crowded party or bar.

"School out already?" the man asked, slinging his thumb through a belt loop on his jeans.

"Um-hmm." I nodded, but I didn't move. Instinctively, I knew that if I tried to go around him, he'd strike as quickly as a snake.

"Seems a little early for school to get out," he said, winking. "Sure you're not cutting class?"

Our voices were having one conversation; our eyes and bodies, entirely another. Adrenaline rushed my veins while I considered and discarded plans: *Don't run; he'll catch you. Don't scream; he'll attack. Don't fight; you can't win.* Something about the way his eyes appraised me told me he knew what I was thinking. And he was enjoying watching my escape options dwindle.

"I'm not cutting," I said. My senses snapped into high gear. A few feet away, a small animal rustled through the bushes and tall grass that lined the tracks. The plastic bag in my hand slowly stopped swinging, like a pendulum winding down. I fought the urge to look around to see if anyone was coming; I couldn't turn my back on this man for an instant.

"See, back when I went to Wilson, I could've sworn we got out at two-thirty," the man said. He slid his thumb out of his belt loop and moved a step closer to me. It took everything I had not to match his movement with a step back.

"It's almost three now," I said, forcing the words out through my throat, which had gone tight and dry. That scar on the man's right temple, combined with something about his voice—which was oddly high-pitched—suddenly revealed his identity. Jerry Knowles, the older brother of my classmate John, who had the same cartoon-character voice. Jerry had spent the last four years in state prison for stealing a car and fighting with the police officers who arrested him. It took a nightstick to the temple to finally subdue Jerry, who was getting the best of the two cops. At least that's what the kids in school always said.

"So you're not skipping school," he said, his voice teasing. Another step closer. "I didn't think you looked like a bad girl."

"I—I need to go to work," I said. My heart pounded so hard it felt like it would explode through the front of my chest.

Another slow, deliberate step.

He was so close now; I could see his scar was starfish-shaped and slightly raised, like he hadn't gotten stitches to pull the broken skin together into a straight line.

"They're waiting for me," I whispered desperately. "They'll come looking for me."

That's when he took one last step. He reached out a finger to stroke my cheek. I couldn't move, couldn't talk, couldn't even breathe. His finger felt hot and rough against my skin. It moved lower, to trace my collarbone.

"Funny, you don't look like a high school girl either," he said as his finger dipped into my cleavage. Jerry was done toying with me. Now he'd reveal the real reason why he'd stopped me. My body's adrenaline took charge, screaming that I had to escape, *now*. I twisted around to run, but Jerry caught me from behind before I'd gone five yards.

"Someone's in a hurry," he said and then laughed, crushing my upper arms between his big hands as his body rubbed up against mine. His breath felt hot against my cheek and smelled sour. My legs went limp with terror.

"Let's take a little walk," Jerry said. Somehow that high, squeaky voice was more frightening than a shout. He forced me off the path, into a cluster of bushes.

"Get down," Jerry said, pushing me roughly to the ground. He leaned over me, in a push-up position, trapping me between his forearms. It was so quiet that Jerry's ragged exhales exploded in my ears. I was vaguely aware of a rock bruising my shoulder blade, but the pain didn't even register.

"Lift up your shirt," Jerry ordered me.

Should I obey or defy him? Which would be worse?

Do what he says, instinct warned me. *Don't make him angry.*

I hiked up my blouse, but only a few inches. My hand froze and I couldn't lift it any higher. Why did it have to be so warm today? I wondered desperately. Why did I have to be wearing this thin shirt instead of a bulky sweater and coat?

"Please," I whispered.

"Please what?" Jerry asked.

"Please don't," I begged.

Jerry leaned closer to me. His flat eyes bore into mine. "Lift up your fucking shirt," he said, spraying flecks of spit on my checks with each *f*.

Then I heard something—the crunch of a twig under someone's shoe.

"Get off her!"

I registered a blur from the left as a guy leapt onto Jerry's back and punched him in the head. Jerry released me and spun around, shaking the guy off.

"Run, Julie!"

It was Mike Dunhill, the skinny boy in my class whose hand always shot up before the teachers finished asking questions.

I jumped up and started to run, to get help, but a sickening sound made me turn around. Mike was already on the ground, and Jerry was kicking him. Jerry must've weighed twice as much as Mike, and he was in a fury. Mike was going to get hurt, bad, unless I did something now. I didn't even remember that I was still holding the bag of ice cream until I reached into it and sent a half gallon of Breyers strawberry sailing toward Jerry's head.

If the ice cream had been frozen, it probably wouldn't have stopped Jerry. He was obviously a man who could take a hit. But that unseasonably warm day turned out to be a gift in more ways than one. The lid flew off, and the softened pink ice cream spattered across Jerry's face and eyes. He stood there, temporarily blinded, his foot raised for another kick. That was all the opening Mike needed. He uncoiled and grabbed Jerry's ankle, yanking him off-balance. As Jerry tumbled backward, Mike sprang up, as if he hadn't been hurt at all, and shot out the side of his hand to clip Jerry in the throat, hard.

"Run!" Mike shouted again, and this time, I obeyed. Together, we sprinted another fifty yards down the track, cut left onto the dirt path leading to Becky's neighborhood, and wove through the streets for a quarter mile, until we'd reached her little single-story brick house. I jabbed her doorbell over and over again, stealing glances behind me, certain Jerry would appear from out of nowhere again.

"Hang on! Geez!"

The door opened agonizingly slowly. Mike and I burst inside, breathing hard.

"What's wrong?" Becky's mother asked while I slammed the door shut and double-locked it.

"It's okay," Mike said. He bent over and put his hands on his knees as he sucked in great gulps of air. "He didn't follow us . . . I checked."

"Who?" Becky's mother asked, looking back and forth from Mike to me. "Are you guys playing a game?"

Tears flooded my eyes as I remembered Jerry's cold smile, and his lazy, insistent finger tracing a hot trail across my skin. Suddenly my stomach lurched and I almost gagged.

Then Mike saved me for a second time.

"All the books I've read about self-defense," he said, grinning at me, "and not one of them mentioned the dreaded ice-cream counterattack. Do you have to be a black belt for that?"

We stared at each other for a second, then started laughing. Mike clutched his ribs and tears ran down my cheeks as we both leaned against the wall, unable to talk.

"Guess you had to be there." Becky's mother shrugged, walking away. That made us laugh even harder, howling and bending over and gasping for breath. And when we finally stopped laughing, I reached into the bag and pulled out the half-melted carton of chocolate ice cream that I'd somehow held on to the entire time.

"Are you hungry?" I asked Mike.

A slow grin spread across his face. "Starving."

I pretended to be fine, and even though I was so jittery my skin felt electric, I must've done a pretty good job, because I convinced Becky's mom it was okay for her to go to her afternoon shift at the pharmacy. The sheriff was on his way to take my statement, and Mike offered to stick around, in case he could answer any questions. But I sensed the real reason why Mike hadn't left was that he knew I was terrified Jerry would somehow spring out from behind the shower curtain the moment I was alone.

I was looking out the window while Becky chattered on about the new Nancy Drew mystery she'd checked out of the library, and I didn't see Mike take our ice-cream bowls to the kitchen. When he suddenly clattered them into the sink, I spun around, my heart nearly convulsing in panic.

"Sorry," he said, even before he looked at my white face. I nodded and swallowed hard.

"So here's the thing." He leaned back against the kitchen counter and casually folded his arms. "All those mysteries Nancy stumbles across? She's like, what, seventeen? Don't you guys think it's a little suspicious that she's already solved a hundred crimes? Shouldn't somebody be investigating *Nancy*?"

I forced a smile, even though my lips felt cold and stiff. "Are you accusing Nancy of exaggerating? Careful; she's Becky's hero, and she used to be mine, too."

Mike raised his hands so his palms were facing me. "I'm just saying *someone* seems to need a little more attention than the average seventeen-year-old. Sure, Daddy bought her a snappy little roadster, but apparently he doesn't care that she's dropped out of school."

I nudged him with my shoulder and managed a smile. A bit later, when Becky was drinking a glass of water and accidentally spilled a few drops onto the table, I watched as Mike reached over, casually wiped it up with his sleeve, and winked at her without missing a beat in his blistering imitation of our chemistry teacher, who seemed to hate not only teenagers but also chemistry and small towns (it probably wasn't the best idea to give a lone white male with anger issues free access to combustible elements, but it's not like we had a lot of teachers to pick and choose from).

Up until then, everything I knew about Mike came from the whispering I'd overheard. *The mother just up and left,* Brenda had told a customer through the bobby pins she held in one corner of her mouth while she fashioned an upsweep. *Course, I might, too, if I was married to that S.O.B. But can you imagine leaving your childr——* Then Brenda had caught sight of my wide eyes and quickly begun talking about the new yellow Lab puppy she'd just adopted.

It was the blessing and the curse of a small town; most people knew you, but everyone thought they knew all about you. Yet I hadn't understood the first thing about Mike.

Later that day, as he walked me home from Becky's, he acted nonchalant, but his eyes swept from side to side more vigilantly than any Secret Service agent's. A few times he even spun around to look behind us. No one would ever sneak up on me with him around, I realized, and for what seemed to be the first time in a long, long while, I breathed deeply and felt my hands uncurl out of fists at my sides.

"Becky was in a car accident, right?" Mike asked as we turned the corner onto my street. It was dusk by now, but the day still held on to some of its earlier warmth, and a few yellow crocuses bloomed like little spots of hope in the yards we passed. "I remember hearing about it."

"Yeah," I said. "Her mom was driving, and it was icy out, and they skidded into a tree. She wasn't speeding or anything. It was just one of those awful things."

We reached my house, and Mike walked me up our concrete front steps. Most of the homes in our town were small but tidy, with neat yards and bright flower bed borders and trimmed hedges. Mine used to be, too, but now the gutters were still clogged with fall leaves and a shutter had come loose and was leaning there lopsidedly, like a party guest trying to hide the fact that he'd had a few too many martinis.

I paused on the top step. I hated to be rude, but I couldn't risk inviting Mike inside. Not even after everything we'd been through together. Mike glanced at the front door, then at me, but he didn't say anything. Maybe he already knew; most people did by now.

"Is Becky going to walk again?" Mike asked, casually sitting down and leaning back on his elbows as he stretched out his legs, like it was completely natural to carry on our conversation out here rather than inside.

"She thinks she will," I said as I plopped down next to him. "But I don't know what the doctors say."

"Jesus." Mike let out his breath in a long, whooshing sound, then winced and clutched his side, despite his claims that his ribs didn't hurt. "Being in a wheelchair is the worst thing I could imagine. I'd go crazy."

"I guess you don't know until it happens," I said. "Becky handles it really well, especially for a kid."

"No. I'd go crazy, Julie," he repeated. "To not be able to move? To have to depend on other people for help?"

He suddenly sprang up and shifted his weight from one foot

to the other, like he was reassuring himself he could still control his body. Mike was in constant motion. I hadn't noticed it at school, but that afternoon I saw: His leg jiggled, or his fingertips thrummed a beat on a table, or his hand wove endless paths through his curly, dark hair. That was probably how he stayed so skinny, despite the fact that he'd gobbled most of the ice cream and raided the refrigerator to make himself two turkey-and-cheese sandwiches at Becky's.

Already, I was learning his mind was as hungry as his body. Mike told me he'd read half a dozen books about self-defense, not because he was worried about being attacked but because he read *everything*. That's how he knew about the vulnerable spot in the middle of the throat: Hitting it hard enough with the side of a rigid hand would stun just about any assailant.

Mike tore through his homework, devoured books at the library, and gobbled up newspapers and biographies of business leaders and World Book encyclopedias. He even read the ingredient lists on the packages of everything he ate (alas, this little habit of his ruined my love affair with hot pink Hostess Sno Balls). He'd skipped third grade, and he'd completed all the high school math courses by the end of tenth grade.

Everything about Mike was quick. Weeks later, when I lay my head on his bare chest for the first time, I thought he was nervous because I could feel his heart beating so rapidly. But that was his normal heart rate; Mike was just wired differently than anyone I'd ever met.

Maybe I would've fallen in love with Mike anyways, because of the unexpected parts of himself that he'd revealed the day Jerry attacked me: his bravery, and the way he'd joked about how brilliant I'd been to hang on to the chocolate ice cream: "I mean, if you're going to use something as a weapon, for God's sakes, use the strawberry! Strawberry's kind of scrappy, but chocolate's too mellow. It's always getting stoned and sitting around listening to Led Zeppelin. You never want chocolate to have your back in a fight."

But there was something else—something he said that day on my front steps—that seemed to pierce me all the way to my core.

Mike frowned at the horizon, as if it wasn't really me he was speaking to. "Someday I'm going to have enough money to do whatever I want. I'm going to have my own company, and my own house, too, not something the bank owns. I'm not going to end up in this crummy town like everyone else. *Nothing's* going to stop me."

I stared at him, unable to speak. Mike had just put into words everything *I* desperately wanted, like he'd peered into my brain and scooped out my deepest, most secret wish. It wasn't so much the money, though at that point I couldn't even imagine owning a house. Funny, because now we have two—in D.C. and in Aspen, Colorado. But the security that came along with money . . . well, I ached for it. The sick, unsteady feeling I'd had ever since my dad had changed—the sense that quicksand was inching closer and closer to me, biding its time before it could suck me down and cover my head and suffocate me—disappeared as Mike spoke.

I looked at him, this scrawny, twitchy guy with crazy curls and jeans with a ragged hole in the knee, and a rush of certainty enveloped me like a warm blanket: With Mike, I'd always be safe, in every way possible.

"See you in school tomorrow?" he asked.

"Yeah," I said. "We've got that history test."

He nodded, then looked down at his feet. "You always sit by the window, right?"

"Right," I said, surprised.

"Except last week." He took a deep breath, like he was gathering himself, then lifted his blue, almond-shaped eyes to meet mine. "Shelby Rowan took your seat first. You looked at her for a second, then you went to the back row. You were wearing a white sweater that day."

I stared at him, speechless. Mike had been watching me? He remembered what I wore? He hadn't shown any fear when he attacked Jerry, but right now, he looked nervous. He was worried about my reaction, I realized with a jolt.

"You sit in the front row, too, right?" I finally said.

Mike shook his head. "I'm right behind you, Julie. I always have been."

Like today, when I desperately needed him there.

I felt a hot rush of shame. "Sorry."

Mike shrugged, but I saw hurt flash across his face. "If you don't play football, no one notices you. God, I hate high school. Do you know how many days until we graduate? Four hundred and thirty-eight if you count holidays and weekends and summer vacation. I've been counting down for years."

It was true; our school did revolve around football, and half the town came out for the Friday night games. Suddenly I remembered: Mike had two older brothers. And they'd both played football; I'd heard their names being chanted by cheerleaders during games.

"I'll save you a seat tomorrow," I blurted.

"Good," Mike said, and then he smiled. His teeth were a little crooked, but on him it was appealing. "I should get going. Will you be okay?"

I nodded. "The sheriff said Jerry's probably already left town. Apparently he was planning on leaving anyway. He just ran into me first. So"—I gave a tight little laugh—"I don't have anything to worry about."

But I was still scared. The touch of that finger was seared into my skin like a burn. And somehow, Mike knew.

The next morning at seven-thirty, he was outside my house with his overstuffed backpack on his thin shoulders, waiting to walk me to school. From then on, we were inseparable.

"High school sweethearts?" people always exclaim after they ask how we met. "How wonderful!"

And it was. For a long time, at least, it really was.

Three

THE FIRST PERSON I saw after I whipped through the hospital's revolving door made me want to spin right back around onto the sidewalk. Dale, the top lawyer for Michael's company, had planted himself in the middle of the lobby, next to a young couple holding a screeching newborn baby. I didn't blame the baby; Dale had that effect on me, too.

Maybe if I ducked my head and sprinted—

"Hi, Julia."

"Oh, Dale!" I squeaked. "I didn't see you there!"

Did the Learning Annex offer a course in the art of the convincing lie? I really needed to take one; even the bobble-headed baby seemed to pause between outraged wails and give me the stink eye.

"Where's Michael?" I asked. I'd talked to Kate on the drive over, and she'd reassured me that Michael was awake and talking. "He won't *stop* talking," Kate had said with a laugh. "That's how I know he's okay."

Still, there was something in her voice, some off note . . .

"Hang on a second." Dale reached out and grabbed my forearm. I looked down at his thick fingers with the coarse black hairs on the knuckles and remembered the fancy dinner party when I'd knocked my glass of '82 burgundy all over a snow white tablecloth. Dale had chortled, "You can take the girl out of West Virginia, but you can't take West Virginia out of the girl." I'd laughed along with the rest of the table, but for the balance of the night, I kept catching myself twisting a lock of my hair around my right index finger. It was a nervous habit from childhood that I'd finally broken in my twenties.

"Which way is he?" I asked, wrenching my arm away and suppressing a shudder.

Dale ignored my question. "There's something you should know." His eyes darted around furtively, as though spies might be lurking everywhere in candy striper uniforms. "Michael is . . . well, he's . . ."

"What?" I asked impatiently. "He's conscious, right? He's okay now."

"Yeah, but . . ." Dale's voice trailed off again.

Sheesh, you'd think Dale was the one who'd toppled over in the conference room and conked his head on the floor. Not that I was taking any satisfaction from that image. Nor was I embroidering it to include someone sitting astride Dale's chest and slapping his cheeks to revive him—*violently* slapping; Dale would stubbornly remain unconscious for quite a while . . .

Priorities, I reminded myself. "Dale, where is he?"

Dale sighed, like I was thwarting his attempts to make pleasant conversation possible, and pointed to a hallway. "He's in the Cardiac Care Unit."

I hurried down the long corridor, my shoes briskly tapping against the linoleum as I followed the signs posted on the walls. Finally I found the heavy gray swinging door leading to the CCU. I lifted my hand to push it open, then froze.

I hadn't stopped moving, hadn't even stopped to think, since I'd seen the flurry of messages on my BlackBerry. After begging

Patrick the blusher to cover the fund-raiser, I'd leapt into the car Kate had sent over with Michael's driver. During the ride to the hospital, I'd talked nonstop with Kate, who'd filled me in on all the details. She'd used the office phone to call 911 as soon as he hit the floor, and when Michael was revived, the dispatcher marked the time, so doctors would know how long he was without oxygen. I was still marveling at Kate's ability to juggle the 911 operator while sending me text messages from Michael's BlackBerry *and* using his cell phone—sometimes I was convinced she had more than the usual allotment of fingers and thumbs, not to mention brains. Then again, Michael needed an extraordinary assistant to keep up with him. He'd gone through seven before finding Kate.

Now, the empty hospital corridor felt too quiet, and my stomach clenched up like a fist. The antiseptic smell—Lysol, probably, mixed in with some bleach—filled my nose and mouth and lungs and made it difficult to breathe. The shaky tone in Kate's voice, Dale's hesitation . . . exactly what was waiting for me on the other side of that door?

I heard Dale walk up behind me, and I snapped out of it, pushing through the door a little too quickly. I nearly bumped into a pretty, dark-haired nurse who was frowning down at a clipboard as she headed toward a circular workstation in the middle of the large room.

"I'm Michael Dunhill's wife," I began.

"Oh!" the nurse said, nearly dropping her clipboard. She quickly looked me up and down, which I'm used to by now. Lots of women check me out to see what kind of woman a man like Michael, who could presumably have anyone, chose to marry. I automatically sucked in and straightened up, hearing the voice of the image consultant I'd hired in a moment of insecurity reverberate in my brain: *A string is pulling the top of your head toward the ceiling! Do you feel it, darling? Stretch, stretch!* If anything, the image consultant—bronzed, whippet-thin, and a perfect advertisement for her own services—had sent me scurrying toward my secret stash of Sara Lee in the freezer faster than ever. No, I'm definitely not a trophy wife, even though I've shed a size and become two shades blonder since leaving West Virginia. On my best days, I'm more like a bronze medal wife.

"Mr. Dunhill is in that room, but if you want to talk to the chief of cardiology first, I can call him." The nurse gestured toward one of the small rooms that ringed the unit. Through the glass wall, I could see Michael lying on a narrow cot, covered by a stark white sheet and surrounded by hulking gray machines.

Something is wrong. The panicked thought roared through my mind until I realized what it was: I just wasn't used to seeing Michael lying down.

I needed to get a grip or I'd probably end up lying on the bed next to Michael, and I wasn't even wearing nice underwear, like generations of mothers have ordered us to do in case of just such a scenario. I was wearing a girdle. Sure, it had a cute name (Spanx) and came in fun colors and was advertised by skinny, playful women, but I wasn't fooled. Anything squeezing me this tightly was either a hungry python or an old-fashioned, no-nonsense, kill-the-evidence-of-those–Sara Lee–cakes girdle.

"I'd like to talk to the doctor first," I said, and the nurse pressed a button on a phone and spoke quietly into it.

"Mrs. Dunhill?" A short, slim man in a white coat came through the swinging door moments later. "I'm Walter Kim, chief of cardiology. I'm overseeing your husband's care."

I couldn't help wondering if he'd have shown up so quickly if Michael had been, say, a garbageman instead of one of the hospital's big donors. "Did he have a heart attack?" I asked. "They just told me he collapsed . . ."

Dr. Kim shook his head. "Michael suffered a cardiac arrest. His heart simply stopped beating. We don't know why. Sometimes it happens out of the blue to healthy, young people. The heart's electrical circuitry just misfires."

"But he's okay now," I said. "He's fine, right?"

The doctor hesitated. "We're monitoring him closely, and we'll need to keep him here for a while. But yes, it seems he was one of the lucky ones. He was clinically dead for more than four minutes, but I've seen cases where people have been in full cardiac arrest for as long as six or seven minutes, and they've been fine. Other patients have suffered some brain damage after less than two minutes. Everyone comes out of something like this differently."

"He just bought that defibrillator a few months ago," I said, shaking my head.

"Good for him," Dr. Kim said. He cleared his throat. "Anyway, I'm sure you're eager to see him now."

"Right." I smiled and slowly walked into the room.

"Hi, honey," I said, moving to Michael's side. I'd gone for a cheery, confident tone, like a junior high school soccer coach might use during halftime to rally the troops, but my voice came out too loudly in the sterile white room, and I flinched.

I reached for Michael's hand, which felt warm. Strange, because the room was cool. An oxygen tube ran into his nose, and a few wires snaked from under his gown to a big heart monitor machine next to his bed.

"How are you feeling?" I asked.

"At least I wasn't attacked by a vicious carton of ice cream," Michael said. Then he winked.

I blinked in surprise. It was our old private joke, the one that had grown dusty from neglect. We used to whisper it whenever we were given a pop quiz in school, or when we ended up sitting next to half-deaf Roy Samuels and his wife— who obligingly stage-whispered the dialogue—at our town's lone movie theater. But we hadn't repeated our joke in . . . how long?

I stared at Michael. He wasn't demanding his cell phone, or railing at having to stay in bed, or clicking through endless e-mails on his BlackBerry. Even when Michael had a raging case of the flu two years ago, he'd dragged himself into work while the poor interns raced around squirting Purell on everything he touched.

For the first time in my memory, my husband was absolutely still.

"I love you," Michael said. He stared meaningfully into my eyes while he said it and squeezed my hand.

I glanced at the nurse refilling Michael's jug of water, and Dale standing vigil in the corner, not even pretending not to eavesdrop. Everyone was staring back at me. Was it because I looked as stunned as I felt, or . . . oh, my God!

"I—I love you, too," I responded belatedly. The words felt rusty and awkward in my mouth. Why was Michael looking at me so adoringly? Was he putting on a show for the nurse in case she talked to the press? I felt wooden and self-conscious, like I was on a movie set and the cameras were rolling but no one had given me my lines. How was I supposed to act?

"They need to keep me here for a few days," Michael said.

"I know," I said, relief gushing through me as I latched on to something practical to talk about. "Is that okay? Because we can get Dr. Rushman here in a minute, and maybe he can override—"

Michael squeezed my hand again, and I stopped babbling. "It's fine." His eyes stayed fixed on mine. Those blue eyes were among the few remaining parts of the skinny teenage boy he'd once been. His thick curls were meticulously shaped now, and his teeth were bonded and whitened. Michael was still thin—still twitchy, too, and he always ate like every meal was Thanksgiving—but protein shakes and daily workouts with his personal trainer had broadened his shoulders and chest with a layer of muscle.

"I'll bring in a laptop," Dale said. He glanced around and snorted, not unlike, say, a large farm animal, if one were pressed to come up with an example off the top of one's head. "Have you moved to a nicer room, too."

"It's not necessary," Michael said. "But thank you."

There was another uncomfortable silence; at least, I was uncomfortable. Michael was stretched out like a sunbather on a Caribbean beach. All he needed was to trade in his IV for a fruity drink with a little umbrella.

"I should run home and get your toiletries and a robe," I said when the silence had stretched out too long. "Is there anything else you need?"

Michael shook his head. He was smiling a dreamy, private smile, like someone had just whispered a delicious secret into his ear.

"It's amazing how little I need," he said. "Why didn't I ever realize that before?"

Dale theatrically cleared his throat.

I get it, Dale, I thought in exasperation. So Michael was acting oddly—there had to be a simple explanation. Maybe he'd been medicated; the faraway look on his face was probably the work of Valium. God knows, every time I swallowed a Valium before an airline flight, I became as loopy as a clown at a kiddie birthday party. That could explain all the moony looks Michael was giving me, too.

Except—why would they give him Valium for cardiac arrest?

"So I'll just go get your things," I repeated, then cringed as I heard how eager my voice sounded.

"Hurry back, okay?" Michael said. "We have so much to talk about. So much."

His eyes hadn't left my face the entire time I'd been in the room, and by now I felt almost frantic. The man lying in bed looked like my husband, but he was an impostor.

"Be right back," I promised Michael. My hand slid away from his and I walked to the door, feeling guilty about the relief that flooded through me as I put space between us.

One thing I've learned about opera is that it's synonymous with passion. It's in the tremulous power of the violins, the lines of the libretto, the crash of fingers against piano keys, and the impossible arc of the soprano's aria. Some of my favorites—*La Bohème, Fidelio, La Traviata*—tell the story of lovers who defy jealous rivals, or scheming interlopers, or layers upon layers of misunderstandings and lies, to end up together against all odds. Even if the ending is sad—and it often is, because death is almost always a main character in operas—it's bittersweet, because love usually triumphs.

But one opera is different. In Rossini's *Barber of Seville,* a beautiful young woman named Rosina is wooed by Count Almaviva. The Count doesn't want Rosina to love him for his title alone, so he pretends he's a drunken soldier (because obviously women can't resist *them*). Later the Count, who could clearly use a few tips from eHarmony, dons another disguise and tries to pass himself off as a substitute music teacher for Rosina. Finally she discovers who he is and agrees to marry him, defying the creepy older guy who wanted her. She and the Count are blissfully happy. But unlike other opera characters, they aren't left frozen in time when the curtain drops.

Mozart picked up their story years later in an opera called *The Marriage of Figaro*. By now, the Count and Rosina have been married for years. The passion they once shared is gone. The magic has evaporated from their marriage, and they barely talk to each other.

I adore Mozart, but I no longer go to see that opera.

Four

KATE HAD DONE IT again. Just as the elevator doors opened and I stepped into the hospital's lobby, I received her text message telling me she'd arranged to have my Jaguar brought to the hospital's parking lot and the keys left at the admissions desk. Whatever Michael paid her, it wasn't enough.

For just an instant, I imagined turning the wrong way out of the parking lot and speeding toward the highway. Any highway, it didn't matter which one. I had a few hundred dollars in my wallet, enough to see me through a week or two's worth of driving if I wanted to stay anonymous and not leave a credit card trail. I could roll down the windows and blare the radio and keep the ball of my foot pressed hard to the gas pedal. There wouldn't be room for anything else in the cocoon of my car, not even the icy sensation that something was coming, something I wouldn't be able to outrun.

I sighed and turned the key in the ignition, feeling my sedan leap to life with a gentle purr. Bad enough that I'd almost forgotten to answer Michael when he told me he loved me. If I went on the lam now, I'd never be named Wife of the Year.

Traffic was light, which was unheard of for D.C., even in the middle of the day, and soon I was heading down our driveway, which was flanked by tall pine trees for privacy. I used my remote control to open our security gate, then left my car parked by our outdoor fountain and hurried to unlock our front door. It took me two tries; my hands were trembling again, even though my sugar buzz from the cupcakes had worn off long ago.

I stepped inside and turned off the alarm as my eyes drank in the bright, abstract artwork on the walls of our entranceway, and I felt the tension in my neck and shoulders ease just a bit. Every time I entered this house, I felt like a guest at the most outrageous hotel imaginable. Maybe that was because I *was* a sort of guest: Michael had paid for it, and a team of decorators had picked out everything from the colors on the walls to the throw pillows on the couches. The decorators had driven us nuts—I'm still awed by their level of excitement about the merits of ivory versus buff-colored swatches—but in the end, they'd delivered exactly what they'd promised. It wasn't a house; it was a showplace, filled with air and light and enormous walls of glass. Massive art deco–inspired chandeliers hung from two-story-high ceilings, and our gleaming main dining room table stretched out far enough to seat twenty-four. Both of our kitchens—the large caterers' one on the main level, and a smaller private one upstairs—were awash in rich granites and copper, and our six bathrooms shone with details like hand-painted tiles and detached glass bowl sinks. "Suitable for embassy-style entertaining," our real estate agent had murmured, gesturing toward the grand rooms, as if we might suddenly decide to stage a violent coup against the ambassador to Sweden.

Michael had kept his vow to succeed, and then some: The little company he'd started in our cramped old apartment's galley kitchen—all-natural, low-sugar, flavored bottles of water—had netted him more than $70 million after its stock went public, just before competitors like Vitaminwater and Smartwater burst onto the scene.

Seventy million dollars. It was impossible to wrap my mind around it—kind of like the reaction I had to black holes in space, or the principles of aerodynamics, or tenth-grade geometry.

But success hadn't slowed Michael down even for a moment. He was branching into new products, like organic energy bars and prepackaged, food-pyramid-friendly kids' lunches, and now it looked like they might someday become as valuable as his DrinkUp Water.

WILL DUNHILL'S THIRST FOR SUCCESS EVER BE QUENCHED? read the headline on the two-page spread in *Fortune,* which was framed and prominently hung above Michael's desk (my unspoken answer: Nope. Even if he swigged down Niagara Falls, he'd still be parched).

I bypassed our elevator and climbed the grand split spiral staircase that led to our master bedroom suite. I hurried into Michael's bathroom and began searching his medicine cabinets and linen closets before finally finding his toiletries bag in a vanity drawer. Let's see, he'd need deodorant, a razor, maybe some face lotion . . . I scooped up a black glass bottle with an indecipherable French name, then noticed two other brands. Which one did he use? I shrugged and decided to put all three into the bag. Now, where was his toothbrush? I searched his medicine cabinet twice before finally spotting an electric one perched by the side of the sink. But Michael hated electric toothbrushes, I thought, feeling strangely off-center. He said the noise made him feel like he was at the dentist's office. When had that changed?

As I stood there, frowning down at the toothbrush, a memory flashed through my mind. Back in our old apartment, the one Michael and I had rented when we'd first moved to town, we'd shared what had to be the world's tiniest bathroom. Michael always showered first, since he sprang out of bed like he'd been awakened by the live end of a cattle prod, and by the time the alarm sounded and I stumbled in, rubbing my eyes and yawning hugely, he'd be shaving.

"Good morning, sunshine," he'd singsong in the voice of a chipper preschool teacher.

"Go to hell," I'd mumble, elbowing him out of the way so I could reach past the plastic curtain decorated with pictures of palm trees and turn on the shower. I'd come alive as the alternating hot and cold water hit me (our water temperature was inconsistent, but I'd decided to pick my battles with our landlord and focus on the broken freezer), then Michael and I would chat through mouthfuls of minty toothpaste and over the roar of my hair dryer. We'd compare our schedules for the day and bump hips like backup dancers as we jockeyed for position in front of the mirror. Michael would hand me my flat hairbrush without being asked, and I'd towel off the bit of shaving foam he'd missed behind one of his ears.

When Michael and I had first toured this house, I'd swooned when I saw my bathroom with the sun streaming in through the skylights and the balcony overlooking our sprawling green backyard. The steam shower was big enough for a dozen people if you were so inclined (just for the record, I wasn't), and the fixtures on the double limestone sinks were as delicately crafted as works of art. The nights when I'd sit down on an exposed toilet bowl at 3:00 A.M. and kick Michael awake in retaliation for leaving the seat up were happily behind us.

On our first morning in the house, I'd stepped onto the sea green porcelain tiles, then curled my toes in delight. "They're heated! Michael, you've got to come feel this!" But across the expanse of our bedroom and sitting area, Michael's bathroom door remained shut; he hadn't heard me. I'd shrugged, then stepped into my oversize Jacuzzi.

Why was I even thinking about this? I wondered, blinking away the old images. I needed to get back to the hospital. I tossed a travel toothbrush into the kit, then tucked a long cashmere robe into an overnight bag. I added jeans and a casual shirt, too, so Michael wouldn't have to put back on his suit and torn shirt. Once he got out of the hospital, he probably wouldn't want any reminders of what had happened today. On the way out, I hesitated, then grabbed Michael's laptop off his office desk. He'd probably be demanding it within a few hours.

I put the bag on the passenger's seat of my car and was pulling out of the driveway when my cell phone rang. I recognized the incoming number and pressed speakerphone.

"Hey, Raj," I said, relieved to hear a friendly voice. Raj was one of Michael's former business school professors, and since he'd joined the company, he'd become close to both of us.

"Julia," he greeted me in his lovely Indian accent. "Quite an afternoon."

"We've all had better ones," I agreed as I programmed the name of George Washington University Hospital into my GPS. I was too shaken to trust myself to find it without help. "But the main thing is, Michael's fine."

"Thank God for that," Raj said. He paused. "I hate to bother you."

"It's okay," I said. "I'm on my way to the hospital now."

"Oh." A strange tone crept into Raj's voice. "You haven't seen Michael yet?"

There it was again: that glimmer of—anxiety? confusion?— that everyone who'd come into contact with Michael since his cardiac arrest seemed to experience.

"No, no, I saw him," I said. "I just ran home to get him a change of clothes."

"How . . ." Raj cleared his throat and began again. "How was he feeling?"

"I think he was looped up on something," I said. "He was definitely calmer than usual." I gave a little half laugh, but Raj didn't join me.

"I was there, you know," he said. "When it happened. I was at the other end of the table, and I'd just turned my back to fill up my coffee cup. I didn't see him fall, but I heard him hit the floor."

Raj didn't say anything else, and I wondered why he'd called. It was almost as if he was waiting for me to volunteer something.

"I'll tell Michael you phoned," I finally said.

"Please do," Raj said. "I'm here for whatever either of you need. Anything at all."

"Thanks," I said. I was about to hang up when Raj's voice stopped me.

"Julia?" he asked. "Did Michael . . . say anything at the hospital?"

"Like what?" I asked. I pulled to a stop at a red light and looked down at the phone, feeling icy fingertips tickling my spine.

"Just checking. It's nothing." His voice changed; grew more forceful. "He seemed a little disoriented, that's all. Call me anytime," Raj said again. "I'll have my cell phone on all night."

I pushed Disconnect, and as I crossed the border from Virginia into D.C., I turned up the volume on my Puccini CD, trying to drown out the troublesome thoughts buzzing in my head.

Five

SO HOW DID MICHAEL and I get from there to here, from being inseparable to becoming near strangers? There isn't a single moment I can hold up and turn around, like one of those prehistoric insects suspended in a chunk of amber, and say, *Do you see it? That's it; that's the precise second when everything changed for Michael and me.* No, our marriage was more like spending an afternoon at the beach while the tide receded. You could be lying right there on the soft sand and not even notice the microscopic changes—the waves pulling back, inexorably pulling back—while the sun warmed your back and the happy shouts of children filled your ears. Then you'd look up from the last page in your novel and blink, feeling disoriented, wondering how the ocean had moved so far away and when everything around you had changed.

By the time my husband collapsed at work, he and I hadn't talked—I mean really talked, one of our all-night heart-to-hearts—in years, which is crazy, because talking was all we used to do. Well, maybe not all. We *were* teenagers, which meant we were so overflowing with hormones that we practically trailed them behind us like bread crumbs, but every day, when the final school bell sounded, we'd race to the banks of the river on the outskirts of our town. We'd spread out a blanket and ignore our homework while we drank each other in. No detail was too obscure or minor to revel in: He hated pickles, I couldn't stand ketchup. "We'll never be able to have a proper barbecue," Michael moaned. "They'll ban us from ever living in the suburbs." We both secretly, humiliatingly, loved the game show *Family Feud.* I told Michael about how I tried to keep my lips tightly clenched for an entire year after some bitches in training on the third-grade playground told me my dimples looked like ugly holes in my face ("I'll put itching powder in their bras," Michael vowed, tracing my dimples with a gentle fingertip. "I'll slip so much vitamin C into their Diet Cokes that they'll turn orange. We'll create an army of itchy-boobed Oompa Loompas, and force them to do our bidding.")

Our conversations were like Russian nesting dolls: With each layer of thoughts and fears and memories we uncovered, we only grew more eager to delve deeper, to tease apart the outer façades, until we finally uncovered each other's hidden, secret parts. We stretched out those delicious afternoons as long as possible, folding up our blanket and shrugging into our backpacks only when mosquitoes began nibbling on us and I imagined my mother's anxious face peering through the living room window.

Though it took him a while to open up, I slowly came to understand how horrible it was for Michael at home. Before they moved out, his older brothers had teased him relentlessly, calling him a nerd and a geek, landing charley horses on his skinny biceps or sticking out a foot to trip him as Michael walked by, engrossed in a book. Worst of all, his dad didn't try to stop the torment. Once when his oldest brother punched him in the stomach, Michael doubled over, then looked at his father for help and caught him smirking.

"I think my dad's jealous that I'm smarter than he is," Michael said, his lighthearted tone contradicting the way his mouth twisted around the words. "And I look more like my . . . my, ah, mother. That's part of it, too, I guess."

Eventually I told Michael about my father, too. He was the first person I ever talked to about it.

Sometimes we just lay silently for hours, our legs, arms, and even fingers entwined, as though we couldn't bear for a single part of us not to be touching. I honestly believe Michael and I saved each other that year, the final one we spent in our hometown.

Now, when I mentally trace the trajectory of our relationship—and I've had plenty of time to do it, lots of silent evenings alone in our home—I realize there wasn't a sharp breaking point or single furious argument that set us on our current path. And yet, a particular evening always comes back to me when I wonder how and why everything changed for us. It was the night I listened to an opera and fell in love for the second time in my life.

I'd heard opera music before, of course, but I'd always flicked past it to a different radio station or talked over it at dinner parties. Go to an opera? I mean, if you were looking for that kind of a thrill, why not just volunteer to referee a shuffleboard tournament on a seniors' cruise?

Then I agreed to take on the D.C. Opera Company as a client on a pro bono basis. It was a win-win: My company could use the tax write-off, and the opera company desperately needed the infusion of cash that my fund-raisers would attract. As a thank-you, the company sent me two tickets to opening night of *Madama Butterfly*.

"Do you want to go?" Michael asked as he looked in a hallway mirror to straighten his tie. He was heading out even earlier than usual that morning; he'd just bought a minority interest in the Blazes, and he was meeting with the D.C. mayor about building a new basketball stadium.

"Sure." I shrugged, yawning sleepily and glancing down at the tickets in my hand. "I should probably learn something about my new client."

"It's Friday night? What else do I have on Friday?" he asked.

I narrowed my eyes. "You better not have forgotten."

Michael smiled and held up his briefcase like a shield against my death glare. "Kidding. I have to go to New York that day," he said, opening our front door and stepping outside, then quickly ducking back in to kiss me. "I'll meet you there."

As the evening approached, I began to look forward to it more and more. At least Michael and I could laugh at the opera snobs—they didn't actually use those silly little glasses, did they?—then, afterward, we could have a late dinner together. I'd surprise my husband, I decided, impulsively reaching for the phone to make reservations at a fancy Italian restaurant where every booth was sealed off with thick velvet curtains.

At five o'clock, I stopped working and took a long, steaming bath in my Jacuzzi. I spent extra time on my makeup, blending a peach blush high on my cheekbones and smoking my eyes; then I put on my new emerald-colored silk underwear. Michael had once told me he liked the way the color brought out the green in my hazel eyes. If my push-up bra lifted and plumped with the enthusiasm it promised, I doubted Michael would be noticing my eyes tonight.

By the time I began to climb the majestic marble steps leading to the opera company's front doors, I felt almost giddy. Michael and I needed to do this more often, I realized, inhaling the crisp air that made me think of bonfires and hot apple cider and the crunch of orange and gold leaves under my feet. How long had it been since we'd had a quiet dinner, just the two of us?

I looked off into the distance at the Washington Monument and nearly laughed out loud, remembering the first time I'd seen it, more than a decade earlier. Michael and I had been teenagers then, freshly graduated from high school and driving toward our new life together in an ancient station wagon with a piece of paneling missing from the side and garbage bags stuffed full of our belongings in the trunk. Every fifty miles or so we'd had to stop and fill the radiator with cold water and check the patched tire to make sure it wasn't leaking.

Then we crossed from Virginia into D.C. and the huge, pencil-shaped monument loomed into view. Michael pulled over to the side of the road and stopped the car while we gaped at it. We'd really done it; we'd escaped our town and our families, and we were crossing the threshold into a brand-new life together.

"I can't believe it," Michael breathed.

I blinked back tears, too overcome to talk.

"I mean, I can't believe they built that thing just to honor me," he said, guiding my hand to his lap. "Isn't it a perfect replica?"

I batted his hand away. "Freud was right about you men," I said. "Do you really think everything is about your anatomy?"

"Absolutely not! Gherkin pickles and Vienna sausages couldn't be more different." Michael leered, and I hit him again, then kissed him long and hard while cars flew past us, honking and weaving in and out of lanes.

But five minutes before *Madama Butterfly* was scheduled to start, the smile dropped away from my face. I'd gotten used to sending our regrets when Michael begged off from dinner parties, and I'd canceled our trip to Paris—the first real vacation we'd ever planned to take. But would he really do this to me tonight, when he knew I'd be standing outside, waiting for him?

As if on cue, my BlackBerry buzzed with a new message: MEETING RUNNING LATE. FLYING HOME IN THE MORNING. SORRY.

I stood there uncertainly, watching a few stragglers hurry inside.

You don't have any right to be upset, I told myself, trying to push back the anger and hurt that instantly flooded me. *You wanted Michael to be successful. So he has to work late; it comes with the territory. You can't change the rules now.*

Michael's unstoppable drive was one of the things that had attracted me to him, back when we'd stood on another set of front steps so long ago. He'd given me the kind of life any woman would dream of; he'd accomplished everything he'd promised to, and then some. How could I complain now?

So I didn't text him back or call him. I didn't let Michael know how much I wanted to be with him. Maybe it was because I couldn't bear to hear what he'd say if I asked him to choose between me and work, or maybe it just seemed easier to let the moment slide by, another wave infinitesimally pulling back. It was too late now, anyway. The night was ruined.

I'd go home and watch a movie, I decided as I began to reverse my climb on the steps. Take off my new dress and put on some soft pajamas. Maybe I'd wander through our wine cellar and pick out a special bottle to savor. The chef who came by our house twice a week always left the refrigerator stocked with all my favorites—Thai peanut noodles, and shrimp quesadillas with fresh guacamole, and all kinds of salads . . . I'd almost done it, almost talked myself out of my mood, like I was cajoling a little kid back from the brink of a tantrum. Then the romantic meal I'd secretly planned—just Michael and me in that candlelit booth—flashed through my mind, and a powerful wave of loneliness almost knocked the wind out of me. I ducked my head and wrapped my arms around myself as I stared down at the steps.

I couldn't go home and dull my feelings with a few extra glasses of chardonnay, like I'd done on so many other nights. But what else could I do?

"Excuse me? Are you coming inside?"

I turned around and saw an usher in a red coat preparing to close the door.

"No—" I began to say, but then my feet took charge, whirling me around and leaping back up the steps two at a time. I slipped inside the tall doors just in time for the usher to lead me to my seat as the lights dimmed.

Ninety minutes later, the lights flicked back on for intermission. All around me, people stood up and stretched and murmured to each other as they began walking toward the lobby bar and restrooms, but I didn't move. I just sat there, blinking slowly, feeling as though I were awakening from a beautiful dream. All the empty places inside of me had been flooded with heat and color. How had I misunderstood it so completely? Opera wasn't stuffy at all; it was messy and passionate and . . . and *real*.

The story told through song was that of a beautiful young Japanese woman named Cio-Cio San who was pining for her American husband, who'd returned to the States and forgotten about her. I hear you, sister, I'd thought as she sang of her pain and sorrow at her abandonment. Hot anger flooded me when the husband's new American wife appeared on the scene, and I brushed away tears as Cio-Cio San realized her husband didn't love her, not in the way she yearned to be loved. Not in the way she loved him.

She's singing to *me*, I thought as she began her heartbreaking aria.

After that night, I secretly bought a subscription for one in the orchestra section, where I was so close I felt like I could practically touch the rustling, jewel-colored costumes; so close I could feel the music swelling like air in my lungs, almost lifting me up out of my seat with its power. Opera quickly became my addiction *and* my therapy, my secret escape from a life that—at least on the surface—was everything I'd ever dreamed of and more.

When I arrived home that night, still hearing echoes of Cio-Cio San's aria, I unlocked the door and my eyes fell on a table in our grand foyer. Crimson roses overflowed prettily in a huge crystal vase. Naddy, our maid, must have arranged them there so I'd see them as soon as I came in.

At least Michael had remembered what he'd murmured in my ear right after we got engaged. He'd given me a single perfect rose—all he could afford—and promised, "I'll buy you a dozen roses for every year we've been married on our anniversaries."

"Even our fiftieth?" I'd laughed, wrapping my arms around him.

"*Especially* our fiftieth," he'd said, tickling my neck with the soft petals.

I walked over to the vase and counted. Five dozen roses, just as Michael had promised. I picked up the little white card and read the message a florist had typed: "I'll make it up to you on our sixth. Love, M."

Ever since that night, I've gone to the opera as often as possible, and I've never been disappointed. But I dream of going back in time to see opera the way it was meant to be. If you skipped back a century or two, you'd forget all about exorbitantly priced seats and lace-trimmed handkerchiefs dabbing at damp eyes and genteel murmurs of "Brava!" Opera, in its heyday, was a bloody, bruise-filled, raucous *sport*.

Audience members booed wildly when they hated a song, and they roared louder than rabid football fans when they approved. Opera halls were filled with shouts and fights and foot-stomping, cheering celebrations. Decorum was nowhere to be found during opera's early, heady days; it was probably cowering under a seat, terrified someone would throw a drink down its throat and make it dance in the aisles.

The people who inhabited the world of opera were completely nuts, which probably had something to do with all the chaos swirling around. Once, when the soprano Francesca Cuzzoni refused to sing an aria written by the composer George Frideric Handel, he grabbed her and threatened to dangle her out a window until she came around to his point of view (she saw it quickly enough). Then there was the guy who watched his wife flirt with a tenor during Wagner's *Ban on Love*. The husband flew into a jealous rage, jumped up onstage in the middle of the performance, and punched out the poor tenor, who could probably at least take solace in the fact that his acting was believable. And I've always loved the story about the woman, who told her rival, mid-performance, that one of the rival's false eyebrows had come off. So the rival ripped off the other one and soldiered on—except her first eyebrow had been fine, so the poor woman went through the rest of the opera looking slightly deranged.

Can't you just see it? All those people, bound together watching the spectacle onstage, strangers becoming friends as they flooded the streets, carrying a triumphant composer on their shoulders, reliving the glow of the most glorious music ever invented?

Nowadays, it seems like the audience is removed from the chaos and madness unfolding behind the scenes. It isn't that the performers have suddenly become less quirky—Luciano Pavarotti was so superstitious that he wouldn't perform until he'd scoured the stage and found a single bent nail—but somehow, the belief that opera is supposed to be as stuffy as a bad head cold has come into vogue.

Why did things have to change?

Six

IT WAS AS THOUGH Michael hadn't moved a muscle. The remote control to the television lay untouched on his bedside table. The nurse and Dale were gone—someone had probably used the Jaws of Life to pry Dale away—and Michael and I were finally alone.

"I brought your things." I plopped the distressed leather overnight bag on the chair next to the bed and unzipped it, then grabbed his toiletries kit and carried it into the bathroom. "I wasn't sure if you wanted your electric razor," I called out. "So I brought one of my disposable ones instead. I don't mean to insult your manhood, but it's pink."

"Julia," Michael said softly. "Come sit down."

"Sure," I said. "Just let me put your clothes away so they don't wrinkle. Oh, and Raj phoned. You should probably call him. He sounded like he was still a little worried."

I shook out Michael's jeans, suddenly feeling an urgent need to fold them. He watched my every move.

"Did you want to call Kate, too?" I asked, rerolling a pair of his socks. I seemed to be afflicted with a mild case of OCD, which could be convenient, because my desk was a mess. "Should she cancel your meetings for the week? Unless you think you'll be up for talking on the phone. You could always call in. And I know you said you didn't need a computer, but I brought one just in case—"

"Julia," Michael said again. His gentle voice cut through my whirlwind of activity, making me stop as abruptly as if I were a robot that had short-circuited. I moved the bag to the floor and sat down, trying to quash the anxiety swelling inside me. Michael reached out for my hand. There it was again—the room was cool and he was only covered by a thin sheet; why was his hand so warm?

"Something amazing happened to me," Michael said, his blue eyes latching on to mine. This nonstop eye contact was making me so nervous my hands felt sweaty—or maybe that was from Michael's odd internal thermometer.

"It's a miracle," he whispered.

"I know," I jumped in eagerly. "If you hadn't bought that defibrillator—"

"Not that part," he said, and I fell silent. The room was so stark and white; sure, it was a hospital, but couldn't they add just a little flair? Was a measly framed print too much to ask for? It would definitely be easier to have this conversation if I had something to look at other than Michael's blue eyes, which, right now, seemed to be the only colorful things in the room. They were so vivid and intense, it felt like they were physically pinning me to my chair.

"Something amazing happened to me," he started again, "when I was dead."

He beamed, looking as if he'd just announced he'd won a scratch-off lottery ticket.

"When you were dead," I said slowly, as though repeating the words would make them snap into clarity.

"Something . . . *happened*," Michael breathed. "I don't know

what to call it. There isn't any word for what I felt, for what
I saw."

I swallowed hard. "Can I get you an aspirin?" I offered.

Michael burst into laughter and reached around with his
other hand, to envelop mine between his.

"We've been scared for so long, both of us have. It kept us
from seeing what was truly important. I know it might sound
strange, but can you just open your heart and listen to me? The
love I felt, but even more than that, the . . . the *understanding*.
I've been living behind a veil for all my life, and it was just
whisked away. Julia, everything I thought I wanted, I already
had. It was already inside me."

Michael blinked back tears as I stared at him in shock. Open
your heart? Living behind a veil? My husband didn't say things
like that; he looked earnestly into my eyes and said things like
"Have you seen my cell phone?" and "I'm thinking about short-
selling some GE stock."

Valium combined with a head injury could do this to a man,
I reminded myself. I'd heard of near-death experiences before,
but I wasn't willing to concede one had happened to Michael.

I didn't believe in the afterlife, or heaven, or whatever you
wanted to call it. And neither did Michael.

We were atheists, for God's sakes—so to speak. We'd been
married before a justice of the peace, and we hadn't set foot
in a church since a friend's son was baptized four years earlier.
Even then, we'd been like a Laurel and Hardy team, with one
of us sitting and one of us standing when we were supposed to
kneel, and both of us heading for the exit when everyone else
was just getting up to take communion. I blame that one on
Michael—he was checking his e-mail instead of listening to the
priest's invitation for the audience to take the holy sacrament.

"Please," Michael begged. "Just listen. I thought I wanted
money. I thought it would make me feel powerful. But it was

never enough. Don't you see? The more I had, the more I wanted. I was a gerbil on a tiny little wheel. I kept going faster and faster, but I never ended up anywhere real. It was all an illusion."

"Did you, um, mention this to Raj or Kate? Or to Dale?" I asked, already knowing the answer.

"Of course," he said. "I want everyone to know. If I can save one person from making the mistakes I did . . ."

I can handle this, I thought, already snapping into crisis mode. This was nothing compared to a temperamental soprano with a fake sore throat. Michael might be out of commission for a day or two, but then he'd become himself again. He'd had a hell of a scare, on top of everything else, and we couldn't expect him to act normally. My mind spun with plans: I'd tell Raj and Kate to take charge of the office. I'd stay in the hospital and keep everyone away from Michael.

"There's so much I need to say to you," he said.

I braced myself for more gibberish about peace and a white light. Peace, by the way, which could come from a little orange pill called Xanax, and a white light which could easily be explained by hitting one's head.

But his next words shocked me.

"Julia, I'm so sorry I was going to skip your birthday dinner. How many of our anniversaries did I miss because I was traveling?"

His hands tightened around mine. "But the worst thing I did was not rush home from Los Angeles . . . I can't believe I stayed around for a stupid fucking meeting the next morning even though—"

I cut him off. "Michael, why are you talking about this now?"

"I wasn't there for you when you needed me the most," he said. "I can't tell you how much I regret that."

Tears filled my eyes, like no time at all had elapsed since that black hole of a night. This wasn't fair; I felt blindsided. Michael and I didn't talk about this stuff, not *ever.*

"I want to make it up to you," he said softly. "All of it."

"Michael." I forced back my tears and kept my voice firm. "We've moved on. It was a long time ago."

"I know, but we haven't moved on," he said.

This was too much; Michael was overwhelming me. How dare he bring up the pain in our past—in my past, really, since he hadn't ever seemed to be affected by it?

"I need something to drink," I said, yanking my hand away from his. "I'm going to the cafeteria."

An old, buried anger burned through me as I rushed toward the door, erasing the protective instincts I'd felt for Michael.

"Wait," he said, struggling to a sitting position. I heard an alarm sounding from a monitor by his bed, but I ignored him. "There's something important I have to tell you—"

I let the door swing closed, cutting off the rest of his words. Let him spout off about understanding and peace like some bearded guy in a toga who handed out daisies at the airport. Let him deal with the fallout, which would probably be a blind item in the Reliable Source gossip column in the *Washington Post*. We'd made it there twice before—when Michael became a co-owner of the Blazes and held a party that brought Shaquille O'Neal to town, and again when we bought our house. Real estate transactions weren't normally considered sexy, but it was a slow news week, and our $9 million house probably inspired the same awe in others that it had in us. The two-paragraph item detailed the hand-painted fresco on the ceiling of our library, and the twenty-seat home movie theater, and the steam room in the home gym.

I could imagine the headline this time: DELUSIONAL MOGUL COMPARES SELF TO GERBIL.

For some reason, Dale's grinning face appeared in my mind. Raj and Kate would keep this quiet, but I wouldn't put it past Dale to plant the item himself.

I pushed the elevator button and rode down to the cafeteria, forcing myself to nod at the middle-aged woman who was riding along with me.

"Beautiful day," she said cheerily.

Sure, I thought, if your husband isn't acting like a lunatic, and the fund-raiser you've been planning for a month isn't probably falling apart, and you've eaten something other than a fifteen-dollar cupcake.

"He said *what?*" my best friend Isabelle asked a few hours later. "Hold on, I need to fortify myself."

She reached over and grabbed the carafe of sangria from the coffee table and filled both of our glasses.

"I've been fortifying myself since I got home," I protested, gulping down another huge sip. "If I get any more fortified I'll fall over."

"Luckily you're sitting," Isabelle said. "Besides, this is basically fruit salad with a little kick. We're being virtuous." She tucked her long legs beneath her. "Now, tell me again, from the top."

She leaned back against the couch, her glossy black hair a stark splash against the white cushion. I knew I could confide in Isabelle; these days, she was my only real friend. That was another complication I hadn't foreseen when Michael suddenly became so wealthy. You couldn't always trust the motivation behind people's kindness. I'd learned that the hard way.

"He said he understood everything now." I waved my hand around and barely avoided sloshing ruby-colored sangria on my couch. Funny how things like that still made me flinch, even though we could buy a new couch any day of the week. *You can take the girl out of West Virginia . . .*

I took a gulp and felt the tangy sweetness of the raspberries and blood oranges explode against my tongue. Isabelle was right; they should sell this stuff in health food stores.

"He understands everything? How annoyingly vague." Isabelle raised one perfect eyebrow. She was the one who'd sent me to Sasha, the eyebrow-shaping guru. I was convinced Sasha was able to charge such outrageous prices because he wielded pointy little instruments an inch away from your corneas. Who would be brave enough to tick him off by questioning the bill? It would be like mocking your brain surgeon's toupee seconds before the anesthesia took effect.

"Oh, and he apologized for everything bad he's ever done to me," I said, frowning. "Suddenly he thinks he's Mother Teresa."

"But the whole idea about an afterlife . . . I mean, doesn't it intrigue you?"

"Look, I know other people have said it happened to them," I said. "But I can't even think about that part of it. I'm too busy worrying about Michael. He's acting so strangely."

"What if there really is life after death?" Isabelle mused. "What if what happened to Michael was real?"

I spun my heavy crystal wineglass in gentle circles, watching my drink turn into a miniature whirlpool. "It seems so freaky," I finally said. "Why would it happen to a nonbeliever? Wouldn't whoever's in charge say, 'Hey, you don't believe, so you don't get in'?"

"I doubt there's a bouncer in heaven," Isabelle said, swatting my knee with a pillow. "Did Michael feel a presence? Did he see anything?"

"He didn't say." The sangria was warming me from the inside as the fear and strangeness of the day receded. Isabelle never questioned her place or her right to belong, and when I was with her, her confidence rubbed off. Being born into money could give a person that kind of poise, I supposed. Her family owned a frozen-food empire—"From vegetables to apple pie," Isabelle had said when I first met her at a dinner party. "Brussels sprouts paid for my years at boarding school." I hadn't known how to respond. Was this rich people humor? Michael's company had publicly issued stock the previous month, netting him all sorts of media coverage, and we'd been thrust into a new world so quickly I was still trying to figure out which of the four forks to use—but then Isabelle had winked. While I was gaping over her long eyelashes, she'd completely disarmed me.

"You know how every kid hates Brussels sprouts?" she asked. "For me it's personal. Because boarding school was really awful."

I laughed then, a surprised, natural laugh, and Isabelle joined in. We spent the rest of the night gossiping about books and the weekend's quickie Vegas wedding between an aging movie star and a cocktail waitress ("Doesn't anyone believe in true love anymore?" Isabelle wondered. "I think those crazy kids are going to make it.") We rolled our eyes as Michael gobbled down both of our desserts along with his own.

"Does he always eat this way?" Isabelle asked me.

"No, I think he's dieting."

"We should kill him," Isabelle decided. "Men have died for lesser sins."

"But then who would drive you home?" Michael asked me.

"Oh—you mean you don't . . . ?" Isabelle fell silent.

"Don't what?" I prodded.

"Sorry, I was just going to say, don't you have a driver? I usually have mine take me to parties so I don't have to worry about driving after a few drinks," she said.

Michael and I looked at each other, and I could see him adding it to his running mental to-do list: Hire a driver. Get a personal chef. Learn about wines (Isabelle's date and another man at the table had spent fifteen minutes discussing the nuances of the white burgundy we were drinking, and I could tell it was killing Michael not to be able to add to the conversation). We were playing catch-up as quickly as we could, and I felt like everyone could see us scrambling.

"What was it like?" Isabelle asked now, leaning closer to me. "I mean, this is really wild. Did he see a white light?"

I shook my head. "I don't think so. We didn't spend that long talking about it. He just said it was an amazing feeling."

"Better than sex?"

"You are the only person in the world who would ask that."

"What else did he say?"

Just then our house phone rang. I picked up the cordless and checked caller ID.

"It's Bettina," I groaned.

"Why don't phone calls come with warning labels?" Isabelle wondered, lazily tracing a fingertip around the rim of her glass. "Answer at your own risk: Contents may be toxic."

Bettina was Dale's wife. She looked like she'd been drawn with a straightedge: her chin-length white-blond hair was always flat ironed, her clothes hung from her frame as cleanly as if she was a wire hanger, and her nose was a sharp triangle. Bettina even spoke in staccato sentences. Once when I was at her house for a cocktail party, she'd casually discussed the merits of the various maids she employed like they were hors d'oeuvres.

"I tried Hispanics. Asians are better," she'd announced as a maid wandered by within hearing distance.

She and Dale were absolutely perfect for each other.

"Just let the machine get it," Isabelle advised.

"No, I'd better take it," I said. "In case there's a work emergency or something."

"Julia, how are you?" Bettina asked. She didn't wait for my answer. "I heard what happened. Incredible!"

"I know," I said, eager to spin the conversation in a good direction. "Michael's doing so well, and he'll probably be out of the hospital by Tuesday."

"I see," Bettina said. "And what will you do next?"

"Next?" I asked. "What do you mean?"

She paused, and I could hear her inhaling smoke from one of her long, thin cigarettes.

"Michael told everyone he wasn't returning to work. Dale said he announced it as they loaded him into the ambulance."

I couldn't help it; I gasped. I could almost see the victorious grin forming on Bettina's lips. She'd probably burn up the phone lines tonight describing my gasp to everyone she knew.

"Didn't he tell you?" Bettina inquired, her tone cloyingly sweet.

What? Isabelle mouthed. I shook my head at her; I still couldn't speak. Isabelle read the shock in my eyes and wrestled the phone out of my hand.

"It's Isabelle. What's going on? Did something happen to Michael?"

Isabelle was quiet as she listened, but I could see her jaw tighten.

"Charming," she said calmly. "Michael nearly died today, and you're calling his wife and upsetting her even more. Have you thought about getting a job at the *National Enquirer*? You've got the perfect touch. Oh, and by the way, you should wear longer dresses. Your knees are getting wrinkly."

Isabelle slammed down the phone: "Vulture."

I finally found my voice. "What did she mean?"

Isabelle shook her head. "She's a pathetic gossip. She's just jealous we didn't invite her to your birthday party. Ignore her."

"Do you really think he wants to quit work?"

"Nah. He would've said something to you first. Maybe he wants to take off some time and travel. He was probably just talking about taking a little break."

"Isabelle," I whispered. "Michael wanted to talk to me about something important, but I got so angry with him because of—well, because of some stuff I can't go into now. I left the room. I wouldn't listen to him . . . I went back an hour later, but they'd taken him away to do some tests. We never got to finish talking."

I could see Isabelle turning the possibilities over in her mind. She wanted to console me, but she'd never lie to me.

"Okay," she finally said. "Here's the plan. Tomorrow morning you go to the hospital first thing and talk to Michael. Find out what's going on. We'll figure out what to do from there."

"You're right," I said. Somehow my voice stayed even, but my mind churned in panic. Michael wanted to quit work? What the hell was going on? What had really happened to him during those lost four minutes and eight seconds?

I reached over and grabbed the soft throw blanket from the arm of the couch, wrapping it around my shoulders. Suddenly I was so cold.

"Oh, God, the party. If Michael's still acting like this . . ."

She shrugged. "So we'll cancel it. More cake for us."

"Would you mind if we did? I just don't know if Michael's going to be back to normal by then," I said.

Isabelle looked at me, and her brow furrowed. "I think this calls for a margarita. I'll make some. Don't worry; you won't get a hangover. They're in the same alcohol family as sangria."

"They are?" I asked dumbly.

"Sure. They both end in *aah*, don't they?"

I smiled despite myself. "But you've got a date tonight," I said.

Don't go, I thought. "You should get going."

"First of all, my date is with a guy named Norm whose pride and joy is his collection of antique rifles. Try and tell me he isn't compensating for something."

"But there isn't anything we can do tonight," I said, taking a slow, shuddering breath. "I'll be fine. Really."

"I'm not leaving you alone to go out with Norm, proud owner of a musket."

I snorted again—but in a graceful way, of course. I'm told they teach my snort in debutante school. "Okay," I said, feeling as though the coating of ice around me was breaking up, allowing warmth to flow back into my body. I felt so absurdly grateful that Isabelle was taking charge that I blinked back tears. But I know Isabelle saw them; she doesn't miss much.

"And secondly," Isabelle said, reaching for my hand and squeezing it. "There *is* something we can do tonight."

She reached for the television remote and held it aloft like a trophy as she smiled her wonderful smile: "*Project Runway*'s on."

I felt the last vestiges of my panic subside. "I may have some chocolate stashed away. Purely for emergencies, of course."

"*Project Runway*, chocolate, and margaritas," Isabelle said. "And suddenly, all is right with the world again."

Seven

"I SHOULD'VE TOLD YOU first."

Michael was trying to look chastened, but his eyes refused to cooperate. They were bright and cheerful, like he'd just enjoyed an exceptionally long night's sleep. But sleep was Michael's mortal enemy; he bitterly resented the four or five hours it stole from him every night. If he could've taken sleep to court for theft, or challenged it to a street fight, he would have.

"You just can't—can't decide something like this without talking to me," I sputtered.

"Julia, honey, I don't have a choice. I feel like I have to do it."

"So you're going to quit? Fine. Then what happens in six months, when you get bored and want to go back to work? I know you, Michael. I promise you you're going to go stir-crazy. It won't even take six months. It'll take six *days*. And then what? If you hire someone else to run the company, things are going to get tricky. There'll be buyouts and maybe a lawsuit—"

"I'm not going to change my mind."

A doctor in a white coat walked in just then, and I turned to her in relief.

"Doctor? I'm sorry, could I ask a question? I'm his wife, and

I need to know what medications he's on. He's not acting like himself."

She shook her head, and her long blond ponytail swished from side to side in a way I considered very undoctorly. "Nothing that would affect him mentally."

"No Xanax?" I asked. "Are you sure? Can you double-check? Because I've been on Xanax before and I'm pretty sure he's taking it. Maybe he got mixed up with another patient."

"The chief of cardiology is personally overseeing his care," she said, wrinkling her pert little nose. "I promise you there's no mix-up."

"Honey," Michael said. "I know it's a lot to take in. But will you just trust me? I promise it's the right thing."

"Sure," I said, tossing a fake smile at Michael. "What about a head injury?" I whispered urgently to the doctor. "He probably whacked his head when he fell."

"I can hear you perfectly well, and I didn't whack my head," Michael protested.

"Don't listen to him," I said to the doctor. "Check his pupils."

Or maybe it was the doctor who'd screwed up, I thought, narrowing my eyes as I appraised her. She appeared far too young and perky to be a real doctor. Maybe she was a resident—but weren't they supposed to be all exhausted and hollow-eyed? I peered at the name sewn onto her coat in blue stitching, vowing to Google her later and maybe, I thought wildly, submit her as a candidate for a *Dateline* exposé.

"Julia," Michael said in a pleading tone. I turned to him, this stranger in a hospital bed who was masquerading as my husband. Not work? Michael never *stopped* working.

"Could you give us a minute?" Michael said to the doctor, who left the room—a bit too slowly, it seemed to me. She was probably about to call her cheerleader friends to gather around a bowl of Jiffy Pop and enjoy the show.

Michael took a deep breath. "I haven't been a good husband," he began, his voice gentle. "I want us to start over. I'm going to make you so happy, if you'll just let me."

I stared at him, so stunned I couldn't speak. Earlier in our marriage, the sincerity in his words might've stripped away the hard protective layers around my heart. Maybe it would've even sent me leaping into Michael's arms, like we were in the closing scene of some Hollywood romantic comedy—the couple that fell in love, lost each other, and then reconciled as the heart monitors beeped wildly in celebration and concerned nurses rushed into the room, then broke into applause.

Michael wanted to start over? His timing would've been funny, if it wasn't so sad. In my wallet was a business card for a divorce lawyer. I'd had it for a while, but I hadn't made the call. The card was a security blanket of sorts; it meant I could walk away—if I was willing to risk leaving behind our lifestyle. But things weren't that bad, at least not yet.

"Let's say you stop working," I finally said, ignoring his question. "What are you going to *do*?"

Michael smiled broadly, like he was a game-show contestant and this was the big bonus question he'd been waiting for. "I'm going to sell my company," he said.

I gasped and grabbed the arms of my chair. Suddenly the room seemed to be shrinking. Nausea rose in my throat, and I closed my eyes against the dizziness that engulfed me.

"Sell your company?" I repeated dumbly.

I didn't think anything Michael could say could shock me more, but I was wrong.

"I want to donate everything I have to charity." He looked at me as if he wasn't just shattering all of our dreams. As if he was giving me a gift. "My company ruined me, Julia, and it almost destroyed us. I know you're not happy; you haven't been in years. The things I've done, the people I've screwed over . . ."

His voice trailed off while my mind flashed to Roxanne, the former publicity director for his company. He could blame his company all he wanted, but it was his affair with Roxanne that had upended our marriage.

"I've gotten a second chance," Michael was saying. "How many people get one? Now I need to fix everything I did wrong in my life."

Eight

I SWEAR THE PRENUP seemed to make sense at the time. It was even—that thudding sound you hear is my head repeatedly whacking itself on a table—*my idea*. But to understand why I wanted a prenup, you first need to understand my relationship with my father.

I was a daddy's girl from the day I was born. And who wouldn't be, in my place? My dad was the first guy you'd ask if you needed help moving furniture or had an extra ticket to a ball game; he was the kind of father who made a Wednesday night dinner seem like a New Year's Eve party.

"Mr. Tolson shoplifted another Snickers bar today," Dad would say, piling his plate high with mashed potatoes and chicken breasts as he recounted his day at the small general store he and my mom owned. "Stuck it right down the front of his pants. He's a genius, that guy. He knows I'm never going to reach down there and risk grabbing the wrong thing."

"Steven!" Mom would admonish him while I cracked up, and then my dad would lean over and kiss her, and Mom would start laughing, too. Mom always said that, when I was a baby, Dad was the only one who could rock me to sleep. As a kid, I was happiest perched up on his broad shoulders. When I became a teenager, Dad and I went out every Sunday afternoon, just the two of us, to run errands. He never once turned on the radio but instead asked me about my teachers and friends. He listened so intently and laughed so easily that he made me feel like I was a good storyteller, too. On Saturdays, when our store was busiest, our little family worked there together. Mom bagged groceries while Dad ran the cash register and I stocked the shelves.

We were happy. Happier than most families, I think. Even though there were only the three of us, our house never seemed quiet or empty, and although sometimes I secretly wished for a sister, I knew I was lucky to have parents who loved me so much.

Sometimes I wonder how and why everything began to change. Dad had always been a man with big appetites, a guy who lived a small life in an oversize way. He devoured second helpings of dinner before Mom and I finished our first ones. People always flocked around him, crossing the street to greet him and slowing down their cars so they could lean out the window and chat when they saw him working in our front yard. Sometimes I wondered: Had this hunger always been buried inside my father, like a seed waiting for the right conditions to break through the ground and grow so big and strong that it cast a dark shadow on the sunniest days?

We didn't suspect anything for so long. The urgent, whispered phone calls; the five percent discount Dad suddenly offered customers if they'd pay cash; even the time our electricity was cut off at home and we had to store our perishables in a neighbor's freezer and eat dinner by candlelight.

"The check must've gotten lost in the mail," my father fumed, while my mother and I watched him silently, somehow unable to ask why the electric company wouldn't have sent a warning and another bill first.

Then, during my sophomore year of high school, a year before Michael and I met, a guy named Brian Lucker swaggered
up to my locker and asked me to his senior prom. I managed
to stop gaping long enough to stutter out a yes. If there was a
handbook for girls' crushes in our high school, Brian would
be the cover boy: He was tall, dark, and a running back on the
football team.

I had some babysitting money saved up, and I decided to use
it to buy my first formal dress. I knew better than to ask my parents to buy me one. The bumper had fallen off their truck after
Dad had been in a fender bender, and they hadn't had it fixed.
Our phone had been cut off for a week the previous month, and
even though Dad muttered about idiots at the phone company
mixing up our bill with some delinquent's, I sensed something
was terribly wrong. My mother wasn't smiling as much as she
used to, and once when I woke up in the middle of the night to
use the bathroom, I walked past her sitting at the kitchen table.
I spoke her name twice before she looked up.

"Hi, sweetie . . . I couldn't sleep so I came in here to get a
snack," Mom said, but the table in front of her was bare.

But whenever I started to get really scared—when the knot
in my stomach grew so big I had trouble eating—Dad would
sweep in the door carrying a box of Mom's favorite dark chocolate–covered caramels and a handful of the glossy fashion magazines I adored. He'd make a production of sitting down with
his checkbook and paying the bills with a flourish. "Are my
favorite girls free for dinner, by any chance?" he'd say, and we'd
head to the pizza place, where Dad would overtip the waitress
and insist on ordering ice-cream sundaes. "Don't skimp on the
fudge!" he'd shout, and people sitting on stools at the counter
would swivel around to look at him as he pumped his fist in the
air and grinned. "We're a family of fudgeaholics and we're not

ashamed of it!" During those magical times, I believed everything would be okay. No, I *let* myself believe it.

A week before I planned to go dress shopping with my girl-
friend, Sara, who'd been invited to the prom by one of Brian's
buddies, Dad surprised me. He was waiting for me outside
of school in his old Ford pickup truck. The bumper was still
missing.

"Thought I'd give you a ride to Becky's," Dad said. "You're
sitting today, right?"

I nodded and happily hopped in, inhaling the faded-wood
smell of Dad's Old Spice cologne. It had been a while since Dad
and I had ridden together. He'd been too busy lately for our
Sunday drives.

"Is Mom at the store alone?" I asked.

"Mmm-hmm," Dad said absently, his eyes on the road.

"It must've been a quiet day. You know, for you to get away,"
I offered, but Dad didn't say anything else. We rode in silence
for a moment, and I could feel tension in the car, as thick and
bulky as a passenger squeezing onto the seat between us. For
the first time, my fingers struggled with the urge to reach for
the radio button.

"I hate to ask this," he finally said, his eyes fixed straight
ahead. "Julie, the thing is, a bunch of people didn't pay their
bills this month. I had to extend them credit. They've all got
families, so what could I do? But I need to pay our suppliers,
and I'm short. It's just for a few days."

I told him where to find the babysitting money I'd been saving in the sock drawer of my dresser and tried to swallow the
sour taste that filled my throat.

Just for a few days, Dad had said. But a week passed, and he
made no mention of the money.

The next Friday, Sara turned to me in gym class while we

waited in line to do the rope climb. "We're on for tomorrow, right?" Her mother had offered to drive us to the next town over, where there was a decent-size shopping mall.

"I'm thinking of getting something cut really low in the back," Sara announced. "I saw this model wearing a dress like that in *Seventeen*. She looked so cool."

I could feel the envious eyes of the other girls on us, but that wasn't why I didn't reply.

"Hello? Julie?" Sara asked, sounding annoyed.

"Sorry," I said. My throat tightened, making it hard to force out even that single word.

"She's thinking about Brian," someone said and giggled.

"Wouldn't you be?" another girl sighed. "You're so lucky, Julie."

"Pick you up at nine tomorrow?" Sara said as we shuffled forward in line. "I'm getting a manicure, too. I want to get going early."

I hesitated, then finally nodded. "Sure."

I approached Dad cautiously that night. He hadn't met my eyes at dinner, and when Mom asked if he wanted more salad, he'd barked at her, then apologized and shoved back his chair and left the table, even though his plate was half-full.

"Dad?" I poked my head into his bedroom. He was lying on top of the teal polyester bedspread, fully clothed. Even his shoes were on. Dad hadn't bothered to turn off the overhead light, and his right forearm was draped over his eyes. For one terrifying moment the thought flashed through my mind that he was dead. Then I saw his chest slowly rise and fall.

"Are you asleep?" I asked softly.

The silence stretched out so long that I almost turned around. Then he said, "Nope."

"I was just wondering about the money I loaned you." I swallowed and looked down at my toe tracing an imaginary line back and forth across the room's threshold.

Dad didn't say anything.

"I could get it out of your wallet," I said tentatively. Dad always put his wallet and keys in a little white dish on his bureau, and I could see them there now. I began to slowly walk across the room. When his voice exploded, it felt like a punch to my gut.

"Damn it, Julie! I don't have the money. Now get the hell out!"

I froze. Dad never talked to me this way; he never talked to *anyone* this way. This was the man who used to toss me high into the air at the river and never fail to catch me as I splashed, squealing and laughing, into the water; the guy who stepped in powdered sugar every Christmas Eve and walked around the house so I'd wake up and think Santa had tracked snowy footsteps everywhere, long after I was too old to believe in sleigh bells and magic.

"Get out!" Dad bellowed again, and as I fled, I remembered his white fingers clenching the steering wheel as he'd asked me for the loan, and him peeling away from Becky's house without even saying good-bye, leaving me standing on the sidewalk staring after him.

I called Sara early the next morning and told her I had a sore throat and couldn't go to the mall. She believed me, because my voice was so husky from crying. Two days later, I told Brian my parents weren't letting me go to the prom after all. He ended up taking another girl, and he ignored me from then on.

Dad never mentioned the money again, and neither did I.

But it wasn't because of a stupid dress that I was so angry at my father. It was because he destroyed our family.

By the fall, creditors were calling our house and store. Dad had borrowed heavily against both, and he wasn't paying his loans. He'd gambled away everything on lottery tickets, on sporting events, on poker games—on any bet he could find. By now he was going to Atlantic City every week or so, too.

"I work hard," he snapped at my mother whenever she voiced an objection. My mom hated conflict, and she was too weak to challenge him when he got angry. He never used that against her until gambling began to consume him—then anger became his most effective weapon in cutting off conversation. "So I take a night for myself every once in a while," Dad would say, his voice rising, just before he slammed the door behind him. "What's the big deal?"

One evening a month or so after the prom I didn't attend, I opened our front door and slipped through the house, intending to go right to my bedroom. I'd been avoiding my parents as much as possible. But I heard my mother's voice in the living room, and something told me to stop and listen. "How much did we lose?" I heard her say.

"It's going to turn around for me," Dad said. His voice was so tight and shrill I almost didn't recognize it. "I swear to you, we're going to be fine."

They were sitting side by side on the couch, not looking at each other. Neither of them had bothered to turn on a light, and the room was so shadowy I couldn't see their faces.

"How much?" my mother asked. "The store? Please tell me you didn't borrow against the store."

"Eliza, I promise you I'm going to win it back," Dad said.

"The house?" Mom asked. Where his voice was shiny and anxious, hers was dull and worn, the flip side of a penny that was glinting in the sun but tarnished underneath.

"I swear to you," Dad repeated feverishly. "I've had a bad streak, but do you know how much I won last week? Two thousand dollars. In one night! I'm so close to turning it around. Baby, just hang on. We'll get back to where we started, then I'll quit."

"Oh, Steven," my mother said, and the desolation in her gentle voice broke my heart.

Nothing stopped him from gambling, not when the bank foreclosed on the general store that winter, not when our pickup was repossessed a few months later, not even when we were evicted from our house and had to move in with Dad's brother and his wife during the summer before my senior year of high school.

If I hadn't met Michael a few months earlier, I don't know what I would have done. Run away, maybe, or quit school and gotten a job so I could move out. Everyone was miserable; my aunt was so angry at our intrusion that she marched around with her mouth in a thin, tight line, barely speaking except when she and my uncle were fighting behind their closed bedroom door, and my mother just looked wan and colorless, as though she'd given up on life and was waiting for it to be over. All the joy had seeped out of us, and the worst part, the part I could never forgive him for, was that Dad didn't stop. He tried to borrow from the neighbors, from his friends, even from the mechanic at the auto shop, a guy with tattoo sleeves on both arms. He put an oil-stained hand on Dad's shoulder and I caught him whispering, "Get help . . . I've been there . . . ," while I stared at a blue-inked Marilyn Monroe flirting on his thin forearm and wondered when I'd started to feel so old.

It felt as though our family had been ripped open and exposed for everyone to see, with our problems spilling out like the ugly gray stuffing of a once-smiling teddy bear. Sometimes Dad stayed away for more than a night, and I knew he'd found his way up to Atlantic City again, probably by hitchhiking. I could barely stand to be in the house at those times, knowing either Dad would come home all manic, trying to make up for a year's worth of pain with gifts and glib charm that would quickly evaporate, or he'd be dark and withdrawn.

Dad and I never went for a ride together again.

So you see, the prenup was my way of trying to protect myself. When Michael and I got married, he was still struggling to get his new company off the ground, and he owed tens of thousands of dollars in loans from college and business school. I earned more money than he did at that point, and I had less debt. I had no doubt Michael would be successful, but as much as I loved him, as much as I wanted to, I couldn't bring myself to gamble on him.

Our prenup was so straightforward that a lawyer drew it up in an hour: We'd be married, but as far as money was concerned, we were essentially two separate people. Whatever each of us brought into the marriage and subsequently earned would remain divided, as though someone had built a brick wall between our finances.

"I understand why you need it," Michael said that day, putting the papers in his desk drawer before he changed into his nicest shirt for our civil ceremony in front of a judge at the courthouse. He knotted his tie, and I saw his Adam's apple bob when he swallowed hard. His neck suddenly looked thin and vulnerable to me, and I felt horrible about starting our married life on this note.

"Let's not think about it again, okay?" he said, not meeting my eyes.

And I didn't, not until the day Michael looked up at me from his hospital bed and told me he wanted to give everything away.

There's an opera called *Arabella* by Richard Strauss, in which a father who has gambled himself into poverty tries to marry off his young daughter to a rich suitor. The daughter ends up with a different wealthy guy instead, but the result is the same—the daughter escapes her father's legacy and gets everything she could ever want.

I see the story of my father and Michael and me twisted up in that opera. But sometimes I wished Strauss had written a fourth act, because I've always wondered what happened after the curtain came down. Did money make her happy? Did Arabella and her husband grow old together, or did they grow far apart?

How did their story end?

Nine

AT TEN O'CLOCK SHARP, I stepped across the threshold of a boutique in Chevy Chase, smiling my thanks at the saleswoman who'd rushed to hold open the heavy glass door for me. I knew I couldn't focus on work today, so I'd asked my assistant to take messages and contact me only if something urgent came up. Instead, I was meeting Isabelle to help her pick out something to wear for her date with Norm, the guy she'd suspected of substituting rifles for a Viagra prescription. Turned out it had all been a misunderstanding: Norm's grandfather had bequeathed him a single Civil War–era musket, and it had arrived by FedEx on the very day Norm met Isabelle, which was the only reason why it came up in conversation.

"You thought I was a gun collector? No wonder you canceled on me! I'm surprised you didn't change your phone number and leave town." Norm had laughed when Isabelle called to thank him for the gorgeous flowers he'd sent.

"He's got potential. Most guys send roses *after* the date," Isabelle said after we'd hugged hello. "Actually, scratch that, most guys don't do that. But they should. Did they stop because of women's lib? Should we be blaming this on Hillary Clinton?"

"Either that, or you could subscribe to the theory that guys like women who don't treat them well," I said, holding up a delicate gold mesh tank top. "Why don't you kick him in the groin tonight and see if he proposes?"

Isabelle fingered the top and wrinkled her nose.

"Fine, but you could get away with it," I said, reluctantly putting it back. I'd never buy it—I was too wholesome-looking for something that exotic—but Isabelle's cat-shaped eyes and angular body let her dress far more dramatically.

"Anyway, so Norm isn't compensating," I said, eager to keep the conversation going so I wouldn't have to think. This was exactly what I needed; some good girl talk to get my mind off what Michael was doing this morning.

"As far as we know," Isabelle allowed. "If I decide an investigation is warranted, I'll give you a full report. We're having dinner tonight. And I decided if he's the kind of guy who sends flowers when I cancel at the last minute, the least I can do is show up wearing something new."

"Noble of you," I said, waving a silky blue empire-waist dress in front of her. Isabelle held it up against her, and we both shook our heads.

My cell phone buzzed in my pocket, and I started so violently that Isabelle grabbed my arm. "Are you okay?"

"Of course," I said, but my voice came out shaky and Isabelle looked at me carefully. It was no use; I couldn't keep up the façade any longer.

"I can't believe Michael's doing this," I whispered, feeling my shoulders slump in defeat. Michael had been released from the hospital yesterday afternoon, and he'd left for his office at 7:00 sharp this morning, as usual. But for the first time, it wasn't because he was itching to dive into work. He was going to begin extricating himself from his company. He'd scheduled a 10:00 A.M., all-hands-on-deck meeting to announce it to his employees.

I glanced at my watch: 10:15. He'd probably already given his speech and assured everyone that he'd do his best to ensure they'd still have jobs. To sweeten his announcement, he was giving every employee a piece of his personal company stock. I mean, why not? Why not throw around the money you'd practically killed yourself to earn like it was confetti at a Mardi Gras parade? His employees were probably hoisting him onto their shoulders and parading him around the office right now, maybe hoping he'd slip off and thunk his head again and decide to hand them the keys to his Maserati.

"Take it!" I could almost see Michael yelling. "I'll ride the bus home! No, take my bus fare, too. I'll walk! But take my shoes first!"

What had happened to him? Why wouldn't he listen to me when I told him he was making a terrible, terrible mistake? I'd alternated between arguing and pleading during these past few days, but nothing I said swayed him. It was as if the old Michael had been replaced by a totally different man, one who wouldn't listen to reason. Everything that had driven him forward in life, all the goals he'd nurtured for decades, had somehow been erased the moment his heart stopped beating.

I picked up another dress and stared at it, but my vision blurred and I couldn't even have said what color it was. I sighed and rubbed my hand across my forehead as exhaustion crashed down on me. I'd barely slept since Michael had announced his insane plan. My eyes felt gritty, and my jaw ached; I'd probably been grinding my teeth in my sleep.

Isabelle was still watching me. "Let's sit down for a minute." She gestured toward the oversize chairs tucked in a corner of the boutique, then turned to the saleswoman who had been discreetly hovering nearby, waiting to whisk our clothing to a dressing room. "Would you mind bringing us two lattes?"

I sank back into the velvety softness of the chair and sighed gratefully.

"I still don't know what I'm going to do," I blurted, like Isabelle and I had been halfway through a conversation. In a sense we were; I knew we were both unable to stop thinking about what was happening. It was the same when my father's gambling addiction became common knowledge. People would look at me, and chat about something innocuous—the weather, or our town's upcoming Fourth of July parade—but I knew an undercurrent always veined through their thoughts, adding another, uglier dimension to their perception of me: *The gambler's daughter. The girl from the ruined family.*

My throat felt swollen and sore; maybe I was coming down with the flu. Or maybe it was from the effort of fighting back tears for so many days.

"I keep turning it over and over in my mind, but it only gets more tangled," I said. "I don't know if I can bear to stay married to him."

"What would happen if you left?" Isabelle asked.

"I could file for divorce, and get a judge to try to freeze his assets." I shrugged. "Of course, that probably means I wouldn't have any of them for a while either. I'd move to a new house, I guess." A very different kind of house. I'd have to live there alone. No, not alone. I'd adopt a cat, a little stray who'd be so grateful that he'd curl up on the foot of my bed every night. I'd name him Ralph, and share cans of tuna fish with him for dinner. That wouldn't be so bad, would it?

"And if you stayed with Michael?" Isabelle asked.

"I don't know. I haven't talked to him much about the future. I'm so mad at him I can barely stand to be around him. I have no idea what he's planning."

"Ladies?" It was our saleswoman. She handed us each a delicate china cup.

"Would you care for freshly ground cinnamon?" she asked me. "Or a blueberry scone? They're warm."

Suddenly, in those simple sentences, everything Michael was making me give up became real: pretty little boutiques with saleswomen who brought me lattes or glasses of icy cold chardonnay in the afternoons. Vanilla-and-lavender-scented Jacuzzis under a sky full of stars. A new car that smelled like rich leather and gleamed from biweekly polishings. We'd had this glittering life for such a short time.

I hadn't even learned to embrace it yet; in some ways, I still felt like a fraud. In the mornings, when Naddy, our maid, came in through our kitchen door, I leapt up guiltily, hiding the evidence that I was reading the newspaper, and raced off to make our bed or wipe down my bathroom sink so she wouldn't secretly think I was a lazy slob. I paid bills the moment they arrived, weeks before they were due, not because I was worried the money would disappear but for the sheer pleasure of writing those checks and knowing there was money to back them up. I still scrutinized the cost of everything I bought, even though I sometimes dared myself to walk into a store and grab something, even just a pair of gloves, without looking at the price tag.

I'd barely dipped my toes into this incredible existence. We'd spent so many years working and planning and striving, and now it was all being snatched away by the very guy who'd made it possible. It was so unfair I wanted to scream. I *had* screamed yesterday while I was driving to the hospital, while I sped down the road so quickly that the trees lining it merged into one hazy, green blur.

"Aah, that tastes good," Isabelle said after she took a sip of latte. "C'mon, Julia. Have some."

I looked at my foam-topped latte, knowing if I asked for anything at all—salted Marcona almonds, a laptop to check my e-mail, a back rub by a strapping Norwegian named Sven who'd murmur in concern over the tension I carried in my shoulders—the saleswomen would all scramble to somehow make it happen.

But never again. Not after today.

I blinked hard and silently repeated the words: *Never again.* I stood up and walked over to a shoe display so I wouldn't have to meet Isabelle's eyes.

"Julia?" Isabelle was up and by my side in one fluid motion. "Are you sure you're okay? You look so pale."

"I . . . I just wanted to see these," I told her, reaching for a pair of shoes. But they were farther away than I'd thought and my hand clutched at empty air. Isabelle said something else, but I couldn't hear anything except the words pounding into my brain like a frantic drumbeat: *Never again. Never again.*

Isabelle was still talking, but her words sounded as garbled as if she was speaking underwater. I gulped in shallow breaths; I couldn't seem to push the oxygen all the way down into my lungs.

"I'm . . . I'm . . ."

I couldn't get out any more words. Then I saw the worry etched across Isabelle's face, and my knees buckled. I heard a saleswoman shriek, then Isabelle's firm voice: "Please give us some privacy." I felt something soft and warm against my cheek; it was as comforting as the blanket I'd loved as a child. I used to rub that threadbare old blanket against my cheek over and over again before falling asleep. I'd kept it for an embarrassingly long time, but my parents never made me feel babyish for wanting it. Now I rubbed my cheek into the softness again, then realized what it was: the rug on the floor. My face felt wet, and I knew I'd hit my nose when I'd fallen. I was bleeding all over this beautiful rug. I should get up, find some tissues, and clean the rug before it stained, but I didn't want to move.

I felt something against my back, as gentle as the touch of a bird's fluttering wings: Isabelle's hand. Then I realized the wetness dripping down my face was tears.

"It's going to be okay," I heard her say, but her voice sounded like an echo from a great distance away. I heard Isabelle make a call on her cell phone, and in what seemed like no time at all, a pair of strong arms was lifting me up and carrying me outside, into the sunlight.

Ten

"IT'S FOR YOU," MICHAEL said, handing me the phone. He patted me on the shoulder and his hand hovered in the air for a moment, as though it was unsure of where to go next. "I'll be downstairs if you need anything."

I ignored him and lifted the phone to my ear to hear Isabelle's worried voice asking, "Are you better?"

I stretched underneath my cool white silk sheet, flexing and arching my toes and feeling my calf muscles contract while images from yesterday morning flooded my mind: Isabelle's driver scooping me up off the floor of the boutique and carrying me to the car; Isabelle with her arm wrapped around me as she made a few hushed phone calls in the backseat of her Bentley; the sharp brown eyes of Dr. Rushman looking at me from behind his wire-rimmed glasses while he pressed a stethoscope to my chest. Dr. Rushman had given me a little orange pill—Xanax, I thought, appreciating the irony—and I'd let its bitterness dissolve on my tongue before giving myself up to the blessed darkness. I'd slept through the whole day and woken at 1:00 A.M. to find Michael dozing beside me. It was one of the few times I'd ever been awake while he slept.

I'd slipped out of bed and wandered downstairs and made myself a cup of coffee. I'd turned on my iPod and slipped in the earbuds and stepped onto our big stone back patio. As the hours passed and I stayed curled up on a chaise lounge, watching the first streaks of color lighten the sky, I began to realize I *was* feeling better. Maybe it was the lingering comfort of the Xanax, but I suspected it was something else, something stronger fighting its way past the fear and confusion: my survival instinct. I'd battled my way out of the dreary, sad life that had claimed my parents. I'd built my own little company from scratch, teaching myself how to incorporate it and advertise and decipher the various taxes. And I'd endured the stark loneliness of my marriage. I was stronger than I'd realized.

And then Renée Fleming's voice had come through my iPod.

I think Renée is the most beautiful opera singer in the whole world. She has thick blond hair and wise blue eyes and a face that manages to combine strength and kindness in equal parts, but it's not her physical beauty that makes her so special. She's a lyric soprano, which means her voice is sweet, rather than, say, that of Maria Callas, whose tones were steely. You'll find plenty of people who argue that Callas was better, or maybe Beverly Sills, but once you hear Renée sing—well, it's impossible not to fall under her spell. The best part is that she seems totally normal, like she could be one of your girlfriends, kvetching about those five pounds she gained on vacation or debating whether John Cusack is hotter than John Mayer.

But the way she works at singing—well, her training regime would put an Olympian to shame. She contorts her body into yoga-like positions, making sure she can hit her high notes when she's bending over and touching her toes, or lying on the floor with all of her muscles completely limp. She memorizes pages and pages of the libretto in all sorts of languages she can't even speak, and when she's up onstage, she's controlling her breathing and remembering how to pronounce foreign words and synthesizing it all with gestures and movements true to her character—and still sending her glorious voice all the way to the last row of a giant opera house. It takes *my* breath away, just thinking of it.

But years ago, Renée nearly threw away her years of training and walked off stage forever. Her marriage fell apart while she was raising two young girls, and then, out of the blue, attacks of stage fright seized her. Renée was terrified she couldn't get through songs she'd sung dozens of times before. She was scared she'd fail. She would physically shake before performances, fighting her fear as hard as she could, knowing terror was the worst thing for her voice. Then one night, she performed at La Scala, and everything went wrong. The conductor fainted, right there in the middle of the performance. And some members of the audience—not many, but enough for her to hear—began to boo her. Can you imagine? You're going through a divorce, you're worried your voice might give out from fear, you've begun to have panic attacks, and you're thinking about just giving up and crawling away somewhere and hiding. And you're standing under a spotlight, a *spotlight* for God's sakes, scared and alone but trying to tough it out, and people are booing you. Wouldn't you quit? Wouldn't you just walk off the stage and never go back?

But Renée kept putting on her beautiful costumes and practicing her deep breathing, and she rested her voice on the days of her big performances. She never ran away. She's still singing to this day, in the languages of Puccini and Strauss and Bizet.

Six months after she was booed at La Scala, Renée went back and sang her heart out. They gave her a standing ovation.

As I'd listened to her and watched the sun rise, I'd thought, If she can endure all that—endure and *triumph*—then maybe I could get through this.

I wasn't going to passively sit back while my husband dictated which direction our lives would take. It was time to start formulating a plan of my own. Right now, I could see only two options: I could try to convince Michael to change his mind, or I could call the lawyer whose card was tucked into my wallet and ask him to contest the prenup. I knew our prenup was rock-solid—I'd made sure of that—but a good lawyer might be able to find a loophole, or get it thrown out in court. I wouldn't be entitled to all of Michael's money, but maybe I could get a chunk.

If only I hadn't been so adamant about keeping our finances separate, I'd thought, burying my face in my hands. I didn't want my name on the title for either of our houses because Michael had taken out big mortgages for the tax benefits, and some part of me still couldn't believe he was so successful. In a way, I guess I was waiting for the floor to drop out, and I didn't want to be hurt in the fall. I was ashamed to admit it, but I wanted to enjoy all the luxuries of our lifestyle without actually being responsible for any of them. Now that precaution was boomeranging back at me.

I'd leaned my head against the couch and imagined telling Michael I wanted a divorce. What would he say? What would his face look like in that moment? I didn't know what it would feel like to walk away from him, but maybe that was just because we'd been together for so long. Maybe I could learn to live quite happily without my husband.

When Renée finished singing, I'd stood up and switched off the music and gone back to bed. I knew I'd need my strength for what was to come.

"I promise I'm fine," I said to Isabelle on the phone now, keeping my tone light. I'd worried her enough lately. "You know me. I was just trying to get some attention."

"Oh, honey, you scared the crap out of me," Isabelle said,

sounding like she was half-laughing, half-crying. "I called last night, but Michael said you were still sleeping."

"I think it just hit me all at once," I said. "I'm never going to be able to walk into a boutique like that again and buy anything I want. Hell, if Michael has his way, I won't be able to splurge at the Dollar Store."

"He really did it?" Isabelle asked.

"Yep," I said. "That's why he's here instead of at work."

I heard a gentle tap on the door, and I covered the phone receiver. "Come in, Naddy."

But it wasn't Naddy. It was Michael, carrying a tray.

"I thought you might be hungry," he said, putting it down next to me on the bed. He'd made me French toast and scrambled eggs and coffee. The eggs looked a little rubbery and overdone, but he'd picked some irises from our garden and put them in a little glass vase in one corner of the tray.

There it was: evidence that Michael didn't know me at all. I hadn't eaten French toast in years; it was Satan's breakfast buffet for the calorie-conscious.

Oh, hell, what did it matter anymore? I thought, spearing a bite with the fork. It was buttery and brown, and it almost melted in my mouth.

So Michael remembered it used to be my favorite. So what? It was going to take more than a few wilted irises for me to forgive him, I thought. Then the flowers made me remember Isabelle's night.

"Let's talk about you for a change," I said. "How was your date?"

I could practically feel her smile over the phone line.

"Nice," she finally said.

"Details," I demanded.

"It was wonderful," she blurted. "I mean, aside from the times when I couldn't stop worrying about you. But we went to dinner, and it felt like we sat down one minute, and the next I looked up and saw we were the only ones left in the restaurant."

"Wow," I said. "I haven't heard you talk about a date that way in . . . well, ever."

"We just have so much in common," she said. "We even both had starter marriages."

Isabelle had gotten married right after college, and divorced six months later. "Why do they let anyone get married that young?" she once asked me. "Marriage should be like a driver's license—you should only get a provisional trial marriage until you're thirty, and then, if you've proved you can handle all the bumps and fender benders, you get the real license."

"I told him about you," Isabelle was saying now. "I mean, not the specific details or anything. But he could tell I was upset when he came to pick me up, and I didn't want to cancel on him again. Dr. Rushman said you'd probably sleep through the night, so I knew there wasn't anything I could do . . ."

"You did plenty," I told her, meaning it. "Tell me more about Norm."

"Are you sure?" She didn't wait for me to answer; I didn't think she *could*. The words cascaded giddily out of her, like foam from the mouth of a champagne bottle. "There was this little boy outside the restaurant when we were walking in, and he was so damn cute in his stroller with one of those fake cell phones he was babbling into, and then he dropped the phone and Norm picked it up and handed it to the kid, and said, 'Sir? I think this call is for you.' And the little boy gave him the biggest smile. It was one of those moments, you know?"

"He sounds great," I said. *Wow.* Was this really Isabelle gushing? Sharp, funny, nongushing Isabelle?

"But the thing is, he's *not* perfect," she said eagerly. "I'd be suspicious of perfect. His nose is kind of big, and he's a little klutzy. He almost tripped walking into the restaurant. But it makes him seem . . . I don't know, more *real*. Then in the car, on the way home, he sang along to the radio, and his voice was awful, but he didn't care. So I sang with him, and you know I never sing in public. I mean, my voice is a misdemeanor in all fifty states."

I just sat there, my French toast growing cold, as I listened. Isabelle had dated dozens of guys since I'd known her—men always flocked around her, attracted by her beauty and money and sometimes, for the most confident guys, her brains, too— but she brushed them off after a few dates. I'd begun to assume she'd always stay single. As my marriage grew more distant, I'd secretly harbored the thought that we'd be single together, in a sense, our friendship deepening with each passing decade. We'd drive each other to the doctor if we became sick, sit side by side on rocking chairs complaining about our arthritis, and crack each other up by yelling, "Can you bend over and get me a drink, sonny?" to the muscular young pool boys Isabelle would hire.

I was happy for Isabelle—wasn't I?—but a shameful sense of betrayal gnawed at me. We were so close. We talked on the phone once or twice a day. We were as comfortable in each other's homes as we were in our own—which meant I was just as worried about scratching her antique furniture or knocking over a priceless vase as I was about my own. Secretly, I'd begun entertaining the idea that, if I left Michael, I could stay with Isabelle until I sorted out what to do next.

"So are you going to see him again soon?" I asked. I pushed away Michael's tray. I'd lost my appetite.

"The day after tomorrow," she said. "He's surprising me. He just told me to dress casually, and he's picking me up at lunch- time. Is it horrible that I Googled him? I had to make sure he hasn't filed for bankruptcy or something awful like—" Isabelle's voice skidded to a stop.

I broke the silence quickly: "I know what you mean."

"Not that it's terrible not to have money," she said apologetically. "I just wanted to make sure that wasn't the only thing he was looking for in me."

There it was: a tinge of embarrassment staining her voice. The first sign of a little fissure between us.

You could argue that a true friendship would endure no matter what, that superficial things shouldn't matter, but I knew firsthand how emotions like envy and pity and guilt were cancers to a friendship. If I tried hard enough, would I be able to stave off my jealousy when I saw Isabelle living the life I once had? Would Isabelle be as happy about meeting me at a corner deli for dinner instead of a five-star restaurant? Maybe at first, but I'd been on the other side of this equation a few years ago, when Michael had made the quick leap from debt-ridden to insanely wealthy, and I still missed the friendship I'd lost.

I couldn't let it happen again, I vowed. Isabelle was too important.

"I'm babbling," she said. "What are you going to do today?"

"Oh, tell me more about last night," I said, injecting enthusiasm into my voice. "What did you end up wearing?"

As I steered the conversation back into safety, Michael tiptoed into the room and took away my tray. There was a note behind the vase of flowers that I hadn't seen until now, and it slipped off, onto the bed, when he lifted the tray.

"I've loved you from the first moment I saw you," it read. "Please give me one more chance."

I crumpled the little card in my hand, not caring that Michael saw. I wanted to hurt him. He was ruining everything.

Eleven

FROM TIME TO TIME, you hear on the news about people—usually men, but occasionally a woman—who suddenly abandoned their lives, as cleanly and abruptly as if they took a pair of scissors and snipped away their pasts. The media always focus on the person who walked away, digging into the crushing pile of bills or the double life with another family, but what I've always wondered is what happened to the folks left behind, the bewildered people just outside the glare of the hot TV lights and the camera flashes.

Imagine: There you are in the kitchen, tossing salad in a wooden bowl while your baby bangs a spoon against the tray of his high chair and the dog hovers nearby, fervently hoping you drop a scrap of chicken on the floor. And while you putter around, absently listening for the sound of a key turning in the lock, the person you love the most, the person you thought you knew inside out, is in the process of walking away from the life you've built together, from the life you've only partly finished constructing.

Some people abandon a life in the snap of a finger, and now Michael essentially wanted to do the same thing by giving up his company, which *was* his life. It staggers me, given what it took him to create DrinkUp, starting from scratch.

When Michael and I first moved to D.C., we were about as broke as it was possible for two people to be. We had six hundred dollars in cash, a car worth about a third of that on a good day, and a couple of Hefty bags with our clothes and shoes and drugstore toiletries jammed inside.

But within a week, Michael landed a job as a waiter at a pizza place—we both agreed he needed to be fed at work or we'd go bankrupt, fast—and soon after that I capitalized on my babysitting experience and got hired as a nanny for a wealthy family with two-year-old twins. Later I'd learn the twins were biters, but at the time, I felt incredibly fortunate to be earning three hundred dollars a week—which, as it turned out, ended up being about fifty dollars per bite.

We lived in a youth hostel at first, until we'd saved enough money for a security deposit, then we moved into a fourth-floor walk-up studio apartment in Tenleytown, where my one luxury was keeping on a kitchen light all night so the cockroaches wouldn't venture out of the cracks around the stove. We bought a secondhand futon that was our couch during the day and our bed at night, and we trash-picked a little kitchen table and two mismatched chairs that we painted sky blue to add a splash of color to our dreary apartment. Then we took out student loans for college and got even broker. But Michael had a telescopic view into the future; he could see that he needed to get deeper into debt in order to climb more quickly out of it. Somehow, between our jobs and financial aid and loans, we cobbled together enough to attend school—Michael at Georgetown University and I at the University of Maryland in College Park. We worked by day, took classes at night, and spent every weekend alternately napping and studying—at least *I* napped, while Michael used a yellow highlighter to mark up his textbooks on the futon next to me.

Michael's grades and test scores were so phenomenal he could've gotten a job anywhere. I always thought he'd do something with computers, or maybe rise through the ranks of a Fortune 500 company. But Michael was determined to never work for anyone but himself. He bided his time, whipping through college in three years and applying to business schools while he pored over the blueprints and mission statements of start-up companies.

"There's always room for a new product," he'd say, pacing our apartment like a 1950s father outside the hospital delivery room. "The trick is finding the niche. Mrs. Fields cookies. Post-it notes. Baby Einstein videos. None of those took a lot of capital; they all started small and exploded. What's missing? What does the market not know it needs yet?"

Our apartment was so tiny he could take only three or four steps before stubbing his toe on our futon frame or dark-wood dresser from Goodwill and cursing before he spun around again, and I hid a smile while I watched him. He felt to me like a greyhound, all coiled energy, every speck of his concentration waiting for the gate in front of him to slide open and reveal the racetrack.

The only thing he needed was an idea. None of us knew it at the time, but one was already simmering in his mind. During Michael's very first semester at Georgetown, his favorite professor, Raj, had used Coke versus Pepsi in a case study about effective advertising strategies.

Much later, Michael would tell me he'd jotted down a question mark in the margin of his notebook as he idly wondered, "Why is it Coke versus Pepsi? Why isn't there something else?" The thought didn't take hold then, though. It lingered deep inside Michael's brain, waiting to be triggered by the perfect collision of circumstances, which wouldn't occur until a sweltering hot afternoon several years later.

By then I'd already started my own little party-planning company, All Occasions, and Michael was in his final semester of business school at Georgetown. My income made our lives a bit more comfortable. We'd moved to a nicer apartment building, one with an elevator and no roaches, and we saw a movie or went out for a beer together every week. We'd bought a living room set that was on sale, and secondhand computers and a television. But most of my money went toward my student loans; I was frantic to get rid of them as quickly as possible, and I doubled down on my monthly payments.

Whenever I thought about our future, I imagined it as a series of stepping-stones: We'd made the leap from West Virginia to D.C., and now to a better apartment. We had a few nice belongings. Next we'd buy a car that had fewer than six numbers on its odometer, and after that, we'd move to a pretty little house. Slowly but steadily, our life would take on a reassuring, solid shape. But Michael was focusing on a very different future. It wasn't that I didn't believe he'd be successful, but we were two poor kids from West Virginia. We were the first ones in our families to go to college. He was the dreamer, I was the pragmatist. How high could we realistically aim?

Every afternoon, when he had a break between classes and his shift at the pizza place, Michael laced up his sneakers and ran, looping through the city's eclectic neighborhoods—Chinatown and Dupont Circle and Cleveland Park—as he tried to burn off some of the energy pulsing through him.

"A drink," he gasped as he flung open the door one unseasonably hot May afternoon.

"Get it yourself, caveman," I said, not even looking up from my computer.

"No, I mean *a drink*," he panted, bending over and putting his hands on his knees. "That's it. That's what's missing. I just went to 7-Eleven to get a drink, and they've basically got four choices: soda, Gatorade and iced tea—which are just as sugary as soda—or plain old water. None of it looked good to me. There's a hole, Julie, right there in the middle of the 7-Eleven case. A giant freaking hole! What if there was flavored water that tastes good? But not as sweet as Gatorade; that stuff tastes as sugary as soda . . . no artificial dyes, but maybe I'll add some vitamins. Health food is becoming trendy; it's not for hippies anymore. I just read an article about it in *Newsweek*. I'll use natural sweeteners instead of high-fructose corn syrup, that's the key . . ."

As he spoke, Michael absently shed his clothes and walked into the shower, and I could hear him still talking over the flow of the water. I smiled and turned back to my computer, knowing his methodical brain would have worked through the kinks in his plan, weighing the potential downsides versus the merits, by the time he turned off the water. He'd already considered and discarded the ideas for a dozen companies.

But within five minutes, he'd called in sick to work and was racing to the grocery store, his hair still dripping wet. He went to three different grocery and health food stores that day, and by the time I went to bed, our kitchen looked like a convention of mad scientists had invaded it. Concoctions filled every pot and pan we owned.

"Take a sip," Michael demanded the next morning, thrusting a spoonful of something lemon-smelling in my face as I stumbled into the kitchen for coffee.

"Did you even sleep?" I asked, already knowing the answer.

"Is it too sweet?" he asked urgently. "My taste buds are shot. I need a fresh palate."

"Not too sweet," I said, licking my upper lip. "But . . ."

"Not quite there yet. I know, I know."

I looked at the ingredients flooding the kitchen—the brightly colored limes and oranges, the thick, golden honey and agave nectar, the jars of liquid vitamins, the stubby roots of ginger and rolled sticks of cinnamon and bowls of dried fruits. Our coffeepot held a light orange liquid, and every one of our mugs and glasses was full; it looked as if Michael was trying to isolate all the colors of a rainbow. *Was that*— I squinted and realized that, yes, Michael had uprooted an African violet and was using its pot as another container.

"How many drinks have you made?" I asked. The competing smells were overwhelming, and I flung open a window.

"Dozens. Hundreds. I've tasted them all. I'm peeing every ten minutes," he said, grabbing a pot off the stove just as the sea green liquid inside began boiling over.

"I've got to run," I said, grabbing an orange to eat for breakfast on the road. "I'll probably be late."

"Can I heat brown sugar into a syrup . . . hmmm? What? Did you say something?" Michael asked, frowning at the little notebook he'd filled with the scribbles that no one but he could decipher.

"Bar mitzvah for the Rosenbaum brat," I said, reaching out to tilt up his chin and kiss him and coming away with a sticky residue on my lip that tasted like blueberries.

When I walked in the door that evening, the kitchen looked even worse, but Michael was smiling. He handed me a glass bottle adorned with a label he'd printed up on our computer.

"DrinkUp? That's the name?" I asked. "What's in it?"

"About ten cents' worth of products," he said, his face bright despite the dark circles under his eyes. "I'm almost there."

* * *

In retrospect, it was a good thing I was so busy at work that month. If I'd known that Michael had stopped going to classes and missed the deadline on an important paper, that he was in the process of dropping out of school, I would've been furious. He was so close to earning his degree; why the rush? Wouldn't his new product seem more legitimate when he had an MBA after his name? And secretly, while I thought the idea for his healthy drinks wasn't a bad one, it didn't seem revolutionary. Personally, I counted myself as a satisfied customer of Diet Coke.

But I was too busy dealing with the Spence stepsisters to keep track of Michael. They were a Cinderella story, but with a twist: Abby, the youngest sister, who was getting married, was homely and awkward. It was as though someone had taken a mold of her father's face—heavy eyebrows, hooked nose, strong chin—and recycled it for her. Abby's stepsister was the maid of honor, and she was thin, beautiful, and had just discovered her own fiancé was cheating on her. Which might've been a form of social justice, except that the pretty stepsister, Diane, was by far the nicer of the two.

"Which ones do you think I should wear?" Abby asked as she held up a glittering, teardrop-shaped earring and a simple pearl encircled by gold.

"I like the pearls," Diane said. "They're classic."

"But you only get to be a bride once," Abby said with a huge smile. "Everyone's going to be looking at me. I think I should go for the sparkle."

"Of course," Diane said, managing a grin. "That makes sense."

"Now let's go over the seating chart again," Abby said, her voice sympathetic but her eyes bright. "Are you sure you want an uneven number of chairs at your table? We could put someone else there instead of just taking away Rob's seat."

Diane blinked hard, and I quickly interjected a question about the centerpieces. That was one thing I hadn't expected about my job. Party planning was the official title, but I was equal parts therapist, referee, judge, and troubleshooter. I loved it, though. Maybe because my life seemed like it was just beginning to unfold, and this gave me the chance to glimpse other people's and imagine which pieces I wanted for myself someday: the lavish anniversary party? No way; I liked quieter celebrations. The first dance to a song that had meaning only for the newlyweds? Yes! The minivan with the gaggle of kids? Someday, maybe . . .

Michael was so busy putting together a business plan for his new idea, and studying for exams—or at least that's what I thought—that our apartment was usually empty when I came home. But later, when I looked back on that time, what I remembered most was the little notes he'd leave for me every day in unexpected places.

"I'll be home before your head hits this," read one on my pillow.

"Meet you inside here at 10:00 P.M. I promise to wash your back." This one was taped to the shower curtain.

And propped up against a single red rose he'd left on our kitchen counter on Valentine's Day: "You were smiling in your sleep when I left. I wanted to watch you forever." That note I tucked into my underwear drawer to save.

A week or so after the Spence wedding (where I'd successfully urged the good-looking but shy drummer for the band to ask Diane for her phone number during a break between sets), I came home to find Michael sitting at our little blue table with four glasses in front of him.

"You look vaguely familiar," I said, tossing my briefcase onto the couch. "Remind me of your name again?"

"I'll be your server tonight. We're having a tasting, madam," he said as he stood up and bowed. He had a dirty old dish towel folded over his forearm; I'd have to withhold his tip. "Please sit down. Tonight we'll be serving Citrus Fruit, Berrywater, Not-Too-Sweet Lemonade, and PuckerUp Limeade."

"Sounds delightful," I said. "And very filling."

"I think you'll find our tasting menu is deceptively light and refreshing." He handed me a cup. "Your first course will be Not-Too-Sweet Lemonade."

I sipped, and my eyes widened. "Michael, it's *good*!"

"You like it?" He dropped his terrible French accent.

"It's tangy and . . . and so *fresh*," I said.

"Right! That's it exactly," he said, the words tumbling out of him in a torrent. "My professor Raj knows one of the former beverage buyers for Whole Foods. She came in and did a guest lecture at Georgetown a few years ago. He thinks he can get me a meeting with her. Here, try this one."

I sipped them all—the lemonade was still my favorite, but Berrywater was a close second—then I started dinner while Michael squeezed into our galley kitchen with me.

"It's not just the ex-buyer," he explained for the tenth time as I swirled spaghetti around in boiling water. "She's a link in the chain. If she likes my product, she might be able to introduce me to her contacts."

"She will," I said. "She'll like it."

"All I need is two minutes with the right person," Michael continued as I drained the noodles in a plastic colander in the sink, leaning over the hot rush of steam to get the poor woman's version of a facial. Later I'd slather half an avocado on my face to complete my beautifying and make Angelina Jolie shake in her shoes with raw, unbridled envy.

"I told you what *Natural Foods Merchandiser* reported, right?" Michael asked as I handed him a spoon and pointed him toward the spaghetti sauce simmering in a pan.

"Tell me again?" I humored him.

"There's been a huge increase in natural foods buying during the past three years. It's poised to explode. I'm going to ride the wave. God, who would've thought all those years of reading food labels would pay off? Remember when I used to warn you about those disgusting neon pink cupcakes?"

"Hey," I said. "They were good!"

Michael smacked me on the butt with a dish towel. "People don't know what they're putting into their bodies. But they're going to start caring, and they're going to get mad. I'll keep my ingredients list fresh and simple and natural. The timing couldn't be more perfect!"

I nodded, even though Michael would've kept talking without any encouragement, and he ladled warm marinara sauce on the noodles before setting our plates down on the wobbly table that barely afforded enough room for them.

"Maybe I should tweak my marketing plan once more," he said, spinning around and heading for his laptop.

I looked down at our dinner, then looked over at Michael, whose fingers were already flying across the keyboard. Michael wasn't eating? That, more than anything, drove home to me how serious he was about this project.

And two nights later, he was waiting when I came home from work.

"Ten A.M. next Friday!" he shouted, handing me an icy cold bottle of Bud Light.

"You got the meeting with the former buyer?" I asked, sinking into the futon—as much as I could sink, given how hard the mattress was—and sliding off my shoes.

"Nope," he said, shaking his head as he sat down beside me and began rubbing my feet a little too vigorously. "The current buyer! I met the former buyer today, and she already set it up. She loves DrinkUp. *Loves* it! I found this guy who designs wine labels for a little winery in Maryland. They're really classy, look"—he sprang up and grabbed a wine bottle and handed it to me—"and he's going to do some mock-up labels for me. He already came up with one concept, but it isn't quite right. I don't care if he has to go through ten drafts. I can't go in there looking second-rate. This is huge. I feel it, Julia. It's finally happening!"

My heart skipped a beat, but not for the right reason. I thought about the costs Michael was incurring—already, before his brand-new company had even made a cent—but I forced myself to swallow my worry. This was Michael's dream; I couldn't tarnish it with my old fears.

I stood up and grabbed his hand.

"We're going out," I said, putting down my beer and pulling him toward the door. There wasn't any question of where we'd go—the pizza place on the corner was all we could afford, since Michael got an employee discount—but still, we splurged on a bottle of Chianti and toasted our future and leaned close to one another over the red-checked tablecloth, our fingers twining together, talking until they brightened the lights and kicked us out.

"It's going to happen," Michael said, his blue eyes darkening with intensity. "I've got a good product, the market needs it, and with Raj's contacts, I can make it work. The next thing to do is get investors—but if Whole Foods likes me, it'll be a snap."

"Definitely," I agreed, squeezing his hand. I hate to admit it, but I still wasn't convinced. Flavored water? *That* was Michael's stroke of genius, the culmination of all he'd learned at one of the country's top business schools? It seemed so . . . so simple.

Twelve

OUR WEDDING DAY WAS absolutely perfect.

By then I'd overseen enough receptions to know that it was
the little moments people kept as cherished memories, not the
splashy, oversize ones. One of the most elaborate weddings I
planned was ruined when the groom got so drunk he spent
half of the party throwing up in the bathroom while the bride
sobbed and her father muttered curses ("I'm not quite sure
what shots to get," the photographer had whispered to me. "A
little direction?").

Michael and I didn't have many friends to invite, and we
both wanted to keep things simple.

"Should we ask your parents to come?" he wondered.

I tried to answer him, but started to cry instead. "I want them
here," I finally said. "But my dad . . . I mean, I know he's sick.
It's like alcoholism. But I keep thinking about how he ruined
my mom's life. I mean, they're still living with my uncle. She's
waitressing, for God's sakes. My mom is pushing sixty and she's
on her feet all day serving hamburgers."

"He stopped, though, right?"

"For now," I said. My dad had quit gambling a half dozen

times before—always with grand promises—but it never stuck.

"It'll hurt them if I don't invite them," I said. "And how can I have a wedding without my parents there? I'd feel so strange walking down the aisle alone . . ."

"We could elope," Michael said immediately. "It'll just be you and me. That's always been enough for us, hasn't it?"

His arms closed around me. "We don't need anyone else. Let's do it soon. Right away. We just need to get our license, but it won't take long. The waiting period's only a few days."

I rested my head against his shoulder. "Just you and me?"

"Next week," he said. "I want to marry you before my Whole Foods meeting. Jules, this is the beginning of everything for us. My company, our new life together . . . let's start it off right."

I looked down at the simple engagement band Michael had given me a few months earlier, when he'd proposed, then I lifted up my face to his and smiled.

I wore a classic cream-colored sheath dress that was deeply discounted because of a torn hem I'd sewed up in under ten minutes, and carried a bouquet of wildflowers that Michael had picked for me. As we stood in front of a justice of the peace reciting our vows, Michael wiggled his eyebrows when I got to the "obey" part, almost making me laugh out loud. But as we were pronounced man and wife, he stared into my eyes for a long moment, and the look in his took my breath away.

He cooked me dinner that night, and we shared a bottle of champagne—the first we'd ever tasted. Afterward he reached for my hand and pulled me to my feet. He pressed a button on our battered old CD player, and we swayed together in our tiny apartment as Louis Armstrong sang "What a Wonderful World."

"I'll buy you a diamond soon," Michael promised as we cuddled in bed. By then we'd both forgotten about the prenup we'd signed that morning. "A huge one. You won't be allowed to walk down the street because the glare will blind innocent by-standers."

"Why are bystanders always presumed to be innocent?" I asked.

"Good point," he said. "I'm sure plenty of them are down-right evil. They deserve to be blinded. I'm going to give you another five carats so we can take them all out."

"But what about you?" I asked, tracing a lazy finger along his jawline, then down the slope of his shoulder. He was still so skinny, but I loved his body. "Are you going to buy yourself a Lamborghini?"

"Maybe a boat," Michael mused.

"You'd have no idea what to do with a boat." I laughed. "You'd crash it on the first day."

"So the Lamborghini," Michael decided. "Unless I buy a backup boat. You know, for when the first one is in the shop."

"And you'll need to add 'the Third' to your name," I pointed out. "It's a requirement for stuffy rich guys."

"Are stuffy rich guys allowed to ravish their wives twice in one night?" Michael asked, rolling from his back to his side to face me.

"It's a requirement," I whispered in his ear. "Read your stuffy rich guy manual."

I wish I could've been there the day Michael circled the Whole Foods parking lot in our rusty station wagon and lugged his four thermoses of DrinkUp into the upscale grocery store. What did the beverages buyer think of Michael, dressed in his best black sweater and slacks, his hair carefully gelled for the first time in his life? Did he look into Michael's eyes and see the intensity burning there, and know that if force of will could guarantee victory, Michael would be a runaway success?

The buyer drank the samples—"He was like a wine connoisseur, Julia, he sniffed first and everything"—and then, right there on the spot, offered Michael a deal: Whole Foods would test out two pallets, or ten thousand bottles, in a trial run for seventeen stores in the Mid-Atlantic area.

"My God! That fast?" I said. "When do they want them?"

"I asked them to give me two months," Michael said, absently tugging his curls back into wild disarray. "Julia, here's the thing. They're not going to pay me for whatever they sell. They're doing me a favor by testing them out. I have to absorb the cost; that's traditionally the way these things work."

I felt my pulse quicken. "So you'll be taking on debt." *More debt,* I thought, my mind flashing, almost like a reflex, to the copy of the prenup I'd tucked in a shoe box in our closet.

Michael didn't seem to hear me. "I need investors, but Raj is going to help with that. He's fronting me some money, too. There's this other guy from my marketing class whose dad is really rich; his name is on a plaque above one of the classroom doors. I'm going to ask him to kick in five thousand. I think if he knows Raj is doing it, and I've got Whole Foods behind me . . . Now I need to rent a place to make the water; this kitchen is too small. I need a U-Haul to get the stuff up to Buffalo—I found a good bottler there . . ." And he was off, again, sprinting for his laptop, while I frowned and stared after him.

By the time Whole Foods let Michael set up a little tasting table in their store, everything had somehow come together. The customers never saw the mistakes and setbacks—the cases of bottles that were labeled upside down, the batches of DrinkUp that turned out too sour before Michael tweaked his recipes for mass production, and the endless hours he spent on the phone, cajoling investors who'd dropped out because the risk seemed too great, finding replacements, and begging his bottler to delay the bill in exchange for a percentage of the first two years' profit. The only thing they noticed was a polite young man in a freshly printed DrinkUp apron, standing there and charming them into accepting a cup as they walked by.

"You look like a soccer star," Michael called to a ten-year-old boy. "This stuff'll give you energy you won't believe when you're on the field. Here, take a cup for your mom, too. It's much better for him than Gatorade, and one bottle has a day's worth of ten vitamins. Now, how about you, sir? Take a sip of my Not-Too-Sweet Lemonade and see if it doesn't remind you of the lemonade stand you had when you were a kid. How'd I know you had one? Because you look like an entrepreneur."

He never stopped talking, never grew tired, never wavered in his belief that his drinks were exactly what customers needed. And they began to believe it, too; I stood near the checkout aisle and saw the carts—not all of them, but some—had bottles of DrinkUp tucked in among the free-range chicken breasts and organic salad greens and pita chips. He'd picked the perfect store to launch his product, I realized, feeling my respect for Michael bump up another notch. I wandered over to where he held court like a carnival barker and snapped a photo as he held a little paper cup aloft. Later I framed it and put it on my desk in my office; it has always been my favorite picture of him.

The pallets sold out quickly—every last bottle—and Whole Foods followed up with an order for ten more. But this time, Michael got paid. And years later, he had the last laugh when Georgetown gave him an honorary degree.

I hate to admit that so many other people believed in Michael before I did. But when he and I got married, I was the richer one. I knew he was planning to hire salespeople to cold-call on grocery stores and gourmet markets. He was desperate to stay ahead of the pack. "When everyone sees me taking off, they're going to jump all over this," he often said, tightening his jaw in his best imitation of a threatening, 150-pound man.

All those salaries, all those flights around the country . . . I couldn't help adding up the costs in my mind, but Michael never hesitated in taking on even more debt, or wooing more backers. His student loans were exorbitant, too.

But it wasn't *my* debt, I reassured myself as my husband methodically built his company by selling bottle after bottle. I'd never be like my mother, wiping down tables at age sixty because I'd tied my fortunes to the wrong man. Michael's company couldn't hurt me.

Thirteen

ONE MORNING AFTER WE'D been married for a couple of years, I opened my eyes to find Michael leaning over me, waving a copy of *USA Today* inches away from my face.

"I'm asleep," I groaned, batting away the paper. The previous night I'd held a beach-themed fiftieth birthday party for a woman who'd insisted on filling the dance floor with real sand. The cleanup had lasted longer than the actual party.

"Look," he whispered.

I yawned and rubbed my eyes. "Oprah's producing another movie?" I asked, scanning the headlines.

"The photo," he said, his voice strangled.

I glanced at him, then sat up straighter. There it was: on the table next to Oprah Winfrey, within reach of her famous bejeweled hand, was the beverage she'd consumed during the interview. DrinkUp's Berrywater.

"Michael!" I leapt out of bed, instantly awake, and flung my arms around his neck.

"Do you know what this means?" he shouted, grabbing me around the waist and hoisting me into the air and dancing me around our apartment. "I've gotten a hundred messages this morning from store owners and customers and suppliers wanting to know where to buy Oprah's water. When the interviewer asked her about it, she said Madonna recommended she try it, and now she drinks it every day. She said it gives her energy. Every fucking *day*! I could've bought ten Super Bowl ads and it wouldn't have done this for my company! Jules, this is it!"

"You did it!" I squealed.

Michael put me down, and I ran over to an open window, leaning out of it and screaming, "Oprah and Madonna love my husband's water! They freaking *love* it!"

A sleepy-sounding voice shouted back: "Tell them to shut up!"

"*We* did it," Michael said, his voice awed and quiet now. We stood there, staring at each other and breathing hard, I in one of Michael's old T-shirts and he in one of his even older T-shirts, feeling the molecules shift and rearrange all around us, and knowing nothing would be the same, ever again.

"Come here, you," I said, my mouth curving into a smile. I wanted to feel his thin arms wrapped around me and hear the sound of his rapid heartbeat echoing in my ears. I wanted to kiss him forever, then take him out for pancakes and champagne. This was the moment we'd dreamed of, back when we'd saved our dollars in an old cigar box. No—we'd never dreamed this high. At least, I hadn't.

Michael wagged his eyebrows. "Exactly what did you have in mind, Mrs. Dunhill? Are you thinking impure thoughts?"

"Come find out." I grinned, but Michael's cell rang again and he snatched it up.

"I saw it," he said, his hand slipping away from my mine as he walked out of the room. "I'll be there in ten minutes. Five. I need to capitalize on this, fast. Here's what I'm thinking . . ."

"I'm sorry, Julie," he whispered, ducking his head back

through the doorway and covering the mouthpiece with one hand. "Tonight. We'll celebrate tonight."

But when I fell asleep that night, naked and cold, the space in bed beside me was empty. By the time I woke up, Michael was already gone, leaving nothing but the faint imprint of his head on a pillow to prove he'd been there at all.

Fourteen

I STARED STRAIGHT AHEAD at the double yellow line stretching out on the road in front of us. Our driver was gone; Michael had given him, Naddy, the gardeners, and our chef glowing recommendations and a year's salary, and our house seemed eerily quiet without their constant bustle. Now it was just Michael and me heading to the grocery store. We were out of milk. Everything was collapsing into a jagged, dusty heap all around us, and here I was doing errands with my husband like it was any other mundane weekend afternoon. Somehow it seemed like ordinary life should've frozen around us, but the car still needed gas and the newspaper kept arriving and the refrigerator grew emptier with each passing day.

When Michael had seen me shake the last few drops of milk into my afternoon cup of tea, he'd stood up from the kitchen table.

"I'll get some more," he'd said. "We're out of orange juice, too. Is there anything else you need?"

I'd shaken my head and turned away from him. But when Michael had picked up the car keys, I'd abruptly set down my mug and headed for the Maserati. I didn't feel like staying in the house.

Now Michael briefly took his eyes off the road to look at me. "I know you're thinking about leaving me," he said. "Anyone would be, in your shoes. Just give me a little time before you decide."

My jaw felt as rigid as concrete; I could barely force out the words: "I don't know." I turned my head to stare out the window. Coming with Michael had been a mistake; I was too upset to talk to him.

"I don't know why I was sent back and given a second chance," he continued, his voice as casual as if he was discussing the passing scenery. "But the minute I opened my eyes and realized I was lying on a floor with everyone staring down at me, everything changed. My cars and clothes and houses looked so useless. Silly, even. What I felt when I died was . . . the *connectedness* of us all, of everyone on Earth, and I suddenly knew I had the chance to help people. To make up for—"

I cut him off; I'd heard enough. "Why can't you give *me* some time before you sell everything?" I asked. "Wait a year. If you still feel the same way, you can sell the company then."

Something flickered in Michael's eyes. I knew that evasive look well; it meant he wasn't telling me something. "I just . . . have to do it now. Right away."

"Why are you being so illogical?" I shouted. "I don't even know who you *are* anymore."

"I know it doesn't make sense to you, Julia," he said, his voice soft. "It wouldn't have to me either, a few weeks ago. But when I was dead—I can't even believe I'm saying 'dead,' because in those minutes I felt more alive than I've ever been—but when I died—"

"Michael! Stop talking about that, okay? You're not floating on a puffy cloud and listening to harp music, damn it. You're here with me, and you're trying to give away everything we own. You've got to deal with reality!"

"It wasn't really like that, but okay," he said a moment later. "I won't talk about that part, not until you're ready to hear it. But can I tell you what the worst thing is for me? I keep thinking about how I wasted all those years with you. I should've taken weekends off. I should've gone to Paris with you. I can't believe I never took you on a honeymoon. Julia, we've grown so far apart . . ."

I turned my head to stare out the window and didn't say anything; too many turbulent emotions were swirling inside me. Anger and sorrow and fear, but something else, too. A glimmer of something that almost felt like hope. For just a moment, those afternoons by the river flashed through my mind. I thought about how Michael and I used to lay together for hours, talking like we'd never stop. *Could* we possibly have that again?

When I'd first seen Kate's message on my BlackBerry, telling me Michael was in the hospital, panic had seized me so sharply it forced the breath from my lungs. The words blurred on the screen as my mind screamed *No!* and my legs gave out like someone had kicked them out from under me. I calmed down considerably during the drive to the hospital, but during those first few raw moments . . .

Maybe some part of me *did* still love him. I tested out the thought, then shook my head briskly, trying to whisk it away. It didn't matter. Michael wasn't trustworthy. I couldn't believe anything he said, when he'd twisted around everything he'd promised once before. For all I knew, in two weeks he'd change his mind again and abandon me to build another company, or change his name to Om and go chant mantras in a yogi's hut.

"I've done so much wrong in my life," Michael was saying.

He slowed to a stop at a red light. "I've focused on all the wrong things. We should have had"—I felt his eyes on me again—"a baby."

I felt an awful wrenching in my chest, and I gripped the leather edges of my seat, *wanting* my fingernails to scratch the expensive material. My anger rose again, so swiftly it nearly choked me. How dare Michael cavalierly toss around the idea of having a child? Whenever we'd talked about it before, he'd always said he didn't want kids. His company was his real baby, the one he nurtured and cherished and watched grow.

"It wouldn't be fair to the child," Michael had said when I'd brought it up. Funny, but even though we'd talked about everything else back in high school, we'd never once discussed whether we wanted to have kids. "We work too much, Julia," he'd said. "Who would take care of the baby?"

"I could scale back," I'd argued. "And lots of people hire nannies."

Michael had shaken his head. "I wouldn't feel right about it," he'd said. "I'm never home. I don't want to ignore the kid like my dad did to me."

At first I held on to hope that he'd change his mind, but as time passed, I didn't bring it up for another reason. Part of me secretly wondered if it would be a good idea to bring a child into our marriage, since Michael and I were so distant. Still . . . the guest room closest to our bedroom was filled with windows that let in swatches of bright sunlight, and sometimes I used to linger in the doorway, seeing painted puffy clouds on blue walls and yellow stars on the ceiling. The crib would be tucked snugly in a corner, away from the windows, so the baby would never feel a cold draft, and an old-fashioned rocking chair with a pink or blue blanket folded over one arm would fit perfectly next to the crib.

But of course, Michael didn't know about any of that, I thought, feeling bitterness rise in my throat. He was never home. He never talked to me anymore. And, the truth was, I'd given up trying to talk to him long ago, too.

"Now you're just going to the other extreme," I said through clenched teeth. My body was so tightly wound I felt like I might explode out of my seat and shatter through the car's windshield. "Why does everything have to be so damn dramatic with you? First you're a workaholic, now you're Mr. Sensitive."

"I've changed, Julia. I'm not the same man."

"I was happy before," I said.

"Were you?" he said gently. "Or did we just substitute stuff for happiness? Did we keep busy so we didn't notice how little was in our lives other than work?"

"Are you gunning for Dr. Phil's job?" I snapped. "You've got the lingo down, but you need to work on your good old boy accent."

Michael hid a grin, which only infuriated me more. "You know the cliché about no one on their deathbed wishing they'd spent more time at the office? It's true, it really is. When I realized I wasn't ever going to see you again, I couldn't bear to . . ." He paused and swallowed hard. "To leave you. Not like this. Not with so much wrong between us."

He paused and kept his eyes on the road while he gathered himself. "It's going to take about three weeks to finalize all the paperwork to give away my company," he said. "Don't decide if you're going to leave until then. Give me one last shot, then you can walk away from me."

"Michael, what if you're making a mistake?" The words shot out of me. "What if a year from now you realize you want your company back?"

I saw his fingers fidget on the steering wheel.

"That's not going to happen," he said quietly. "I'm not going to lie to you, not ever again. I'm worried about you, too, Julia.

I'm worried you care so much about money that it has twisted things for you. I just want us both to see that we can be happy without it. We don't need it. We never did." He reached over to put his hand on top of mine, but I yanked mine away. I saw him flinch, but I didn't care. I *wanted* to hurt him.

"I don't think I love you," I said, carefully enunciating every word. He thought he knew what I needed? He didn't know me at all. The glimmer of hope disappeared, like a bit of bright confetti sinking into murky water and swirling down a drain. "I haven't loved you in a long time."

"I don't blame you," he said. "But can't we just talk about—"

"I don't want to talk to you!" I yelled. "You're ruining everything, Michael. You promised me so much." My voice broke, but I kept on, the words tumbling out practically on top of each other.

"You swore you'd give me a good life. Remember all those days by the river? We promised each other we'd have everything we ever wanted. And then we got it all and you left me. You were never home. You never wanted to be with me. You *lied* to me, you broke our vows! And I got used to that. I made peace with it, damn it! Now you're changing the rules again. You're not the only one in this marriage."

"I'm sorry," he said again, as though those two words could erase all the empty years between us.

"You didn't go anywhere. You hit your head!" I shouted. "The electrical activity in your brain didn't stop right away when you died. You just had some kind of crazy dream."

"It was real," Michael insisted. "The most real thing I've ever felt. As real as that tree," he said, pointing out the window. "As real as the air we're breathing."

"You checked your BlackBerry when everyone else was kneeling to pray at that baptism," I reminded him. "And when it buzzed, you clasped your hands together to hide it and frowned at the guy in front of you."

"Julia, I believe in something now. I don't know what to call it, but I felt love . . . it was there; it existed, wherever I was—"

"Let me out," I suddenly demanded, fumbling for the door handle.

Michael glanced at me in surprise, but he kept driving.

"Stop!" I yelled, and his tires screeched against the pavement. I yanked open the door and scrambled out, onto the sidewalk.

"I don't think I can be with you for three more seconds, let alone three weeks," I said as I slammed the door shut as hard as I could. I spun around, shaking with anger. Why did Michael get to play God, just because they'd allegedly met? How dare he try to decide what was best for me. This was the worst thing he'd ever done, even worse than the time I'd picked up his BlackBerry and read that e-mail from Roxanne, asking if he could sneak out of work early and meet her again . . .

I walked quickly, my breath coming in hot gasps, my shoes slapping furiously against the concrete. After a few minutes I calmed down enough to take a look around. I recognized the area, and I knew that, in another couple of blocks, I'd reach a little strip mall with a bar. Perfect, I thought as I picked up my pace again. I'd sit at the counter, sip a cold beer, and figure out what to do next.

I pushed the door of the bar open with so much force that it banged against the wall.

"Sorry," I muttered to the bartender, who barely lifted his eyes from the sports page of the *Washington Post*. This place was exactly what I needed, I thought as I climbed onto a stool. It smelled like stale beer, and the walls were paneled in something that was supposed to pass for wood but looked more like plastic. The floor felt sticky under my feet, and a beat-up pool table ate up most of the space in the middle of the room. I couldn't bear to be anyplace fancy and shiny right now; I wanted my surroundings to match my insides. At my usual restaurants— the Old Angler's Inn or The Palm—the waitstaff would recognize me and rush to offer me the wine list and anticipate my every need. Here no one would bother me. I'd be invisible.

"Sam Adams, please," I told the bartender, who reluctantly folded down his paper.

"Need a glass?" he asked, popping the cap and handing it to me. In answer, I lifted the bottle to my lips and chugged a third of it down.

He shrugged and went back to his paper. Maybe he was used to frazzled-looking women storming in here and swilling beer like they were pledging a fraternity. I gulped some more, and the bartender absently slid a dish of peanuts closer to me.

"Don't get too invested in that article," I warned him, waving my bottle in the air and liking how tough I sounded. "I'm going to need another one in a minute."

The phone in my pocket vibrated just then, and I took it out and looked at the caller's name before answering.

"Where are you?" Isabelle demanded.

I squinted and read the sign over the mirrored wall behind the bar. "Joe's Bar and Grill. Isn't that a perfect name for a bar?"

"Do they serve vodka?" Isabelle asked.

"Joe, do you serve vodka?" I called to the bartender.

"I'm Neil. And yes."

"I'm on my way," Isabelle said.

"Excellent," I said. "Because I left my purse in the car and I'm not sure I can make enough hustling pool to pay off my bill."

"Maybe we can hustle together," Isabelle said.

John Mellencamp's voice was wailing out of the speakers too loudly for me to have noticed it before, but now I picked up something straining Isabelle's voice.

"Are you okay?" I asked as a wave of guilt flooded me. Isabelle had rescued me enough lately. And wasn't her big date today? "Michael shouldn't have called you. You don't need to come down here."

"Michael didn't call me," she said. "And no, I'm not okay."

"Starter fucking marriage," Isabelle said four vodka shots later. Which meant she actually said "starter fuckamage," but I knew exactly what she meant.

I tossed back a shot in solidarity and followed it up by sucking on a sugar-dipped slice of lemon.

"I can't believe he lied," I said, licking the extra sugar off my fingertips. "Men are assholes. Not you, Joe! You're the only guy we like."

He poured us another round; by now he knew better than to ask if we wanted a refill.

"You're not driving, right, ladies?" he asked.

"She has a driver," I said, jabbing Isabelle in the upper arm with a little more force than I'd intended. "I don't. My goddamn husband is giving away all our money."

"Husbands suck," Isabelle agreed. "Especially the one I've been dating."

"So he picks you up, takes you out for a romantic picnic he allegedly made himself even though you recognized the sandwiches from Balducci's, and then pulls out his wallet because he's uncomfortable sitting on it," I recapped.

"Yup." Isabelle cracked a peanut, popped it in her mouth, and promptly spit it out into a napkin.

"Joe, how often do you freshen up the peanuts?" she called.

"Every day," he lied. "And it's *Neil*."

"I got a new outfit," Isabelle shouted back at him. "I *waxed*."

By now he was at the other end of the bar, reading the help

wanted section, and I could only hope we hadn't sparked his desire to change jobs.

"If the asshole's going to pretend to be single, he shouldn't carry a photo of his wife in his wallet," I said. "That's basic Adultery 101."

"I don't think he was planning on pretending," Isabelle said. "I mean, we both stared at the photo when he tossed his wallet down on the blanket and it flipped open. He could've just said the picture was of his sister or something if he wanted to keep on lying."

"A photo of his sister in his wallet?" I wrinkled my nose. "I think that's worse than him being married."

She laughed for the first time since she'd come into the bar with bright red spots of anger high on her cheekbones and a dark stain on her shirt. ("I meant to throw my wine at *him*," she'd said. "I guess I was sitting a little too close to him." "How close?" I'd asked. "In his lap," she'd said.)

"So why aren't you speaking to Michael?" Isabelle asked now.

"All of a sudden he's regretting that we didn't have kids." I picked up a peanut and bounced it against the bar. "Can you believe it? Today he told me he was sorry he didn't take me on a honeymoon."

"And?" Isabelle prodded.

I looked at her questioningly.

"That's pretty much it."

She paused. "Look, I know I'm the president of the Anti-Men Club right now, but I don't get it," she finally said. "Hate Michael because he wants to give away all his money, sure. But because he's apologizing for not spending more time with you and for not having a baby?"

I sighed and slumped down on my stool. That was the part I'd been turning over and over in my mind, too. Why hadn't I gotten furious at Michael years ago for all of those things? If they meant so much to me, why hadn't I fought back then?

"Here's the thing," I finally said. "Marriages have all these unspoken rules. You know which part of the newspaper each of you gets first, which side of the bed you sleep on, and exactly how far you can push one another before a little disagreement turns into an ugly fight. It's like every marriage is a country, with its own customs and rituals and bartering systems. And one of the big things is that you both know what's off-limits to discuss. Michael and I don't talk about kids. We don't talk about the honeymoon we never had. We're not close enough to go there. We haven't been in years, Isabelle."

I rolled my shot glass between my palms, wishing it was full again, but Neil was avoiding eye contact with us and I couldn't really blame him.

"Talking about stuff—really deep stuff—isn't something Michael and I do anymore," I said softly. "It is possible to live with someone and not really know them. It's easy, in fact. I can tell you what kind of underwear Michael likes and what his computer password is. He knows I'm terrible at remembering people's names, so he has to jump in and greet them first. We know all the superficial details about each other, like the kinds of things they quiz immigrants on during citizenship tests. But does knowing how many stripes are on the flag teach you anything about living in America?"

Isabelle nodded. "I get it," she said after a moment. "You guys just seemed . . . I don't know. As happy as anyone, I guess. I mean, I know he fooled around with that little bitch, but that's been over for a while, right?"

I shrugged. "Yeah. But I still check his e-mail and voice mail all the time. Such a lovely, trusting marriage we have."

And Isabelle didn't know all of it, I thought as my eyes skittered away from hers. There were some parts of our story that I was too ashamed to share even with her.

I cleared my throat. "Anyway, if I get dragged into having all these deep talks with him, we'll have to go through the pain of figuring out what went wrong with us. Why *didn't* we go on a honeymoon? Every couple does, if they have enough money. And"—my voice dropped; I couldn't bear for even Neil to overhear me—"why was I willing to trade less of Michael for more money? I think I hate Michael because he's forcing me to think about all of those ugly questions."

We sat there in silence for a moment, then Isabelle exhaled loudly and said, "Well, hell. What are we going to do next?"

"You'll be fine. There are lots of other guys out there," I said, sweeping my arm around to encompass the room. Two white-haired men sipping Miller Lites at the other end of the bar smiled obligingly at Isabelle, and one lifted his beer mug in a toast.

"Maybe that's what I need," she said. "I mean, not *them*."

She paused and squinted, then shook her head. "Definitely not them. But a normal guy. All the men I know are too rich. It warps them."

"You sound like you've been talking to Michael," I said. "You know, it *is* possible to have money and still be a decent person."

"Obviously," she said. "Look at me."

"Point taken." I held up my glass for another shot, and Neil reluctantly shuffled over with the Smirnoff bottle.

"So Michael thinks you should have had kids? There's still time, you know. I mean, if that's what you want."

"I don't know what I want anymore." I thought about the stacks of holiday cards we got every year, and how I'd begun to dread opening them and seeing the photos of children—babies in tiny Santa suits, and older kids posing on the beach or clustered with their parents in front of a Christmas tree. The sharp longing those photos conjured in me was one of the reasons why my fingers kept reaching for the divorce lawyer's card in my wallet. If I left Michael, maybe I could start over with someone else . . .

I sighed and stretched out my arms, trying to shake off the thick, heavy feeling that had settled over my body. The room's two windows were covered by neon signs that allowed only a little sunlight to filter inside, catching the dust motes swirling in the air and adding to my sense of gloom.

"Michael wants me to give him three weeks before I decide anything. It's like he wants to live the rest of the month in suspended animation, without thinking about the future. But there's no way I'm doing that. I'm calling a lawyer tomorrow morning to see what I'll need to do if I decide to file for divorce and go after some of Michael's money. I have to be ready to fight him, Isabelle."

She nodded. "I was wondering if you'd try to do that. I probably would, in your place."

"So I guess that pretty much rules out me having kids with Michael." I blinked hard, twice, then glanced at Isabelle.

Something in her expression made me blurt out a question I wasn't planning on asking: "Do *you* want kids?"

She started to say something quick and light, then she cut herself off and began again.

"Actually, I, ah, had one, once." She looked down into her empty glass. "A baby. I was eighteen." She held up a hand to cut off my murmur of surprise, still not looking at me.

"I didn't know who the father was. I could narrow it down, obviously, but it wasn't like I had a boyfriend, let alone anyone I really cared for. You didn't know me back then, Julia. I got pregnant the summer after I graduated from high school, when I was living in my parents' house. I'd been at boarding school since I was thirteen, and by then I figured out they'd shipped me off to get rid of me, not because they thought it was the best thing for me.

"Maybe it was a form of revenge, maybe I was looking for attention any way I could get it—take your pick. I'm sure a shrink could come up with a whole smorgasbord of theories, especially since one of the guys I slept with was old enough to be my father. I screwed anyone I could find: the lifeguard at the country club pool, my tennis instructor, one of the young guys who did our lawn. Even a lawyer at my father's company."

Her voice grew rougher. "I couldn't believe it when I missed my period. I thought about an abortion. I knew girls who'd had them, in school. I got a brochure and everything. But for some reason I couldn't bring myself to do it."

I wanted to reach out and cover her hand with mine, but I sensed she was a thin layer away from tears, and I knew even a gentle touch would push her through it.

"I deferred college for a year, and traveled. At least that's what my parents told their friends, who probably knew they were full of shit. I grabbed a credit card—I was a rebel, but I still needed Daddy to pay my way—and I went to live in Seattle. I wanted to put a whole country between my parents and me. I lived in a little apartment and worked part-time in a used bookstore, and for the first time in my life, I just breathed, you know? I learned how to make vegetable soup from scratch. I'd never cooked before, so I ruined the first few batches, but I finally got it. A pinch of cinnamon—that was my secret. Funny . . . I haven't thought about that in years. I read a lot, and on Saturdays I took long walks along the water and got hot chocolate afterward.

"Part of me wanted to keep her." Isabelle's voice almost broke, but she fought past it. "But I was still so screwed up, there wasn't any way I could've raised a child. There was another girl I met at the adoption agency who was giving up her baby, too, and she kept talking about the couple she'd picked, how they'd be able to give the baby anything it wanted. You'd look through the files and see these people who had already established college accounts, and they'd include pictures of their houses and the room for the baby, but I kept searching the files, flipping past those postcard-perfect parents, until I found a woman who was an art teacher. Her husband was a physical therapist, and they'd already arranged their schedules so one of them could always be home with the baby."

Isabelle smiled sadly. "Do you know what I did? We met at a restaurant to talk, and afterward, I pretended to leave, but I snuck back around the side of the building and followed them. I wanted to see what they acted like when they didn't think I was watching. You should've seen me, Julia: I'd brought along this big bag with a hat and sunglasses and a jacket so the couple wouldn't recognize me. Of course, I had this huge belly I couldn't disguise, so I'm sure the jig would've been up if they'd just turned around, but they didn't. They walked a block or so to their car, and when they got there, they didn't get in right away."

Isabelle's eyes grew faraway, and I knew she was back on that street corner, scared and confused and eighteen years old, seeing it unfold all over again. "They stood on the sidewalk, and then they reached for each other at the exact same time and hugged. Her head was resting on his shoulder, and I could see him whispering something into her ear. The next morning, I signed the papers. I never even saw my baby. I never held her, or kissed her good-bye. I *couldn't*. But I know"—Isabelle finally lost the fight and her voice broke—"I know she's a girl."

Now I reached out to her; I couldn't bear not to.

"For a while I self-destructed," Isabelle said, wiping her eyes with her knuckles. "I did some drugs and stopped eating. I kept staring at babies when I passed them on the street, wondering if she'd be about the same size. Finally I moved back home. It became easier to stop thinking about her then."

"I had no idea," I said, squeezing Isabelle's hand and wishing I could think of something comforting to say.

"No one does," Isabelle said. "Except probably this friend of my mother's who grilled me about my year abroad. She kept asking if I'd seen the Sistine Chapel or the Louvre like she was a private detective, and finally I snapped, 'No, I spent most of my time in the red-light district in Amsterdam. You haven't lived until you've tasted the brownies there.'"

We both laughed then, and I handed Isabelle a napkin.

"This isn't the one I spit the peanut into, is it?" she asked, a smile trying to fight its way through her tears.

Oh, Isabelle, I thought as I blinked back tears of my own. This was what I loved best about her; her spirit never stayed hidden for long. She always strode confidently into parties, casting around her perfect smile and slipping into conversations as easily as if she were diving into a cool, deep swimming pool. She jaywalked across busy streets, her long legs drawing whistles and stares, and gave the finger to anyone who honked in protest. Once, when a store manager was berating a young salesman for putting the wrong scarf on a mannequin, Isabelle interrupted with a steely smile: "Actually, I like that one much better. Yours looks like something my aunt Bertha would wrap around her curlers before going out to get her newspaper. Actually, *is* that Aunt Bertha's scarf?"

I'd always seen her strength and poise; but somehow, I'd missed the vulnerability that lurked just beneath it. Or maybe I hadn't missed it; maybe Isabelle had kept those jagged parts of herself hidden until *I'd* revealed just how vulnerable I was as I lay sobbing on the boutique carpet. Maybe friendships had rules, just like marriages, and Isabelle and I were in the process of rewriting ours.

"The adoption is open, but the parents and I haven't had much contact. They send me photos every year along with a little note about how she's doing. Her name's Beth, and she's so beautiful. In her first school photo, she had this tiny red headband holding back her hair, and the next year she looked completely different—she had bangs and her cheeks had lost some of their baby fat. Now she's tall and slim, and she probably has a boyfriend and is thinking about applying to colleges. I put all the photos in an album, but I only look at them once a year, on her birthday. I toast her with champagne, and I flip through the album and watch her grow up. There's just one thing I did. Actually that I *didn't* do . . . and I'm ashamed of it," Isabelle said slowly.

"So tell me," I said, keeping my voice light.

"That day in the hospital, when her parents came to take her away, they stopped by my room first and said they were going to tell her about the adoption as soon as she was old enough to understand it. I promised I'd write a letter for them to give to her. I started to do it dozens of times, but every time, I just froze. I couldn't think of what to say. . . . And the longer I waited, the harder it got. I kept thinking, What if she hates me for giving her up?" Isabelle's voice was so soft I barely heard what she said next. "And maybe now she hates me for not writing. Maybe they all do."

I couldn't stand to see the pain in her eyes. "She doesn't," I said firmly.

Isabelle glanced over at me in surprise.

"You found incredible parents for her," I said. "That was the most loving thing you ever could have done. Isabelle, Beth knows you love her. She *knows*."

After a moment, Isabelle nodded slowly.

"When everything happened with Michael, the first person I thought of was Beth. What if I get really sick or die? Or what if she does? What if I miss the chance to tell her I love her because I was too afraid?"

"You could still write the letter," I said after a moment. "It isn't too late. You can tell her you were scared to write before, if you want to. Just tell her the truth. It doesn't have to be perfect."

Isabelle squeezed my hand. "I think I have to."

We sat there awhile longer, still holding hands, listening to Bruce Springsteen's gritty, haunted voice singing "Thunder Road."

"Do you think we've scared Neil off for good with all this sobbing?" Isabelle finally asked.

"Probably," I said, wanting to see her smile again. "But there's one good thing. I think the two guys at the end of the bar have given up on you. I'm pretty sure they think we're a couple."

Isabelle laughed—not a big laugh, but at least she'd stopped crying. "And I just noticed something else," she said, squinting at Neil and wobbling slightly on her seat. "He brought his twin brother in to work with him. Now we won't have to wait as long for refills."

"Another shot?" I suggested.

"Only one?" Isabelle asked indignantly.

She signaled Neil, then looked at me, and I saw sadness cast a shadow across her face again. "I think you should give Michael his three weeks before you decide if you're going to divorce him," she said softly. "Anything could happen during that time. Maybe he really has changed. But even if you leave, at least you'll know you gave it a chance. Trust me, always wondering about someone you walked away from is the hardest thing in the world."

* * *

"I have something to tell you," I announced, marching into our living room. I tried to sound dignified, but my hiccups weren't doing me any favors.

Michael was sitting on a chair near our great white stone fireplace, not reading a book or watching television or anything. Just sitting, as still and quiet as a statue.

"I'm not going to let anything inferte—finterfere . . . mess up my job," I said. "I've got a big event in a couple days. But after that I'll spend a little time with you. I won't make a decision about what I'm going to do for a few weeks. But I'm not promising anything. I don't think I'm going to be able to get over this."

Michael stood up so quickly he was like a blur—or maybe that was the vodka creating complimentary special visual effects.

"Thank you," he whispered.

I turned around and staggered toward our bedroom. I needed ten hours of sleep, one for each of those shots.

"I'll bring you some water and aspirin," Michael said, grabbing my elbow and helping steer me into the bedroom.

"I love my heated bathroom tiles," I told him.

"I know you do," he said.

"I'm gonna take them with me," I said, collapsing onto the bed. "If I leave you."

"Okay," he said, easing off my shoes.

"Don't try to humor me," I said. "I see right through you."

"Do you need anything? Some crackers?"

"You're giving away all your money and you offer me a saltine," I muttered, rolling over and putting a pillow on my head to block out the light. "Charity begins at home, you know. How about a spare million or two to go with the crackers?"

I felt Michael leave, and a moment later, he was back, forcing a glass of water and two aspirin into my hand.

"You'll feel better tomorrow if you drink this," he said.

I finished the water and flopped back onto the bed, my eyes closed.

I felt Michael hovering above me. "I know none of this makes sense to you now," he said, pulling a quilt over me. "I know you don't believe me when I promise you that you'll always have everything you need. But you'll see. You don't have to be scared, Julia."

His hand was on my forehead, softly stroking, and it felt so comforting. My mom used to do that when I was a little girl, home sick from school. Her fingers were long and thin and cool, and their steady rhythm always made me feel better.

I miss my mom, I thought.

"I know you do," Michael said, and I realized I'd spoken the words aloud. "We'll go back to West Virginia to visit her, if you want."

I rolled away from him.

"I love you," he said, and that was the last thing I heard before I fell asleep in my clothes, the touch of my husband's fingers still lingering on my forehead.

The opera is a perfect place to hide. No one cares if you sit in your seat crying, as long as you're quiet about it.

A few nights after I told Michael I'd give him his three weeks, I slipped out alone to see *Cavalleria Rusticana.* It wasn't just the tragic story of the tenor Turiddu and his love, Lola, that made me weep, though. I couldn't help thinking about the backstory of the composer, Pietro Mascagni. He was a dirt-poor piano teacher when he wrote it for an opera competition, hoping a win would reverse his fortunes. Like so many artists, he was incredibly self-critical, and he ended up despairing of his work. But his wife believed in him, and she secretly mailed it to the judges. He won, and just like that, his life turned around.

And now mine seemed to be spinning around, too, but in the wrong direction.

Fifteen

"I'LL ALWAYS HAVE MY cell phone on," I reminded Gene, my thin, energetic, twenty-eight-year-old assistant, who was never too far away from a freshly opened Red Bull.

"Got it," he said, eager to get back to the game of Internet Scrabble I'd interrupted. He'd flipped screens when I approached, but he was so slow that I'd ruled out a future career in espionage for him. "I'll call you if anything important comes in."

"Don't tell clients I'm working from home," I instructed him. "Just say I'm out for the moment."

"Sure," he said.

"You can e-mail me, too," I said. "And I'll check in every day."

"Gotcha."

"Even if you don't think it's anything important, you should double-check."

Gene nodded.

"It's just for three weeks," I confided. "Then I'll be back in the office full-time. And I'm only doing this because it's such a slow month."

Gene's fingers began drumming against his desk.

"Right! So, I'll just, ah, grab something off my desk," I said, stepping into my office before I flopped down on the couch and Gene started scribbling on a pad and making thoughtful noises and billing me by the hour.

My company didn't take up much space, just two rented rooms in one of the dozens of nondescript tall office buildings within walking distance of the White House. The outer room held Gene's desk and a few leafy plants and a pretty peach-and-white striped couch, and just beyond that was a bigger room, where I worked and held client meetings. It was sunny and bright and the perfect space for my little company. Unlike in my house—or my soon-to-be-ex-house—I'd picked out everything in here, from the soft mossy green paint on the walls to the big antique desk with dozens of tiny drawers that held everything from paper clips to my illicit stash of Hershey's Kisses.

Funny how I'd stumbled into such a perfect job, I thought as I straightened the chairs around the glass table in the center of the room. Unlike Michael's—he'd planned every aspect of his company—mine had started as a fluke.

I'd become good friends with a woman named Stephenie after we sat next to each other as freshmen in English lit at the University of Maryland. When she got engaged during her senior year, she asked me to help pick out her dress since her sister and mother lived out of town.

"I can't afford to spend too much," she'd said. "Just a couple hundred dollars. But it's my wedding day, you know?" Her voice had grown wistful. "I want something special."

"Let's go to a consignment store," I'd suggested.

We'd ended up driving to five that weekend, but none of the dresses were right. Stephenie was Rubenesque, all generous curves and auburn curls and pale, pale skin. She needed something simple and well cut, but everything we saw was covered in lace and flounces and spangles, as if a group of kindergartners had broken into the craft closet and gone wild.

"Holy God," I'd muttered under my breath, whipping through the racks. "What bride-hating sadist invented puffy shoulder bows?"

"Usually it's the bride who's picky about these things," Stephenie had joked as she'd modeled yet another gown and I'd shaken my head.

"It's not that bad, is it?" she'd asked, frowning as she ran a finger over the stiff white skirt with sequins affixed.

"No, it's worse," I'd joked. "Just one more store. Then we'll quit for the day, okay?"

When we walked into I Do, I Do, it was almost as though a magnetic pull steered me to the dress. I gently lifted the padded hanger from its rack, barely daring to hope. I'd seen only a flash of rich ivory, a gentle swirl of a train . . . I held it up and smiled. This was it. The shawl collar, the elegant sweep of silk—this dress was like nothing we'd seen before. It was old-fashioned and romantic, softly pretty and unique.

"Really?" Stephenie had asked, wrinkling her nose. "Isn't it kind of . . . *plain*?"

"Just try it on," I'd begged, crowding into the dressing room with her and fastening the tiny hooks up the back. "A little altering here and there . . . Don't look yet," I'd commanded, smoothing out the train. "Okay. Now."

"Oh, my God," she'd said, twirling in front of the mirror. She didn't say anything else; she just kept spinning and spinning, like a windup ballerina dancing in a jewelry box, while I'd watched her and smiled.

"How did you know?" she'd asked later in her car, her dress draped protectively over her lap. She wouldn't let go of it for a second. "I never even would've taken this off the hanger."

I'd thought about the fashion magazines Dad used to bring home for me, and how he'd sit next to me while I flipped through the pages.

"A thousand bucks? For a dress?" he'd say. "Tell me why that dress is worth so much more than the one in the window at Sears."

I'd push the magazine closer to him. "See all the beads around the hem? They're hand-sewn. But you're right; it's way over-priced. Look at how the armholes gape. Not in that picture; the model's arching her back to compensate. But on the next page her body's more relaxed, and you can see the dress isn't well cut. Now, this jacket is worth every penny. You could wear it to the fanciest party ever, or you could wear it over jeans. Check out the buttons. They're like little pieces of jewelry; every one is different."

"I swear, Julie, you could design this stuff yourself," Dad would say, shaking his head. "You see things nobody else does. Now how about my sweater? Is it couture"—he pronounced it "cootie-yer"—"material?"

"Absolutely," I'd say with a laugh. "You could strut down a runway right now."

Then I'd flush with pleasure and secretly start thinking maybe I really could do it, someday, maybe I could figure out a way to go to design school or just buy some material and start sewing my own stuff . . .

Stephenie had been staring at me. "Are you okay? I was asking how you knew this was the dress."

I'd swallowed hard. "Just a feeling."

The idea for my business didn't gel until after Stephenie told me her grandmother's cameo necklace, which she'd been planning to wear as the "something old" part of her outfit, was missing—stolen by a nursing home aide, the family suspected.

It really wasn't so hard to find something similar; a Saturday morning walking around flea markets and antiques shops, and then I was pointing at a glass case, saying, "That one. Can I see that one, please?"

When I gave the ivory-and-rose cameo to Stephenie as an early wedding present, she cried. I helped Stephenie cut corners everywhere at her wedding, and brushed off her thanks; the truth was, I loved every minute of it. The bridal bouquet was pale pink cabbage roses bought wholesale and tied with silk ribbon from a five-and-dime, and I discovered dusty cases of champagne glasses at a store's going-out-of-business sale. "They're less expensive than plastic, and so much nicer," I'd told her. "If you want, you could hire someone to wash them after the toast, then give away pairs as favors to your guests, maybe tied with some of that ribbon."

"So we don't have to spend money on favors!" Stephenie had exclaimed. "Brilliant! But do you know what I'm really worried about? The caterer's bill. That's going to be the biggest expense."

I'd thought for a minute. "You know, you could just do cake and champagne if you had an evening ceremony. It would be so romantic; you could use little votive candles everywhere."

Her eyes had lit up. "Perfect!"

One of Stephenie's cousins approached me at the reception, raving about the wedding and asking if I could help plan hers— "I'll pay you, of course." Soon after that the jobs just began trickling in by word of mouth. Weddings, retirement parties, birthday bashes, bar mitzvahs—I did them all.

But I hadn't talked to Stephenie in years.

I walked over to my desk and opened the drawer that held the *Washington Post* clipping describing our house. Stephenie had called me when the story ran, her voice shot through with tight, high notes of surprise.

"I had no idea," she'd said. "I mean, I know Michael was

really excited about his new business, but . . . the paper said he's worth seventy *million*?"

"Yeah," I'd said, and I'd tried to pull off a laugh. "It kind of surprised me, too."

"I mean, you couldn't spend that much money in a lifetime, could you?" Stephenie had marveled, almost as though we were gossiping about someone else, some celebrity we'd seen in films and posing on the red carpet.

We'd chatted for a while longer, but by the time we hung up, it felt like one of the seams binding our friendship had split open. I tried to hold our friendship together—I believe we both made an effort. But our lives had veered into completely different directions, stretching us apart even as we reached out to one another. Stephenie had a baby daughter by then and was clipping coupons to make ends meet, and once when I met her for coffee, I'd seen her eyes linger over my new Hermès Kelly bag.

"Did Michael buy you that?" she'd asked, tentatively touching the supple leather, as though it was an exotic animal that might bite.

I'd nodded quickly, then offered to get her a coffee.

"I can buy my own," she'd said defensively.

"No, of course you can," I'd blurted, embarrassed. "I just meant since I was going to the counter anyway." I'd tucked my purse under my chair and wondered if I should bring my old one, which I'd bought at T.J.Maxx, the next time we met. But then I realized that would make things worse.

I was to blame, too. I still flush with shame when I remember how I didn't invite Stephenie to the first big dinner party we gave at our new home. Part of me knew she and her husband, who worked as an electrician, wouldn't be comfortable with our new crowd. And a smaller, uglier part of me wanted to

show off our house and everything in it—our newly acquired
Picasso sketch and enormous flower arrangements and private
chef making sushi in our gorgeous kitchen—without worrying
if it seemed ostentatious to my old friend. I didn't want to see
her mentally adding up the money we'd spent; I had to work
hard enough not to do that myself. That night was our coming-
out party, and I wanted to revel in it.

She'd found out about the party—I'd foolishly let it slip the
next time I saw her—and I still remember the hurt flashing in
her eyes.

"It was just a business thing," I'd lied.

"Sure," she'd said too casually. Then she'd begun talking about
her new playgroup, and the other moms she'd befriended, and
it was my turn to feel a sharp pang of jealousy between my ribs.
By then Michael had told me he didn't want children.

Our calls and e-mails grew more and more sporadic, until
they trailed off completely. I still missed her, though, and I
thought—hoped—that maybe she missed me, too. Now I'd be
on the flip side of that same equation. The people we social-
ized with, except for Isabelle, would drop me. Michael would
become an anecdote at dinner parties, gossiped about and ruth-
lessly analyzed before people forgot about him and moved on
to the next juicy story. Besides, I couldn't run in those circles
any longer. I almost laughed, imagining hosting a dinner and
inviting Bettina and Dale to my new place.

"Sit anywhere you'd like," I'd say grandly, gesturing to
the cushions on the floor. "The rump roast will be done in a
minute."

Well, maybe that part alone would be worth losing all our
money, I thought, reluctantly smiling. I was about to leave my
office and head home when my cell phone rang.

"I did it," Isabelle blurted as soon as I'd found my iPhone
in my purse and answered. "I already sent the letter. I put it in

an envelope addressed to her parents along with a note asking them to give it to her whenever they decided it was a good time."

"Isabelle! That's huge! Are you okay?" I asked.

"Yup," she said. "I hadn't realized how fear was keeping me frozen in place, you know? Now I can see how another five years might've slipped by, and then maybe five more . . . and who knows? Maybe I never would've done it. It would've been the single biggest regret in my life. Well, except for that spiral perm I got in the ninth grade."

The laughter in her voice conjured my own. "How do you feel?" I asked.

She paused, and when she spoke again her voice was serious. "I think about her all the time. I keep imagining her parents bringing her the letter, maybe at night when she's in her bedroom studying. I wonder what her room looks like. I wonder if she's in the popular crowd at school, or if she feels like an outsider. For some reason I imagine she'll carry the letter around in the pocket of her jeans, so she can take it out and look at it whenever she wants."

"What did you write?" I asked, before quickly adding, "You don't have to tell me if it's private . . ."

"No, it's okay. I kept it simple. I took your advice and told her how scared I was to write before. I described what I felt like when I was pregnant—how she seemed to dance inside of me whenever I turned on music—and why I picked her parents. And I wrote that if she ever wanted to get in touch, I'd love it."

"It sounds perfect," I said.

I could hear Isabelle take a deep breath. "So now the ball's in her court."

"I'm at the office, but I was about to head home," I said. "Want me to swing by there on the way? We could have a celebratory drink. Or are you still hungover from the other night?"

"Yes," Isabelle said. "And yes."

I looked down at the *Washington Post* clipping I still held in my hand, then crumpled it into a ball and tossed it in the trash can as I held the phone tight against my cheek with my other hand. No matter how this turned out, I couldn't stand losing Isabelle. I'd find a way to fight through the awkwardness. I had to.

Sixteen

AS I PULLED UP at our security gate, after leaving Isabelle's house, I saw a small knot of people—five, maybe six—clustered around Michael. He'd stopped his car outside the gate and was standing there chatting with them.

"What's going on?" I called, putting my own car in Park and stepping out as a twinge of fear worked its way down my spine. "Michael?"

A photographer whipped around, and a bright flash temporarily blinded me. By the time I could see again, Michael was by my side, holding my elbow. "A story went out on the AP wire this morning," he said quietly. "I'm giving them a statement. I might as well do it now; they've been calling my cell phone all morning."

"A statement?" I asked in confusion, just as a middle-aged woman with gray hair called out, "So you confirm you're giving away one hundred million dollars?" She pushed her glasses up higher on her nose and poised a pen above her little spiral notebook. "That's your entire net worth?"

I wrenched my arm away from Michael's grasp. *Don't answer,* I wanted to shout, but it was already too late. He was nodding as camera flashes exploded again.

"Can you tell us exactly what made you decide to give it all away?" A man's voice rose above the din.

Michael hesitated, and I suddenly remembered the last time we'd stood in front of the media, after he'd bought an interest in the Blazes. Back then we'd had a savvy publicist waiting to usher us away if the questions turned unpleasant or went on too long. Now we were on our own, and I felt trapped. I had to make Michael see that going on record would make this almost irrevocable, that if—no, *when*—he finally came to his senses, he'd regret making his decision so public. I had to stop it.

"I died recently, for four minutes and eight seconds," Michael was saying, as casually as if he were recalling a sudden change in the weather. "You remember my cardiac arrest, right? It made the local papers. When I came back to life, I realized everything I once valued didn't matter. Money is completely meaningless to me now."

The reporters scribbled furiously in their notebooks as two photographers moved in closer, their cameras zeroing in at dueling angles on Michael's face. My God, how had I gotten here? I felt like one of those cheating politicians' wives, standing at a press conference while the intimate details of our lives were rolled out for the world to hear. I knew my face must look just like so many of theirs: grim, shell-shocked, uncomprehending.

"Michael, let's *go,*" I said, tugging his arm.

"Did something happen to you?" someone asked. "Did you have a near-death experience?"

Michael paused, and everyone fell silent. A group of geese flew overhead, heading south in anticipation of the coming winter, and one let out a loud honk, making me flinch.

"I don't know what to call it," he finally said. "But yes, something happened."

"What was it like?"

Michael had never before struggled to express himself; his

lightning-fast mind always sorted through his vast vocabulary and zeroed in on the precise words he needed. "I can't—can't really explain it," he said now. "It was beautiful. I don't know what else to say. Some of it is private . . ." He glanced at me. "I can't talk about it. Not now."

"Where is the money going?" another reporter asked. "Which charities?"

"I'm keeping a little bit for some immediate expenses. Everything else will be sold at auction, including our houses. I'm going to ask Christie's to handle it. It'll go to a lot of charities. Doctors Without Borders, Habitat for Humanity, cancer research, as well as a number of smaller ones . . . I've got a list inside."

He was calling Christie's? He had a *list*?

I instinctively jumped into my car and hit the remote control to open the security gate. Just before I pressed down on the gas pedal, the passenger-side door flew open and Michael jumped inside.

"Why the hell did you have to *tell* them?" I yelled as the gate swung open, agonizingly slowly, and I sped through it, wishing I could mow down the reporters. I rubbed my hand roughly over my face, feeling furious with myself for not stopping it. But everything had unfolded so quickly; I'd been blindsided.

"It just seemed easier to give them a quote and get rid of them," Michael said and shrugged. "They would've kept calling if I hadn't."

"You should've talked to me first." I struggled to keep my voice even. I couldn't scream at Michael; I needed to stay calm and rational. It wasn't too late; maybe we could call the reporters and get his statement retracted . . .

Michael glanced at me. "Honey, I'm not going to change my mind," he said quietly. "If you decide to stay with me, it can't be for my money. I won't have any."

I felt a fresh surge of anger. "So you expect me to work while you sit around the house?" I asked incredulously, skidding to a stop in front of our house. "Oh, wait, scratch that, we won't *have* a house."

"Julia, it's not going to be like that at all."

"So you *are* going back to work? Because that's the only other option I can see in this whole fucking nightmare you've created."

I saw different emotions play across his face before I got out of the car and slammed my door.

"I can promise you one thing," he said, getting out, too, and facing me across the hood of the car. "I need to sell my company, but you'll never have to support me."

"So you'll get some sort of job?" I asked. "A consultancy or something?"

Michael seemed to choose his words carefully. "I would love to do that. To work less, and be with you more."

I stormed toward the house, feeling my frustration swirl into a sharp peak. Michael could probably make a ton of money as a consultant. He obviously wasn't averse to earning a living; so why was he so hell-bent on giving away all his DrinkUp profits?

"What *is* it, then?" I finally asked. "Why do you have to sell the company? It's like it's suddenly your . . . *enemy* or something."

Michael fitted his key into the lock and swung the door open before answering.

"In a way, it is," he said, standing aside to let me enter our house first. "I'm not proud of my company anymore. I think it ruined me. I got so caught up in it that I turned into someone I didn't like. I'm ashamed of some of the things I did."

I could think of one or two things, I thought, my mind helplessly flashing to his former employee Roxanne's knowing smile as her eyes raked up and down me . . .

"You killed yourself to build that company," I reminded him.

Michael smiled a kind of half smile. "Literally, right? Listen, I would love it if we could just sit down together and talk. Hold hands, maybe."

My God, he was like a sixth-grader with a crush.

"Tonight, maybe we could pack up a picnic and watch the sun set."

No, he was a Hallmark card—one that had been rejected for being too sappy.

I opened my mouth to say something to move us past this ridiculous moment, but instead, something completely unexpected emerged in a strangled whisper.

"Why do you love me so much now?"

Michael just looked at me, his eyes filled with sadness.

"There were so many times you could've been with me," I said. "Not even special occasions, just regular nights when you could have come home early so we could've had dinner together and talked."

"I know," Michael said. "I'll never get that time back. That makes me sadder than anything else." He paused and looked down for a moment. "There's something else I need to tell you," he said, meeting my eyes again. "From here on out, I'm only going to be honest with you about everything."

Something in his voice made me nearly flinch, but I forced myself to lift my chin and stare at him. After all, what else could Michael do to me?

"I told you I wanted to go back to work," he said. "And I will, if I possibly can. Julia, I'd love to build a new life with you. But . . . I don't know how much time I have left."

Relief made my body sag. This was Michael's big, honest announcement?

"None of us do, Michael," I said. "*I* could die tomorrow, or next week."

"It's different," he said. He inhaled a slow breath, and that look came into his eyes again—the one that always did when he talked about those missing minutes. "I just had this sense . . . while I was there . . . I was being allowed to come back, but not for long. . . . You see, time doesn't really have meaning there—"

"Who told you this?" I interrupted. "The head angel? Was he walking around like a gym teacher with a whistle around his neck and a clipboard, putting everyone into lines and telling them whether they could stay or go back?"

"Not exactly," Michael said. He grinned. "It was much nicer than gym class. No one gave me a wedgie there."

"Do you have any idea of how crazy this is?" I walked into the living room and flopped down on a chair. "You're telling me you might not live much longer, but because there's no concept of time in the afterlife—it sounds kind of like a preschooler's brain in that way—you have no idea if you'll be here for another five years or fifty. Michael, *come on*. Don't you hear how nutty this all sounds? I know what happened to you was terrifying—"

"It wasn't scary at all," he cut me off.

"Fine," I said. "But can't you just slow down a little? Why does everything have to change all at once?"

He moved over to kneel on the floor beside me. This was how he'd proposed, I remembered with a start. He'd just walked over and knelt next to me one morning while I was reading, and he'd pulled an inexpensive gold band out of his back pocket, and I'd shouted "Yes!" before he'd even said a word. "I was going to ask you tonight," he'd said. His voice was muffled against my shoulder. "I was going to buy flowers and cook you dinner and everything, but when I walked into the room and saw you, I couldn't wait another minute."

A few years after we married he bought me the big diamond,

but I always wore that plain engagement ring next to it, every single day.

"Let's not argue anymore," he said now. "I can't bear to waste any more time with you."

"So you want me to fall in love with you again, even though you think you're going to leave me?" I asked. Even though I didn't believe a word of it, I felt a tear trail down my cheek. "But that's so . . . *mean.*"

"Oh, Julia, don't you see?" he said, and his eyes were so clear and blue. "I had to come back for you. Because of you. I'll only be truly at peace when I know you're going to be okay when I'm gone."

I used to believe that all of the biggest moments of my life were tangled up in opera. But I know it was pure coincidence that the station our Bose radio was tuned to began playing *La Bohème* later that day. *La Bohème* was the Italian composer Giacomo Puccini's first big hit, and it has always been one of my favorites. It's the story of four young guys, all broke, who live together in a crappy little apartment in Paris—well, as crappy as a Parisian apartment can be. A neighbor named Mimi knocks on their door one night because her candle has blown out—I know, I know, it sounds like a cheesy pickup line to me, too—and she ends up falling in love with one of the guys. The thing is, she's dying of tuberculosis. Her boyfriend, Rodolfo, struggles with his conflicting feelings. Their relationship is intensely complicated, and the way they sing to each other, with longing and passion and sorrow . . . Well, if you can sit through it without pulling out a tissue, then you must be made of steel. Rodolfo and Mimi become estranged, then passionately reconcile. Things would be easier if they just separated—their future together is so complicated, their love always intertwined with the pain of their mistakes and transgressions against one another—but they can't. They're as necessary to each other as oxygen. But no matter what happens, looming over their heads is the knowledge that death will soon separate them.

Like I said, pure coincidence.

Seventeen

I'VE ALWAYS LOVED THE ritual of balancing my checkbook. The day I received my first payment from my nanny job, I walked straight to the bank and opened a checking account, pride making me stand taller than usual. Every month after that, I sat down to balance my account with my supplies spread out around me: a calculator, a yellow legal pad, and a freshly sharpened pencil. At any given moment, I could tell you almost to the penny how much I was worth.

I'd established a personal budget with that first paycheck, and it became a game to see if I could beat it, if I could save more every week than I'd projected was possible. I'd once read that writing down expenses and calories was the best way to keep track of both, so I kept a little spiral notebook in my purse and dutifully noted every bottle of Suave shampoo and newspaper and pair of socks I purchased (Snickers bars were best consumed under the radar, I'd decided. There was only so much note taking a girl could do, and given the energy level of the twins I was caring for, splurging on chocolate seemed virtuous compared to my other option, which was mainlining speed).

Sometimes, if I worked late, the twins' parents gave me cab

fare home. "Should we call you a taxi?" they'd offer. "Oh, don't bother. I'll just walk a block to Wisconsin Avenue and hail one," I'd say cheerfully. "There are so many at this time of night." Then I'd head for the bus stop, fingering the crisp, folded bills in my pocket.

By the time Michael's company stock went public, I'd added two more bank accounts under my name: one that automatically withdrew savings from my checking account every month, and another devoted solely to All Occasions. I took great satisfaction in watching the sums in all three accounts steadily grow.

It might seem odd that, when I was in Michael's world, I drank criminally expensive wine and bought clothes I saw in *Vogue* layouts, but when I was at work, I debated whether to upgrade my office computers or stretch them out for another year. But I never considered asking Michael to buy things for my company or pay the rent on my office; somehow I felt it was critical to keep a fire wall there. I'd built my company all by myself, and even though it was nowhere near the roaring success that Michael's was, I liked being the only one in control of it. Now I was grateful I'd never asked him for help; it meant I'd have a true picture of my assets and expenses.

I took a fresh legal tablet out of the box of twelve that I'd purchased years ago and then stacked the already-used pads back into the bottom of the box. These yellow pads were the closest thing I had to a diary. All anyone could ever want to know about my thoughts and fears and hopes was in the pictures doodled in the margins—a frowning face for the time a client's check bounced, a bunch of balloons for the office party for five hundred that would net me fat commissions, and thick, excited lines drawn under the numbers when my savings account broke five figures.

I'd spent a few hours on the computer in the middle of the night when I couldn't sleep, researching the costs of houses in areas circling D.C., like Del Ray and Silver Spring, so I knew the ballpark costs. "Mortgage," I wrote on the top of my page. That would be my biggest expense. "Office rent. Utilities. Food. Car." What else? I nibbled on the rubbery pink pencil eraser, then wrote, "Insurance. Clothing. Miscellaneous. Savings."

My fingers moved over the calculator's buttons for a few minutes, then I jotted some more figures on the page. I didn't need to look at my tax returns to know exactly how much money I earned each year, and I wrote those sums in a column next to my projected expenses.

Even if the worst happened and our prenup held up—if I didn't get a dime of Michael's money—I'd still have enough, I saw, relief flooding me as my eyes flickered across the page. I could live in a perfectly pleasant house, pay all my bills, even tuck away a bit every month. Somehow, instead of depressing me with the prospect of downsizing so drastically, the knowledge was oddly liberating. I'd felt dependent on Michael—tied to him by the gilded ropes of his wealth—but now I knew that, no matter what he did, I'd be safe.

I leaned back in my chair and drew up my knees, wrapping my arms around them. I didn't need Michael. The question was whether or not I wanted him.

He'd left a few minutes earlier, saying he had to go into his office and tie up some loose ends. Before he'd gone, he'd invited me to have dinner with him, and something in his expression reminded me of how he'd looked back in high school, when he'd offered to stay with me at Becky Hendrickson's house.

I'd felt sharp tears prick my eyes, which had infuriated me.

"Just go," I'd said brusquely. "I don't know if I'll be here when you get back."

He hadn't tried to argue; he'd turned around and silently walked to his car. But after a moment, I'd gone to the window and seen him sitting in the driver's seat, his head resting on the steering wheel. He'd stayed that way for several minutes before starting his engine.

Now I stood up and stacked my yellow pad back into the box. Suddenly I felt at loose ends; I needed to get out of the house. It was an unusually warm day for late fall, and I wanted to be outside. I'd go to Great Falls and walk until my mind cleared, I decided impulsively, scooping up my keys. I hadn't been there for a while, but I'd always loved hiking along the green trails and rocky banks of the Potomac River; it was a little bit of wilderness draped around the stone and asphalt that dominated D.C. I used to go there after we moved to town because it reminded me of our river in West Virginia. Sometimes I'd pack a water bottle and sandwich and take long walks on Sunday mornings. Michael came with me at first, but once he began creating DrinkUp, he stopped. Remembering that erased the ache I'd felt in my chest when I saw him slumped in his car.

Half an hour later I was pulling into the parking lot at Great Falls Park. I grabbed my iPod out of my purse and tucked the buds into my ears as I headed for the main walking trail. It was quiet today, since it was a weekday afternoon and most people were still at work. After a few minutes, I glimpsed something between the trees—a big flat rock jutting out over the river's edge. It looked like the perfect place to sit and think, to lose myself in the endless rush of water. I pushed back a few prickly branches, feeling a quick burst of pain as a thorn caught the skin of my palm. As I drew closer, I could see a boy was already on my rock. He was small and skinny—maybe ten years old—with an elfin face dominated by huge blue eyes. By the boy's feet was a dog, and it was hard to tell who was more scruffy.

"Hi," the kid said cheerfully as I passed by. "This is a cool spot, isn't it?"

"Mmm-hmm," I grunted. I wasn't in the mood for conversation.

He threw the stick into the water, and the dog leapt in after it.

"Do you live around here?" the boy asked. Clearly he was lacking a filter that prevented his thoughts from flying out of his mouth like popcorn. An adult I could've glared into silence, this kid would probably mercilessly grill me about why I was so grumpy.

"Yes," I said. "Well, sort of. Not for long, though, I think."

He nodded, like it all made perfect sense.

I glanced out over the water, then did a double take. "Hey, I don't see your dog."

"I know," he said calmly. "His name's Bear. I'm Noah, by the way."

What was it with this kid? Hadn't he ever gotten the stranger danger lecture?

"Are your parents here?" I asked. I looked at my watch. "Shouldn't you be in school?"

"School's been out for half an hour." He dug into his pocket and came up with a cell phone. "And I'm allowed to come here alone if I call my mom when I get here and before I leave."

He looked up at me, and his forehead wrinkled. "I'm twelve, you know. You thought I was younger, didn't you?"

"Of course not," I lied. "I was going to guess thirteen."

I scanned the rippling surface of the water again, more slowly this time. Where was that sandy head? I felt a stab of fear: Had the dog gotten tangled up in something below the surface?

"Aren't you going to ask me what my favorite subject is?" Noah said. "Adults always ask me that. I have no idea why."

"Bear can swim, right?" I said, fighting to keep my voice calm.

"Like a fish," Noah assured me. "Math, by the way. It's my favorite. The problem with everything else is that there is rarely a perfect answer. Math has just one answer, and you get to figure out what it is. That's the fun part."

I shaded my eyes with my hand.

"Shit! I mean, shoot! I don't see Bear anywhere." I jumped down from the rock and began running along the waterfront. This boy's dog was going to die on my watch, and the kid didn't even seem to care. He'd been under for how long now—fifteen seconds? Twenty?

"Algebra's really cool," Noah called.

I ran faster, tripped over a tree root, and sprawled on the ground.

"Are you okay?" he asked. My God, was there something wrong with him? He seemed bright enough, but didn't he understand what was happening?

"Noah, I don't see your dog!" I yelled. Sickening images flooded my mind: Bear struggling underwater, his legs tangled up in roots, his paws helplessly clawing toward the surface . . . How much longer could he last?

I could tear off my shoes and dive in, but I'd never find him in time. The river was too big. There wasn't anything I could do, and in another few minutes, Noah would realize what was happening, and—

"Good boy, Bear!" he shouted. The dog was swimming toward the rock, the stick clenched between his teeth.

Bear climbed up onto the rock, Noah threw the stick again, and the dog dove into the water. *Dove.* When he finally broke the surface, Bear was fifteen yards away from where he'd entered.

"Told you he could swim like a fish," Noah said as Bear spotted the stick and went under again.

I sat there in the dirt, rubbing my sore kneecap through the fresh tear in my jeans as Noah clambered over and stuck out a hand that hadn't been acquainted with soap and a running sink in a while. He helped me to my feet, and I brushed myself off. It was impossible to be mad at this kid. Freckles danced around his cheeks and nose, and his lips curved up even when he wasn't smiling. He wasn't cute in a traditional sense—no one would ever hire him to pose for a Pottery Barn Kids catalog— but there was something immensely appealing about him. He reminded me of someone I couldn't quite put my finger on.

Bear climbed back onto the rock, then raced over to me, planting two muddy paws on my pants and almost knocking me back down.

"Down!" Noah commanded. The dog ignored him and tried to French-kiss me.

"It's fine," I said, and in a way, it really was: at least Noah and Bear had distracted me from the mess of my life.

"Do you want a chip?" the kid asked, holding out a crumpled bag.

I shook my head and recoiled from the evil carbs like he'd offered me a sample of nuclear waste. The boy reached into the bag and pulled out an oval chip, just slightly brown around the edges, and bit into it. It looked greasy and salty and crisp. I'd skipped lunch, I realized as my mouth watered.

Oh, hell. I'd probably burned off a few hundred calories in the last five minutes from stress alone. "I'd love a chip," I said, climbing onto the rock again.

Noah passed me the bag, and I pulled out a few, greedily shoving them into my mouth. I hadn't had a potato chip in forever. They were even better than I'd remembered.

"I'm always hungry, too," Noah observed as I licked the salt off my fingertips.

I plopped down next to him. Maybe his upbeat mood would be infectious, and it wasn't like I had anything better to do today.

"I can't stop eating potato chips," he confided. "I'm already on my second bag today. Isn't it funny that salt makes you feel thirsty, but when you're thirsty, you crave salt because it helps your body hold on to water? I learned that in science class."

"Interesting," I lied again.

"It's this circular thing," Noah said. "I can't figure out which came first."

"Yep," I said, because Noah didn't seem the type to let a conversation end until he'd wrung it dry. "Kind of like the chicken or the egg."

"What do you mean?" Noah asked.

"Oh, it's just this question that doesn't have an answer," I said, waving around my hand. "Which came first, the chicken or the egg?"

"Well, duh. The egg."

I smiled indulgently, sensing a teaching moment. "Ah, but who laid the egg?"

Noah frowned.

"Don't worry. Even adults can't figure it out," I comforted him. "That's why it's this famous question."

"The egg came first," Noah said impatiently. "Hens lay eggs. Adult male chickens are called roosters, but some people use the term *chicken* interchangeably for any adult fowl, so asking about the chicken or the egg might include males, who don't lay eggs."

I gaped at him.

"Now, if you'd asked me, 'Which came first, the hen or the egg?' That, I wouldn't have an answer for."

"But . . ." I couldn't think of what to say. It was probably best to move on from this teaching moment.

"What are you listening to?" Noah asked, pointing to my iPod.

"Wagner," I said, relieved to be back on more comfortable ground. "He was this German opera composer."

"Do you like him?"

"I like his music, but no, I don't personally like him."

"Why not?"

I rubbed my finger over my iPod's screen and thought about how to answer.

"Well, he was so anti-Semitic that Hitler loved him, for starters," I said slowly. "I've always wondered how such a terrible human being could create such a thing of beauty."

"Can I listen?"

I shrugged. "Sure." I unwrapped the earbuds from around my neck and handed them to Noah. After a moment, he closed his eyes, and when he opened them again, he was smiling.

"I like it," he said.

"Me, too. Not everybody does, though. Hey," I said as a thought struck me, "did you ever see the Star Wars movies? They're kind of old, but—"

Noah cut me off. "It's only one of my favorites. The special effects are kind of funny now, though. I mean, they're so obvious. Like when Han Solo's ship goes to warp speed? It's just these lines of white on the screen, and they're supposed to make you feel like you're flying."

"Next time you watch it, notice how there are these little bits of music that play when a certain character comes on-screen. Like with Luke Skywalker, the music is kind of brave and bright, right? Well, those are called leitmotifs. Wagner is the guy who created the idea of leitmotifs, but he did it for opera characters."

"Seriously?" Noah leaned over and picked up a stick, then flung it far out into the river. Bear sprang off the rock and landed in the water with a terrific splash. "Cool. Is Wagner still alive?"

"Nope," I said. "He died a long time ago."

"Hmm." Noah pondered this for a moment, then said, "Hey, I've got a trick question. Say you go out to dinner with two friends. You each pay ten dollars, but then the waiter realizes he overcharged you because the bill was only twenty-five dollars. So the waiter goes and takes five bucks out of the cash register, and he gives you each a dollar back, but he keeps two dollars for himself as a tip. So you've each paid nine dollars, and he gets a two-dollar tip. But that's only twenty-nine dollars total. What happened to the missing dollar?"

I blinked rapidly a few times. *"What?"*

"Think about it. If you can't figure it out, I'm usually here after school. I'll tell you the answer next time."

"Next time?" I repeated dumbly.

"I'll bring more chips," Noah said. He tossed the stick into the water again. Didn't that dog ever get tired? Didn't the kid ever stop talking?

Noah looked over at me and grinned. And when the dog's head broke the surface, I could swear he was doing the exact same thing.

Eighteen

"IS IT WRONG TO want to bitch-slap a saint?" I asked Isabelle a few hours later as I cradled the phone between my ear and shoulder and popped a medicinal chunk of dark chocolate into my mouth. I'd come home and taken a long, hot shower after hanging out with Noah, but by the time I'd gotten dressed and dried my hair, Michael still hadn't returned from the office.

"Trouble in paradise?" she asked.

I wandered into our living room and sank onto a couch, wincing as I bent my scraped knee. "How do people *do* it?"

"Oh, honey, I've been waiting for us to have this little talk. First the man takes out a condom, but only after buying the woman lots of dinners and complimenting her shoes. But of course he can't like them so much that he wants to walk around in them, because that would mean we'd need to have a whole different kind of talk—"

"How do people stay married?" I interrupted.

"You're asking me? I was married for six minutes, and I think we were both drunk for five and a half of them."

"Do you know anyone who's happy? Who's really in love with their spouse?"

Isabelle considered it. "Posh Spice? What does she have to complain about?"

"But didn't Becks hit on their nanny or something?" I asked.

"I think that was Jude Law. What is it with hot celebrities lusting after their nannies anyway?" she mused, just before breaking into an off-key and off-lyric rendition of "Just a spoonful of medicine makes the sugar go down."

"Stop it," I ordered. "Don't even think about taking up a new career. As either a singer or a nanny."

"But those Beckham boys need a helping hand at home," she said. "I'd institute shirtless Fridays for all fathers in that house. Think of the laundry they'd save. Nudity is very Scandinavian, you know."

"They're British," I said.

"Same continent."

"Take Dale and Bettina," I said. "What brought them together? Do you think they were ever in love?"

There was a long silence.

"Perhaps they're not the best example," Isabelle said. "You weren't just thinking of them having sex, were you?"

"Thanks for putting that image in my mind," I said. "Hang on while I go dip my brain in a bucket of bleach."

"Look, marriages are strange," she said. "Did I ever tell you about the woman I know whose husband cheated on her for four years? They worked it out, if you can believe it. She says she loves him more now than she ever did before."

"She forgave him?" I asked incredulously.

"To hear her talk about it, they started over. And this time around, they're doing things differently. They go see a counselor every week, even when things between them are good, then they go out for dinner afterward. It's a little annoying being around them, frankly, because those saps are always holding hands."

"I don't know if I could ever be that forgiving," I said. "It seems kind of weird. I mean, with Michael—he had a fling. But four years?"

"She says they almost became strangers in their first marriage. She's glad the affair happened, in an odd kind of way. It ripped them apart for a while, but now they're happier than ever. She said if she had a choice—to live out their lives in their old marriage, or go through the pain to get to this one—she'd choose this one any day of the week."

"But I bet her husband didn't give away all of their money," I said.

"Yeah, he's loaded," Isabelle said. "Actually, I think most of the money is hers. Hedge funds."

"I never dreamed Michael would be this successful," I said slowly. "When we moved here, I figured we'd both make enough money for a house and a couple cars, maybe take a nice vacation every year. But I never imagined . . . this."

Even though I knew Isabelle couldn't see me, I swept out my hand to encompass our living room in cool tones of blue and cream and rose, with its three separate groupings of furniture. "Someday it probably *will* feel like a dream, though," I said, almost to myself.

"So he's definitely going through with it?" Isabelle asked.

I sat up abruptly. "Why do you ask that?"

"I was just wondering if after his . . . experience . . . started to wear off, if he might rethink things."

"Isabelle, that's just what I was thinking," I said excitedly. "It makes sense, right?"

"I don't know," she said, drawing out the words. "Maybe not, if what happened to him was powerful enough. I was just wondering."

I lay back down and stared up at the ceiling. "Yeah. I guess we'll find out. So what are you up to today? Still thinking about Beth?"

"Every minute. She should have the letter by now. I know her parents said they were going to tell her about the adoption, so it's not like I'm going to come as this big surprise. Or maybe I am; maybe she doesn't think about me at all. Anyway, I'm trying to stay busy. In fact, Jake just drove up, so I need to run—literally," she said. Jake was Isabelle's personal trainer, but he was fifteen years older than she, and he had the wiry body of a long-distance runner. Since he was a competitive swimmer, he also had the unsettling habit of shaving his body. "It's just not right," she'd once complained. "Isn't having a crush on your personal trainer a requirement for women? I mean, how else do you motivate yourself to show up?" Instead, Jake was madly in love with Isabelle and aggressively spotted her when she lifted weights.

"Are you wearing spandex, you little tease?" I joked.

She snorted. "I'm just hoping he doesn't make me do endless squats like last time. He was panting more heavily than I was. Plus I'm just narcissistic enough to like the attention."

"Maybe it's better than getting a hot young guy so you don't have to primp before you work out," I said. "Think of the time you're saving."

After we hung up I lay there for a minute, then stood and stretched my arms over my head, scanning our living room as if seeing it for the first time. I tried to imagine what my life would look like if I left Michael. I'd decorate my own house, cook my own meals, take my car to Jiffy Lube to have the oil changed. Maybe I'd start dating, and fall in love again. I might even re-marry. Michael and I would become nodding acquaintances, the type of people who exchanged holiday cards but didn't talk for the rest of the year.

I was surprised by how much the thought hurt. I pictured myself running into Michael decades from now—his dark curls gone gray, a different wedding ring gleaming on his hand as it closed around the handle of a cane—and I squeezed my eyes shut against the image.

"Hi."

I turned and saw him standing there. I'd been so lost in my thoughts that I hadn't heard him come in. We stared at each other for a moment, and I could feel him gauging my mood. But I only felt numb, and very, very tired; my turbulent emotions seemed to be giving me a temporary reprieve.

Then my stomach rumbled. "You said something about dinner?" I asked.

Michael nodded. "I'll even cook, unless that scares you away."

"Okay," I finally said, and I smiled despite myself. A temporary truce it would be. "All I've had since breakfast is a handful of potato chips, and I'm starving."

Nineteen

THE SECURITY BUZZER RANG at 9:00 the next morning, taking us both by surprise.

"Are you expecting anyone?" Michael asked, and I shook my head. He stood up and walked to the video screen hidden inside a closet by the front door. He was wearing jeans and a sweatshirt, and his feet were bare. Michael had, without a doubt, the world's ugliest feet—big and knobby and stark white—and he'd always been embarrassed by them. He had drawers full of expensive socks, and he even wore them to bed. But apparently now he was embracing all of God's creations, even the ones with unsightly bunions.

"Is it a Jehovah's Witness?" I asked brightly. "Hang on, let me get you a tambourine and you two can run off together."

Michael gave a laugh-snort, then pressed a button and spoke through the intercom: "Can I help you?"

I stood up and walked over to look at the screen. It was a woman driving a small four-door car that looked like it had seen better days. "Oh! Sorry! I, um, made you these," she said, struggling to thrust a wicker basket out through her car window and holding it up toward the camera. "They're homemade. Oatmeal chocolate-chip cookies. I hope you aren't allergic to anything. I didn't put in nuts just in case. I know it isn't much, but I just . . . I wanted to give you something . . ."

"Do you want to come up to the house for a minute?" Michael asked, and she nodded.

And why not? I wondered. Why not act as if it was totally normal to have a stuttering stranger show up on your doorstep with a basket of cookies? In Michael's world, maybe it was, just before unicorns started high-stepping in a chorus line and the skies rained down lollipops.

Michael held open the front door as the woman got out of her car and approached us. She appeared to be in her early thirties and was plain-looking; her face was round, and her eyebrows were so blond they seemed to blend into her white skin. She looked around our entryway as her mouth hung open like a B-list actor expressing surprise. I knew just how she felt; I'd done the same thing the first time we walked in here while the real estate agent hid a smile and started mentally spending her commission.

"My twin sister died," the woman blurted. "I'm sorry, I didn't even tell you my name . . . It's Sandy."

"Come sit down for a minute," Michael suggested.

"I don't want to bother you." She hesitated.

"You're not. Please, come in."

He led her to our library, which was smaller and cozier than our living rooms. It had walls of bookshelves and a cluster of furniture forming a half circle around a slate fireplace. She sat down on a buttery yellow leather couch, and Michael sat across from her. I followed them in; it felt disrespectful to do anything else. But I sat as far away from him as possible, on the other end of the couch.

"I'm—um—I used to work as a paralegal, but I quit when Shannon was diagnosed with ovarian cancer. I took care of her. Now I'm a substitute teacher."

Michael nodded and kept his eyes trained on her face.

"Shannon and I felt like twins—we *were* almost twins," Sandy said. "Irish twins, I guess you'd call it, since we were born eleven months apart, and the funny thing is, we really are Irish. But that's not what I wanted to tell you. It's just still hard, you know, to talk about it. *Her.* To talk about Shannon."

Sandy took a shuddering breath. "I'm telling this all out of order, aren't I? Our parents died when we were in college. It was a small plane crash. Dad was a pilot in the Air Force before he retired, and he kept a little plane for weekend rides. It was their twenty-second anniversary, and they were out by themselves. After that, Shannon and I just had each other. We were always close before, but . . . then, we were the only family we had."

"You must miss her terribly," Michael said, his voice gentle.

Sandy nodded and squeezed her eyes shut. "I ache with missing her. I'm not married or anything, so . . . I don't know, sometimes I think it makes things worse that I'm not married and don't have kids, but then other times I don't think anything would help."

"I'm so sorry," Michael said.

"Thank you," Sandy said. She didn't try to stop the tears this time. They overflowed and slid down her soft-looking cheeks. "No, I mean, *thank you.* All that money you're giving away . . . I read you were giving some to cancer research. I can't believe you're doing this. You're going to help so many people, people like Shannon. You're going to save lives."

Michael reached over and took Sandy's hand. "I hope you don't mind my telling you this," he said. "But I believe your sister is safe and loved."

Sandy's head snapped up, and she held her breath for a moment, and suddenly, I realized this was the real reason she'd come.

"You do?" she whispered. "You think she's still . . . around . . . somehow? And that she's okay?"

"I do," Michael said. "With all of my heart."

"Is that—is it because that's what happened to you?" Sandy asked. "After your heart stopped?"

"Yes," Michael said simply. And the honesty and the—well, I guess you'd call it the *faith*—filling up that one word didn't make Sandy's tears stop. But something in her eyes changed, softened.

"I just wish I could tell her I love her," Sandy whispered. "I wish so bad I could hug her one more time."

She was crying even harder now. I stood up and found a box of tissues and put them down next to her.

Michael nodded. "You will," he said. "Someday. I really believe you will. After you've lived a long time, and maybe had those kids, and done all the things you need to do here."

Sandy put her face into her hands and her shoulders shook, but her weeping was different now. Softer. After a moment, she stood up.

"Thank you," she said again, quietly this time, and she left without another word.

After a few moments I went into the kitchen for some chamomile tea, but I couldn't get Sandy's face out of my mind.

She believed Michael. She didn't even know him, but she trusted him completely. Yet I couldn't. I'd never believe Michael had gone to another dimension, or heaven, or whatever he wanted to call it. How could you go to a place that didn't exist?

But maybe the other things he'd said had a hint of truth, I thought as I stirred honey into my tea. Like that I cared so much about money that it had somehow warped me. He hadn't used those exact words, but I knew what he meant. *It hurt,* I thought in surprise. I wasn't a pampered snob—if anything, I felt more insecure now than I ever had before in my life—but others might see me that way. My shyness in fancy social situations could look like haughtiness: Did people watch our driver open the car door for me to slide inside and sneer, not seeing me flush with embarrassment as I tried to pull the door shut behind me, having forgotten once again I was supposed to let the driver do it?

Suddenly I remembered a client named Margaret, for whom I'd thrown an eightieth birthday party at the request of her family. It was a big bash—she had seven kids and twenty-four grandkids—and I'd handed her a glass of golden, bubbly champagne as she stood there, surveying the room full of smiling faces and getting ready to slice into a giant coconut cake.

But the knife had stayed still in her hand as she'd turned to look at me.

"Inside, I still feel sixteen," she'd said, almost in wonder. "How can I be eighty years old when I'm still a girl?"

I'd looked into her faded blue eyes with the deep wrinkles bracketing them, and suddenly felt a kinship with her. Secretly, that was exactly how *I* felt: What people saw when they looked at me didn't reflect who I was inside. At my core, I was still a girl without money, a person who worried she didn't fit in, someone who walked around with a silver sliver of fear buried deep inside her, like a bit of shrapnel even the most skilled surgeon would never be able to remove. Whenever I woke up at night, it took me long moments to reorient myself, to realize that we weren't in our old apartment with the roaches and peeling linoleum floors, and that I didn't have to cook spaghetti three nights a week to save money.

I shook off the memory and took a sip of my tea. It was too hot and it burned my tongue, but I barely felt the pain.

Because by then I was walking back toward our library, and I saw Michael still sitting on the couch.

Something about the way a shadow darkened his face, the tilt of his head . . . All in a rush, the day came back to me when I'd come home to see my father sitting on a couch in the exact same position, confessing to my mother how he'd thrown away everything we owned.

Michael thought I cared too much about money, but he didn't understand, I thought, gripping my mug so tightly my fingers hurt. Why couldn't he understand? Yes, it was horrible when my father gambled all our money away. But even worse, so much worse, was everything else I lost when my father abandoned me. When he stopped loving me.

Twenty

WEST VIRGINIA WAS ONLY a few hours away, but I rarely went back home to visit. Shortly after Michael and I eloped, though, I made the trip—mostly out of guilt over not inviting my parents to the wedding. They'd just moved out of my aunt and uncle's place and were living in a house owned by an elderly woman who had vacated it to move in with her daughter. In exchange for rent, my father, who'd always been handy, was fixing it up after years of neglect.

Those twenty-four hours were among the worst in my life. The shabby little house couldn't contain the tangle of feelings swirling around inside it, and although we all tried to be upbeat—to gloss over the anger and hurt in our shared past, if only for a day—we kept stumbling. Every conversation felt stilted, every memory held a hidden land mine, and the distance between my parents and me seemed to have grown exponentially since I'd left, leaving a gap that felt impossible to traverse.

It was obvious my father was trying, in his own awkward way, to fix things between us by repairing tangible problems: He changed the oil in my car, hurried out to buy a box of

Lipton's when I asked if there was any tea in the house, and insisted on carrying my overnight bag up the stairs to the guest room.

"I just painted it last week," he said, and I smiled and pretended that I loved the rose petal pink shade on the walls. It had been my favorite color, but that was when I was sixteen—the last year my father and I had really known each other.

My dad seemed to feel the need to constantly stay in motion, as if by doing so, he could find relief from the heavy emotions pressing in on us. "After I change the oil, I'll put a little air in your tires," he said as he wiped my car's dipstick on his old canvas work apron.

"That would be great," I said, not letting on that I'd filled them up at a gas station before I left D.C. I sat on the grass next to him and chatted a bit about my job and Michael's new company, but it felt strange. My father did odd jobs around town, cleaning gutters and repairing leaky sink faucets, and here I was talking about the dinner for a hundred people that I'd organized at a fancy country club. My successes only seemed to put his failures in stark relief.

After a while my voice trailed off and I stood up. "I should check on Mom and see if she needs help with dinner."

She'd cooked a pot roast along with steamed carrots and baked potatoes—the kind of simple, hearty food she'd always made while I was growing up—and the smells brought my childhood rushing back. I remembered the countless times I'd banged open our screen door after school and had caught a glimpse of my mother turning around from the stove, a long wooden spoon in her hand and a smile washing over her gentle face as she caught sight of me.

Now she was scrubbing dishes in a sinkful of soapy water. When I went to help, I saw how red and chapped her hands had become, and the sunlight streaming in through the window over the sink highlighted the sharp new lines creasing her face. Even the pan she was holding looked crummy and old. Suddenly a rush of fury at my father overpowered me, even though by now I understood more about his disease. He was probably genetically predisposed to having a gambling addiction, I'd learned by reading a psychology journal. The traits I used to admire in my father—his constant chatter, his loud, almost forced laugh at gatherings, even the way he scarfed down food—were tied in to an anxious disposition, which was often an underpinning for the illness.

But understanding my dad's addiction didn't make it easier to accept. My mother had worked so hard all of her life; she should be retired by now, sitting on a porch and working on the knitting projects she loved, even planning a big trip for the first time. Instead she stood for eight-hour shifts, hustling for tips.

"Sit down," I ordered my mom. "Let me wash that."

She shook her head and kept scrubbing at a stubborn spot. "It's fine, honey. You just relax."

But none of us could.

Our initial unease only deepened as we exhausted our superficial chatter, and every time a silence fell over the dinner table, we all began talking animatedly at once, which only made things more awkward. At one point my mom asked about Michael's new company.

"He's sorry he couldn't come. He's working crazy hours, trying to get it off the ground," I said. Back then I could laugh about it, imagining it would be a temporary thing. "But hey, I've got an idea. Why don't you come visit for a few days? I could show you around D.C."

"That sounds like fun!" my mom said. "Steven? What do you think?"

I let only one syllable slip out—"Oh!"—but those two letters conveyed so much: surprise that my mom had invited my father when I'd intended the invitation for her alone, and a hint of disappointment, too.

Dad quickly took a bite of pot roast.

"You should go alone," he finally said, dabbing his mouth with his napkin. "Go have fun."

"Of course you can both come," I said. "You *should*. It's just with Michael working all the time, I thought it could be a girls' weekend. That's all."

"Sure," my dad said lightly, but he didn't meet my eyes.

That night I went to the bedroom and lay in the darkness as memories flashed through my mind: Dad stocking shelves in our general store and juggling cans of soup to make me laugh. Dad flipping me in my pink footsie pajamas over his shoulder and carrying me around the house, shouting, "Where's my Julie-girl? I can't find her anywhere!" Dad coming home late at night to my aunt and uncle's house, his face drawn and dark, while I lay on the thin, stained mattress of a rollaway cot, feigning sleep.

Around midnight, I heard the stairs creak and realized someone else was awake. I could tell by the heavy tread that it was my father. I impulsively threw back the covers and hurried after him.

I caught up to him in the kitchen.

"You couldn't sleep either?" he asked, and I nodded, suddenly feeling tongue-tied. He went to the refrigerator and pulled out a carton of milk, then filled a saucepan and put it on a burner.

"This always did the trick when you were little," he said. He opened a cabinet, took out a box of cinnamon graham crackers, and put a few on a plate, then folded a paper towel into a perfect triangle.

"Here you go," he said, tipping the milk into a mug and setting everything on the kitchen table.

"Aren't you going to have some?" I asked.

He shook his head. "I'm not hungry."

I wasn't either, but I couldn't reject his midnight snack. I dipped a cracker in warm milk and began to eat.

"I'm glad you came home," he said, settling into the chair next to mine. He gave a half smile. "Your mom brags about you all the time. The way you put yourself through school and started your own company. I always knew you'd do something special, Julie."

I shook my head and started to tell him I wasn't special; the other young people who lived in our apartment building all seemed to be doing bigger things. One was a legislative assistant to a U.S. senator, and another worked at the World Bank and spoke three languages.

But then I thought about my parents' life: this small kitchen with the linoleum peeling up in a corner of the floor; this crappy little house that they didn't even own; this tiny town, where the big news was the grand opening of a new building for the bank next summer.

"Thanks," I said. The soggy cracker seemed to expand in my mouth, almost choking me, but I forced it down.

"You'll be able to sleep now," he said when I'd finished the last sip of milk. He took my dishes to the sink and switched off the light, and we both headed upstairs. But he was wrong; I lay awake for hours, staring up at the ceiling in the room filled with the tangy smell of fresh paint.

"Come to D.C. soon," I said to my father the next morning as he carried my bag back down to the car. It weighed only about five pounds, but he wouldn't let me do it.

"Sure, that sounds good," he said, but I knew that he never would. I wanted to stay longer, to find a way to connect with my parents, and yet I was desperate to leave. As Dad was putting my bag in the backseat, a blue car pulled up behind us, dislodging a little cloud of dust.

"I was hoping to catch you," a middle-aged woman said when she got out. "I brought by some grout for the bathroom floor." She looked from my father to me. "Is this your daughter? She must be; she's got your eyes."

My father nodded. "This is my Julie," he said, putting a hand on my shoulder. "Julie, this is Debbie. She owns this house. Her mom taught you second grade, remember? Mrs. Nix?"

I smiled. "Of course I do. Your mom was a great teacher. How's she doing?"

"Not so good," Debbie said, her shoulders raising and lowering on a sigh. "She's in a wheelchair now. Her mind's still pretty sharp, though, at least on most days. But your dad's a really good man. He installed a ramp and widened the doorways so she could live with me instead of in an institution. He wouldn't even let me pay him for the work, just for the materials."

I looked at my dad, and because it was true, I swallowed past the lump in my throat and said, "He is. He's a good man."

After his company's stock went public, Michael bought my parents their own house, just two blocks away from where I'd grown up, and he set up automatic monthly deposits into their checking account. It meant my mother could finally retire.

"What if my father loses it?" I asked. "He doesn't have such a good record of keeping houses, you know."

Michael shrugged. "I'll buy them another one."

In that moment, I felt so awash in love and gratitude to Michael for saving my parents that I couldn't speak. Knowing they were taken care of eased my guilt for not visiting more often. I sent gifts instead—a fancy coffeemaker for my mother, a beautifully crafted pipe for my dad, a pair of plush bathrobes—and

I called them every single week. I pretended that was enough, even though I knew better.

But when my marriage collapsed inward, I didn't have room to think about anyone or anything else. It began simply enough—with another woman's name in place of mine, and a lingering look—and it grew and grew, until it overshadowed everything good in my marriage: the way Michael looked into my eyes before he kissed me on our wedding day, the sweet notes he used to leave me, the painful but well-intentioned foot rubs he gave me when I kicked off my high heels.

Maybe every relationship contains an invisible, constantly shifting scale that measures the good and bad it holds. Things between Michael and me were so wonderful for so many years that sometimes I wonder if the bad was quietly building strength all along, waiting for the right moment to claim dominance and violently pull everything over to its side.

Twenty-one

I HONESTLY BELIEVED MICHAEL wasn't doing anything but working during all those late nights at the office. I didn't grow suspicious when my calls to his cell phone went unanswered, or when he packed his bags and headed out for frequent overnight trips. The only cliché that was missing was lipstick on his collar, but I still didn't catch on, not until the evening when Michael and I went to a fancy political fundraising dinner downtown.

It was a work event masquerading as a social one; business cards were passed around faster than the crab puffs and mini quiches, and everyone's eyes skimmed past the person they were talking to, in case someone more important was in the next group over. It was the sort of event that I hated but that Michael thrived on. I'd almost begged off from it, but I'd spent so little time with my husband that I ended up changing my mind. Maybe I'd convince him to leave early, I thought. We could sneak a bottle of wine into the back of our limo and have the driver take us on a nighttime tour of D.C.'s monuments.

But from the moment we arrived, Michael was swept into conversations that pulled him away from me. By then he'd joined the boards of a half dozen charitable foundations, and meetings consumed most of his evenings. He seemed to be on a first-name basis with half the people in the room. It had taken me a while, but it finally dawned on me that being rich wasn't enough. What Michael really craved was power. He loved donating huge sums to politicians and being invited to events where members of Congress mingled with celebrities and elite journalists. He adored giving speeches about business development and new marketing techniques; no matter how busy he was, he always stayed and took dozens of questions from the audience, growing visibly more expansive as everyone hung on his words. It was as though Michael had finally been permitted to join an exclusive club after years of having its members toss him their keys and order him not to dent the Porsche or Mercedes when he parked it.

He was in his element again tonight. After we accepted cocktails from a passing waiter, a guy I vaguely recognized as a former secretary of commerce walked over with his chest puffed out in the self-important manner of both mating bluebirds and D.C. politicians. He vigorously pumped Michael's hand—hand-shaking was practically a sport in Michael's new crowd—and when the conversation turned to the ever-sexy topic of the U.S. census, I slipped away before I keeled over from boredom. I wandered through the room, checking out the flowers and nodding in recognition at a waiter who had worked some of my events. Eventually I found a table lined with rows of little calligraphed seating cards. I spotted Michael's name quickly enough—he was at Table 12, right by the podium where the president elect would be speaking—but I couldn't seem to find my card. I scanned the rows of names twice, then a third time—and suddenly my vision blurred and the voices in the room became distorted and dark, like a record being played backward.

Roxanne Dunhill, Table 12.

I grabbed the edge of the table to steady myself, then snatched up the card, as if by doing so I'd be hiding the evidence, camouflaging my anger and shame.

"Ready?" Michael asked, coming up behind me and putting his hand on my hip. I shook it off.

"What's wrong?" he asked. I twisted around to face him and silently held up the card with a trembling hand.

He frowned at it. "They made a mistake." He shrugged. "Wait a minute. You don't think . . . ?"

"I don't know what to think," I said, my voice shrill and too loud. I stood there, silent and shaking, as another couple wandered over and found their cards and then walked away again.

"Someone made a mistake," Michael repeated.

"Someone thought she was your wife. Why would they think that, Michael?"

Michael spread his hands out to the sides in an expression of innocence, even though he couldn't prevent the nervous facial twitch I'd seen so many times before, like when he'd been caught trying to slip me a note in twelfth-grade English class, and the occasions when he'd fibbed his way out of social engagements that didn't interest him. His voice was *too* firm, too confident—and the net result was the opposite impression of the one he'd been trying to give. He was lying.

Had I known this moment was coming? I wondered. I'd felt something—an instinctual warning that felt like a mild electric shock—when I met Roxanne, the public relations manager Michael had hired a few months earlier. Something about the way she looked at him and smiled before skimming her eyes appraisingly over me made me draw in my breath and move

closer to my husband. But later I'd dismissed it as an inconsequential crush on her part. She was young, had the body of
a ballerina and the name of a porn star, and was probably in-
fatuated with Michael. It wasn't my favorite recipe, but I could
choke it down.

That's what I told myself again a few weeks later when I
opened the morning paper to see a photo of them in the owners' box at a basketball game. I hadn't gone—Michael had invited me, but I wasn't feeling well and I'd begged off, knowing
it would be a long, rowdy night. Roxanne stood next to him in
the photo, her nails grazing the sleeve of his rolled-up white
oxford shirt. He was looking straight at the camera, but she was
smiling up at him.

She looked like a cat, I'd thought, trying to objectively assess
her triangular face and big, long-lashed eyes. Michael probably
found her attractive—who wouldn't?—but he was twisted away
from her in the photo. He was watching the game, while she
watched him.

What would I have seen if the camera had snapped a few
moments later? I wondered. Would his dark head be bent closer
to hers? Would her hand still be lingering on him, maybe moving up to caress his biceps?

But there were lots of people around them in the photo, including employees from Michael's office and the other team
owners. It didn't mean anything, I'd told myself, folding up the
newspaper and tucking it deep in the recycle bin. It *couldn't*.

"Julia. This is silly." For a moment, I thought Michael was
reaching out to embrace me, but instead his hand grabbed the
seating card out of mine. He tore it up and shoved the scraps of
paper into his pocket.

Julia. He'd been introducing himself as Michael and calling
me Julia for years, as if our old selves were skins we shrugged
out of when we moved to D.C. I'd stopped by to meet him

for lunch at Georgetown University one day and discovered his classmates were calling him by his full name.

"Mike sounds like a little kid," he'd said with a shrug when I'd asked about it. "Did you ever think of calling yourself Julia?"

I'd rolled my eyes, but later that night, I tested out the full name on my birth certificate, which no one, except a substitute teacher in school, had ever used before. I wrote it down on a piece of paper and said it aloud. It sounded elegant and sophisticated, I thought, even though using it made me feel like I was stealing someone else's identity.

Now Michael was nodding hello to another man across the room while I stood there, feeling nauseated from the onslaught of hurt and jealousy.

Didn't he care how I felt anymore? Who *was* he?

"I want to go home," I said. I wrapped my arms around myself, feeling as if I might splinter into a thousand pieces.

"Julia, come on," he said, lifting his hand to wave at someone else. "Everyone's waiting for us."

I looked at him in disbelief: he cared more about what people thought than he did about my feelings. I weighed the only two options I could see: storm out, or follow him to our seats. The organizers of tonight's event assumed Roxanne was his wife. I wondered what they'd seen or heard.

A waiter walked by, and I grabbed a glass of white wine off his tray and gulped a third of it down without tasting it.

"Sweetheart," Michael said. His tone was pleading, but his smile was firmly in place. If anyone glanced at us, they'd have no idea what was unfolding.

I looked around the room and realized no one in here was a true friend. If I left, people at our table would gossip about my empty seat, but no one would miss me. Would Michael leave, too? I wondered. Or maybe he'd stay the whole night, charming everyone at our table after murmuring a quick explanation about how I'd suddenly taken ill. A few years ago, I wouldn't have had to question how he'd react.

I was wearing a two-thousand-dollar Issey Miyake dress and my earlobes hurt from the weight of my diamond-encrusted hoops. My husband was one of the most successful men in a room full of newsmakers. Yet I'd never been so miserable.

"Please . . . ," Michael said as the band struck up and the president elect and his wife walked in. Now everyone was on their feet, clapping and cheering, but in a minute they'd all sit down and Michael and I would draw attention.

I threw back my shoulders and walked to Table 12 and sat there for the rest of the damn night, smiling and chatting with the men seated on either side of me. I pretended to listen to the speeches, though I couldn't have repeated a word of them. I clapped until my hands hurt, and smiled until my cheeks did, too. I drank another glass of chardonnay, then another, trying to make the image of her delicate hand against his sleeve dissolve. But it never did.

As the president elect's words turned into a low, buzzing sound inside my head, I kept seeing the face of Rosina, the woman whose story was originally told by Rossini and picked up in Mozart's opera years later. By then, she and the Count had been married for years, and they'd grown estranged. He tried to cheat on her with an employee.

Rosina found out about it, too.

I confronted him later that night—I yelled and I cried and I demanded to know what had transpired between them—but Michael denied everything. By now his face was a smooth mask, his features arranged in an expression of innocence.

"You're having an affair," I said. I walked up to him, got in his face, and spit out the words again, hoping to shock the truth out of him. But he just shook his head.

"It was a mix-up," he said. "You're making a big deal out of nothing."

But I wondered. Of course I wondered.

As I lay in bed, I thought about the time, back when Michael and I were living in our old apartment, when I went out for "Sake Sunday" at the Japanese restaurant next door with three women who lived in the building. We'd all become friendly through the usual neighborly encounters—signing for one another's packages, or watering plants if someone was away—and they'd invited me to their weekly gathering a few times before, but Sunday evenings were popular wedding times, and I almost always had events booked.

Even though I was a newcomer to the group, our rapidly disappearing cups of hot sake helped fold me into their intimate conversation. Marnie, one of the women, had separated from her husband a few months earlier, and she'd finally dropped off the last load of his things at his new place before coming to happy hour.

"A few CDs, a pair of his underwear that had somehow gotten mixed into my drawer, and some frozen pizzas that he loved but I could never stand. It felt so strange to see him in his new apartment," Marnie said, her right hand unconsciously rubbing the bare finger on her left one. I could still see the slight impression the ring had indented into her skin. "My parents tried to talk me out of it. My sister did, too. Everyone thought he was a great guy . . . but he didn't make me happy. The little things he did—the way he slurped up cereal in the morning, and threw the newspaper all over the floor when he'd finished with it—just drove me nuts."

"I have to pick up after my husband all the time, too," one

of the other women said. She was a few years older than the rest of us and had been married the longest. "It's something I've learned to live with."

"Oh, he cleaned up the newspaper after he'd read the whole thing," Marnie said. "But the way he left it scattered on the floor, instead of taking two seconds to just fold it back up in case I wanted to read a section . . ."

She glanced around the table and flushed. "It sounds like I'm nit-picking. Maybe I am. . . . I just always thought—if you love someone, shouldn't you be able to overlook that sort of thing? But I never could, with Brian. I think we'll be much better friends than we were husband and wife. Sometimes at night, hearing him breathe through his open mouth drove me crazy. . . . I felt like I had to leave before I started to hate him. That sounds awful, doesn't it?"

"Why did you marry him?" I blurted, emboldened by the four cups of the vaguely medicinal-tasting sake.

Marnie leaned in, putting her elbows on the table. Her honey-colored hair swung forward, framing her oval face. "I dated this bad boy before Brian. He cheated on me, got drunk all the time, started a fight at a bar once when a guy flirted with me . . . he was a nightmare. But God, was he sexy. . . ." Her eyes grew dreamy. "Anyway, I think I saw Brian and I knew he wouldn't do any of those things. I didn't see him for who he was, I saw him for who he *wasn't,* and that was why I married him. It wasn't fair to him. He deserves better."

"My marriage . . ." The woman who cleaned up after her husband cleared her throat and took another sip before starting again. A bit of lipstick was smeared on her front tooth, and I wanted to gesture for her to rub it off so she wouldn't be embarrassed when she noticed it later, but she was staring down at her sake cup. "My marriage isn't a fairy tale. Whose is, though?"

"Everyone has to put up with some crap," Marnie agreed.

"The husbands do, too. I know Brian got tired of me being so bitchy. . . . But when I started fantasizing about sleeping on the couch—and you guys should see our couch, it kind of sags in the middle—it was pretty obvious. I couldn't stay married to him or we'd both go crazy."

"I don't think I could leave my husband," the woman with the lipstick on her tooth said. "Not that I want to," she quickly clarified, "but unless he did something really awful, like hit me, I couldn't just go."

"If he hits you, you have to leave," the third woman said.

"Or if he verbally abuses you," Marnie added. "Then you walk away."

If he gambles away all your money, you go, I thought, wishing once again my mother had been strong enough to do just that.

"But what do you do if the lines aren't that clear?" the first woman unexpectedly asked, still looking down at her glass. "Say your husband breaks the promise he made on your wedding day, and he stops cherishing you. Maybe he loves you, but he doesn't act like he's in love with you. Should you divorce him then?"

Somehow I sensed the answer was vitally important to her, despite her earlier protestation that she wouldn't be able to leave her husband.

"Everyone has to compromise to some extent," I said carefully. "But if you're unhappy more often than not . . ."

"Doesn't Ann Landers or Dear Abby or someone always tell you to ask yourself if you're better off with or without him?" Marnie added.

"But what if you don't fantasize about sleeping on the couch?" she asked, finally lifting up her eyes. They roved around the table to land on each of us in turn. "What if things aren't terrible, but they aren't great either? What if you're not happy, but not terribly unhappy either? How do you know what to do?"

I refilled everyone's cup while I thought about it. "I think you'd know if you needed to leave," I finally said. "You have to trust yourself."

We moved on to lighter topics soon after that, but I couldn't forget her confused, pleading eyes. She was stuck in that fuzzy middle place—not happy, but not terribly unhappy either—and she was desperate for an answer. Maybe when she was alone, she mentally listed the good things in her marriage, then counted up the bad parts. She probably listened to her friends complain about their husbands and thought, Well, at least he doesn't do *that*. Her husband's fidelity or disinterest in golf might buy her a few days or weeks of unexpected gratitude. Maybe she even had moments of grace mixed in with the dreary days—times when her husband unexpectedly threw an arm across her in sleep and pulled her closer to him, or cracked a joke about a movie they both hated. It might be impossible for her to answer the advice columnist's deceptively simple question.

At the time I felt so sorry for her, with her sad eyes and smear of lipstick on her tooth. But it wasn't long before I knew exactly how she felt—before I *was* her.

Part Two

Twenty-two

I ONCE READ A newspaper story about what happens to the human body just before a big accident. Say you're driving through an intersection, absently dangling your hand out the window to catch the breeze and doing your best Alicia Keys impression while she backs you up on the radio. Then, out of the corner of your eye, you glimpse a guy in a truck barreling through the red light, and in that fleeting, frozen moment, your brain calculates the trajectory and speed of your car and his truck and screams a warning: *You're going to be hit.* That's when your body snaps to attention and scrambles to protect you. Blood rushes toward your internal organs, to give them added cushioning at the moment of impact. Instinct pulls your arms up, to cover your vulnerable head and face. *Let's focus on the priorities, the things it would hurt most to lose,* your body is basically instructing itself—and that's exactly what the doctors do, too, when you're rushed to the ER. Sometimes a minor injury like a sprained shoulder or broken toe won't even be noticed until long after the internal bleeding is stopped and surgeons ensure that your pupils can still contract in a bright light and that you know the correct day of the week.

When Michael announced he wanted to give everything away, that's exactly what I did: I focused only on the big hemorrhage, the potential loss of the company and our houses. I didn't think about the smaller pieces. Then one day I went into my dressing room to change my shirt and it hit me with the force of a thunderclap.

How could I have forgotten?

I spun around and peeked into the bedroom to make sure Michael wasn't around before locking myself inside my dressing room. My eyes swept past the glass-door closets where my clothes and shoes and purses were artfully displayed as I hurried toward a back corner. I moved a shelfful of sweaters onto a chaise lounge, then stared at the section of bare wall I'd uncovered. I pressed a spot I'd long ago memorized, and part of the wall silently slid aside to reveal a secret panel. I dialed the combination of the safe and waited until I heard a click and the heavy metal door swung open.

I reached in and took out the velvet boxes containing the sapphire-and-platinum teardrop earrings and matching necklace Michael had given me for my last birthday. I laid them on the shelf, and then reached in again. My solid gold bangles were here, too, I thought as my hand closed around their reassuring heft, and my ropes of onyx and white pearls. I reached in again and pulled out the cases containing my diamond tennis bracelet, two Rolexes, and chunky emerald ring. Next came my diamond hoop earrings, my Tiffany tourmaline cuff bracelet, my grossularite and platinum brooch—one by one, almost reverently, I opened the lids and laid the jewelry boxes on the shelf. The platinum choker encrusted with gems in every color of the rainbow—probably the most valuable piece of all—had been delivered to me the day after Michael's company's stock went public.

These belonged to *me*, not Michael, since he'd given them to me as gifts for birthdays or anniversaries or special events. No matter what happened in the future, I could take my jewelry with me.

I closed my eyes, feeling a physical lifting sensation, as though I'd come in from a rainstorm and flung off a soaking wet wool coat. I'd never had my jewelry appraised, but I knew that, if I had to sell it, even taking into account a hefty drop in value for a resale, I'd still walk away with a fat six-figure check. Enough for a big down payment on a house in a lovely neighborhood, with a chunk left over to tuck away in the bank for emergencies.

If I decided my future didn't include Michael . . . My fingers lingered over the delicate craftsmanship of the stones and precious metals. Even if I couldn't find a way to break the prenup, I'd have this gorgeous, glittering safety net.

I started when I heard Michael's voice outside the dressing room door: "Julia?"

"Just a minute," I shouted. I scrambled to pile the boxes back into the safe, then shut the door and slid the panel to cover it. I quickly put the sweaters on the bare shelf, then ran to the door and flung it open.

"Hi," I panted.

"Are you okay?" Michael asked.

"Sure. I was just changing my shirt," I said. "It's colder out than I thought."

"Oh." Michael looked at me strangely. "But isn't that the shirt you were already wearing?"

"I, um, couldn't find anything else . . ."

Michael's eyebrows shot toward the ceiling as he scanned my dressing room, which was as well stocked as any boutique.

"Anyway, did you need something?" I asked quickly.

"It's such a beautiful day," Michael said. "I packed up a snack. Want to go for a walk?"

I shrugged a shoulder, feeling more kindly disposed toward him than I had in a long time.

"Sure," I said. "A walk sounds great."

It was nearly four o'clock in the afternoon when we left, and without planning it, I found myself driving toward Great Falls. I hadn't intended to bring Michael here, but I didn't feel like strolling the streets of D.C. Someone might recognize Michael and force us into a conversation I didn't want to have. So I suggested we go to the spot where I'd met Noah. He'd said he often went there after school, and I was hoping we'd catch him. Maybe it was because I still felt awkward around my husband and I knew Noah's chatter would bridge the gaps in our conversation. Or it could've been because something was drawing me to Noah, as steadily and persistently as the ocean's undertow.

Besides, I still couldn't figure out the solution to that stupid problem about the waiter and the missing dollar.

We got out of the car and walked in silence for several minutes. It felt strange to be in this quiet space with Michael, and I was as self-conscious as if we were on a blind date. I made sure there was plenty of room between us while we walked. I didn't want my hand to brush against his and give him the wrong idea.

When I spotted the skinny form throwing a stick to Bear, he waved us over. His wave grew more vigorous when he spotted the picnic basket Michael was carrying. From the moment we joined him, Noah was the one who steered the conversation, screeching around corners and taking shortcuts through bumpy fields, while Michael and I hung on for dear life.

"This is soo good," Noah said, gobbling up half my sandwich and looking beseechingly at the chocolate-chip cookies Michael had packed. I handed him a few and smiled, then stretched out my legs on the rock.

"So I read about that opera guy, Wagner?" Noah said. He had a smudge of chocolate on his nose, and somehow, more had found its way into his spiky brown hair. "It took me a minute to Google him because I spelled his name with a *V* at first. Then I figured it out."

"Really?" I felt a flush of pleasure. I'd never shared opera with anyone before, and the thought that Noah liked it was unexpectedly lovely. "What did you learn?"

"I think I know why he was such a jerk," Noah said. "He couldn't get away from the number 13."

I wrinkled my nose in confusion. "What do you mean?"

"Take his name, Richard Wagner. It's got thirteen letters, right? He was born in 1813. And guess how many operas he wrote? Thirteen."

"I think you're right," I said, reaching back in my memory.

Michael looked back and forth, like Noah and I were speaking a foreign language he couldn't translate, but he didn't interrupt us.

"I am right," Noah said cheerfully. "And there's more. Add up the numbers of his birth year, 1813. It comes out to thirteen. And did you know he was exiled from Germany?"

I closed my eyes. "I think so. I read about it . . ."

"For thirteen years," Noah said. "His first opera, the one I can't pronounce? *Tann* something?"

"*Tannhäuser.*" I nodded eagerly. "It was a disaster . . . people booed him like crazy."

"March thirteenth," Noah said. "That's when it came out in Paris."

"My God," I breathed.

"Told you I love numbers," Noah said. "The guy died on the thirteenth of February, too. Can you blame him for being such a jerk? He must've had really bad luck all his life. He probably kept slamming his fingers in the piano cover by accident, and tripping over his own feet. Maybe the reason he didn't write more operas was because he accidentally burned the ones he wrote in the fireplace. Think about it, all those thirteens? The guy had to be pretty miserable."

Noah was grinning, like it was all a great joke, as Michael and I gaped at him.

"You . . . you figured this all out from Google?" I finally said. "Did it take you a long time?"

"You mean the stuff about burning the operas? I was just kidding."

"The numbers, Noah, all those thirteens. How long did that take you to figure out?"

Noah shrugged. "I dunno. A couple minutes, maybe."

"How'd you do it?" Michael finally spoke up, his voice quiet but with a taut undercurrent of interest running through it.

"Sometimes when I see something, like some long boring story"—Noah flashed me a grin—"no offense, but some of the stuff about his life was kind of boring, you know, like that boat trip he got stuck on, but anyway, the numbers just float up at me. Even when I'm not looking for them."

"Do things like that happen a lot?" Michael asked, leaning forward slightly.

"Yeah," Noah said, gobbling down the last cookie. "I read about math a lot, too. That's probably why I think about it so much."

"I think there's a little more to it than that," Michael said, almost under his breath, shaking his head.

"Most people only see numbers in boring places," Noah said blithely. "Like their checkbooks, or"—he looked down at the fingers he was licking clean—"they count on their fingers. But numbers are everywhere."

"Where do you see them?" Michael asked.

By now I felt like the outsider in the conversation; I *always* counted on my fingers. I mean, didn't everyone?

Noah looked at Michael for a moment, like he was taking measure of whether Michael was truly interested or just humoring him.

"Math is all around us right now," Noah said. He pointed at a tree. "It's in there."

"How?" I asked. Noah's dog could swim underwater—who knew, maybe he'd found a tree that could spout multiplication tables.

"See, there was this guy named Fibonacci? He was from Italy?" Noah said, his already high voice rising to helium levels at the end of every sentence. "Anyway, he came up with this series of numbers. It goes 1, 1, 2, 3, 5, 8, 13, 21, 34, 55. The thing that's special about it—"

"Every number is the sum of the previous two numbers," Michael interrupted. "Eight is 3 plus 5. Thirteen is 8 plus 5."

Noah's eyes widened in surprise. "That's right. How did you know?"

"Math used to be my favorite, too, kiddo," Michael said.

"I read in this book that you can find Fibonacci numbers everywhere in nature," Noah confided. "And it's true. If you count the petals on a flower, it's usually a Fibonacci number. And if you look up into that tree—actually, a lot of trees, not just that one—and you count up from a low branch to the next one directly above it, there's usually a Fibonacci number of branches between them. I've found the numbers making patterns in pinecones, too."

Noah ducked his head and grinned. "Once I even found Fibonacci spirals in the cauliflower my mom was going to cook for dinner. I tried to convince her to let me keep it, but she made me eat it anyway."

Michael and I just looked at each other. I'd heard of child prodigies; Mozart wrote the opera *Bastien and Bastienne* when he was twelve. And by the age of fifteen, Rossini could go to an opera, then come home and write entire arias—both the vocal and orchestral parts—from memory. But I'd never met one before.

How was it possible that this little kid wearing a stained shirt, this scruffy, skinny guy who spent every afternoon throwing a stick for his dog on a rock out in the middle of a river, possessed such a magnificent brain?

"There's one other place I found Fibonacci," Noah said, and now he turned to look at me. He looked kind of shy for the first time since I'd met him, as if he was offering up a gift he wasn't sure I'd like. "I thought of you since you love music so much. When I was Googling opera, I learned there are thirteen keys in every octave. On a piano, eight keys are white and five are black in each octave, and the black keys are grouped in twos and threes. They're all Fibonacci numbers. Every single one of them."

He'd thought of this for me? This sweet little boy who'd held my iPod earbuds and closed his eyes and curved his lips into a smile while he listened to Wagner?

Who are you? How do I know you? I wanted to ask him. Because I'd met Noah before, somewhere. I was certain of it. He felt so familiar.

Suddenly Noah jumped up and threw a stick into the water for Bear. "Did you bring anything to drink?" he asked hopefully. "All those cookies made me a little thirsty."

"Sure," Michael said. He fumbled for the picnic basket, pulled out a bottle of DrinkUp, and poured some into a paper cup. "Here you go. . . . Hey, Noah? Do you see your dog?"

"He's fine," Noah and I said in unison.

Michael's brow furrowed. "But I don't see him—"

"Trust me," I cut Michael off. "So, Noah, tell me the answer to that problem. It's driving me crazy."

Noah grinned. "So you go to lunch with two friends, and you each pay ten dollars toward the bill, right? But then later, the waiter realizes the bill was only twenty-five dollars. So he gets five dollars out of the cash register, and on the way back to your table, he takes two for himself as a tip. He gives you each a dollar. So, you and your friends pay nine dollars each, which adds up to twenty-seven dollars. And the waiter has two, which makes twenty-nine. What happened to the missing dollar?"

Michael laughed.

"You know it, don't you?" Noah asked.

"Why don't you explain it to him, just in case," I said impatiently.

"It's like an optical illusion," Noah said. "It's a trick question. The two dollars should be *subtracted* from what the customers pay, not added."

I thought about it for a minute. I still didn't totally get it, but then I forgot all about Noah's trick question. Because at that moment, as I looked back and forth between him and Michael, it hit me: the person Noah was a dead ringer for was a young Michael.

Twenty-three

EARLY THE NEXT MORNING I flung the sheet away from my sweaty body and sat up, my breath coming in quick gasps. "It was just a dream," I said aloud. I looked over, but the other side of the bed was empty.

"Michael?" I called out, my voice cracking. He didn't answer.

I'd been restless all night long. After lying awake for hours, I'd finally drifted off, but I'd never dipped fully into sleep. Instead I felt suspended inside the thin membrane separating sleep and wakefulness. My dreams had been dark and turbulent—I'd been swimming with Noah in the river, and he was arcing high into the air, like a porpoise, the sunlight turning the drops of water on his pale skin into diamonds. Then he slipped under the surface, so cleanly and suddenly he didn't leave even a ripple behind. I dove deeply, blindly reaching for him, but my arms kept closing around nothing, and then I saw him through a burst of bubbles. I kicked as hard as I could, diving deeper into the water, but Noah's face turned into Michael's and he spiraled away from me, to the bottom of the river. He was smiling; how could he be smiling when he was drowning?

"Please don't go," I'd been crying in my sleep.

I didn't know why I'd had a nightmare about losing Michael. It could have been because of what he'd said about not knowing how much time he had left. Or maybe I was beginning to realize that, at the end of these three weeks, I wouldn't stay with him.

I climbed out of bed and put on my robe, trying to shake away the shadowy images clinging to the corners of my mind.

Michael wasn't in his bathroom, or the sitting room. I hurried downstairs, the thick carpets absorbing the sound of my footsteps.

I saw a silhouette by the French doors and stifled a scream. "You scared me!" I said when I realized it was Michael.

"Sorry," he said, turning toward me. He gestured toward the glass doors. "I was just watching the deer."

I'd never seen deer in our yard before, probably because our gardeners had an arsenal of tricks to keep them from snacking on our manicured flowers and shrubs. I'd once heard them discussing wolves' urine and foul-tasting chemicals. But the gardeners were gone, and rain must've washed away their toxic sprays.

I walked over to Michael and saw there were at least a dozen animals moving through our yard with the graceful steps of dancers.

"Look at the little ones," he whispered. Four fawns, their soft brown coats dotted with snowy spots, rooted their noses into the grass. One chased another to a far corner of the yard, then they raced back, hurdling a row of butterfly bushes with ease. A doe sensed our presence and lifted her head, but after she appraised us, she seemed to decide we weren't a threat, and she bent her head to eat again.

"It's incredible," I breathed. "There's this whole other world all around us, and we never noticed it."

Michael looked at me but didn't say anything.

"Don't even think for a second that's an analogy for anything else," I said, and he laughed. He lifted his arm, as though to put it around me, then he slowly let it drop back to his side.

I wondered what I would've done if he'd tried to hug me. Michael always used to bury his face in my hair when we embraced; it was a habit of his I'd loved. "You switched shampoos," he said to me once, shortly after we'd started dating. "Now you smell like green apples." Still reeling from my parents' abrupt withdrawal, I'd hungered for the way he cherished the tiniest details about me: the mole on my left shoulder, the tiny but stubborn cowlick in the back of my hair, the way my eyes took on the hues of certain shirts I wore.

I might've stopped him if he'd tried to touch me . . . or maybe I would've let myself feel his arms around me again, for a moment. I looked up at his profile and swallowed a sigh.

This was how it had been with Michael for too long, I thought, suddenly feeling as tired as if I'd been battling insomnia for months. My yearning juxtaposed with anger at him for not giving me more—and at myself for wanting it. Being with him was a constant push and pull. Nothing about our relationship was simple now.

"I think the deer are leaving," Michael was saying. "Want to go outside and watch the sun rise?"

I considered it for a moment. I knew I wouldn't be able to go back to sleep, and I didn't feel like being alone. "Sure," I finally said.

Still in my pajamas, robe, and slippers, I followed him into our backyard. "Oh, my God," I said upon catching sight of the rock-lined pond. How could I have forgotten? I ran toward it, grabbed a small plastic container resting between two of the rocks, and reached inside for some pellets. I felt relief as greedy, gaping mouths came to the surface and gobbled up the food. I threw in more pellets and watched them disappear as flashes of orange and white and red and black zipped through the water.

Michael was staring into the pond, an inscrutable expression on his face. "I didn't even know we had fish."

"Seriously?" I couldn't believe it. "Michael, we stocked them two years ago."

I reached back in my memory, seeing the gardeners approach me about it one morning as I lingered over coffee and the Style section of the *Washington Post*. Michael wasn't home, but surely he'd walked by the koi pond sometime in the past two years. It was only fifty or so yards away from our house. He had to have occasionally looked down instead of always staring at the spot in the distance where he wanted to go next, hadn't he?

"Move it, Pugsley," I ordered, tossing in another handful. "You've had enough."

Michael grinned. "You named them?"

I looked over my shoulder at him. It was a small secret, but I felt reluctant revealing it. He was suddenly so eager to know everything about me, and perversely, his eagerness made me want to hold back. It was my way of punishing him for not being interested before, I realized. I wanted to show him the distance between us wasn't that easy to bridge; *I* wasn't that easy. Finally I shrugged and kept my voice light: "The littlest one is Nemo, and that pretty one with the long fins is Cinderella. Pugsley is the breakfast hog."

"Speaking of breakfast, want to eat out here? I could bring us a tray."

"I'm not hungry," I said, "but I could use something to drink."

"Coffee?" Michael asked.

I shook my head. "I'm more in a juice mood."

"Be right back." Michael lightly jogged toward the house as I looked after him. For years my husband hadn't touched a stove, laundered a sock, or filled a tank of gas. Now he was my personal cabana boy.

I heard a little splash and tossed another pellet into the water. "Just one more, Pugsley," I warned. I never could resist his puffed-out cheeks. He looked like a toddler who was threatening to hold his breath until he got his way. "But after this, you need to clean your room, understand?"

Pugsley eyed me, then swam off with a shake of his tail that I interpreted as fish-speak for "Make me!" I grabbed the net by the side of the pond and skimmed the leaves and sticks from the surface. See, this was why Pugsley never listened; he knew I'd cave and do his chores for him.

After a few minutes, I spotted Michael coming toward me, clutching two bottles of DrinkUp and carrying a plate covered in aluminum foil.

"Provisions!" he announced as he got closer to me. "I brought some croissants and jam in case you changed your mind. Sorry I took so long. Dale called when I was inside."

"What did he want?" I reflexively wrinkled my nose, as if a bad smell had just wafted by on a breeze.

"It isn't important," Michael said. "Even if Dale thinks it is."

"Is something up with the company?" I asked casually. I picked up the net again and began clearing some imaginary leaves.

"A former employee is complaining about something. It's nothing. Dale said he's just trying to get some money. Let's not let it interfere with the day. Some lemonade?" He held up a bottle.

Interesting, I thought as I slowly nodded. It was strange that Dale had called about something so inconsequential. Dale was the company's top attorney, and he had a vested interest in seeing that Michael stuck around, since Dale might be out of a job after Michael left. Could Dale be casting around for excuses to lure Michael back to work?

Maybe, I mused as I sipped the lemonade I'd helped taste-test to perfection in our tiny kitchen so many years ago, Dale could turn into an unexpected ally.

"What are you thinking about?" Michael asked. "You're a million miles away."

"Hmmm . . . ?" As I looked up at him, our herb garden caught my eye. "I've got an idea. Let's find some fresh mint to put in the lemonade."

"Good idea." Michael followed me to the little patch lined with straight green rows. "Is that it?" He pointed to a cluster of stalks that shot up straight into the air.

I shook my head. "That's lavender."

Michael dropped to his knees and leaned close to the plant and took in a deep breath. "Julia, have you smelled this stuff? It's incredible!" I thought about telling him the gardeners used to cut fresh stalks and put them in a vase in our bedroom all the time, but I refrained.

"I can't believe how good this smells," Michael said, his eyes shut. He stayed there for a long moment, inhaling and smiling like the poster boy for the Get High on Life campaign. He was wearing old jeans and a faded Georgetown University long-sleeved shirt, and his hair was growing out into wild curls; somehow it made him look like a college student again. Like the Michael I used to adore. I'd felt numb toward my husband for so long; now he was conjuring such sharp emotions in me that it felt like the ground beneath my feet was constantly shifting.

Finally Michael stood up and pulled a smaller, shinier leaf from a plant in the next row over and rubbed it between his fingers. "What's this one?"

I leaned in for a sniff. "Basil. And here's the mint." I tore off a few sprigs and handed one to him. He dropped it into his bottle, then led me to a nearby hammock that was strung between two strong poplar trees.

"Want to sit for a bit?" he asked.

I shrugged. "Sure."

He held the side steady for me as I climbed in. We nearly tipped over when Michael got on, and I clung to the side of the hammock until we stabilized. "I've been wanting to ask you something," he said, stretching out his legs. "Do you like your job—I mean *really* like it?"

"Of course," I said without even having to think about it.

His brow had been furrowed, but it smoothed out with my answer. "Good," he breathed. "What was the best party you ever threw? I don't mean the fanciest one, or the most expensive. Just the one you liked the best."

"Oh, I don't know," I said, hanging one of my legs over the hammock's side and using my toes to push off against the ground and swing us back and forth.

"Come on, I really want to hear it," he said.

There wasn't any reason not to tell him, other than to punish him by denying him the conversations he'd once withheld from me. Which, come to think of it, was a pretty appealing reason, even if it did make me feel about as mature as Pugsley.

"There were so many of them," I finally said, casually crossing my arms behind my head, as if I'd only been sorting through my memories during the long pause. "I guess I can rule out weddings. There's always some battle leading up to the day, between the mother and the bride, or maybe if the parents are divorced and remarried, there's drama about the photos and who gets to sit where. And sometimes relatives get upset if they're not allowed to bring kids. . . . I don't know, it seems like there's always something. The day itself can be magical—"

I smiled as I thought of something.

"Tell me," Michael said.

"Whenever the bride starts to walk down the aisle, everyone turns to look at her. But I never do," I said. "I look at the people surrounding her. There's so much hope and love in the room. Sometimes there's an older couple reaching for one another's hands at the exact same moment, or the father of the bride trying to choke back tears—"

Michael was staring at me.

I cleared my throat, feeling inexplicably annoyed at him. And at myself, for letting him in even this much. "Anyway, weddings are great, but I can't ever forget all the stress leading up to them."

"Anniversary parties?" Michael asked. "Are they any better?"

"Usually," I said. "By then everyone has mellowed out. But nothing's jumping out at me as a favorite. Let me think . . ."

I reached back for the memory. "There was this family reunion," I began, then I looked up at the sky and frowned. The clouds were thin and gray, and the air held a hint of winter, which was less than a month away; it felt like a storm was coming.

Michael was watching me intently, as if my favorite celebration was significant in some way only he knew.

"The family reunion," he prodded.

"It was for three brothers, who all lived really far apart," I began again, getting caught up in the images of that day despite myself. "They'd grown up in Virginia, and one still lived there, but another had moved to England and one was all the way in Australia. Anyhow, they'd all gotten married and had kids, and somehow time just slipped away from them. They wrote holiday cards and called, but they hadn't seen each other in years. They wanted to reconnect, with each other and with their families. So they invited everyone—their parents and aunts and uncles and cousins and new in-laws—and it ended up being forty people.

"They were my easiest clients ever, but that's not the only reason why they were the best. They didn't care about the food or the decorations, they just wanted to be together and have fun. So before I planned anything, I called them up one by one and asked about their memories of growing up. They had this great childhood. They were outside all the time, playing stickball and kick the can and football. There was a creek behind their house where they went fishing every weekend, even though they never once caught anything. I'm not even sure there were fish in that creek. But it wasn't about the fish; it was about the three of them, digging for worms and casting their lines into the water and catching fireflies in jelly jars when it turned dark. Once they even tried to make a raft, like Huckleberry Finn. It sank before they'd gotten ten feet away from shore."

Michael laughed.

"I rented a National Park building—really more of a cabin—that was surrounded by picnic tables and outdoor grills and soccer and baseball fields. We brought in stuff for old-fashioned games, like three-legged races and horseshoes and softball. Then we served up giant bowls of buttered corn on the cob and watermelon wedges and hot dogs and burgers. When it got dark, all the kids hunted for sticks and made s'mores over the grills. Most of the adults did, too."

"Were the brothers happy?" Michael asked. "Were they able to find each other again?"

I nodded. "I hired a photographer, and she took pictures all day long. I made copies of one and gave it to each of them afterward. It shows the three of them toward the end of the day, and they're standing together in front of the fire. She shot them from the back, and the one in the middle had his arms draped around each of his brothers. I paired it with a photo of them as kids and gave them all framed copies."

"After all those years, nothing had really changed, had it?" Michael asked.

"I don't know when they'll see each other again," I said, and the thought saddened me. "The one in Australia—his wife is from Sydney, and her family all lives there. Their kids are in school and they've set down roots. I doubt they'll move. The brother who lives in England was talking about maybe getting transferred back to the U.S. sometime, but who knows if it'll happen. I just—I wanted to give them that one day. Maybe it will be enough for them, for the next five or ten years."

"I wish I'd had that, with my brothers," Michael said softly.

I looked at him, shocked. Michael didn't talk about his brothers or family, not ever.

He looked down at his hands and absently rubbed at a smear of dirt on his palm, then lifted his eyes to mine. "Did I ever tell you what I did the day after my company's stock went public?" he asked. "I had all these reporters calling to interview me, and my day was stacked with meetings. Everyone wanted a piece of me. But I made them all wait. I told my secretary to hold my calls and not let anyone into my office, no matter how urgent they said it was. Then I sat down at my desk and took out my checkbook and I wrote my brothers and my parents one check apiece. But not big checks. I gave them each a thousand bucks. And every month after that, I sent them checks, too, always for the same amount. A thousand dollars."

He took in a breath, then continued. "I took my time signing them, and I addressed the envelopes by hand. I put them into the mailbox myself on the first of every month and watched them drop in, one at a time. I wanted my family to be reminded as often as possible that I'd done better than them. That I was the only success story in the family. And I wanted them to worry that the checks might suddenly stop coming. That's why I didn't send a bigger amount; I wanted them to depend on me, to realize that if they bought a new car or a couch or something, I was all over it. I wanted to be in their faces as much as possible, without being around them."

I didn't say anything. I didn't know how to respond.

"I didn't tell you because part of me was ashamed," he said. "I was pretending to help them out, but it was really all about my ego. I mean, when I signed the checks, I even made my signature bigger than usual. It was like, 'Let's see you bastards ignore me now.'"

We'd tried so hard to leave West Virginia behind, but we'd failed, I realized. Moving on requires more than a change in geography. As hard as Michael worked, as much as we acquired, our past had been with us all along, breathing over our shoulders and watching our every move. It was a third person in our relationship, and just like any interloper in a marriage, it had driven us apart.

"Are you going to get in touch with them again?" I asked.

Michael shook his head. "I wrote them all letters explaining everything with a final check. And I set up college accounts for their kids. But they haven't called me. Maybe they're angry they won't get any more money. Maybe they don't know what to say. I don't know, but I'm not going to worry about it.

"The only person I want to focus on is you," he said simply.

Damn it, I'd forgotten this; how being with Michael both energized and relaxed me. How the passing hours grew light and slippery as we talked. He'd lulled me in, somehow, and made me forget everything while we talked. But now the uncertainty of our future came rushing back, stronger than ever.

"What if I can't ever forgive you for giving everything away?" I asked. *Keep calm,* I instructed myself. *Don't argue with him; just plant seeds to make him doubt what he's doing.*

"I know you don't see things the same way I do. I think it would be impossible for you to, without experiencing what I did. I just want us to be together without worrying about money for a while."

I felt my nails bite into my palms.

"I'm not getting there," I told him. "What you're doing is making me focus on money more, not less."

"Julia, I know what this is costing you," he said, his voice low and urgent. "I know you better than anyone—at least I used to. I hope I get to know you that way again. And maybe I'm not doing this perfectly, but it's the only way I know how."

I started to say something, then abruptly glanced up at the sky as it rumbled a warning. "It's going to rain."

"But look." Michael pointed up to the trees. The thick, leafy branches provided a canopy over our hammock. "We're completely protected."

"You want to stay out here?" I asked.

He nodded. "Stay with me?"

"Seriously?" I asked. If the rain came down hard, we'd be trapped—we were a few hundred yards from the house. "We could still make a run for it."

"Julia, we don't have to be anywhere, do we? We've got our provisions." Michael held up his mint-spiked lemonade and smiled. "Let's just wait it out, okay?"

I swallowed a sigh and lay back in the hammock. Before long, I'd forgotten my frustration again as Michael told me stories about the early days of his company, like the time when he was so absorbed thinking about a big meeting that he didn't see a height restriction sign on a parking lot entrance ramp and crashed the top of a DrinkUp truck into the concrete roof. "The parking lot attendant's face was priceless," he confided. "I'm sure he was thinking, This idiot's a millionaire but he can't read a giant sign above his head?"

"How'd you get the truck out?" I asked.

"Much more slowly than I got in," he said.

I laughed, then noticed Michael focusing on the trees overhead.

"What is it?" I asked.

"I've been counting branches," he said. "Noah's right. I keep finding Fibonacci numbers."

"He's a great kid," I said, wondering if talking about Michael's brothers—his tormentors—had made him think of Noah. He knew firsthand how smart, awkward kids could wind up as targets; I know we were both hoping Noah had it easier.

"Please don't get mad at me for saying this," Michael said. "But I keep wondering, if we'd had a son, if he'd be like Noah."

I waited for the surge of anger, but it never came.

I want a baby. The thought roared through my mind, and I nearly gasped. I'd buried my hope for years, trying to suffocate it, but it had only grown stronger with the passage of time. Just last month at Starbucks, I'd stood in line behind a young mother holding a little girl, and I couldn't stop staring at the baby's liquid brown eyes and fat cheeks. I could almost feel the downy warmth of her head against my own shoulder. The barista had to ask twice for my order, and it was only when the mother turned around to look at me that I broke my eyes away, flushing in embarrassment.

Now I looked at Michael and began to say something, but then a few words flashed in my mind, just as they had dozens—*hundreds*—of times before, and I felt like I'd been sucker punched.

"I want your lips, your hands, your body . . . can we sneak out early tonight?" Roxanne had written to Michael in an old e-mail. That single line summed up the biggest reason I'd never pushed Michael to have kids. Bringing one into our shell of a marriage wouldn't be fair.

The rain came down harder, soaking the ground and creating muddy puddles while I thought about Michael's affair. It had been over between them for quite a while; I was certain of that because I still snuck onto his BlackBerry and reviewed the calls on his cell phone. Such a wonderful marriage we had, I thought bitterly, and I shifted my legs over so they weren't brushing against his anymore. Being with Michael was an emotional cha-cha-cha; every time we stepped forward together, we marched just as quickly backward. Talking to him made it impossible to ignore our past hurts and betrayals, just as I knew it would.

Maybe Michael had changed, I thought. I studied him as he stared up at the trees. But would it last?

The rain finally tapered off. We were walking back to the house when the world seemed to flip upside down around us.

"I know you need to stay on top of everything at the office," Michael said. "But you don't have anything special planned for the next—"

An explosion, loud as a thunderbolt, cut off the rest of his sentence.

My eyes shot skyward as I instinctively lunged forward. Michael was just standing there, frozen, but somehow I knocked myself into him with enough force to send us both sprawling a few feet before we hit the ground. I landed awkwardly on top of Michael, and my jaw smacked into the back of his head. At the precise moment we tumbled to the ground, something crashed down behind us, forcefully enough to make the earth shake.

We lay there in the mud for a few seconds. Then Michael slowly got to his feet and reached out his hand and pulled me up onto my shaking legs.

"Are you okay?" he asked, brushing back my hair to look at my face.

"Not a scratch. You?"

He nodded.

"It would've hit me," he said, staring down at the tree limb, his voice unnaturally calm.

I looked up and saw the jagged break where the limb had

ripped away from the tree: twenty, maybe thirty feet off the ground. It was about a foot thick and six feet long, tapering to thinner, leafy branches at the end. But the thickest part—the most dangerous part—had landed near us.

"The rain must have weakened it," I said. I rubbed my sore jaw and took a step closer to the limb as I peered down at it. "It was probably rotten."

"It doesn't look rotten," Michael said, bending down to examine it. He touched the jagged end with the tip of a finger, then looked up at the tree again.

"It might have killed me," he said slowly. "If it had hit me in the head."

"But it didn't. Come on," I said, feeling an overwhelming urge to get away from this spot, fast. I tugged on Michael's arm. "Let's hurry before the rain starts again."

He stared at the limb for another few moments, then we walked back to the house, the air around us thick with words we weren't saying.

Twenty-four

I WAS STILL TREMBLING a few moments later when my cell phone rang.

"Can you come over?" Isabelle asked after my fumbling fingers found the Answer Call button.

Her voice sounded even shakier than mine. I gripped the phone tighter. "Are you okay?"

"Beth just phoned. I—I'm going to Seattle to see her." The quaver in her voice that I'd mistaken for sad tears was actually caused by happy ones, I realized.

"Ten minutes," I promised. "Don't move."

"Was that Isabelle?" Michael asked as I hung up.

I nodded. "It's kind of a long story." The thought flashed through my mind that it was another example of how far apart Michael and I had grown: he knew so little about my friendship with Isabelle.

He studied my face for a moment, then grabbed my car keys off a hook by the front door and tossed them to me. "Tell me about it when you get back, okay?"

I sped down our driveway, managed to hit mostly green lights (one was reddish green, but definitely more on the green side), and pulled up in front of Isabelle's house thirteen minutes later. I took her front steps two at a time and pounded on her door. She flung it open immediately—she must've been standing there waiting for me—and I gave her a huge hug.

"It's crazy, isn't it?" she asked.

"Completely. In the best possible way."

"Come on, I'll tell you about it while I finish packing." I followed her upstairs, into her bedroom suite—an area that managed to be both cozy and spacious at once, with scattered rugs in warm earthy colors, a stone fireplace, and a sitting area that was bigger than the entire first floor of the house where I'd grown up. "Tell me what I need. Warm socks, right?"

"And don't forget an umbrella," I said. "It always rains in Seattle. Oh, my God, you're going to Seattle!" My brain had felt so sluggish that I seemed to be trailing a few beats behind in our conversation, kind of like I always used to in aerobics class.

She tucked another sweater into an already-bulging suitcase, then zipped it shut. She opened a matching, smaller Vuitton bag and laid it on her bed. "I probably shouldn't bring all this," she said, stuffing in an armful of socks. "I can buy anything I forget, I guess. . . . I just can't think straight. I still can't believe she called. It's happening so fast."

"What did she say? Did she just come right out and ask you to visit?"

Isabelle shook her head. "I was the one who suggested it. I didn't even know I was going to say it. But all of a sudden I blurted out the idea of going to Seattle to meet her. At first she seemed surprised, then she said she'd like that."

"How long do you think you'll be gone?"

Isabelle smiled. "As long as Beth wants me. I left the return ticket open-ended. She deserves it, Julia. I have to tell her how difficult it was to give her up, and that it wasn't because of *her*. And I want something more than a few photos. I need to see her. I can't believe she's sixteen years old and I'm finally going to see her."

So that was it, I thought. Isabelle's life had turned around in the space of a day. Everything she'd wondered about for so long was waiting for her, just an airplane ride away.

"So her family still lives in the same place?" I plopped down, cross-legged, on the bed next to the suitcase.

Isabelle nodded. "They never moved. I didn't see their house, but there were photos of it in their file in the adoption agency. She's an only child. They've got two French bulldogs. Beth told me"—Isabelle grinned, and I could hear in her voice how much she loved saying her daughter's name; how she turned that single syllable into a caress—"she told me her father's mildly allergic, but because she loves animals so much he takes Claritin every day so she can have her pets."

"You really did it," I said. "You picked such great parents for her."

Isabelle ducked her head, almost shyly. "I don't want to assume too much, you know? I could tell she mentioned her dad because she felt loyal to him. And I'm fine with that; I don't want to swoop in and act like I've got any claim on Beth. But if there's even a little bit of room for me in her life . . . I mean, if she wanted to talk to me from time to time, or maybe I could visit now and then and take her out to lunch . . ."

"You just put in twenty pairs of socks," I told her, shooing her away from the suitcase. "You've got bras, right? Shoes? A coat? Medicines?"

Isabelle nodded distractedly.

"You definitely don't need these," I said, pulling a pair of fishnet stockings out of the tangle of socks.

"Present from an ex," she said, narrowing her eyes. "He wanted me to install a stripper pole in my bedroom. He saw something about women doing it on *The Tyra Banks Show*."

"But it would go so well with your décor," I told her. "Did you dump him because of the stripper pole or because he watches Tyra Banks?"

"Both," she said, frowning absently at her suitcase. "Anyway, after I visit Beth . . . I don't know, but I feel like something has been missing for a while now. I don't know if I can do this anymore."

"Do what?" I asked, taking out some socks and standing up to toss them back in her drawer.

"*This!*" Isabelle spread out her arms, like a little kid who was pretending to fly. "My life! I'm thirty-four, and what do I have to show for it? I spend the money my grandfather made—not even the money, I just spend the interest on his money—and I dabble in charity work. I play tennis and go to parties and shop and travel. I'm busy every day of the week and it's not enough. I'm bored, Julia. I'm bored out of my fucking mind, and I have been for a while. I didn't think my life would turn out like this. I don't even know how it happened. I've just been drifting along, and suddenly, almost half my life is gone.

"I don't know what I'll do when I get back. Maybe I'll get involved in a charity—really involved; not just show up at a benefit in a pretty dress and write a check—or hell, maybe *I'll* adopt a child and bring all of this full circle. You've got a job you love, and you've got a good man who adores you. And he does adore you now, Julia, no matter what happened before."

I ducked my head and busied myself folding clothes into her suitcase so Isabelle wouldn't see the emotions flooding my face. She didn't know everything that had happened between Michael and me; maybe she wouldn't sound so optimistic if she did.

"I need something more in my life, too," she was saying.

I nodded slowly. "Can I take you to the airport?"

"I'd love it," Isabelle said. She stood up again and opened

another dresser drawer, adding a pair of drawstring pajama bottoms decorated with little red hearts to her suitcase. I'd given those to her for her birthday last year, I remembered, and then we'd gone out to a belly-dancing class and laughed so hard that the instructor's face had tightened and her shockingly flexible middle had stopped swiveling and she'd asked us to leave.

"What else do I need?"

"Socks?" I suggested, and she threw a pair at me.

"Maybe pack some pictures of you at different times in your life to show her? She might like to see a childhood photo of you."

"Great idea. I'll just grab an album," Isabelle said. She started to leave the room, then turned back to look at me. "Families come in all shapes and sizes these days, don't they?" she said. "It wouldn't be so strange if Beth wanted to have a relationship with me, too, would it?"

I saw the uncertainty and longing on her face, and I stood up and walked over to Isabelle and hugged her.

"She's going to love you," I whispered. "And her parents . . . they sound like the kind of people who'll welcome you into their lives if that's what Beth wants."

"I'm scared," Isabelle said.

I thought of the days stretching before me without my friend's constant phone calls and funny texts. I imagined Beth and her family reaching out to Isabelle, and folding her into their lives. I was so happy for Isabelle, but if she started spending a lot of time in Seattle, especially if Michael and I separated . . . I'd just miss her so much.

We were splitting into different directions, like Stephenie and I had long ago.

I'm scared, too, I thought but didn't say.

* * *

It was dusk by the time I arrived home. I turned off my Jaguar and sat in the sudden silence, rolling my neck around in slow circles to work out the kinks. Then I paused, my head tilted back, to stare up at our house. Our lush lawn, such a brilliant shade of green that it almost looked like the fake stuff they put on miniature golf courses, stretched out to both sides for an absurdly generous distance, by D.C. standards, before meeting the neighbors' property lines. A few floodlights had turned on automatically, and they illuminated the marble columns and grand steps flanking our front door. The play of stark white light against the shadows made our entranceway appear even more imposing than usual. All that space, all that silence . . . so different from my house in West Virginia, where our neighbors lived so close by that all Mom had to do if she needed to borrow a lemon or a scoop of Tide was bang open the screen door—we never kept our front door shut in good weather, and neither did anyone else—and call out. If I was running late to school, I scrambled over our picket fence and cut through the yard behind ours, stooping to pet the fat little mutt who lived there. Sometimes, if he woke up from his morning snooze to look at me with mournful brown eyes, I'd slip him a bite of my biscuit with bacon. We didn't have much of a backyard to speak of, but in the front, Dad had tied a rope around a thick branch of our oak tree and hung a tire swing. Neighborhood kids gathered there while Dad pushed us so high that, if we stretched out our legs, our feet almost grazed the roof of our house.

"Where do you summer?" someone asked me at the first dinner party Michael and I ever hosted. I can't remember who asked—we had a woman named Holiday and another named Etienne at our table, and I was still trying to recover from it—and I'd taken a careful swallow of my lemon sorbet before answering.

"I've always summered on a tire swing," I thought about saying grandly, imagining the women murmuring to each other, "Did she say Charleston?" "No, no, it must've been the name of their yacht."

Instead I mumbled something about staying in town, and I saw, or rather *felt,* Michael's awareness of the conversation from his seat at the other end of the table. A month later, Michael bought the house in Aspen, sight unseen. We sometimes managed to go there for a full week in August—but since Michael always brought along a laptop and cell phone and his Black-Berry, it wasn't a vacation, just a relocation. Once we'd even flown in around noon, only to have Michael get a call from the office right after lunch. He'd jetted out within the hour, meaning he'd actually spent far more time in the air than on our vacation.

Now I opened my car door and stepped out onto the grass, still gazing up at our house. What would it be like to leave all of this? I wondered as my eyes traveled over the peaked roof and elaborately constructed decks and sprawling side patios. Would I miss it during every single moment, or would I adjust? I wouldn't miss having a full-time maid, I decided. Even if I'd worked at a reception until 3:00 A.M. the night before, I always felt too guilty to relax when I knew she was nearby, cleaning toilets or hand-washing my lacy bras. And despite the fact that we'd had a sommelier come to our house for a dozen wine-tasting sessions, I still couldn't taste the difference between a twenty-dollar chardonnay and one that cost ten times as much.

Some things I wouldn't mind giving up, but I'd probably glance around our—or *my*—new place, seething with resentment as I noticed chips in the plaster walls and the overflowing laundry basket. Every time the dishwasher broke or my car overheated, I'd mentally curse Michael.

I didn't know what it would feel like to step back toward our old life, but I did know that moving here, to this breathtaking mansion, wasn't anything like what I'd expected. It was the first time I'd admitted it, even to myself. I'd thought living in this house would erase my fears, heal my old wounds—that my new setting would transform me into the kind of confident, poised woman who *should* live here—but somehow, I'd always felt as if everything was only temporary, a rug underneath me that could be yanked out at any time. I'd never felt like I truly belonged here.

Still, that didn't mean I wanted to give it up. Certainly not my Jacuzzi and heated tiles.

I headed up the front steps, but Michael swung open the door before I could fit my key in the lock.

"What's wrong?" I asked.

His eyes looked strained, with dark shadows underneath. It was the first time I'd seen him truly agitated since he'd come home from the hospital.

"It's noth—" Michael started to answer, then he looked at me and shook his head. "I made this vow when . . . when everything happened. I want you to know everything about me, even the stuff I'm ashamed of. I'm never going to lie to you, not ever again. Julia, I'm worried."

I just looked at him and waited while my mind clutched on to those words, *not ever again*. Exactly how many times had he lied to me before?

"After you left for Isabelle's, I kept thinking about Dale's call. I had this feeling that something was really wrong, so I had the papers faxed over. This kid got injured on the job a few months ago. Dale handled it; no, I *let* Dale handle it. That's what Dale does; he makes problems disappear. The kid got into an accident when he was driving one of our trucks, and we paid him off, Julia. He injured his brain. Something is wrong with his short-term memory now. He's twenty-four years old, and we pushed him to settle fast. He didn't know what he was doing. His family is poor and unsophisticated, and they took the money."

I took off my coat and silently hung it in the closet as I processed what Michael was saying. "How much did you give him?" I finally asked, turning to face him.

"Seventy-five thousand. We're covering all his doctors' bills and he'll get a little workmen's comp, but he's not going to be able to get another job—not one that pays much, anyways. Maybe he could wash dishes or something. Bag groceries. I don't know. We screwed him, Julia. This kid isn't going to have a normal life, and it's because of us."

"It was an accident, though," I pointed out.

"But we should have taken care of him," Michael repeated, using his fingertips to rub circles in his temples, something he did to ease the pressure when he had a bad headache. "The truck's brakes failed. It was a fluke, but we were the ones who abandoned him. It was *our* truck. He was just trying to make a living. He was a hard worker; I checked his files. I wanted to see what happened. When Dale called the other day, he made it sound like the kid was just after a quick buck. But I called the doctor who treated the guy, and he's going to need help for the rest of his life. He won't be able to live alone, ever. He might forget he turned on a stove burner or something. What kind of life is he going to have, Julia?"

I was quiet for a moment. "Can't you do something?" I asked. "It's not too late, is it?"

"I'm going to try," Michael said.

I thought for a moment of Dale's clammy hand on my arm in the hospital, and the way his eyes always followed Michael at the events we'd attended together.

"Why would Dale spin it that way?" I wondered. "Why wouldn't he tell you the truth?"

Michael exhaled a short burst of breath that sounded almost like a laugh. "Dale hates me, Julia."

I blinked in surprise. "Why do you say that?"

Michael looked at me wryly. "Honesty, right? Dale's jealous as hell. He wanted what I had. He wanted my money, my life. I *liked* his jealousy, Julia. I fed off it. I knew how greedy and cunning he could be. But I could control him, so he never worried me."

"And now?" I asked.

"Now I can't control him anymore," Michael said simply. "And I have no idea what he's going to do. But I'm not going to waste time thinking about Dale. I need to figure out how to help this kid."

For some reason, I thought of Becky Hendrickson. I remembered Michael reading aloud one of her battered, beloved Nancy Drew books while she watched him with eyes that seemed too old for her face. I tried to reconcile that image with one of Michael agreeing to pay off—to *cheat*—a twenty-four-year-old man who had nothing but the shell of a life before him.

"You need to make this right," I told him.

Michael nodded. "I don't know how, but I swear to you I will."

Twenty-five

"HOW'S SEATTLE?" I CRADLED the phone between my neck and ear as I lay down on a couch, settling in for a long talk. Isabelle had been gone for only twenty-four hours, but I'd never missed her more. "And how's Beth?"

"Gorgeous. Both of them," Isabelle said, and I could hear joy ringing through her voice like a bell. "She met me at the airport. God, she's so self-possessed and mature for sixteen! She just walked right up to me at the baggage claim and smiled and said, 'Hi, I'm Beth.' Like us meeting was the most natural thing in the world."

"What was she like? Does she look like you? What did you talk about?"

"Slow down, Katie Couric." Isabelle laughed, and I knew then that everything had turned out fine. "She's tall and slender and thoughtful, and yes, she looks a little like me. But mostly she looks like herself. She seems so at home in her skin. I wasn't that way as a teenager, not at all, even though God knows I tried to fake it. But I did it with cigarettes and low-cut shirts. Beth's confidence comes from her eyes. She looks right at you when you talk to her."

"What did you say to her? Was it easy to talk?"

"So easy! She had all these questions about why I put her up for adoption and what my life was like back then. She's a thinker, Julia. Her dad says she loves crossword puzzles and Sudoku and games like Scrabble. I'm a puzzle for her, too, in a way. I can see her digesting everything I say and fitting it into what she knows about me."

"She sounds great," I said. "Did you spend any time with her parents?"

"Yes, after she picked me up, she took me back to her house for a while. She lives in a real house, you know? It's small and homey, and there are books everywhere and knitted blankets on the backs of the couches. They all have funny mugs to drink coffee; Beth gives her dad a silly one every Christmas. This year's says, 'Sleep is a symptom of caffeine deprivation,' and they told me everyone tries to grab it first in the morning. It's kind of a running joke, to see who can get it first. Isn't that the cutest thing you've ever heard?"

Isabelle hadn't had any of those silly little moments that strengthened the fabric of a family when she was growing up, I realized. She'd had maids and nannies and then, practically the day she hit thirteen, a set of Gucci luggage and a plane ticket to a boarding school.

"She'd just gotten her license and it was one of the first times she'd ever driven alone, when she came to pick me up at the airport. I love it that I'll always be a part of that memory for her. And have I ever told you I've got a theory that you can see people's personalities in the way they drive?"

I covered a laugh with a cough: Isabelle was a maniac behind the wheel. She drove with her left leg hitched up on the seat and one arm dangling out the open window. Once she'd clipped a hedge as she rounded a corner and we carried a leafy branch with us for the next few miles, sticking out of the side of the car like a flag.

"Oh, go to hell, I know what you're thinking! Anyway, Beth lets people into her lane when they flash their turn signals but she isn't a pushover. This guy cut her off on the highway, and she really laid on the horn. Anyway, the parents . . . well, I could tell they were nervous. The mom—Diane—offered me coffee about four times, once right when I was in the middle of taking a sip of some she'd just made me. I don't blame them, though. I mean, we'd only met once sixteen years earlier and I was a teenager then. How were they supposed to know I wasn't completely loony?

"It said so much about them, that they wanted Beth to meet me even though they didn't know what I might bring into their lives," Isabelle said. "They put her first, Julia."

"So did you," I reminded Isabelle.

"Don't be nice to me or I'll start crying," she said. "That's all I've been doing lately. First it was in relief that Beth's turned out okay—better than okay, she's incredible—and now it's because I feel so lucky. I get to have a tiny little piece of her life. I get to love her, too."

"How long do you think you'll stay?" I asked. There was a tiny quaver in my voice; I hoped Isabelle hadn't heard it. I'd had another nightmare last night. Michael and I were in the car together, and he suddenly stood up and went through the windshield—he didn't break the glass, he just sort of *melted* through it—and then he walked away from me. I'd tried to go after him, but the car doors were locked, and no matter how many times I pushed the button to release them, they wouldn't budge. Michael kept walking while I pounded on the window, and even though I could hear him whistling a cheerful tune, he didn't hear my screams. I'd woken up gasping for breath, and I hadn't been able to go back to sleep for hours.

"I'm not sure. Probably another few days," Isabelle was saying. "I'm at the hotel now, but I'm going to see Beth for dinner tonight. How are things there? Has Michael won you back yet?"

I turned her question over in my mind, trying to think about how to answer it. How could I explain that Michael and I were treating each other as carefully and politely as seatmates on a cross-country train ride? That sometimes I worried I'd fall back in love with him, and other times I was certain I'd leave him even if I did?

"Things are pretty much the same," I finally said. "I'll fill you in when you get back. Tell me more about Beth."

"It's funny, we're all trying to be so sensitive to each other's feelings. I asked the parents if I could take Beth out for dinner and they fell all over themselves saying yes. Then I was worried they secretly wanted to come, too, so I kept assuring them they were welcome. They were like, 'Do you want us to come? Because we can, if you want. But if you'd prefer to go alone . . .' Finally Beth just started laughing and took charge. She said she'd go to dinner with me alone this time. Julia, she said *this* time. Like there might be a next time."

"Why shouldn't there be one?" I asked. "If you and Beth both want to see each other again . . ."

"But then when her mom left the room to clear away the dishes, Beth said it would be good for us to talk alone. I sensed there was something . . . worrying her. She was trying to be casual, but get this—she started chewing her thumbnail."

"Her right thumbnail?" I asked.

I could hear the smile in Isabelle's voice. "Just like me, when I'm upset."

"So you'll help her, whatever it is," I said. "And then you'll take both of you out for a manicure."

Isabelle was quiet for a moment.

"Now that I've seen her . . . Julia, I can't bear to lose her. If she's coming to me for help, I can't mess it up."

"You won't," I told her. "You're doing everything perfectly. You're available for Beth, and you're being considerate of her parents and their feelings. Why wouldn't they want you in their lives, Isabelle? All of them?"

She paused, and when she spoke again, her voice was small. "I guess I'm not used to that. To family. Mine was so messed up that I don't know how a real family works. Maybe I think I don't deserve to be welcomed into one."

"You do," I said. "You do deserve it."

I hadn't ever really thanked Isabelle for everything she'd done for me, not just these past few weeks, but long before then, too. So I said it to her now, using different words: "You're my family, Isabelle. You have been for a long time."

Twenty-six

"GIVE ME A HINT," I said. "You know I hate surprises."

"You do?" Michael's brow creased.

"No," I admitted. "C'mon."

"I'm taking you to a lavender farm so we can sniff it all day long." Luckily Michael spoke again before I could harm him bodily. "Kidding, kidding. It's something I hope you'll like. That's all I'm going to say."

I settled into the backseat of the taxi again, and we drove in silence for another few minutes, then I spotted the signs for Dulles airport. Michael leaned forward and whispered something to our cabdriver, then handed him a few folded bills. The taxi pulled up to United Airlines, and Michael said, "Close your eyes."

"*Michael,*" I complained.

"Please?" he asked.

"Fine," I said. I heard the sound of fabric sliding across the seat and the door opening, and then, a moment later, the metallic bang of the trunk slamming shut. I squinted through one eye and saw Michael talking to someone standing on the curb.

"Okay. You can look now. I don't want you to expect too

much," he said, reaching his hand to help me out of the cab. I hesitated, then let him. "I didn't book a fancy hotel. We're flying coach. And it's only for three days. I'm doing it the way I should've years ago. I just . . . I really wanted you to have this, Julia."

"Where are we going?" I asked.

But he wouldn't say another word—not through the crowded security line, or when he bought us each a big bottle of water and a fruit and cheese plate at a kiosk, or even when we got in line to board the plane.

"Don't look," he said, handing me my ticket as we waited. "Can you not tell her where we're going?" he pleaded to the gate agent. "It's a surprise."

She smiled and tore apart my ticket, handing me the smaller end. "Enjoy your trip."

Fifteen minutes later, we'd settled into our seats, then I felt the plane gather force and soar into the sky. After a few moments, the female captain's voice filled the cabin, telling us about the clear air ahead and expected arrival time.

"It looks like smooth flying all the way to Paris," she concluded.

I turned to Michael. He was smiling.

"We're going to Paris?" I spun around and looked out the window, half-expecting to see the Eiffel Tower already.

Then my head snapped back toward Michael. "But I didn't pack—" I began.

"I did it for you. I checked our bags at the curb."

"My office—?"

"Gene knows how to reach you. He told me it would be a slow few days and that you wouldn't miss anything."

"I can't believe you did this," I said.

"Is it okay?" Michael asked, his brow wrinkling. "I didn't want to assume too much . . ."

I slowly nodded, then rested my forehead against the tiny, cold window and watched the landscape below us grow smaller and smaller, until it disappeared beneath a burst of white clouds.

For the next seventy-two hours, I told myself, I wasn't going to think about my maddening, increasingly complicated marriage, or the decision looming over my head at the end of the month. This wasn't real life; it didn't count. I'd dreamed of seeing this city for years, and I wasn't going to let anything ruin it. I wanted to surrender to Paris.

As soon as our plane landed, we dropped our bags at our small, quaint hotel in the Latin Quarter, then we wandered through the city, eating hazelnut gelato from a little shop that boasted a dozen homemade flavors. The old buildings, in shades of blue and gray stones, were still damp from a recent shower, and looking at them made me feel like I'd tumbled into a watercolor painting. I forgot my jet lag and fatigue as we walked for hours, wandering in and out of shops and stopping on a bridge over the Seine to gaze at the boats passing below. *"Pardonnez-moi,"* a young woman murmured as she brushed by me while I stood at the intersection of three narrow cobblestone streets, and I looked after her as she passed, whispering the words and feeling their grace on my tongue.

As the sun began to set, we bought fresh baguettes from a street vendor who sliced them open and filled them with a delicious white cheese I didn't recognize. He pressed the concoctions against a hot grill before wrapping them in waxed paper and handing them to us, and we gobbled them down for dinner right then and there.

"Are you getting tired?" Michael asked, handing me a bottle of water.

I hated to admit it. "Just a little."

"How about we get a bottle of wine and sit down for a while?" he asked. "There's a shop right here."

The proprietor spoke perfect English, and he recommended an inexpensive pinot noir. We ended up drinking it on the tiny balcony of our hotel room, where we could still soak in the sights and smells and sounds.

"Cheers," Michael said, tapping the water glass he'd swiped from the bathroom against mine.

I thought about what to toast to as I watched a guy roar down the street on a motorcycle, a woman seated behind him with her arms wrapped around his chest, so close together they almost seemed to be one person. I didn't want to make this trip about our past or our future.

"To Paris," I finally said.

That night I slept so soundly I couldn't remember dreaming, and the next morning, we awoke early and hiked to the Arc de Triomphe, then drank steaming bowls of café au lait at a sidewalk bistro as we watched the old city come alive. "The women here are gorgeous, don't you think?" I said to Michael as I watched a girl stride by our outdoor café, her sheath of shiny auburn hair swinging with each step. Around her neck was a cherry-colored scarf tied in an artfully careless way I knew I'd never be able to replicate.

"Yes," Michael said. But when I glanced at him to see if he'd noticed the same girl, he was staring at me. I looked down and took the last sip of my milky coffee, feeling both annoyed and pleased.

When we'd finished our basket of croissants, we strolled to the Eiffel Tower, then wandered through the Louvre before succumbing to jet lag and going back to our hotel for a quick nap. We took hot showers and ventured out again an hour later, ravenous from all the walking, and feasted on roasted oysters and niçoise salads. Later that night, as we took the long route back to our hotel, we stumbled upon an old-fashioned merry-go-round, right in the middle of the city.

"Want to take a ride?" Michael asked, and I silently nodded. I'd never been on one before. He bought a handful of tickets, and I wandered among the horses before finally choosing one with pink and purple and silver painted ribbons wound through its mane. I leaned my head back, feeling the breeze as we spun around, and Michael nearly fell off his horse trying to grab the brass ring.

This isn't real life, I reminded myself as he stood on his horse's saddle, elaborately bowing to me while I laughed. *This is just a reprieve from it.*

On our last night, we found a bistro and dipped chunks of bread and crisp vegetables into hot cheese fondues. "This has been nice," I said to Michael after I'd eaten the final rich, tangy bite. "Thank you."

"Just nice?" He pretended to clutch at his heart, then motioned to the waiter for another bottle of cabernet. "If we had come here for our belated honeymoon, I would've taken you out to a romantic dinner and told you all the things about you I love."

"Unless you were checking your BlackBerry," I said, keeping my tone light. I drained my wineglass and nodded my thanks at the waiter who refilled it.

"Touché," he said. "But sadly true. Here are the things I should've told you: I love the way you drink the same cup of coffee all morning long. You take one sip, then put it down and forget about it for an hour. Then you reheat it in the microwave and have another sip. I've never seen someone ration a cup of caffeine the way you do."

"That's the best you would've come up with?" I said lightly. "And they say romance isn't dead."

"I'm just getting started," he said. "I love the way you get into fights with your scale; I heard you call her a bitch one morning."

"Must've been around the holidays," I said. "She's always out to get me then."

"I love the way you barely seem to lift up your feet when you walk, yet you never shuffle. You walking across a room is the most graceful thing I've ever seen," Michael said. "I love the tiny freckles on your nose that come out when you've been in the sun; they form an almost perfect triangle. I love the fact that you have laugh lines—don't worry, they're so faint I doubt anyone else could see them—but you don't have even a hint of one frown line."

I swallowed hard as I looked at him. This was the Michael I'd ached for, the guy who found everything about me endearing. Who made me feel special.

"And I love your generous heart," he said. "Any other woman would've walked away from me long ago."

A sudden sound made me twist around in my seat: A piano player had just started his set. He was squeezed into a corner of the small restaurant, separated from us by maybe a half dozen tables decorated with red cloths and little votive candles. I was glad he'd started to play; I didn't want to think about all the reasons why I might leave Michael right now.

"More wine?" Michael lifted up the bottle, and I nodded. And because I wanted to taste champagne in Paris, I had a glass of brut, too.

I could blame what happened next on the alcohol, or on the fact that Paris acted like Michael's wingman by setting a ridiculously romantic scene: It was an unseasonably warm night, and we'd thrown open the doors to our hotel room balcony. The long white curtains fluttered in the soft breeze, and the royal blue candles in the big candelabra on the dresser made the room glow with a soft light.

After Michael locked the room door behind us, he looked at me, and even though he didn't say a word, I felt him asking a question. I'd lost count of how long it had been since we'd last had sex—an occasional fumbling in our darkened bedroom late at night was what passed for our love life these days.

Michael didn't say a word, he just traced my cheekbones and nose and chin with his fingertips, then he slowly began to unbutton my blouse. And I repeated to myself, *None of this is real.*

I woke up in his arms early the next morning.

"Hey, you," he whispered into my ear, his voice huskier than usual.

I sat bolt upright, clutching the sheet to my chest, scenes from last night fluttering through my mind: Michael's fingers gently running over my belly and thighs, his warm lips against my neck, him moving rhythmically inside me while I gripped his shoulders and wrapped my legs around his waist and cried out.

His hands were *still* on me, resting possessively on my stomach, I realized, and I sucked in my breath sharply. I jumped out of bed, taking the sheet with me and leaving Michael naked and exposed.

"What the hell?" I shouted. "You bring me to Paris and get me drunk and have sex with me?"

"Julia, calm down. We didn't do anything wrong."

"Obviously not, Michael. We're married. It's not like we were *cheating.*" I flung out the words like weapons. "I had too much to drink. This doesn't mean I'm in love with you, or—or that I'm going to stay with you!"

"Julia . . . please, honey . . . just hang on a second," he said. By now he'd scrambled off the bed and found his shirt on the floor and was pulling it over his head. I tore around the room, grabbing my jeans and sweater and boots, like we were in a race to get dressed in some bizarre postcoital TV game show.

"Can we just talk for a second?" he asked as I shrugged into my clothes.

But I couldn't bear to be near him. I snatched up my jacket and purse and slammed the door, leaving him standing in the middle of the room trying to put on his boxers, with one leg ridiculously high up in the air like a flamingo.

My mouth tasted sour and my head was pounding and I knew my hair was a mess; I was like a college kid doing the walk of shame after dollar shooter night at the local bar. I found an open bistro and hurried inside, ordering coffee and bottled water while avoiding eye contact with the waitress. No one would believe I'd just had sex with my husband; I was acting as stressed and jumpy as if I was wearing a scarlet *H* for *Hussy* on my chest. I hurried into the restroom while I was waiting for my beverages and did damage control, wetting a paper towel to rub over my face and slicking on a coat of pink lip gloss and running a brush through the snarls in my hair. My cheeks and eyes were blazing and, I saw as I leaned closer to the mirror, I had a little rash from Michael's beard stubble rubbing my chin.

I tilted my forehead against the mirror and shut my eyes. I couldn't believe I'd slept with him. I'd thought I was being so logical as I held Michael at arm's length, letting him woo me and put his heart on the line while I coolly considered whether to take him back. Now I'd blurred the rules; I'd twisted a new set of kinks into an impossibly knotted situation.

I straightened up and walked back to my table and slowly sipped my beverages while I gathered myself. I knew I'd have to go back to the hotel sometime—our plane would leave later that afternoon—but I needed a few hours alone. I finally paid my bill and rose from my table and wandered outside and found a nearby park. I collapsed onto a wrought-iron bench and wrapped my arms around myself as I watched an old man in a tattered coat throw bread crumbs to a flock of hungry pigeons.

I shouldn't be so upset, I told myself. Having sex with Michael didn't change anything; it didn't mean I had to stay with him. It didn't give him an edge. I was still in control of my own decision. So why was I blinking back tears?

It was because it was so good.

It wasn't just a physical release; Michael kissed all my sensitive parts, the ones he knew so well, from the backs of my knees to the insides of my thighs to my eyelids. He told me over and over again how beautiful I was, how much he loved me. I *felt* his love; it was almost a physical presence in the room. And the way he looked at me, with such tenderness in his eyes . . . it was as if he was seventeen again, and he was discovering me for the first time. Afterward he rubbed my back, and when I curled on my side, too exhausted to stay awake any longer, he fitted his body alongside me and twined his fingers through mine. Just like he used to do, when we first fell in love.

Making love with Michael forced me to realize what I'd be giving up if I left him. We could be good together, like we were before. And yet I still didn't know if I could live with him, or ever trust him again.

I looked up as a pair of young mothers walked past me, pushing babies in prams and chatting animatedly, and suddenly I discovered kids surrounding me. Two toddlers chased the pigeons, and another floated a little yellow plastic boat in the outdoor fountain. Still more were heading into a school across the street that looked more like a museum, swinging their book bags and calling to one another in their high, young voices.

If I stayed with Michael—if we found a way to work out all of our issues—would we have kids? I wondered. What kind of father would he be? If he took on a consultancy job, and worked less, and we somehow managed to reconcile everything that had happened in the past, reveal all of our secrets and not let them destroy us . . .

If I stayed with him, I thought, burying my head in my hands. If I could forgive him for giving all our money away, and for everything that had happened before that.

I knocked on the door to our room and heard Michael's footsteps a moment before the door swung open.

"Hi," he said. He studied my face but didn't ask any questions about where I'd been. "I got you something." He handed me a little paper bag. I peeked inside and saw a green beret and felt my throat tighten. I'd admired one yesterday at a kiosk, but I hadn't thought he'd noticed.

"Thanks," I said, clearing my throat. "I guess it's time to go?"

"I already packed both of our bags," he said, gesturing. "But I left out your toiletries."

I nodded. "I just need to use the restroom."

I pulled my hair up into a ponytail and quickly rinsed off in the shower, then brushed my teeth and smoothed moisturizer on my face, my fingers carrying out the familiar rituals while my mind tried to sort out what to do next. I wasn't ready to talk to Michael; I needed space. I put on my clothes again and covered my eyes with oversize sunglasses.

We stood in the elevator like strangers, with enough room between us to comfortably fit two other people. The bellman had already called a taxi, and it was idling outside the hotel. I climbed in and stared out the window as we began to move, looking at the wide Seine, the gorgeous bridges, the narrow streets and the woman running through them in utterly impractical pink high heels. I instinctively reached for Michael's arm to point out the woman, then let my hand drop back into my lap.

I knew Michael had hoped this trip would bring us together, yet right now, I could barely stand to be near him.

Twenty-seven

I TURNED OFF MY cell phone as I settled into my airplane seat, and I didn't turn it on again for nine long hours—until after we'd landed and caught a taxi back home. Later I'd wonder what might have happened if I'd been able to answer when Isabelle called. Maybe I could've figured out a way to convince her to come home. To *help* her.

But I'd been floating high over the Atlantic Ocean, still feeling the red burn of Michael's whiskers on my cheeks and pretending to doze against the back of my seat so I wouldn't have to meet my husband's eyes.

"Remember how I thought Beth wanted to talk to me about a boyfriend?" Isabelle's message began. I dropped my suitcase onto the floor of my bedroom at the jagged sound of her voice.

"I couldn't have gotten that one more wrong. She asked me to go. She wants me to leave, Julia. She was totally polite about it—she said she's happy I came out and that we got to talk, but now she needs space. God, I thought . . . Well, you probably know what I thought. I had this whole crazy fantasy of coming out every month, and taking her to lunch, and talking to her on the phone every week. . . . I was even thinking she might end up going to college on the East Coast, and I could see her all the time. Dumb, huh?"

I closed my eyes against the pain mingling through her words.

"I mean, I didn't get in touch with her for sixteen years, so it's not like all of a sudden we can have this spontaneous relationship. She was kind enough not to say it, but I could tell that's what she meant. I was a 'surprise,' Julia. That's what she called me, which is sort of ironic because that's exactly what she was for me, sixteen years ago. And now she's got this whole life, this whole perfect, happy life, which is exactly what I wanted for her, but the thing is . . . what I hadn't thought about was . . . Julia, she didn't miss me at all."

A tear rolled down my cheek as I listened to her.

"I held it together, and when she dropped me off at the hotel after dinner, I just told her to call anytime she wanted. And she looked at me with those clear eyes and then she hugged me and didn't say anything. God, I just need to go somewhere." Her voice broke on kind of a half laugh, half sob. "I'm going to take a cab to the airport and see where the next plane is heading. Maybe I'll go to Spain and learn to flamenco dance. Maybe I'll go to the South of France and just lie on a beach for a month—"

The message cut off, but I held the phone to my ear for another beat, as if by doing so, I could keep clinging to Isabelle.

"Julia?"

Michael was reaching out for me, and for the second time in as many days, I let myself feel his arms around me. But this time it was different; there wasn't any passion in his embrace. He just held me, while I cried for my best friend and her broken heart.

"I can't believe her daughter wouldn't want to have a relationship with her," I said later, blowing my nose into the tissue Michael had handed me. "Maybe if she were difficult or crazy . . . but it's *Isabelle*. Who wouldn't want Isabelle around?"

Michael nodded slowly. "I don't think their story's over, though. Look at it from Beth's point of view: Isabelle's been building up to this for years, but Beth didn't know about that. She needs time to adjust."

"So you think Beth will call her?" I asked.

Michael leaned back against the headboard of our bed and rubbed the bridge of his nose. "Either that, or maybe send a note. I have this feeling she'll get back in touch once she sorts out her feelings. It was probably really intense to get the letter and then have Isabelle there a few days later. I can't imagine how emotional that would be. Maybe Beth feels like she needs to be loyal to her parents. Maybe she does just want a little space. But I think she'll write again. They can start over again, and maybe take it more slowly next time."

"I hope so," I said. "If you could've heard her voice, Michael . . ."

"I was wondering . . ." He paused and cleared his throat. "If Isabelle feels even more alone because you were with me when it all happened."

I looked up at him in surprise; I hadn't expected him to be so perceptive. I'd had only half of Michael's attention for so long that I'd forgotten how it felt to have his focus on me—how he saw all the dimensions and nuances that other people usually missed.

"I thought that, too," I said. "I feel so guilty. I was off with you in Paris while she was dealing with all of this."

"She's lonely, isn't she?" Michael asked.

I nodded. "She doesn't let a lot of people see it. But yes."

He looked at me for a moment. "Loneliness was what drew you two together, wasn't it?" he finally said. "I had my company, but you didn't have anyone or anything."

I shrugged. "She's the best friend I've ever had," I said simply.

"She'll come back," Michael said. "I promise you she'll be back."

As Michael was loading the dishwasher later that night and I was losing a staring contest with a pint of Häagen-Dazs, he turned to me. "There's something I've always regretted."

Somehow I knew exactly what he was going to say next. The entire evening had been tinged with melancholy, ever since Isabelle's call, as if setting the stage for this moment.

"I never went with you to visit your mother."

This was what Michael and I had been heading toward ever since he'd fallen to that conference room floor, I realized. For a brief moment I wanted to follow in Isabelle's footsteps—to run away, as far and as fast as I could. But instead, I lifted my chin. "Let's go."

"Right now?" he asked.

I looked at the clock, did a quick calculation in my head. "We can get there by ten. It won't be too late."

"I'll get the car keys," he said, quietly shutting the door of the dishwasher and turning off the kitchen light.

Twenty-eight

read the sign on the side of the road, but it was the only thing welcoming us. Our old town was so quiet that the lone noises on Main Street were the hum of our engine and the sound of our wheels spinning against the pavement. I rolled down my window, not caring that the night wind instantly made my eyes water, and stared as memories passed by: There was Covey's Diner, where my family sometimes ate blueberry pancakes with warm maple syrup on Sunday mornings. And just off that side street was our little brick library, where Donna Milson always greeted me with smiling eyes behind her thick oval glasses, showing me the stack of books she'd set aside for me. There was the pharmacy where I'd slunk in at the age of thirteen, my eyes downcast and my face hot, to buy maxi pads. "You might find these more comfortable," Christy the cashier had said, casually putting back my jumbo pack of pads and picking up a thinner brand. She'd slipped a Hershey's bar into my bag, too, without charging me.

West Virginia was often a punch line for jokes, but some of the finest people I'd ever met lived here. It wasn't my hometown I'd been desperate to escape from; it was the pain of my final year here. People had tried to reach out to me during that time: Donna had dropped off a few books at my house after I avoided the library, but I'd stuck them, unread, in the return slot one night after the library was closed. Two of our neighbors, a retired couple who shoveled the whole sidewalk on their block whenever it snowed, had approached me one afternoon with a tin of banana bread and an invitation to talk, but I'd brushed them off with a mumbled excuse about homework. The only person I allowed in was Michael.

"Are you okay?" Michael asked, and I nodded and adjusted the delicate bundle in my arms.

He made a few quick turns before driving down a road that ran adjacent to a small cemetery dotted with simple white headstones. "Let's park here," I said, gesturing. Michael extracted the keys, and I slid out the passenger-side door and waited for him to walk down the little stone path with me.

The moon overhead illuminated the graveyard, and even though I'd been here only once before, I found my way quickly as I wove through the rows of headstones. I stopped by a weeping willow tree and knelt down. I reached out with a fingertip and traced the carved letters on her headstone. BELOVED WIFE AND MOTHER read the inscription, followed by the dates of her birth and death.

I closed my eyes and remembered what had happened on the night that she died:

A shrill ring cut through my sleep. My hand reached out in the darkness, fumbling across the nightstand and knocking a half-full glass of water to the floor before I snatched up the phone. I squinted at the clock in the darkness: 2:00 A.M. My chest squeezed around my heart, as though trying to cushion it from the coming news.

"Julia?"

My father. But it didn't sound like him.

"It's Mom," he said.

"What happened? Is she okay?"

But I already knew, even before he said the words, "Mom's gone."

It was a stroke, my father told me in a choked voice. But Mom was barely in her sixties; didn't older people have them? I leapt out of bed and paced the bedroom, clinging to the phone with both hands. I felt too numb to cry, too frantic to sit still, too dazed to ask anything other than"Why?" over and over again.

Later, I pieced together what happened: Mom had gone to a friend's house for a walk after dinner. "Do you have your ice cream?" Mom had asked as they'd stepped out the front door. The friend had looked at my mom, thinking she'd misheard. "Did you ask if I had my car keys?" the friend had asked, wondering why she would need keys when they were just going out for a walk. Mom hadn't answered. She'd stumbled twice in the first block of their walk. Her friend had suggested they sit and rest for a while, then they'd walked back to Mom's house—her friend just *walked* her home, so slowly, too slowly, while Mom's brain cells were dying—and Dad was there. He'd taken one look at Mom's lopsided smile and rushed her to the car and driven straight to the hospital. But it was too late.

"Can I see her?" I asked my father, clutching the phone in my still-dark bedroom. It had been almost two years since I'd visited my mother. How had it been that long? I should have made her come stay with me more often. I should have gone to her.

I'd tried to think of the last thing I'd said to her. Did I tell her I loved her, or had I just hung up the phone with an absent-minded "Bye"?

"I can be there in a few hours. Just don't let them . . . take her anywhere," I begged. I hung up and reached for my cell phone on the bureau, as one clear word fought its way through the fog in my mind. *Michael.* He'd know what to do. He'd help me get to my mother quickly.

First I dialed his cell phone. I had to redial twice because my fingers were shaking so much. No one answered, but it was possible Michael had turned it off because he'd gone to bed. I managed to choke out a message, begging him to call me right away.

Where was he staying tonight? I closed my eyes and tried to focus; I couldn't even remember which city he was in. Had he told me the name of the hotel?

I stumbled to my computer and turned it on, and the screen filled the room with a weak blue light. I scrolled through my e-mails, trying to find the latest one Kate had sent with Michael's schedule for the week. Usually I ignored those e-mails, but I didn't delete them until the week was through.

L.A. He was in L.A.

I found Kate's notation of the hotel and the phone number and dialed blindly, asking the front desk to put me through to his room. The phone rang once, twice, then three times. I almost dropped the receiver when a woman answered.

"Michael?" My voice was almost a plea.

"He's in the shower," Roxanne purred, a victorious laugh in her voice. She paused a moment to let that sink in. "Can I, ah . . . *help* you with something, Mrs. Dunhill?"

I still have no memory of what I did during those next moments. I must've put the phone back in its cradle at some point, and I know I blindly grabbed handfuls of clothing to throw into a suitcase. All the wrong things, it turned out later. I didn't need exercise pants and high-heeled boots and wispy spring scarves to say good-bye to my mother.

I sped to the hospital still in my nightgown with my winter coat thrown over it, depending on my GPS to guide me. A nurse in a white uniform let me in and directed me to my mother's room. I hurried to her bedside and dropped to my knees, holding her cold hand and kissing it over and over again. I lay my head next to hers while my tears soaked the pillow and mingled with her hair.

After a while—maybe a half hour, maybe much longer—I stood up. There was a blanket on the foot of the bed, and I pulled it up and tucked it around my mother, as gently as she'd done to me on so many nights when I was a child. I'd been a restless sleeper, and my mom always woke up in the middle of the night, creeping into my room to pull the covers up from the foot of my bed, half-awakening me as I burrowed into the warmth that felt like her love.

Someone put a hand on my shoulder and whispered that it was time to go.

"Where?" I wanted to cry. Both of my homes had been destroyed: the one in West Virginia, and now the one in D.C., too. I didn't have anywhere *to* go.

Then I realized the hand on my shoulder belonged to my father, and I jerked away.

"Julie, honey," he began.

I looked at him and felt the ugly words rise in my throat, threatening to choke me. I felt dizzy with grief and anger. It was my father's fault; everything was his fault. His gambling had ruined her life, and now the stress of it had killed her. But I somehow kept the words back as I stumbled out of the room, realizing that, on some level, my father probably knew it, too. Speaking the words aloud would be pointlessly cruel.

He stood in the doorway, watching me go, his hands outstretched. "I love you," he called.

Funny, Michael had said the exact same thing to me before he'd left for his trip with Roxanne.

I ran to my car and drove to the outskirts of town and sat there, staring at the horizon as the sky changed from black to gray to purple to blue, all the colors of a bruise. I thought about the letters Mom had sent me every month—letters, when everyone else in the world relied on e-mail and impersonal texts—always handwritten on pale yellow stationery. Those notes never hinted that this was coming; her writing was never shaky or unclear. They were relentlessly cheerful, with chatty updates about what was going on around town. "I've planted some daffodils this spring, and they look so pretty in the front yard," or "Do you remember Sadie Robinson? She has three little girls now and they're the cutest things, walking down the street all in a row together like little ducks."

I'd always written her back, and called, and even invited her to come with me to New York, cajoling her with promises of a nice hotel and shopping on Fifth Avenue, but she wouldn't. She didn't want to leave my father, and she knew things were too awkward between us for him to come. My mother's loyalty was her downfall, I realized. She could have had such a different life.

Just then my cell phone rang. I looked down and saw Michael's number flashing. It was almost 9:00 A.M. So it had taken him this long to get back to me, I thought, feeling my mouth twist in bitterness. Was Roxanne still beside him in bed?

I picked up the phone and weighed it in my hand. I'd unwittingly followed in my mother's footsteps, despite my vow that I'd have a very different kind of life, I realized. I, too, was bound to a man who'd keep hurting me.

The phone rang again, and I hurled it out of my car window as hard as I could, watching it shatter against the pavement. I tried to imagine starting over without Michael, but I felt paralyzed. I could see myself yelling at him, confronting him with the evidence I'd gathered, but then what? It was like watching a movie that suddenly went dark, midscene. I had no idea what I'd do—how my life would play out—without Michael.

I sat there for hours. In the end, I finally drove home, and when Michael walked in the door that night, I turned away as he tried to comfort me. He misunderstood, assuming I was angry because he'd stayed for his morning meeting instead of rushing home right away. "I'm sorry," he whispered over and over, but I wouldn't talk to him. I ran into the bathroom and locked the door and stayed there, curled on the floor, for the entire night. I felt as though the outer layer of my skin had been scraped off, and the slightest touch or sound would send arrows of unbearable pain shooting through me. I knew I couldn't handle confronting him, not now, not while I was mourning my mother. I couldn't bear to hear what was between Michael and Roxanne. What if it wasn't just a fling? If he truly cared about her, then maybe he'd leave me. Just like my mother had left me, and before her, my father. I'd have no one.

A day later, Michael asked when the funeral would be held, and then I did scream at him. I watched him recoil from the gritty, horrible sound of my voice: How could he think I'd go to the funeral and see my father, who'd probably try to borrow money from the priest who performed the service?

"Go back to L.A.," I hissed at Michael as my mind filled with images of his body wrapped around Roxanne's slim, lithe one. "Why'd you even bother to come home?"

He lifted up his hands, as though he was surrendering, and walked out of the room. "Whenever you want to talk," he started to say, but I slammed the door behind him . . .

Now I laid the bouquet of yellow tulips I'd been carrying on my mother's grave. They were her favorite flowers, but she never bought them for herself. "Too expensive," she'd say, reaching instead for a more practical potted mum, something that would last for months.

Every week since she'd died, I'd had a dozen tulips sent to her grave. But this was the first time I'd brought them here myself; I hadn't been back to my hometown since that night. And other than cursory phone calls on holidays, I hadn't reached out to my father. I still hadn't forgiven him. Something had twisted inside of me that night, turning me into a person I didn't recognize. The little girl who rode around on her dad's shoulders, giggling uncontrollably while he pawed his feet at the ground and neighed like a horse, had died that night, too.

I looked up from the simple words on her headstone to face Michael.

"When my mom died . . . ," I began. I couldn't continue; it felt like something sharp was lodged in the center of my chest.

"I wasn't here for you," Michael said. He knelt down next to me. "I should have flown back first thing. I can't believe I went to that damn meeting. Julia, I'm so sorry."

It was time to finally deal with this, too.

"It wasn't the meeting so much as the fact that Roxanne answered your phone in the middle of the night," I said abruptly. "In your hotel room in L.A."

I raised my eyes to look at him. Honesty, he'd promised me. If he dared lie to me, here by my mother's grave . . .

"She answered my phone?" he said, confusion and then something else, something darker, flitting across his face.

"You had an affair with her," I said. Anger bubbled just beneath my skin, making it feel hot and tight, and I crossed my arms over my chest.

He squeezed his eyes shut for a moment.

Here it comes, I thought.

"Oh, God, I have to tell you this. I did lie to you . . . about some things, before . . . But you didn't say anything about her answering my phone. Julia, why didn't you tell me?"

I sidestepped that question; I had a very good reason, but

not one I was prepared to reveal now. "Don't you dare lie to me again."

"There was this one night," he began. "It wasn't in L.A., though. It was a month or so before your mother passed away. We were all in New York, a big group of us from the company. I'd had a couple drinks at dinner, and then we went to the bar for some cognacs. Afterward we went back to the hotel and she and I ended up alone in the elevator. She started kissing me. We stopped when the doors opened and there were people in the hallway so we ended up going into our own rooms."

He swallowed hard. "But, ah, she knocked on my door later that night."

I stared at him, feeling my insides harden.

"We kissed again, and this time it went further."

He looked away from me, and I could see him fighting to hold back his emotions and keep his voice level.

"She started doing other things. Rubbing up against me and touching me. I . . . I took off her blouse . . . but then I looked down and I saw she had a condom in her hand, all ready to go. And all of a sudden"—he met my eyes again—"I realized I couldn't go through with it."

"You weren't having an affair?" I asked incredulously. "So why did she answer your phone? She was in *your* room. I called you the night my mother died, and she said you were taking a fucking shower!"

"Julia, whenever I go to L.A. I always stay—stayed—in the same hotel. I get the penthouse suite. It's huge. There's a dining room and living room and sometimes I hold meetings there, especially if we're working late. People are always in and out of there."

It had been 2:00 A.M. my time, but 11:00 on the West Coast. Not out of the question for late meetings, for the old Michael.

"Sometimes when it got late we ordered up room service,"

Michael was saying. "I don't know why I didn't answer the phone, but maybe I didn't hear it ring or figured it was the kitchen calling. I could've been on another call, or having a conversation with someone else. Maybe I *was* in the shower, if I'd just gotten back from the hotel gym or something. But do you really think I'd let another woman answer my phone if I was cheating on you?"

"You didn't sleep with her." I sidestepped his question, wanting to stay on the offensive. "But you flirted with her. You had a great time stringing her along, didn't you? You did everything except fuck her."

"Julia, the man I was— You're right, I liked being pursued. It was all about my ego. But she didn't want me, she only wanted what I could give her. And the truth is, I didn't even like her that much. That night in my hotel room, I came to my senses. I know what I did was horrible—but I stopped it after a couple of minutes. I *did* stop it."

Michael reached for my hand, but I pulled away. I'd constructed a completely different story in my mind during all the times I'd imagined his night with Roxanne; I'd never anticipated this one.

"I think she wanted you to know something happened," he was saying. "She was trying to get between us, Julia. Otherwise why would she say that to you? She was a little bit . . . off."

She *had* been trying to get between us, I realized with a jolt. The very first time I'd met her, her predatory look at Michael was designed to unsettle me. If he really had been in the shower . . . Well, technically, she would've told the truth. But her voice sent a very different message, one that was unmistakable. She *wanted* me to think they'd been intimate. She wanted to ignite something between Michael and me.

Then I spun around with a fresh accusation on my lips: "But she sent you e-mails! She said she wanted your lips and body!"

Before Michael even said a word, I closed my eyes and heard his earlier words echo: "She wanted more."

She'd been pursuing him, not sending him a love note. Just like Noah's riddle about the waiter and the missing dollar bill, the true answer depended on your point of view. *It's like an optical illusion*, Noah had said. I'd viewed her e-mail through the lens of what I'd *expected* to see, I'd kept my eye on the deck of cards instead of the sleeve.

"What happened after that night?" I asked.

"She sent me messages for a while. Phone messages and e-mails. I was stuck. I couldn't fire her because we'd been intimate—to a point. I couldn't push back too hard. And she was close to Dale; when things went wrong for the company, the two of them worked together to keep it quiet. I knew her well enough to know she could've made things . . . difficult. But Julia, you're the only woman I'd ever kissed, up until then."

He paused and swallowed. "I've got to tell you this part, too. Dale saw us. He was in the hallway when I came out of her room. It was almost as if he was waiting for me. He was the one who probably called to change your name for the place card for that dinner—it's the only thing that makes sense."

"Why?" I asked again.

"It was his way of letting me know he had something on me, too. I think he wanted to screw with me any way he could. And I liked knowing I could outsmart him, but more than that, I knew his fortunes were tied to my company. I knew he was trapped. *I* got to bully a bully for once, Julia. I got off on it."

He sighed. "But back to Roxanne."

"Do me a favor," I said tightly. "Don't ever say her name again."

"Sorry," Michael said. "After that night I made sure we were never alone. I ignored her e-mails. After a while, she took another job—I kind of helped nudge that along by recommending her at another company.

"Julia." He reached out and cupped my cheeks with his hands and made me look at him. "There's one other reason I stopped it, the most important one of all. . . . I kept seeing your face." I stared at him, and the realization swept over me: He was telling me the truth. I could *feel* it.

Tears blurred the words on my mother's headstone. I stood up and ran, my breath creating white puffs in the night air, like tiny ghosts. Michael chased after me, calling my name. I finally stopped and leaned against a gnarled oak tree. My legs felt so weak I didn't trust them to hold me up.

"Julia, I'm so sorry. Please believe me."

"I do," I whispered.

"You're shaking," he said, wrapping his arms around me. I leaned into his warmth for a second, then I pulled away, before he could.

"You didn't have an affair," I said. I forced myself to look into his eyes and say it: "But I did."

Twenty-nine

IT ONLY HAPPENED ONCE.

No, I'm not being honest. Twice. It happened twice.

Okay, okay, three times. But the third time doesn't really count because we didn't finish.

If you were trying to get revenge on your husband for having an affair, what kind of a man do you think you'd pick? Maybe a hot young surfer with shaggy blond hair and a tattoo of a heart on his smooth, tanned chest, right? You'd probably pick someone sexy and virile, someone to make you feel young and gorgeous and desirable—all the things your husband had stripped away from you.

But I picked a man who was exactly the opposite of that.

I was in my early thirties, and I didn't want to be compared with nubile college coeds who could casually do the splits while peeling a banana. *I* wanted to be the more desirable one. I wanted a man to whisper in my ear that I was beautiful, that he couldn't keep his hands off me. The way Michael used to.

So I had an affair with a totally average guy. I met Brad through work; he was a chef at a catering company we sometimes booked, and he made the world's most decadent chocolate-covered strawberries. At first, I don't even think he knew that I was the wife of one of the richest men in town; I didn't wear my big diamond or other expensive jewelry to work, and Michael never came to my events. To Brad, I was just Julia, the woman who raced around like a maniac with a clipboard, growing more and more frantic as the time for the wedding or party approached, and then, like an actor walking out onto a stage, morphed into someone else entirely, someone calm and smiling, who could fill in for a missing bartender and mix cosmopolitans, or expertly duct-tape a wobbly table leg.

A couple of weeks after my mother died, I oversaw an evening wedding reception. After the bride and groom sped away and the guests had all left, I stood in the middle of the empty room, watching the cleanup crew vacuum red rose petals and break down the chocolate fountain. Michael was in town that night for a change, which meant I wanted to be anywhere but home.

I hadn't confronted him. I was planning to gather evidence first, to protect myself in case he and I divorced. I'd found the name of a good private investigator, and I was going to call him the next morning. Michael was leaving for another business trip that week; it would be the perfect time to have him followed. Then I'd research the best divorce lawyers and see if Michael's infidelity would make our prenup invalid.

Yet the thought of it all—the battles and accusations and hurt awaiting me—made me feel as though I were splitting open from the inside out. I was so exhausted that I seemed to be constantly walking through a thick cloud of fog, and it was seeping into my brain, too, making my thoughts feel heavy and damp. Even brushing my teeth in the morning was an effort, and chatting on the phone with clients—forcing my voice to be light and bright—left me so worn out that I sometimes put my head down on my desk and catnapped in the middle of the day. I was sinking into a depression, I realized. I'd lost my mother and my marriage in the same day, and I wasn't strong enough to bear it.

The worst moments came when I wondered if Michael had fallen in love with Roxanne. Maybe he'd willingly throw me a few million so he could walk away from our marriage.

She'd called late last night, but she hadn't left him a message; I'd seen her number on his cell phone log while Michael was in the shower, and I'd deleted it, my finger viciously pressing the button over and over again, as if I could somehow erase her, too.

I walked outside the hotel ballroom, my shoes crunching on the scattered birdseed everyone had thrown at the laughing couple as they departed, and I spotted a favor someone had dropped on the ground. It was a cookie glazed with the image of the newly married couple. *Liam and Lisa,* the pink script on the bottom read. But someone—maybe even the bride herself, in her pointy heels as she ran for the car—had stepped on the cookie, and there was a jagged break between their faces. I looked down at it for a long moment, then reached into my purse and felt around for the cold metal of my keys.

"You're not going to eat that, are you?" a voice said. I looked up from the cookie and saw Brad leaning against the outside wall of the building, smoking a cigarette. "I could cook you something better, you know."

I forced a laugh and put the cookie pieces into a trash can, then walked over to stand next to him.

"Want one?" he offered, tilting his pack of Marlboros toward me.

I instinctively started to shake my head, then said, "Why not?"

He lit it for me. His fingers were long and graceful and seemed like they should've belonged to another man, someone who played the piano or painted landscapes, not a slightly pudgy guy whose blond hair was thinning on top. But he was funny and kind, and sometimes he slipped me little tidbits of the treats he was cooking at receptions—a scallop browned so perfectly that the top layer was almost caramelized, a slender stalk of baby asparagus dipped into lemony hollandaise sauce, one of those scandalously good strawberries encased in alternating layers of dark and milk and white chocolate.

Now those talented fingers reached toward me again, to light my cigarette. I inhaled and managed not to cough; I hadn't smoked since college, when I used to occasionally have cigarettes between classes with Stephenie. She'd quit when she decided to get pregnant, and without a smoking buddy—someone to feel illicit with—I'd dropped the occasional habit, too.

"You did a great job, as usual," Brad said.

"The weather helped," I said, looking up at the sky. It was clear and cool, and there wasn't any breeze at all. "Brides hate it when it rains, even though it's supposed to be good luck."

I looked over at Brad and was surprised to see he'd inched closer to me. Or had I been the one to move?

"A few of us are going to Matchbox for a drink," he said. "Want to come along?"

I didn't even have to think about it. "I'd love to."

A drink turned into three, and the waiters and catering staff we'd come with slowly began to leave Matchbox, trickling away in pairs and trios, and then it was just me and Brad. The crowd had thinned out, and we'd nabbed two barstools, but it was still crowded enough that we had to sit with our seats jammed close together. Brad's knees were spread open, and mine were between his. We were as close as it was possible to be without touching.

I was different that night; something was fueling me from within, some need I couldn't quite identify. It wasn't lust or anger or a desire for revenge, but a murky sense that I *had* to do this. I surreptitiously unbuttoned an extra button on my shirt, and I laughed harder than usual. I held Brad's brown eyes over the rim of my dirty martini as I took slow sips and licked my top lip afterward. When my cell phone buzzed, I reached into my purse and turned it off without even checking to see who'd called.

Then Brad's leg grazed mine, and the air between us suddenly turned electric. I knew it was a test; the evening was about to go into one of two directions. I could squeeze my knees together more tightly, or get up and go to the bathroom, or do any of a dozen things to shift course. But I didn't. I let my leg relax against his, and through his jeans and the thin silk of my wrap dress, I could feel his warmth. By not moving away, I'd traveled down the second path.

"Want to go somewhere else?" Brad asked, and I nodded without saying anything. We paid the bill, and I looked around, suddenly panicked I'd see someone I recognized. But the lights were dim and I knew I was safe. Besides, I hadn't done anything. Not yet.

We stepped outside, and Brad put his motorcycle helmet on my head and fastened the strap under my chin. I climbed on behind him and wrapped my arms tight around his waist. As we sped away, I emptied my mind of everything but the rush of explosive sound.

He lived in an apartment in Adams Morgan, just off a strip of Eighteenth Street filled with hip restaurants and bars. As soon as I crossed the threshold into his place, I panicked. Brad shut the door behind me, and I felt as if I was being sealed inside. *I can still leave,* I told myself frantically. It wasn't too late.

"Do you want something to drink?" Brad offered.

I shook my head, suddenly unable to speak. I was still standing there in the hallway, wearing my coat and clutching my purse in front of me like a shield. If he'd stepped toward me or said something suggestive, I might've even whacked him with my bag, like a little old lady, and then run away screaming. But what Brad did was so surprising it completely disarmed me.

"Can I make you something to eat? You barely ate anything all night."

"You noticed?" I asked in surprise. My voice sounded rusty, and I cleared my throat.

"Come here," he said gently. He took away my purse and put it on his couch, then led me to the kitchen with both hands. He left on my coat; maybe he knew I wasn't ready to shed even that layer of clothing yet.

"Sit down," he said, pulling out a chair.

He opened his refrigerator and began rummaging through it, narrating the contents.

"Let's see, fried chicken, fettuccine primavera, pumpkin soup . . ." Then he looked at me and made a decision. "An omelet."

I loosened the buttons on my coat but kept it on. I knew I wouldn't be able to eat anything, but as I watched Brad's fingers mince chives and slice thin, even strips of Jarlsberg, I felt my body slowly relax. He cracked three eggs with one hand and gently folded in the ingredients with the other. It was a virtuoso performance; he knew his little kitchen so well that he moved around it with the economy and grace of a dancer, sliding a drawer shut with his left hip while opening the refrigerator with his right hand, then swirling sizzling butter in a cast-iron pan with an expert flick of his wrist. Here, in this inexpensive apart-ment with open windows that let in the sounds of the city—honks and yells and revving engines—Brad was quietly, intently focused on making the perfect omelet. His white dress shirt had become untucked, I noticed. He slid the omelet off the pan with a well-practiced motion of his wrist, and it landed exactly in the middle of a cerulean blue plate.

Then he fed it to me.

That's what did it; the tenderness with which he forked off a bite and lifted it to my lips melted my last defense. Every bit of his attention was focused on me. I hadn't realized how hungry I was until that first bite of omelet filled my mouth. It was so light and fluffy it was almost a soufflé.

We could still recast this evening as nothing more than a mild flirtation brought on by too many dirty martinis, I told myself, even as my hand closed around Brad's over the fork. I could button up my coat and kiss him on the cheek and go hail a cab, then send him a joking e-mail tomorrow about being so drunk that he had to feed me like a baby. "Next time I'll bring a bib," I'd write.

Then I remembered that husky voice with a secret smile in it answering Michael's hotel room phone, and I suddenly leaned forward, almost as if I was tipping over, and rested my head on Brad's chest and closed my eyes. He began stroking my hair, running those fingers through it and massaging my neck and scalp. After a few minutes I lifted my face, still with my eyes closed, and he bent over and kissed me.

If he'd rushed things—if he'd tried to unbutton my shirt, or grabbed my ass—maybe I'd have run to the corner of the street and hailed down a taxi and hurried home, after all.

But he took his slow, sweet time. Eventually I let Brad's gentle fingers undress me, and then I followed him into the bedroom. I didn't feel passion, but that wasn't why I'd come here tonight.

With Brad everything felt different. His chest was covered in thick, curly blond hair, whereas Michael's was smooth. He whispered in my ear while we had sex, telling me how much he wanted me. Michael and I never talked much during sex, but sometimes, early on in our relationship, we looked into each other's eyes. Brad's lips felt thicker, and he used his tongue more when he kissed, and he smelled different, too. He brought the

aroma of everything he'd cooked that day into bed—his fingernails smelled faintly of raspberries as he brushed back my hair,
I tasted cognac on his tongue, and his skin seemed steeped in
spices.

Afterward, Brad wrapped his big arms—so different from
Michael's wiry ones; not better or worse, just not the same—
around me and held me for a while, spooning me from behind.
I waited for the flood of guilt, but it never came. I didn't feel
much of anything at all.

After a while, I slipped out from under the covers and got
dressed while Brad propped himself up on an elbow, watching me.

"I guess you can't stay," he said.

"No," I whispered. "But I'll come back."

During my third visit, Brad began to talk about us going
away together for a weekend. "I could rent a room at this great
little inn in Virginia," he said as he traced tiny circles around my
belly button with a fingertip. "We'll eat and drink and stay in
bed all weekend." I pulled away and looked at him in surprise.
That's when I saw in his eyes that this meant more to him than
a few illicit nights together.

"I can't. I'm sorry," I said, hoping my tone conveyed the fact
that I was also apologizing for not feeling the same way about
him. I hadn't ever considered that maybe Brad wanted more
from me than I did from him. That he wanted an actual relationship.

"You could leave him," Brad said, getting out of bed. He
walked over to look out the window, keeping his back to me.
His voice was casual, but his posture was tense.

"Leave Michael?" I asked. My voice sounded strangled, and I
cleared my throat.

Brad shook his head. "I didn't even know his name. You
never talk about him, Julia."

I sat up on the bed and leaned over to retrieve my shirt from the floor. I toyed with the tiny pearl buttons so I wouldn't have to meet Brad's eyes when he turned around. My body felt heavy from the half bottle of good red wine I'd drunk, and my eyes were gritty and tired. I suddenly saw myself as if from above— naked except for my gold wedding band, my mascara smeared and my hair disheveled—and guilt finally overwhelmed me. But I didn't feel it because of Michael. It was because of what I'd done to Brad. I'd thought he understood this was just tempo- rary; I'd thought he was benefiting from it as much as I was. I'd been sexist, assuming that, because he was a guy, he'd be happy to have sex with no strings attached. How little I'd known about him, after all.

"It's complicated," I finally said. And now I'd made it even more so. "I can't leave him. Not now, anyway."

"He's really rich, right?" Brad abruptly pulled on his Levi's. "Someone said something about it the other day. About wonder- ing why you worked, when your husband had all that money."

"Brad, it isn't like that," I said, even as a shameful little voice inside me asked, It isn't?

"I loved Michael before he had any money," I protested. "We've been together since high school."

"So why are you sleeping with me?" Brad asked.

I looked down at my shirt again, not knowing how to answer.

"I should go," I finally said. "I'm sorry."

Brad shrugged, as if he didn't care, but I could see him fight- ing not to speak. He probably wanted to say something cruel and cutting; I'd hurt him, and now he wanted to lash back. But he was too nice a guy to give in to the urge. I'd made such a mess of everything.

I left Brad's apartment without another word, and I didn't see him for months. Once I called him late at night, but my voice abandoned me when he answered and I hung up. I still didn't know what to say to him, how to explain what had happened between us. It would be months before I figured it out for myself.

By the time we worked on another job together, Brad was clearly over what had happened—over me. He smiled at me, and quickly squeezed my arm in greeting, and then turned his attention back to the pastry-wrapped filet he was cooking. After plating the artisanal cheeses with fig spread and setting out the mini berry cheesecakes for dessert, he took off his apron and washed his hands. I caught myself staring as those elegant fingers caressed one another. Then I heard someone call his name, and I turned to see a nice-looking woman with glasses and short blond hair walk up to the outskirts of the reception area. Her eyes searched the crowd, and when she saw Brad, she smiled in a way that told me everything I needed to know. They left together a few minutes afterward, and Brad never once looked back at me.

I was relieved—so relieved—that he didn't hate me. And I was lonelier than ever.

Otello is considered by many to be Verdi's finest opera. The Moor Otello becomes convinced his wife, Desdemona, is cheating on him after he assembles pieces of evidence. Of course he's dead wrong. But an interloper named Iago—someone a lot like Dale—whispers in his ear, goading him and fueling his suspicions.

I'll always wonder what would've happened if I'd chosen to talk to Michael during that raw, terrible time. Would I have changed the whole course of our marriage? Maybe I could have thrown down his cell phone and held his BlackBerry hostage until we'd pieced together exactly what had happened, not just with Roxanne but between the two of us.

It took me a long time to figure out why I cheated, but I finally realized it didn't have anything to do with revenge. It was because I was facing an impossible choice: If I forced Michael to admit he was having an affair, I knew I wouldn't be able to stay married to him. But if I left him, I'd lose everything—our house, our cars, the luxury I'd always craved. By having my own affair, I'd managed to carve out another option. I could pretend to myself that I'd evened things up, somehow, and stay married to Michael and keep clinging to our glittering new lifestyle.

I think part of me did it because I still loved Michael and couldn't bear to let him go, as warped and crazy as it sounds. But another, uglier part of me was willing to trade love and trust for security and luxury. I never told anyone, not even Isabelle, about what I'd done. In my mind, Michael's offense was worse—he cheated first. That's how I tried to justify it, anyway.

Creating my own secrets meant I'd never have to force Michael to reveal his. So I let the silences and misunderstandings grow and multiply, like mushrooms in a damp forest, pushing Michael and me further apart than ever.

Thirty

"I, AH, DIDN'T EXPECT to hear that," Michael said. He tried to smile, but it turned into a grimace.

"I'm so sorry." I reached out a tentative hand, then pulled it back. I had no right to touch him.

"Give me a minute, okay?" Michael turned away from me and stared out over the rows of simple headstones.

"I should've talked to you," I said, my voice pleading. "It's just that when I thought you and Roxanne . . . but that's no excuse."

"No," he said fiercely. I could see tears glistening in his eyes. "It was *my* fault. I abandoned you first."

"But I was the one—"

"Julia, what kind of person was I?" Michael slid down against the tree and slumped onto the ground next to me. "I drove you to an affair. I cheated that kid out of a real settlement. I toyed with Dale just for the fun of it, and I rubbed my family's face in my money even though they probably could've used some real help financially. . . . *What* did I turn into?"

He buried his head in his hands, and I could barely hear what he said next: "I never thought I'd end up like this."

"Michael, listen to me. You're a good person," I said, but he just shook his head.

"Everything is snowballing, Julia. The more good I try to do, the more I realize how many people I hurt. I almost lost you. I *did* lose you, for a long time, and the worst part is, I didn't even know."

"With Brad . . . it didn't mean anything," I said, hating myself for using the tired cliché. "I didn't love him. I barely knew him."

Michael slowly nodded, but I knew he wasn't with me. He was somewhere else, maybe watching Brad and me tangled together in the warm sheets of a bed. I knew those images would torture Michael; I'd spent enough nights fighting away similar ones.

He was still sitting on the ground. His nose was red from the cold, and a knitted cap barely contained his crazy brown curls. This was the town where everything had started for us so many years ago; it couldn't be where things ended, too.

I love you.

The words just sprang into my mind. Maybe I'd never stopped loving Michael, but now it felt different. I loved him despite the injuries we'd inflicted on one another, because of the bad times as well as the good ones. I loved him even though he wanted to rip me away from the extraordinary life he'd given me, and while part of me longed to cling to it, another part was suddenly excited about what lay ahead of us, about what else we might build together starting from scratch. Our love was richer and bumpier and more complex than it had ever been before.

I opened my mouth to say the words aloud, but then my breath shot out of me, as forcefully as if I'd been kicked in the gut.

"What is it?" Michael said, lifting his head at the sound of my gasp. "Julia?"

He twisted around to follow my gaze.

It wasn't an apparition; it was him.

The tall form, the gray tweed coat, the quick walking pace . . . I was desperate to run away, to put as much distance between us as possible, but my legs refused to move.

"Julia?" Michael asked again. His hand tightened on my arm. "Do you feel sick? Do you want to leave?"

I made myself look one last time, and that was when he passed under a streetlight and I realized the person wasn't my father, after all. It was just another man walking down the sidewalk outside the graveyard.

I leaned against Michael, feeling my body tremble.

"It's okay," I said more to myself than to Michael.

"Should we go?" he asked, his eyes searching my face, and I silently nodded. He held on to my arm the whole way to the car, and I held his, too, unsure of which one of us was holding the other one up.

"We'll get past this," Michael said, and I didn't know if it was a promise or a vow. "We're going to be okay, Julia."

We drove home without stopping, our car moving quickly down the dark, lonely roads. Only a few tractor-trailers and other nocturnal travelers passed us, the flashes of their headlights briefly washing over our faces. We exchanged polite questions—*Are you hungry? Need a restroom stop?*—before falling back into heavy silences.

I knew Michael had been completely honest about Roxanne. When he'd said it was enough for him to know she wanted him, I'd instantly recognized the truth in his statement—it was even more convincing than the intensity of his voice or his clear, unwavering gaze. It meshed perfectly with the secret, wounded side of my husband that nobody but me knows about.

I closed my eyes and thought back to the time, a few months

after Michael's company went public and its stock price soared, when I came home from work and discovered his Maserati—so new that the temporary tags were still on—parked in front of our house.

I'd looked at the clock on my car's dashboard in surprise: It was only 6:15 P.M. Michael hadn't gotten home this early in years, literally. I'd called his name as I walked through our front door, hearing my voice echo in our two-story, marble-floor foyer, but he didn't answer. I'd climbed the steps and checked our bedroom, then wandered down the hall to his office.

That was where I found him, standing in the middle of the room and staring up at the wall he'd filled with framed press clippings: the *Fortune* article, a photo of Oprah Winfrey and her bottle of DrinkUp, a three-column profile in the *Washington Post's* Business section.

Something in his expression had made me speak gently: "Michael?"

He'd turned to me with dull eyes. "My mother called today."

I'd taken a step backward in shock, then instinctively hurried closer to him.

"What did she say?" I'd asked.

His mouth had twisted into something meant to pass for a smile. "She wanted to congratulate me on my success. It seems she always knew I'd make a name for myself. Which is funny, since she never mentioned that little premonition before. All of a sudden, she wants a relationship."

He'd glanced back up at the wall, and his voice sounded so harsh I barely recognized it: "Gee, I wonder what made her change her mind?"

I'd wrapped my arms around him, wanting to absorb his hurt. "What did you say to her?"

"I told her I was busy, and that I'd call her back."

"Will you?" I'd asked.

He'd shaken his head. "Ever since I've been twelve, all I've ever gotten from her is a crappy birthday card. I can't tell you how often I used to dream that she'd come back for me. Do you know one of the most clear memories I have? I was six or seven, and my brothers were fighting as usual, and my dad was sitting on the couch flicking through the television channels with his beer gut hanging out. And my mom had this painting she really liked—it wasn't anything fancy, just a picture of the ocean, I think, but it was one of the few nice things in our house— and one of my brothers threw something and it shattered the glass and ruined the painting. Tore the paper. And my mom just stood there and I saw her look around at them, and then at my dad, and her face . . . it kind of crumpled. I heard her whisper, 'It wasn't supposed to be this way.'"

I'd hugged him tighter. "Did she leave right after that?"

Michael had nodded. "A few weeks later. I know she was really young when she married my dad, and she didn't plan on her life turning out the way it did. He must've looked good to her when she was a teenager; he was a big football player, a popular guy. The thing is, I *get* how she felt, Julia. I know she probably woke up one day and realized she'd married a guy who'd stopped maturing in high school and had created little clones of himself. I didn't want that life either. I knew exactly what she meant when she said it wasn't supposed to turn out like this; I know why she left them. But *me,* Julia? Why did she leave me?"

His voice had grown dangerously soft. "She got herself a brand-new family. She has a little girl and a baby boy with her new husband."

I'd looked up at him incredulously. "She told you that?"

He'd shrugged. "She wants me to meet my half sister and brother. She invited us over for dinner. Just one big happy family, sitting around the table and catching up on old times: 'Hey,

Mom, remember how I spent that first Christmas after you left sitting next to the phone all day because I was so sure you'd call and say you were coming back for me?' I would've killed to have her call me back then. Today I told my secretary to never put her through again, no matter what she said."

I'd rested my head against his chest, hearing his heart pound wildly against his ribs. His arms were around me, but his hands were still clenched into fists. "I don't blame you," I'd whispered.

We'd stayed like that, in the middle of his office, for a long time. After a while Michael had given a sigh that sounded more like a cut-off sob, and he'd said something that broke my heart: "You are the only person in this whole world who loves me."

The next morning he'd gotten up early, showered, and put on a beautifully cut navy suit and crisp white shirt. He'd considered three ties before finally choosing a blue-and-red one, then he'd retied it twice, until the knot was perfect.

I'd leaned against the doorjamb, watching him get ready. "Are you okay?" I'd finally asked.

He'd walked over and kissed the top of my head. "I will be," he'd said. "As long as you never leave me."

For a week or two, it had brought us closer together. Michael had called me in the middle of the day from work just to say hi. We'd taken a Jacuzzi together late one night and shared a bottle of wine. I'd rubbed his back when he couldn't sleep, until the tension finally left his body and he dozed off for a few hours.

But soon we began to slip away from each other again: Michael stayed later and later at work, and started to travel more. My jobs often fell on weekend nights—the rare times he was home—and our BlackBerrys and cell phones refused to stay silent. Michael bought an interest in the Blazes, then joined the charity boards. The invitations started pouring in, and our life just grew and grew. It became so big that it seemed, somehow, to swallow our marriage whole.

Thirty-one

"ISN'T THAT YOUR PHONE?" Michael asked the next morning. Neither of us had slept much. Sometime around midnight, I'd reached over for his hand, and after a moment, his fingers had closed around mine. I'd almost wept with gratitude.

"I think it's yours." I walked over to the bureau to check.

"Just let it go to voice mail," he said. "It can't be important."

Michael's cell number was private, which meant even though a few especially persistent members of the press were still wooing him for exclusive interviews, their calls came through the house. Only a handful of people knew his cell number, and they were all employees at his company. Or his soon to be former company. His mobile rarely rang these days.

Something was drawing me to it, whispering that I needed to answer it.

"Are you sure?" I asked, my hand lingering on the phone.

He shrugged. "Go ahead."

"Julia?"

Dale. Somehow, I wasn't surprised.

"What's up?" I asked briskly.

"Just wanted to give Michael a heads-up," Dale was saying,

his words coming out as thick and smooth as dribbles of oil. "That kid who crashed our truck?"

Revulsion gripped my stomach. "The brakes failed, Dale." I struggled to keep from shouting even as I suspected that Dale *wanted* me to shout, to lose control of myself. "It wasn't his fault."

Dale continued as if I hadn't even spoken. "He's going to sue. It won't work, you know. We can bury him in paperwork, and delay until his legal bills mount up. He might get someone pro bono to take him on, but even so, we're covered. Everything is watertight."

"Is that what you called to say?"

"Just wanted to let Michael know," Dale said. "It's his signature on all the paperwork."

I hung up the phone without saying another word. Michael was sitting on the bed now, watching me.

"The guy who was in the accident is going to sue," I said. I walked over and sat down next to him. "The one who lost his memory."

"I don't blame him," Michael said simply. He drew his knees to his chest, then wrapped his arms around them. "He *should* sue. I deserve to be sued a dozen times over."

He looked over at me. "This isn't the only time I've done something like this." His voice was almost mechanical, it was so emotionless.

I frowned. "What do you mean?"

"A few years after I started the company, there was a problem with the glass our supplier gave us for the bottles. On the manufacturing lines, bottles kept shattering—they were under pressure and heat, and if the glass had been good, everything would've been fine. But it was thin in parts. It was substandard."

"So the glass shattered . . ." I prompted him when his voice drifted off.

"There's this whole safety procedure in place for when something like that happens. You're supposed to shut down the line, throw out any open bottles within six feet of the shattered one in case shards of glass flew into other drinks, clean everything off . . . We did it, the first few times. But more kept shattering. One after the other, going off like little bombs. I flew up to Buffalo the second I heard. At first I thought we'd be okay. We could weather it; we could get new glass. But the supplier vanished. We had orders flooding in—it was after Oprah endorsed us, and we had hundreds of new accounts. I had to get those drinks out, Julia.

"We cleared everyone out of the plant except a few people and gave them huge bonuses to keep quiet. We kept running the bottles through the line, and more shattered—I can still hear the noise they made; it was this huge, ugly pop, as loud as a car backfiring—and we threw out the bottles on either side of the broken ones and we kept running the line. We didn't stop it. We didn't throw out every bottle within six feet."

I saw kids in soccer uniforms drinking Michael's tainted lemonade; pregnant women twisting the lids off Berrywater at picnics, grandfathers popping into convenience stores on hot days to grab PuckerUp Limeade. *Oh, Michael,* I thought.

"I would've gone under. I would've lost everything," he said, his voice still oddly robotic. "We settled sixteen cases. Dale handled each one; he was on an airplane within an hour of us hearing a complaint, with a blank check in his pocket. Somehow, he convinced every single person to keep quiet, except for one woman who lived next door to a reporter for a local paper in Anniston, Alabama. Roxanne shut it down somehow, though. She met the reporter, pretended she was in town for another reason. She convinced him it wasn't a story. And so everyone who found a piece of glass in their drink got ten thousand dollars, fast, and no one knew how widespread it was. Most people spit it out without swallowing it. Only one guy got sick, and he got a hundred grand."

I put my hand over Michael's, but he didn't seem to notice.

"I wanted to tell you, but I thought if something happened, something bad"—*if someone died,* I thought, and I knew Michael was thinking it, too—"you might've been considered complicit. If we were sued, they could've gone after you."

"You must've been so scared," I said. I almost said I wished he had talked to me, but I couldn't lie to Michael either, not anymore. If I had to choose between letting a few bottles go out with shards of glass in them and losing the whole company, watching as Michael was overtaken by debt and lawsuits he'd never be able to pay off, I didn't know what I would have done.

Maybe I'd been more like Michael than I'd thought.

"Do you see why I have to fix this, Julia? I have to help that kid now. If I can just do right by him . . . But I made copies of the paperwork and brought it home and I've gone over it a dozen times. I don't think we can change anything. If I had anything left, I'd give it to him. But my lawyers have already parceled everything out. I'm turning over the deed to this house to Doctors Without Borders. The D.C. public schools are planning to buy a bunch of computers for their classrooms with the money from my cars. The pound is hiring a new investigator for animal cruelty complaints, and I committed twenty million to cancer research. . . . There isn't anything *left.* I've already committed everything I have."

He leaned back against a pillow and stared up at the ceiling. "I keep thinking I should go talk to him."

"What would you say?" I asked.

He shrugged. "I could apologize. I could explain that I was wrong."

I mulled it over. "I hate to say it, Michael, but wouldn't that give him more ammunition in the lawsuit?"

"Maybe," he said.

I looked at Michael and saw the worry etched on his face. A few days ago, I'd heard him phone a lawyer he'd known for years, begging him to check the papers for an escape clause. "No, you don't understand," Michael had said. "I *want* the settlement to be invalid." He'd faxed over the papers, and an hour later, when his phone rang, he'd snatched it up. "I see," he'd said, cradling the phone between his shoulder and ear and massaging his temples with his fingertips again. Another headache, I'd thought, and I'd slipped some Tylenol into his hand.

"Michael?" I said now. "I think you should go see him. Screw the lawyers."

He looked at me—really looked at me—for the first time since I'd revealed my affair. "I was hoping you'd say that," he said, and a trace of a smile appeared on his face.

Thirty-two

WHEN I WAS NINE or ten years old, my father and I went out on a Sunday afternoon drive and saw a woman standing by the side of the road. She was wearing a sensible brown coat, a brown loafer on her left foot and, on her right one, a fuzzy pink bedroom slipper. Her hair was disheveled on the right side, too, but combed on the left, as if someone had drawn a line down her middle to create two completely separate people.

"Isn't that Mrs. Underwood?" I asked as Dad slowed the car. She'd taught me ballet for a couple of years, until I decided I liked kicking around a soccer ball with the neighborhood boys better than pliés.

"Mrs. Underwood?" Dad rolled down his window. "Can I help you with anything?"

She looked at us, and I saw relief flood her face. "I can't seem to find my way." Despite her smile, her voice shook, and she was gripping her pocketbook with clenched fists.

"Hop in," Dad said cheerfully, gesturing for me to get in the backseat. He got out and walked around the car and gently took her by the elbow. "Here we go. Julie and I will get you home safely, don't worry. You were just out for a walk, weren't you?"

Mrs. Underwood nodded unsteadily. "A walk."

"Why did you go so far?" I asked, and even before I'd finished speaking, my father cut in, his voice loud enough to drown mine out.

"Well, I don't blame you for waiting for a ride back. The weather turned unexpectedly cold, didn't it?"

By then I understood nothing about this made sense: not Mrs. Underwood's fuzzy slipper or Dad's implication that she was waiting by the side of the road because she was expecting someone to come along and offer her a ride.

"What was your name again, dear?" she asked me, twisting back to look at my face.

"Julie," I said quietly, and then I knew better than to ask any more questions.

"I'll just see you inside," Dad said as he pulled up in front of her little bungalow. "Julie, can you wait here?"

He jumped out of the car without waiting for my answer, and I watched as he approached her front door, which was wide open despite the chill of the day. He stepped inside and didn't emerge for about fifteen minutes.

"Sorry, kiddo," he said as he climbed back into the car. "We're going to have to wait a bit longer."

"Is Mrs. Underwood okay?" I asked.

"Come on up front with me," Dad said instead of answering. He waited until I was seated, then he twisted sideways on his seat to face me. His eyes were wet, I realized with a jolt. My dad, who was always laughing.

"Sometimes when people grow older, they have problems with their memory," Dad began. "It's normal to forget things. Your grandpa once put his hat in the refrigerator. Grandma asked him if he wanted her to heat it up for dinner."

I giggled, and Dad smiled, too, even though it didn't erase the sorrow from his expression.

"But most people just forget little things here and there. Maybe a name of someone they knew long ago, or where they put their keys."

"You do that now," I pointed out.

He pretended to swat at me. "It gets worse when you're older. But what's happening to Mrs. Underwood is different. It's a disease called Alzheimer's."

"Is there medicine she can take to get better?"

Dad shook his head. "No, honey. And she's going to get worse. She's going to keep forgetting more and more things." He peered out the window and raised an index finger. "Hang on a second, okay?"

He jumped out of the car and walked over to a blue Honda that had pulled up in front of Mrs. Underwood's house. A young woman stepped out, then opened the back door and picked up a toddler. I saw Dad approach them and talk for a few moments, then the woman turned her face away from her little boy's and wiped away a tear.

Dad put his hand on her back and patted it a few times, still talking, then she finally nodded and went into Mrs. Underwood's house.

"Who was that?" I asked when he climbed back into the car.

"Her daughter," he said. "I found her phone number taped up on the refrigerator and I thought she should come over and check on her mom."

"Does she live alone? Mrs. Underwood?" Sometimes I still got scared of the dark, and I imagined Mrs. Underwood lying in bed alone, looking around and clutching the top of her sheet with both hands, just as she'd been clutching her pocketbook. Suddenly ending up in a strange place and not remembering how you'd gotten there sounded terrifying.

"She lives alone now," Dad said. "But she's going to move in with one of her kids. They're worried about her. They're going to take care of her."

"She looked afraid," I said in a small voice.

Dad nodded. "It's scary to lose pieces of yourself, which is kind of what's happening to her. Try to remember that she had a good life, Julie. And she still has people who love her, no matter what happens."

Brightly colored cards wishing Scott Braverly a happy twenty-fourth birthday were still displayed on a table in the living room.

"What's your name?" he asked, giving me an easy smile. He was a big guy with a close-cropped Afro that didn't hide the thick scar curving around the top of his right ear. He wore a burgundy Redskins' football jersey and jeans, and I could see him passing Sunday afternoons around the television with a group of friends, shouting directions at the athletes and gobbling down buffalo wings and nachos.

"It's Julia," I said. It was the third time he'd asked.

His wife, Kimberly, gave me an apologetic smile. I couldn't believe it when she'd opened the door and shaken our hands and fussed about putting away our coats. She was treating us like we were invited guests in her house. I don't know what I'd expected—maybe that she'd slam the door in our faces instead of offering us squares of an Entenmann's coffee cake and some decaf.

I hadn't known Scott was married. Would that make things better or worse for him? I wondered. Physically he and his wife weren't alike—Kimberly was petite and had dainty features—but somehow, sitting side by side on their blue denim couch, they looked right together. There was a photo on the mantel with younger versions of them at what looked to be their high school prom. So they'd been together for a long time. Would Kimberly stay with him and learn to compensate for his condition, or would she eventually grow so frustrated and overwhelmed that she'd walk out?

They lived in a condo in Alexandria, Virginia, in an area halfway between million-dollar luxury waterfront town houses and a run-down public housing complex. Their home reminded me a bit of the second apartment Michael and I had rented together—the nicer one, without the bugs. The living room was a good size, and the kitchen looked as if it had recently been remodeled. Kimberly worked as an administrative assistant at a trade association, she told us.

"His mom comes over during the day," she said, as casually as if she were discussing child-care arrangements for a toddler. "We're lucky she lives close by."

I saw Michael close his eyes for just a moment. He hadn't been able to eat any dinner before we came here.

"Do you have a big family?" I asked Scott. I wanted him to say yes, to hear that there were brothers and sisters and aunts and cousins who'd step in to help him. But he shook his head. "No, not really."

Michael cleared his throat and wiped his palms on his pants legs.

"I came here to tell you how sorry I am," he began. Kimberly watched him with sharp brown eyes, and I saw then that, although she'd welcomed us inside, she hadn't yet made up her mind. She didn't know who to blame for what had happened to her husband.

"I never should have signed those papers," Michael said. "I failed you. You deserved more."

Silence hung in the room. I wondered if Scott would remember bits and pieces of this conversation, or if it would be wiped clear from his mind, like when a teacher erases a blackboard to create a fresh slate for the next morning.

"But it isn't over yet." Kimberly frowned. "I thought that was why you were here. About the lawsuit."

Michael shook his head. "I understand you want to sue. I don't blame you. I'm just here to apologize."

Kimberly let out all her air with a *whoosh*. She was still frowning. "You didn't come here to offer us more money? To see if we'd settle?"

Michael shook his head. "I wish I could. But I've promised everything I have to other people. But if there's anything else I can do—"

Kimberly batted her hand at him, cutting off his words.

"That other man told us to sue. He said we might get more money from you."

No one said anything for a long moment.

"Other man?" Michael finally asked, his voice perfectly even.

"The black-haired one who works with you? He came here a few weeks ago. What was his name? Dan? Dave? Something with a *D*."

Dale.

A small, high-pitched noise came from the hallway, and I spun around, almost expecting to see Dale standing there, rubbing his hands together and cackling like a cartoon villain. But it was just a tiny girl in pink footsie pajamas, yawning and stumbling down the hallway. My breath caught in my throat at the sight of her.

Kimberly stood up and reached for her daughter, but she ran to her father.

"Ashley's a daddy's girl," Kimberly said fondly. "Always has been, from the day she was born."

"She's beautiful," Michael said. I just nodded and watched Ashley nestle her head into the crook of Scott's neck.

"Hey, sweetie," he was saying, his voice as gentle as a lullaby. "Did we wake you up? Want me to get you a bottle?"

"Well. We should go and let your daughter get some rest." Michael stood up quickly, and so did Scott and Kimberly. Scott was still holding Ashley in his left arm.

Then Scott did something that surprised me; he stretched out his right hand. Instead of shaking it, Michael clung to it, sandwiching Scott's big hand between his smaller ones.

"I'm sorry," Michael said one final time, then he almost ran out of the apartment.

I caught up to him by the elevator.

"Can you drive?" Michael asked.

"Of course." His hand trembled as he passed me the car keys, making them jingle.

We got into the car and drove toward home in silence. In the distance I saw the Washington Monument, pale and majestic against the night sky, and I remembered how it had felt to arrive in this town with Michael for the very first time. How our entire lives had stretched out before us, and anything had seemed possible.

Bitterness rose in my throat as I realized I wasn't surprised that Dale wanted to hurt Michael, to shame him. I could picture Dale considering different methods, as if he was turning around a ripe red apple, contemplating where to sink his sharp teeth first. Dale knew the new Michael cared more than anything about being a good person. Encouraging Scott to sue was the worst thing Dale could do to Michael, but not because of the money. It was because a lawsuit would force Michael to think about the type of man he'd been before.

We were pulling into our driveway when Michael finally spoke.

"The papers from the lawsuit? They were delivered to me today, when you were in the shower. Scott isn't just suing the company, Julia. He's suing me personally."

Thirty-three

REGRET SEEMED TO BE eating Michael alive. Gaunt spaces were developing beneath his cheekbones, and his pants were starting to sag around his hips. His high-speed metabolism peeled the weight off of him so quickly it was shocking. I kept offering him bland foods, like bananas and grilled cheese sandwiches, but he never managed to choke down more than a few bites before he pushed his plate away. His insomnia was back, too; whenever I woke up in the middle of the night, I heard him restlessly moving under the covers.

Ever since Michael had collapsed in the conference room, it was as if a new man, who was in many ways his emotional opposite, had slipped inside his skin. But now Michael was more haunted than ever. The difference was, the focus of his obsession had flipped from success to his failures.

"I wanted so badly to fix things," he'd whispered once when his movements woke me up and I asked if he was okay. His voice sounded raspy and worn in the darkness of our bedroom. "But I can't."

Michael had always been visually oriented; once he'd told me that, when he read a novel, he saw the scenes skimming by, as if on a movie screen. I knew that trait must be tormenting him now as images of Brad and me entwined together played out in his head, and as he imagined little Ashley nestled in the crook of her father's neck.

As the days passed, Michael started to make an effort to act normally, to sit with me on the couch and sip the cup of coffee I'd poured for him and talk, but the questions he peppered me with during odd moments revealed his inner torment.

"Did you stop loving me?" he asked me one morning right after I finished brushing my teeth.

I wiped my face with a warm, wet washcloth to buy time while I thought about how to answer him as gently as possible. "I don't know," I finally said as I wrung out the washcloth and hung it over a towel rack. "I guess I didn't feel like there was much love left in our marriage. I loved the you from long ago, and I loved what we once had, but . . ." My voice trailed off.

"I was so oblivious," he said. "At work I was on top of everything. I knew every single thing that happened at my company. I had the figures on how many units we sold in Connecticut every month, and I could tell you exactly how our social media expert was going to leverage Twitter to appeal to younger consumers. But with everything else, with everything that mattered . . ." He shook his head.

I thought again of Noah's illusion, and how my point of view had shaped the words on Roxanne's e-mail, molding them into the picture I'd expected to see. The same was true for our marriage, in a way; Michael and I had switched vantage points, and now I was the cheater, the one who'd lost faith in us, while Michael had held tight to it all along. I thought back to the endless nights when I'd imagined Michael and Roxanne together as sickening feelings flooded me. Now I'd passed along all that pain to him.

"We stopped talking," he said. He wore a T-shirt and boxers, and his legs looked thin and pale in the bright light. He was still standing next to me in the bathroom, like we used to long ago when we got ready for the day ahead. Our eyes met in the mirror, and I wondered if he was thinking back to those times, too.

"I know we did," I said. "I used to blame you, but we were both at fault. I should've fought harder for us, for our marriage. I think having all the money, having this house—I viewed it as a trade-off. If you didn't work so hard, I wouldn't have gotten all of this, so I let your late nights slide. Maybe on some level I was scared we'd lose it if you slowed down."

Michael nodded slowly. "I know you haven't understood why I wanted to sell the company, but do you see now? Just a little bit? It was toxic for us, Julia. The way we were living—it ruined our marriage. If I hadn't—"

The phone rang, cutting him off.

"I'll get it," I said, keeping my voice casual.

I hurried into the sitting area off our bedroom, before the caller could leave a message. I'd turned off the ringer on the downstairs phones yesterday after the third reporter called, but I'd forgotten about the upstairs phones.

"Hello? He isn't in right now," I lied, keeping my voice low. I turned my back to the bedroom, hoping Michael couldn't hear.

"Who is this? His wife? What do you think about the lawsuit?" The reporter's questions were as quick and fierce as the rattle of a machine gun. I hung up while she was still speaking.

Michael's story had barely faded from the headlines, and now it was back. Reporters had discovered the papers filing the lawsuit. It hadn't taken long; maybe they'd been tipped off by Scott and Kimberly's lawyer, or perhaps Dale had placed a few anonymous calls. The latest twist in Michael's saga had proved irresistible to the press: I'd picked up the *Washington Post* yesterday to see a quote printed on an inside page in big, bold letters: HE CAME TO VISIT, BUT HE DIDN'T OFFER US ANY HELP. HE JUST SAID HE WAS SORRY. The story also showed a photo of Scott with his daughter.

As I put down the phone, I sensed someone behind me, and I turned to see Michael standing there.

"You don't have to hide what's happening from me," he said. "Kate called on my cell yesterday. She wanted to warn me because she'd gotten messages from the press, too."

"I'm sorry," I said. "I thought I was helping."

"You know what's crazy? Six months ago, the bad press would've killed me. I would've been launching a huge offensive, trying to shut down all the stories. But now I could care less. All I can think about is that it doesn't matter how much money I gave away. I helped some families, but look at how badly I hurt one. It erases everything good I did."

"Michael, it *doesn't*," I said. I'd never seen him like this; he looked beaten. Dark circles ringed his eyes, and his posture was weary.

He made a little gesture with a shoulder that wasn't quite a shrug.

"Do you want to go somewhere today?" I asked, trying to distract him. "We could go out to the hammock again. Or to Great Falls. Noah might be there."

"Sure, maybe in a little while," Michael said, but there wasn't any enthusiasm in his voice. He turned away from me and stared out the window. And I realized that I was losing my husband all over again.

Thirty-four

MICHAEL HAD ASKED ME for three weeks, and I was passing by our kitchen calendar when it hit me: Less than one remained. I stopped and stared at the four white squares marching across the page. They were all blank, which seemed fitting. I never could have anticipated what had happened to us in the past seventeen days—how could I plan for what lay ahead?

I poured myself a glass of water and sat down on a stool at our sea green granite island, remembering the time I'd served on a jury and two eyewitnesses were called to testify about an armed robbery at a convenience store. The robber was about six feet tall, the first witness said. He was closer to five foot nine, insisted the second one. Their testimony kept diverging, spreading apart and twisting back together like the double-helix strands of DNA, as lawyers took them through the crime beat by beat.

They'd gotten so many little details wrong. At the time I'd wondered why. They'd both been there and seen and heard everything.

During closing arguments, the prosecutor had instructed us jurors to focus on one critical fact: Both witnesses agreed the suspect sitting before us had pointed a gun at the clerk and stolen the money.

"It's not unusual to get confused by little details," the lawyer said, coming over to stand before the jury box. He was an average-looking guy in every way: medium height, ordinary close-cut brown hair, nondescript features. But I remember his light blue eyes meeting mine as he said, "The eyewitnesses agree on the most important fact, the only one that counts. They have no doubt at all that this man"—he whirled around and pointed at the accused—"held up the convenience store. *That's* what matters. *That's* what you need to remember."

The core truth of our marriage, the most important thing for me to remember, was that Michael and I loved each other. Our love had gotten pushed aside and bruised and buried, but it had always existed.

I took a final sip of my water and stood up and walked into the living room, suddenly thinking of Isabelle. I'd been e-mailing her regularly, and she'd sent back a reply, saying she was traveling through Italy and didn't have regular access to a computer. "I like your notes, though," she'd written. "Keep them coming even if I don't always write back, okay?"

I'd reread her e-mail a dozen times, trying to gauge her emotions through the scant words. Then I'd typed back, "Every day. I'll write you every day until you come home."

Now I thought of all the regrets she carried, for not reaching out to Beth sooner. For not taking a chance.

Sometimes following the path that looked the safest was what led to the most hurt, I realized.

Through the French doors I saw my husband standing on the stone patio, his hands jammed into his jeans pockets. He was staring off into the distance. I leaned my head against the glass and studied him. We'd been together for more than half of our lives, I realized. I'd met Michael when I was sixteen, and

I was about to turn thirty-five. In a way it felt as though we'd lived several completely different lives together: our time growing up together in West Virginia, the years we'd spent building our companies in D.C., and finally our move to this house—the culmination of so many of our dreams.

I didn't know what would happen during the next half of our lives. But it didn't matter what we did, or where we lived. I just wanted to spend it with him.

I rapped on the glass door, but he didn't hear me. I knocked again, louder this time, and when he turned around, I motioned for him to come inside.

"Is everything okay?" he asked as he walked into the living room.

I looked at him for a moment, wondering if I'd have the courage to go through with it.

"Jules?" he said, and I took a step backward in shock.

Michael had given me the nickname when we'd first met, but he rarely used it nowadays. I didn't believe in signs, but it suddenly struck me that one of the turning points of our marriage had come when I'd painted the wrong picture from a handful of words in an e-mail. And now, for the second time, it was as if a word had been spun through a kaleidoscope and reshaped into something with a whole different meaning.

"Come with me," I said. .

Something in my expression must have told him not to ask questions. I led Michael up our spiral staircase and into my dressing room; then I pushed open the door to my closet. I walked to the back corner and moved the sweaters onto the floor and opened the safe.

For just a moment, I heard an echo of the words Michael had said when he'd asked me to elope: *It'll just be you and me. That's always been enough for us, hasn't it?*

I hope so, I thought now. *I think so. Yes.*

I pulled out the velvet boxes and began to pile them haphazardly on the chaise lounge. "My jewels," I said. "Give them to Scott. Or have Christie's auction them off for him. Whatever you want."

"Wait," Michael said, his eyes huge. He reached for a box and opened it, and I saw the gleam of my diamond hoop earrings. "You want me to take your jewelry? But I don't—I never—"

"Please do it right now. This second." My throat tightened, and I knew I was about to cry. "Just take it all away. I'm going to walk out of here so I don't have to watch, okay?"

Michael was lifting up the earrings, and the sunlight streaming in through the windows flashed across their facets, sprinkling tiny rainbows around the room. He'd given me those for my birthday—but no, that wasn't technically true. When the jewelry store manager had rung our doorbell, I'd assumed Michael had arranged the delivery of my gift because he knew I'd be thrilled by the ceremony of it all: the little black velvet box being delivered along with a bottle of champagne that I assumed was a promise for us to drink that night. I'd put them on immediately and kept them on much later, when I changed into a silky white nightgown. When I finally heard Michael's car pull up in front of the house, I'd greeted him at the door, posing like a fashion model with my hip jutting out.

"Hey, you," he'd said. He'd drawn back, looked at my earrings—I'd tucked my hair behind my ears for full effect—and smiled. I'd grinned back at him.

"You forgot something," he'd said.

"Oh, yeah?" I'd answered, a teasing note in my voice. I don't know what I expected him to say—maybe that the earrings would look better if I wasn't wearing anything at all—but instead he reached up and touched one of my earlobes.

"You're not going to sleep in those, are you?"

I'd just stared at him for a moment, realizing he'd never

before seen the earrings. I should've known that Kate picked out all of my gifts and bought my birthday cards before putting them in front of Michael to sign in his illegible scrawl. My husband never would've made time to go to Harry Winston or Cartier and linger over the glass cases, trying to decide what I'd like best. And if he'd picked out my cards, they probably would've been silly instead of romantic.

At the time I'd told myself it didn't matter. I'd still opened the bottle of champagne and Michael and I had made love that night, and I'd never said a word. I'd told myself I was the luckiest girl in the world, to live in this house and have a husband who could afford such an exquisite birthday gift. Who cared if he didn't have time to pick them out?

I'd pretended my jewels were a mixture of a consolation prize and a reward for everything that was missing in my marriage, but they were just symbols of all that was wrong with it.

"Are you sure? You could think about—" Michael started to say.

My eyes were still on the earrings, but I was seeing a little girl in pink footsie pajamas, running toward her father as he spread his arms wide.

"Michael, please take it right now. As in this second. Get it out of here. Because I really don't want to change my mind, and if you stay here much longer I'm scared I might."

He took one look at my face, then he slipped the diamonds back into their box and scooped everything into one of my oversize purses and walked out the door.

I was soaking in my Jacuzzi when Michael came home. First I'd run for an hour on our treadmill, blasting music on my iPod, which seemed determined to torment me. I'd suffered through ABBA's rendition of "Money, Money, Money," but when Madonna started singing "Material Girl," I'd leapt off the treadmill and gulped down two glasses of water, chased by a finger of the wildly expensive Scotch we kept at the bar. I drank more water, decided it was working against me, and went for the Scotch again.

I'd still have enough, I told myself as I wiped my cheeks and blew my nose. I repeated those words like a mantra as I remembered the figures I'd drawn on my yellow legal pad. I'd never go hungry, never lack a nice place to live, never need to make a dress out of drapes like Scarlett O'Hara.

Even though I was scared, I knew I had to do this. It wasn't penance for having an affair, or for not trusting Michael. The reasons were tangled and a bit murky, but I sensed they had as much to do with helping me as they did with saving Michael. I had to trust him, to trust *us*, and this was the only way I could prove to both of us that I was ready to do it.

"Hi," Michael said as he entered the bathroom. He sat down on the edge of the Jacuzzi.

"What did you do with it?" I asked.

"Christie's is going to auction it off," he said. "Apparently they expect it to go for even more than it's worth because of the—I guess the celebrity associated with it all."

I winced. "Remember how you told me a while ago you were always going to be honest with me? You can skip the brutally honest part."

"Then I went to see Scott and Kimberly," he continued. "She met me at the door again, and this time I couldn't wait to get inside. I told them this had nothing to do with the lawsuit. They could go ahead with it if they wanted. But now I *know*, Julia. I know money won't be a problem for them, at least not for a long time. What you did—what you gave them—was bigger than what I did when I gave everything to charity. It meant more."

"It wasn't just for them," I said. "It was for their daughter. And you. And me, too."

Michael smiled. "I know."

He reached down, and I saw then that he'd brought a brown paper bag into the bathroom. "I got you something. It's not much . . ."

I looked into the bag and saw a half gallon of Breyers chocolate ice cream.

"Seems like a fair trade," I said. "You know, a million bucks' worth of jewelry for some ice cream."

"I thought about strawberry, but I figured that was only worth about fifty grand," he said.

"You know what you'd do if you really loved me?" I asked. He shook his head.

My throat was raw and sore from crying. Ice cream would be just the thing.

"Grab a spoon and get your ass in here and join me," I said.

Thirty-five

WHEN I WOKE UP the next morning, our bedroom was full of flowers. Michael had snuck out to the wholesalers before dawn to buy armloads of daisies. He'd put each one into its own Dixie cup. They were stacked all over our bureaus and night-stands and tables, covering every square inch of surface, and still more filled the counters in my bathroom. It felt like waking up in the middle of a garden.

He kicked off his shoes, then climbed into bed next to me, fully clothed. I'd forgotten all about what day it was until he said, "Happy birthday."

He gave me a gift every single hour. At ten o'clock it was a song—his voice cracked twice, and he tried, without much success, to rhyme *Julia* with *beauteous*—and I laughed until I cried. At noon, he baked me a chocolate cake.

"You got the mix with the pudding in the middle?" I said, hoisting myself up onto the kitchen counter and reading the back of the box. "I'm touched."

"Nothing but the best for my girl," Michael said. He looked

down at the mixing bowl and fished out a piece of eggshell. "You like your cakes on the less crunchy side, right?"

By one o'clock that afternoon, we were back in bed, my head resting against his chest again. But now his clothes were strewn on the floor next to his shoes.

"So what comes next?" I asked. "We're broke. And we're not even young and broke. We're rapidly approaching middle age—especially me, since I'm officially thirty-five as of a half hour ago—and it isn't nearly so romantic-sounding. Somehow I don't love the idea of carrying our stuff around in trash bags anymore."

"Well, I didn't give away *your* luggage," he pointed out.

"Hmm," I mused. "I might be able to spare a duffel bag. Just don't get greedy."

"And to think I sprang for the mix with the pudding in it," he said. "I could've baked you a dry cake, you know."

"Fine, two duffel bags," I allowed.

"So, what next? . . . . Well, once I transfer this house to Doctors Without Borders, they're going to sell it, but it'll probably take a while."

"It's shocking that people aren't clamoring to buy it," I said. "I mean, who doesn't have a spare ten million lying around?"

Michael smiled. "So we'll stay here for the time being," he said. "Is that okay?"

"Sure. I need to go back to work next week," I said. "I've gotten a few calls about upcoming events."

"I know I told you I'd get some kind of job," he said. "But first can I come work with you? Just for a while?"

I raised an eyebrow. "Seriously?"

"I'd love to see you in action," he said. "I want to get to know that side of you."

"So I get to order you around," I said. "Tell you exactly what to do."

"You can even start right now," he said, kissing my neck, then moving to a spot just behind my ear. "Is this to your liking, ma'am?"

"I like the way you think," I told him. "Keep this up, and I may even name you employee of the month."

My three o'clock gift was a picnic in our backyard. We were lying on a blanket with the remnants of our snack—cheese and grapes and French bread and bottles of sparkling water—spread out around us.

"I know you've always doubted that heaven exists, but doesn't my cooking make you reconsider?" Michael asked, handing me a piece of the cake. The middle had kind of collapsed in the oven, so he'd loaded on extra frosting to make the top appear even.

Instead of laughing, I lay back down on the blanket, my face to the sky. "I never did ask you about what happened," I said. "On the day that you died."

"Oh," Michael said. He lay down next to me and folded his arms behind his head. If he thought it was odd that I wanted to know now, after all this time, he didn't show it.

"It started out as just another day," he said. "I can't even remember everything I did that morning. I know I drank coffee with two shots of espresso on the way in to work, because I did that every day. I must've gone through a few dozen e-mails, taken some calls. And then it was time to roll out our new product, this cranberry-oatmeal energy bar. We were all in the boardroom, and then, suddenly, I wasn't."

I turned my head to the side so our faces were closer together. It was cloudy out, and the afternoon was chillier than I'd expected. The air was filled with the promise of the winter that would be coming soon. I was wearing jeans and a thin sweater, but no coat, and I wrapped my arms around myself and rubbed my upper arms.

"I think I was terrified to die, before. I think it's one of the reasons why I kept moving so fast. If I made enough money, if I was important enough, if I took up enough space—maybe I'd cheat death, somehow. Maybe it wouldn't be able to catch me. Crazy, huh? But the thought of not being here, of not existing, was so frightening."

I hesitated.

"Where did you go?" I finally asked.

"I don't know what to call it," he said. "The name probably doesn't matter. But it was as easy as walking from one room into another. *Easier.*"

I closed my eyes, trying to imagine it, but I couldn't stop thinking about whether I could interrupt Michael and run inside to get a sweater. A sudden sharp breeze made the little hairs on my arms stand up at attention, and I shivered.

"I understood so much in those minutes," he said. "I felt love and I felt loved. I was connected to everyone who has ever lived or died. And we *are* connected, Julia, because even though we speak different languages and live in different places, we all experience the same joy and grief and anger and embarrassment and love. Emotion is the only thing we all share, and it's the only thing we take with us when we go. After I died, I knew I was in a transitional place, and that I'd be moving on to another phase. Someone was with me, too. A presence. I knew it was safe and kind and warm."

"*Someone?*" I asked. "Like, a person?"

"Yes." He paused. "It was your mother."

I sat bolt upright and sucked in my breath.

"Julia, baby, it's okay. She sent me so much kindness. Her eyes . . . the way she looked at me. I think she was giving me her love, filling me with it, so I could bring it back to you."

I couldn't speak.

"She let me know I could come back, and that she would welcome me when I came the next time, and then I'd go on. I think others were waiting for me, in the next phase."

"Michael, this is insane." I could barely force out the words.

"I know," he said quietly. "But Julia, it happened."

I buried my face in my hands. "Why didn't you tell me before?"

"I wanted to. But I didn't think you wanted to hear it."

"Michael, I don't believe this. I mean, I know you think it happened, but it's crazy. Do you hear how crazy this is?" I started to shiver, and I wrapped my arms around myself again.

"Yes," he said simply.

I lay down again and stared up at the sky. My teeth were chattering—from cold or something else—and I couldn't stop shaking.

"I don't know if I can believe you," I finally whispered. "It doesn't make any sense. How was my mother there? How is that even possible?"

"I just wish . . . ," Michael began to say, then his voice trailed off.

"What?" I whispered. I felt a tear slide down my cheek. I missed my mother so intensely I felt as if I were being torn in two. I closed my eyes and remembered her, as vividly as if she were sitting next to me:

My mother's sweet, musical voice calling me in to dinner as I jumped rope in front of our house.

My mother hugging me after I'd graduated from sixth grade, then snapping a photo of me in the white, lacy dress she'd sewn herself.

My mother sitting on the edge of my bed on my birthdays, retelling the story of the day I was born. "You had such a big cry for so tiny a baby," she'd always say. "And the minute I heard you wailing,

I reached for you. I tried to pull you right out of the doctor's hands. I didn't want you to be sad, not even for a moment."

"Julia, I wish so much I could explain how it felt." Just as Michael said those words, the sun broke free from a giant cloud and beamed its warmth onto me, beginning at my feet and moving up my legs, then over my stomach and my arms and neck.

My mother, pulling a blanket up over me when I was cold at night.

I looked at Michael, my eyes wide. He was staring back at me, an expression I'd never seen before on his face.

"That's it," he whispered. "Just now, when you were so cold and then the sun came out? Julia, that's exactly how it felt after I died."

Thirty-six

TWO DAYS LATER WE were leaving the river, walking along the path toward the parking lot with Noah and Bear. Michael and I held hands as Noah walked about ten yards ahead of us, still throwing a stick for Bear.

"Do you think Bear ever gets tired?" I asked Michael.

"He's equal parts motor and dog," he said. "That's how I always used to feel—at least part of me."

"Which half did you relate to?" I asked innocently.

Michael pulled me closer and mock-growled in my ear.

"What do you want to do tonight?" I asked as the path curved around to run parallel with a busy street and Noah pulled a thin nylon leash from his back pocket and whistled for Bear.

"I'm actually a little tired," Michael confessed.

"You?" I said in surprise. I think it was the first time I'd ever heard him admit to needing rest.

"Here, boy!" Noah was calling. But something had caught Bear's attention, and his head was turned in the other direction, away from us. It was a squirrel, frozen in place on the path ahead, I noticed absently.

"You haven't heard from Isabelle again, have you?" Michael asked.

I shook my head. "I'm still writing her every day. I miss her so much. I was thinking maybe I could fly out to meet her for a few days, wherever she is. I could e-mail her and offer, at least."

"Good idea." Michael's hand tightened around mine.

"Can we stay in tonight?" he asked a moment later.

"Sure," I said. I glanced up at him and frowned. "You don't have another headache, do you?"

"No, that's not it," he said.

"So we'll stay home," I said. I looked at him again; he did appear kind of pale. "We'll take a Jacuzzi and go to bed early. Remember, you're going to start working for me. You'll need your rest."

Michael leaned over and kissed the top of my head, then breathed in deeply. "Coconut with a hint of lime mixed in," he whispered. "My Julie."

Bear suddenly took off after the squirrel, which sprang to life and veered to the right, heading directly toward the double-lane street.

"Bear!" Noah ran after his dog, and Michael dropped my hand to join the chase. Noah was still fifty feet from the road, and he looked like he'd catch up to Bear in plenty of time; his thin legs were a blur.

But then Bear's easy lope changed to a full-on run. His head was down and he was tightly focused on the squirrel. His instincts, honed by generations of ancestors, told him little animals were prey; they didn't warn him to look out for the relatively newer innovation of cars.

I looked wildly to the left and right and saw traffic. Too much traffic. People were rushing home from work, probably chatting on cell phones and checking BlackBerrys. It was almost dusk, and scattered trees lined the area between the path and the road. Could the drivers see Bear and Noah running toward them?

I began sprinting even though I knew I'd never reach them in time.

"Noah!" I screamed, cupping my hands around my mouth. "Stop!"

I couldn't see any of them now; they were weaving among the trees, all three of them. I ran faster, seeing our picnic basket ahead of me, where Michael had dropped it. The crackers we'd packed to eat with cheese had fallen out; something about the sight of those white squares scattered on the ground made me stumble and almost fall. The white envelopes tumbling to the ground as Bob the mail-room guy ran to get the defibrillator, the day Michael had died . . .

I heard a squeal of tires and I squeezed my eyes shut even as I kept running, my shoes kicking up dirt and my hands clawing the air, as though I could grab clumps of it and propel myself forward faster. When I finally broke free from the trees, all of the cars in both directions had stopped. My head whipped from side to side, but I couldn't see anyone—not Michael or Noah or Bear. Drivers were getting out, and one woman was shouting into her cell phone and waving her hand in the air.

I kept running and finally reached the street. I wove between the cars until I spotted Noah, lying against the curb, his arm bent up at an awkward angle.

I tried to scream, but his name came out as a croak.

"I'm okay," Noah said. He straightened his arm, wincing a bit, then flexed it again. His eyes were huge as he slowly stood up and looked at me. "Michael pushed me out of the way. I didn't get hit."

Then I looked back and saw Michael lying on the street between two cars.

* * *

My favorite part of any opera is the aria that usually comes toward the end. In Italian, *aria* means "air," and it's an apt description. Everything winds down during those long moments, and the stage is still and hushed. The only thing that matters is the bittersweet sound. I've never been able to listen to an aria without crying, because to me, an aria wraps all the emotions of that opera—and all of the feelings in life, really—into one glorious song.

I told Michael I loved him as I held his head in my hands, and his eyes flickered open for a moment. He heard me; I know he did.

Thirty-seven

WHEN THE DOORBELL RANG the next morning, I slowly opened my eyes, then lifted up my head from the couch. My mind felt dull and foggy, and it took a moment to process the noise and understand what it meant.

Michael.

He'd died once before and returned to life, and somehow, some way, he'd done it again. The policeman who'd tried to pull me away from my husband's body, the young woman who'd bolted from her car and wrapped a crinkly silver emergency blanket around my shoulders while repeating "I'm so sorry," and the EMT who'd put two fingers on Michael's neck while looking up at his colleague and silently shaking his head—they were all wrong.

Michael had come back to me.

I scrambled to my feet and ran toward the door, but I slipped on the glossy wood floor and fell to my knees.

"Wait!" I cried out, crawling to the foyer. I grabbed the edge of the table across from the front door and pulled myself upright as my heart leapt furiously in my chest. My fingers fumbled with the locks, and I flung open the door. Bright sunlight hit my face, sending tiny arrows of pain into my eyes and blinding me for a moment. All I could see was a tall, thin silhouette.

"Michael," I tried to whisper, but my throat closed up.

"I hope I'm not disturbing you," the man said.

As my eyes adjusted, I saw that he was maybe in his early seventies, with thinning white hair and a polished wooden cane. He was a stranger.

I felt my whole body collapse inward. I clung to the doorframe as the terrible knowledge crashed down over me, even more swiftly and powerfully than it had yesterday: Michael was dead. Nausea rose in my throat, and I almost gagged.

"I know this is a terrible time," the man was saying. "Please accept my condolences. I wouldn't intrude under any other circumstances, but I'm Michael's lawyer. My name is Jonathan Boright."

I couldn't breathe. His face swam before my eyes as I grew dizzy.

"I'm so sorry," Jonathan said. He reached out and patted my arm. "I can come back another time."

He began to turn around but stopped when I blurted, "No!"

I'd spent the night curled up, trembling, on a couch in our living room. I couldn't bear to be alone any longer. "Don't go," I said. "You can come in. Please."

"I won't keep you long," Jonathan promised. I let go of the doorframe and slowly led him into our library, feeling as achy and worn as if I'd aged sixty years overnight.

"May I sit down?" he asked. I blinked and realized we'd been standing silently for several moments.

"I'm sorry, of course. I—"

"It's okay," he interrupted me, again with a grandfatherly pat on my arm. "I understand."

He opened his leather briefcase and slid on a pair of bifocals before rustling through some papers. He was sitting in the exact spot where Michael had been, just days ago. If I closed my eyes, I could see him again, stretching out his arms and inviting me to join him. I sank onto the couch next to Jonathan; my legs couldn't hold me up any longer.

"I won't bother with all the legal mumbo jumbo," he said in a gentle voice. "Your husband's life insurance policy was valued at two million dollars. You're his sole beneficiary."

It took a moment for my mind to unscramble his words. "He had . . . life insurance?"

"He had that policy in effect for quite a while," Jonathan said. "He told me many times that he wanted you to be taken care of no matter what happened to him."

I shook my head. "I never . . . but he never . . . he didn't say anything."

Jonathan patted my hand with his bony, spotted one, and I turned my hand over so I could clutch his.

"I lost my wife three years ago," he said softly. "You can hold on to my hand as long as you want."

I nodded and felt tears flood my eyes. "Were you married a long time?"

"Yes," he said simply.

Three years; I couldn't bear to think about this kind man being in pain for so long. "I'm sorry," I said.

He inclined his head. "Me too, for you." He cleared his throat. "But I'm here to talk about what Michael left for you. There's a stipulation in the policy that it doubles if his death was an accident, which it most assuredly was. So the final amount will be four million dollars."

Jonathan reached over with his other hand and put a small pile of papers in front of me.

"How long ago . . . ?" I began to ask, but I couldn't formulate the rest of my sentence.

"He bought the policy years ago. I can get you the exact date if you need it?" His voice rose questioningly.

I shook my head. "It doesn't matter . . . I'm sorry, I just—" My voice broke.

"He came into my office one day right off the street, and he bought the policy then and there," Jonathan said. "His company was already doing quite well, but he told me he wanted something extra as a cushion for you just in case he ever hit a rough spot financially. He paid the premiums every year. And then after—" Jonathan bowed his head and began again. "After his cardiac arrest, he made an appointment to come by one afternoon. He told me what had happened. He said he wanted to make sure everything was up-to-date, and that the policy was still in effect. I assured him it was paid through the end of the year, but he wanted to see it for himself. He asked me so many questions about it, until he was satisfied there were no loopholes. Such a sharp mind."

"He was so smart. He was so good." My lips trembled, but I forced out the words; it was important to say them.

"He loved you very much," Jonathan said. He reached into his pocket and handed me a crisp white handkerchief. I hadn't realized tears were flowing down my cheeks. Michael would never be an old man with a cane; I'd never see him that way. I wouldn't wake up tomorrow morning with my head on his chest, listening to his rapid heartbeat echo in my ears.

I wanted to run out of the room screaming, but my limbs felt so leaden I was pinned to the couch.

"He told me he wanted to make sure his wife would never have to worry about money. And there won't be any problems with the insurance company. I'll take care of everything and notify you as soon as we receive the check. It should be just a few weeks."

I nodded and fought to inhale as my lungs constricted.

"I'll need your signature," Jonathan reminded me gently, motioning to the papers. "Unless you'd like to have them reviewed by another lawyer first?"

I shook my head and blindly scrawled my name.

"It seemed almost as if he was . . . expecting this," Jonathan said. "I hope you don't mind my saying that. He asked me to call you immediately if anything happened to him. Not to wait a minute. And last night, when I saw the news on television . . ."

Then something jolted me out of my daze, and the world around me zoomed into crisp focus: Yesterday was exactly twenty-one days after Michael's cardiac arrest. Three weeks. The precise amount of time he'd asked me to give him as a final gift.

Had he known? How could he have known?

I stared at Jonathan as he put the papers back into his briefcase.

"This should take care of everything," he said. "But there was one more thing Michael wanted me to tell you." He smiled. "Michael said you'd understand what he meant. When you need it, there's more Breyers chocolate ice cream for you in the freezer."

I squeezed my eyes shut. "Thank you," I said when I could speak again.

"I should let you be," he said.

Please don't go, I thought, panic rising within me. *Please don't leave me here all alone.*

"Would you like some water?" I asked. "Or . . ." I tried to think about what someone might want to drink. "Tea? Maybe some juice?"

I could see Jonathan start to reflexively say no, then he looked around, as if seeing the big, empty house for the first time. He was the first person who'd ever walked in here who hadn't seemed to be awed by it.

His eyes finally settled on me. "I don't have any other appointments today. Tea sounds just lovely," he said.

Thirty-eight

"HOW DID YOU GET here so fast?" I asked.

"Chartered a jet," Isabelle said, like another woman might've said, "I hit all the green traffic lights." She tossed her coat over the banister and wrapped her arms around me.

I'd been waiting for this moment, I realized. I'd been desperate for her to come.

"Sweetie, I know this might sound odd, but Michael called me a few weeks ago—right after his cardiac arrest—and asked if you could come stay with me, just in case anything ever happened to him."

"He did?" My voice failed me. Again it struck me, he knew. Somehow, he knew.

I cleared my throat and asked, "What did you say?"

"I said, 'Of course not.' What am I, running a hotel?"

I blinked in surprise, then started laughing. I leaned over and clutched my stomach, and then tears streamed down my face, as quickly as if someone had turned on a faucet to release them.

"Oh, honey," Isabelle said. She wrapped her arms around me again, holding me upright. "I'm here. Just let it out."

"I can't do this," I whispered into her shoulder. "Not without him."

"You don't have to do a thing," she said. "I'm going to take care of you. Come stay with me, Julia. For as long as you want."

"I keep thinking he's going to walk in from another room," I sobbed. "How can he be gone? How can someone be here one moment and not the next?"

"I don't know. It isn't fair." Isabelle smoothed back my hair, making soothing noises.

"Will you come home with me?" she finally asked. "I can't stand to think of you all by yourself, or I could stay here . . ."

I took a deep, shuddering breath and tried to think. Would I be able to leave the home Michael and I had shared? But Michael wasn't here, in these cold, elegant rooms. The places where I'd go to be with him were the banks of both of our rivers, outside under the shelter of a tree when it rained, and in the warmth of the sun.

"Let me just pack a bag," I said. I tried to think. "I need a toothbrush."

"Julia, what kind of heiress do you think I am?" she asked. "I can spare an extra toothbrush. Let's just go, honey."

I didn't move from bed during those first few days. I couldn't eat, or even talk. I just drifted in and out of sleep, my memories and dreams blurring together into one. I saw Michael as a teenager, sliding into the seat next to me in school, and then he was winking as he stirred the batter for my birthday cake. He spun around the merry-go-round in Paris, reaching up for the brass ring, and then lifted a wineglass to toast me, his eyes serious and loving. Sometimes I woke up calling out for him in the darkness. Then the sadness would come, wrapping so tightly around me that I felt suffocated. But something else was always there, too: Isabelle's voice.

"It's okay," she would whisper, holding a glass of ginger ale up to my lips. She smoothed damp washcloths over my face and hands, and murmured soothingly. "I'm right here."

Then, on the fifth day, she opened the curtains, letting sunlight into the room.

"I'm going to help you sit up," she said, reaching an arm behind my back.

"No," I said. I put my forearm over my eyes. "Not yet."

"No isn't an option, honey," she said. "It's time to get out of bed. Come on."

My entire body ached, but somehow, with her bracing me, I made it to my feet. She handed me a fuzzy blue robe and a jar of brown-sugar body wash, and led me to the shower, which was already running and filling the room with white steam.

"Do you need help getting undressed?" she asked, and I shook my head.

"Then I'll be right outside the door when you finish."

I stood in the steaming water for a long time, soaping my hair and slowly rubbing the sweet-smelling wash into my skin. After I turned off the water and wrapped myself in the robe, I found my pajamas had been swept away and a pair of sneakers and new Juicy Couture sweat suit had replaced them on the vanity.

"Just a short walk," Isabelle cajoled, waving a roaring blow-dryer at my hair. "We'll go to the end of the street."

I groaned but gave in, and was surprised by how good the fresh air felt on my face. After a few minutes, my steps came more surely, and before I knew it, we'd gone a half mile.

"Does it ever get easier?" I asked as we turned around to head back home. "When you lose someone you love?"

Her eyes darkened, and I knew she was thinking about Beth.

"Yes," she said. "But it never gets easy."

I nodded. "I think you have the right idea," I said. "We'll just keep putting one foot in front of the other, okay?"

She squeezed my shoulder. "It's all we can do."

We walked in silence awhile longer.

"Tomorrow I think I need to go by the house," I said. "I should check on things."

"Want company?" Isabelle asked.

I hesitated, then shook my head. Somehow I knew I needed to do it alone.

"I'll be okay," I said. "I won't go for long."

This house had never been a home, I realized as I piled the accumulated mail on a table, dislodging a thin layer of dust. I walked up the spiral staircase, my hand trailing on the banister, and stepped into our bedroom. My eyes took in the his-and-her bathrooms on opposite sides of the huge room, and the enormous California king bed. Why had Michael and I ever thought we needed so much space?

This house was emblematic of our problems: so gorgeous on the outside, but inside it, we never could find each other.

I found an overnight bag and packed a few things—my favorite cozy socks, the picture of Michael in his DrinkUp apron holding a sample cup high in the air like he was making a toast, and a journal with a pretty cover so I could capture some memories of my husband before they faded even the slightest bit. I listened to the messages on the answering machine—some from reporters, some condolence calls, and one from Noah's parents, saying over and over how grateful they were to Michael for saving their son. They wanted to meet me, they said. I jotted down their number, promising myself I'd call back soon.

I rinsed out a glass in the sink and put it in the dishwasher, then opened the refrigerator and cleaned out the wilted lettuce and spoiled milk. As I wiped down the shelves with a sponge, I remembered something. I opened the freezer and saw it, tucked in the very back. I pushed aside a package of frozen spinach that I'd been pretending I was going to eat someday and pulled out the tub of Breyers chocolate ice cream.

As I carried it to the counter, I realized something was taped to the lid. I sank into a chair and stared down at it. It was a note on a piece of white paper, folded into squares. My name was written on it in Michael's familiar scrawl. Suddenly a great ache of missing him crashed down on me. I folded my arms across my stomach, curling into myself. Finally I reached for the note.

My Julie,

I know, baby. I miss you, too. I miss you so much.

Here are some of the things I'm remembering: Walking you home from Becky Hendrickson's and knowing I'd already fallen in love with you. Dancing in our old apartment to "What a Wonderful World." Feeling you in my arms as you slept. Seeing you in Paris in the candlelight. How you looked—so terrified but determined—when you gave away your jewelry. I know exactly what that cost you, and I'm not talking about the money.

I know you thought I was crazy for giving everything away, but Julie, I knew this day was coming. I couldn't give you the year you asked for because I suspected—no, I knew—that I didn't have that long. But at least it was long enough for us to find each other again. And I promise you this: We'll find each other for a third time, someday.

I want you to promise me a few things. Eat ice cream.

Smell lavender. Throw away that bitch of a scale for good. Go to Paris again, or maybe Australia, but also sit in your yard at night and just look up at the stars.

I want you to fall in love again. Please have children. You'll be such a good mom.

I love you. I took that with me, remember?

And I'll never stop loving you.

M.

Thirty-nine

"I WAS SCARED TO see you," Noah said. I could feel his thin body shaking. "I thought you'd be so mad at me."

"Never," I said, hugging him tighter before pulling back and looking him in the eye. "Noah, it wasn't your fault. It wasn't anyone's fault—not the driver of the car that hit him, or Michael's for running into the road, or even that silly squirrel's. It was just an accident."

"Do you think it hurt him a lot?"

I shook my head. "He didn't seem to be in any pain. And Noah, he wasn't scared. Michael wasn't afraid to die."

I let go of him, and he threw the stick for Bear again. Even though it was colder now, with patches of snow on the frozen ground, Bear leapt into the water as eagerly as ever. Instead of a dive, he belly flopped this time, his paws splaying out in all directions and water splashing high into the air. He took a moment to look around and spot the stick, then he sank under the surface.

"Do you believe that our souls go somewhere after we die?" Noah asked. His little brow furrowed as he looked up at me. "Do you think that's where Michael is right now?"

"I don't know what I believe right now," I said slowly. "I *want* to believe in something, though, and I never did before."

"A lot of the greatest mathematical minds believed in life after death," Noah said.

Bear broke through the surface and snatched up the stick, then began paddling back to shore.

"And I once read about this guy named Galileo, and he said everything in the universe is written in mathematics," Noah said. "And it's true. It's not just Fibonacci numbers. Sometimes it makes me wonder: Do you think I see math everywhere because someone or maybe something created the world that way, or do you think I just like math so much I impose it on everything I see?"

"Now that," I said, taking the dripping stick that Bear offered up as if it was a priceless heirloom, "is an excellent question."

"Kind of like the hen and the egg," Noah said.

"Exactly."

"Hey, Julia?"

"Hmmm?"

"Did you bring anything to eat?"

"Aren't we supposed to go have dinner with your parents after we walk Bear?" I asked.

"Yeah," he said. "But that's an hour away."

"Check that bag, kiddo," I said. "I was thinking we'd have a little predinner junk food snack."

He grinned. "I'm glad you came back."

I looked out at the rushing water, and lifted my face to feel the gentle winter sun. "Me, too," I said after a moment, and I felt Noah's warm hand slip into mine.

The next day, I sat on a cushioned window seat upstairs, watching a procession of shiny sedans and stretch limousines and older, inexpensive cars file into the long, circular driveway. It was raining out, and the steady drizzle meant umbrellas blocked my view of mourners' faces as they exited their cars and approached the front door.

I'd planned hundreds of events during the past few years, but my husband's funeral was by far the most difficult. For days, I'd agonized over what Michael would have wanted. A small outdoor ceremony? No service at all? I'd been desperate to honor his wishes, but I didn't know what they were. Finally I called Kate, Michael's former assistant. Somehow, her calm voice and sensible suggestions steadied me enough to make decisions, to dial the familiar numbers of caterers and chair rental companies and explain that this time, it was me who needed their services.

Kate had recommended we hold the funeral here, in this historic mansion usually rented out for weddings. Not surprisingly, it was the perfect choice: The main room stretched the entire length of the building, but faded Oriental carpets and big fireplaces on both ends softened the space and made it seem cozy. Lit candelabra on the walls filled the room with a yellow glow that was more welcoming than bright overhead lights.

Michael wanted to be cremated, it had specified in his will, with his ashes scattered in our river in West Virginia. Someday soon, I would fulfill his final request alone, but today was about letting others say good-bye to Michael.

"Honey?"

I turned toward the sound of Isabelle's voice.

She stood in the doorway. "It's time to begin," she said.

This was the room where brides prepared themselves for their weddings, perhaps waiting for those very words. Some of them had probably curled up in this window seat, wearing a dress the opposite color of mine, anticipating the moment when they'd be joined to the man they'd chosen.

I didn't realize tears were rolling down my cheeks until Isabelle moved closer and tucked a tissue in my hand. I held on to her arm as I stood up, then we walked downstairs together. As I moved toward the front row of folding seats, I saw Dr. Rushman and a few of the Washington Blazes players, their heads towering above the others in their rows. I spotted Noah, tugging on an uncomfortable-looking blue-and-red striped necktie, sitting in between his parents. A former U.S. senator, recognizable by his prominent nose and thick mane of white hair, tapped out a message on his BlackBerry before tucking it into his breast pocket. And toward the back was Sandy, the young Irish woman who'd brought us homemade cookies and told us about her sister who'd died of cancer. Nearly all of the three hundred chairs I'd rented were full. Kate was right; we had needed this space.

The service was simple. Raj, who was perhaps Michael's only true friend at the office, told funny stories about their early days in the company together, like the time Michael worked straight through the night, and early the next morning, wandered over to the refrigerator and ate the entire sheet cake intended for someone's birthday. "He ran out to Giant and got a new one an hour later," Raj said. "No one even knew about it, at least until now."

Kate had originally demurred when I'd asked her to speak, until I reminded her how much Michael had depended upon and liked her. She gave a beautiful tribute, her voice cracking as she recalled how Michael once gave her a holiday card that included a check for her daughter's college education.

Then Noah stood and walked to the front of the room. I felt my lips curve upward as I got a better look at him; someone had tried to tame his hair, but his cowlicks were putting up a valiant fight.

"Michael saved my life," Noah began in his sweet, high voice. "I was chasing after my dog Bear, and all of a sudden, I was in front of a car." His chin began to tremble. "I was so scared. I knew I couldn't get out of the way fast enough. And then Michael was there. He lifted me up and pushed me. And I was safe. I wish—" Noah was crying hard now, but he managed to get the words out. "I wish I could tell him I'm sorry. And thank you. Because we were becoming friends, and I really liked him."

When Noah finished, he returned to his seat and I saw his parents reach out for him. The room was silent for a long moment, except for a few murmurs and sounds of people blowing their noses.

Then the music began.

The love song written by Puccini was my last gift to Michael. I'd never get to see an opera with him, but I could give him this. I could share the light and the hope and the heart of its music with Michael.

I mouthed the words from *La Bohème* as I closed my eyes and saw my husband again: "Ho tante cose che ti voglio dire, o una sola ma grande come il mare, come il mare profonda ed infinita . . . Sei il mio amor . . ."

I've so many things to tell you, or one thing—huge as the sea, deep and infinite as the sea: I love you.

"Julie?"

I turned around, surprised by my old nickname, and found myself staring into the eyes of Michael's father. Impossibly, he was unchanged by time. I gasped and almost took a step backward, before I realized it had to be one of Michael's brothers.

"I wanted to convey my respects," he said. I nodded, thinking it spoke volumes that I had no idea which brother he was.

"The checks Michael sent . . . well, they meant a lot," he said. His cheeks reddened and he lowered his voice. He rubbed his rough, workingman's hands together. "Not sure we deserved them, though."

I held his eyes for a long moment as understanding passed between us, then I nodded. People change, I could almost hear Michael saying. At least someone from Michael's family had come to the funeral. "Thank you," I said at last, before turning to the next person waiting to talk to me, a dark-haired man in his forties or fifties.

"I'm Carl Shevinski, from Johns Hopkins University," he said, giving my hand a gentle squeeze. "I never met your husband, but I wanted to be here. The gift he gave us for stroke research is the single biggest donation we've ever gotten. He was an incredible man."

I couldn't speak for a moment. Stroke research. In honor of my mother.

I took a deep breath, willing my voice to remain steady. "I'm glad you came," I finally said.

He started to say something else, but I didn't hear him. I'd caught sight of two people approaching me from the other side of the room. My heart began pounding so loudly it drowned out his words, and I felt a white-hot rage course through my veins. I couldn't believe either of them had dared to come.

Isabelle, I thought wildly, and looked around for her, but she was caught up in a conversation. She couldn't see what was about to unfold.

"My condolences," Dale said. Roxanne stood next to him, staring at me with those wide cat eyes, not saying a word.

"What are you doing here?" I whispered, almost choking on the words. I was so angry I wanted to lunge forward and push them out the door.

Roxanne finally spoke. "We came to pay our respects."

"Your respects?" I echoed incredulously. They'd tried to ruin Michael, to ruin us. And now they were stealing away the peace I'd received from his funeral service.

"I want you to leave," I said.

Dale raised an eyebrow, but he didn't move. My rage intensified as I realized I was powerless. I couldn't create a scene, not here. Had Dale counted on this?

Suddenly, I felt an arm slip across my back, and a deep voice said, "I believe the lady told you to leave." I looked up and saw Scott Braverly.

Dale's brow creased, then he placed him. "Scott, right? We met a while back. We chatted a bit about your lawsuit against Michael."

Scott's wife Kimberly intercepted Dale's hand as he extended it toward her husband. She batted it down, like it was an insect. "Michael and Julia did right by us," Kimberly said. "Things got mixed up for a while, but he fixed it. There is no lawsuit against Michael. And now you need to leave."

Suddenly Isabelle was standing on my other side, and Noah was in front of me, his thin arms spread out protectively. Another voice cut through the crowd like a knife, clear and elegant and unmistakably firm. "You really should be going, Dale. Don't you need to start looking for a new job?" It was Kate.

As I looked at the little army surrounding me, a laugh formed deep inside of me chest and bubbled out of me.

Dale spun around and walked off without a word, and after a beat, Roxanne followed.

"I'll just see that they make it to the door," Scott said, removing his arm from my back and giving me a wink. I nodded my thanks.

"Can I get you a drink?" Kate offered.

"How about a cookie?" Noah suggested. "I've been checking on the food, and they just put some chocolate ones out on plates."

"You okay?" Isabelle asked gently.

I looked into their dear faces, one by one, then exhaled deeply, feeling the tension leave my body. The room was filled with the good smells of fresh coffee and just-baked breads and roasts. And people were waiting to talk to me, to share their own memories of Michael.

"Yes," I finally answered. "To all three of your questions."

Epilogue

I PARKED BY THE curb and turned off my car and studied the house for a moment. I'd been here only a few times before, years ago, and now the small, wooden bungalow had been repainted in a pretty shade of blue. Someone had added a front porch, and a few leftover blue and white Christmas lights decorated the front bushes. They looked so pretty I wondered why people didn't leave lights out all year long. Celebrating shouldn't be confined to just December.

I got out of the car and stretched my arms up over my head, feeling my spine make a satisfying little pop, then I checked my purse to make sure the manila envelope was still inside. I slowly walked up the steps and lifted the brass knocker, letting it thud a few times against the door, and hearing my heart echo the sound.

There wasn't any reason to be nervous, I told myself. I stood up straighter, and after a moment, I knocked again.

Silence.

I couldn't help smiling. It had taken me months—no, make that *years*—to get to this moment, and now no one was here. Next time I'd call first.

I'd walked back to my car and was just opening the door when I heard him call my name, a question in his voice. I turned around.

"Hi, Dad," I said.

He was standing by the corner of the house, wearing gardening gloves and holding an aluminum ladder.

"It's you," he said after a moment. "I was getting a branch off the roof. I thought I was imagining things."

"I got your card," I said. "I wanted to thank you."

He put down the ladder, then took off his gloves and rubbed his hands against his khaki trousers. "I drove up right away when I heard. Julie, I'm so sorry."

"You drove up?" I asked. "To D.C.?"

"You weren't home. I waited for a couple days . . . and then I wanted to come to the funeral, but I wasn't sure . . ." His voice trailed off.

"You waited for me?" I felt my forehead wrinkle. "You mean at a hotel?"

He shook his head. "I brought a sleeping bag, just in case. And I turned on the heat in the car when it got cold," he said.

I swallowed hard, thinking of him parked outside my house for so long.

"I wasn't home for a while, and I didn't think to go through the mail until a few days ago. That's why I didn't answer your card sooner."

He ducked his head. "I wish I'd been there for you."

I took a deep breath. "You would have been, if I'd let you."

I don't know which of us took the first step toward the other, but suddenly I was hugging my dad. He was so much thinner now; my arms could fit all the way around his waist and touch each other. But he still smelled like Old Spice.

"I can't believe you're here," he said, his voice muffled by my hair.

"I need to tell you something." I brushed the tears off my cheeks and leaned back to look up at him and saw the worry spread across his face.

"No," I said. "It's good news."

Earlier I'd done the math and figured it out: Paris.

I reached into my purse and handed him the envelope. He opened it and took out the slippery piece of paper. He stared at it for a long moment, then his eyes grew wide.

"Is it—are you—?" he asked.

I nodded. "It's your grandson's first photo. He'll be here this summer."

Isabelle had already bought a full wardrobe of miniature shirts and pants and shoes—yes, shoes—and I'd woken up from a nap yesterday to see her stacking boxes of diapers in a closet.

"What?" she'd asked when I'd raised an eyebrow. "Girl Scouts taught me to be prepared."

"First, you were never a Girl Scout," I'd responded. "And second, I'm not Octomom. Do you think we need eight *cases* of diapers?"

I'd already asked her to be my birthing partner, and she was insisting that the baby and I live with her for as long as we wanted. "I was the one who said families come in all shapes and sizes," she'd reminded me. "Why can't we create a new one?"

"But what if you meet someone?" I'd asked.

"Then I'll kick you out on the street and stop taking your calls, of course," she'd said. "Come on, Julia. I've got seven bedrooms. Let's just take it day by day, okay? I want you here. I want *both* of you here."

I'd looked down and put a hand on my stomach. It had started to curve, just the tiniest bit, like the beginning of a smile. "Is being constantly hungry a normal side effect of pregnancy?"

"Let me check," Isabelle had said. She'd reached into a shopping bag and pulled out a half dozen books.

"Isabelle!" I'd laughed. "Can we just make some sandwiches and fruit salad?"

"Oh, great. Every other pregnant woman wants ice cream. I get stuck with the only one with healthy cravings," she'd groaned. "I need to gain my sympathy weight, you know. Don't deny me that."

Now my father looked back at the sonogram photo as I pointed out the baby's head and his round little torso. At four months, he was the size of an orange, one of the books said. But he was getting bigger and stronger every day.

I thought back to that morning in Paris, when I'd run out of the hotel room and had suddenly seen children everywhere. Michael had forgotten to pack my birth control pills for the trip, and neither of us had thought about protection that night.

Had I known, even on some subconscious level, that inside of me cells were busily multiplying, laying the groundwork for this little person to be formed?

"He's perfect," my father said. He shook his head. "You're having a son. I can't believe it."

I stared at my father as he looked at the photo again. His face was deeply lined, and gray had overtaken the brown in his hair. His canvas coat looked too big for him; he probably hadn't bothered to buy a new one after he'd lost weight. My mom had always been the one to cook and clean and buy socks when my father wore holes in the heels of his old ones. It must have been hard for him to learn to live without her.

He'd aged so much since I'd last seen him.

He caught me watching him and suddenly asked, "Will you—I mean, would you want to come inside for a bit?"

I took a deep breath, and he quickly said, "I'm sorry. You probably need to get going."

"Dad?" I put my hand on his arm. "I thought I might stay with you for a couple of days. I wanted to see if you'd make the baby's crib. Then I was hoping you could come to D.C. next month and help me paint his room."

He looked at me for a moment, then my dad reached out and held me in his arms for a long time.

Acknowledgments

The first person I need to thank is Seth Goldman, the "TeaEO" of Honest Tea. Seth graciously welcomed me into his office—twice!—plied me with delicious drinks, and answered my questions about how someone could start a successful beverage company from scratch. Of course, my character is nothing like Seth—and my fictional DrinkUp company isn't even remotely based on Honest Tea, which, by all accounts, is one of the most honorable businesses around. Remember: my book is pure fiction! And, incidentally, Honest Tea is addictive.

I'm still pinching myself over my good luck: Not only do I get to write novels—a pretty fabulous job in itself—but also I'm surrounded by the smartest, kindest people in publishing. My editor, Greer Hendricks, is the type of woman I'd pick out of a crowded room as the one I'd want to be friends with—and she constantly amazes me with her editorial vision, creativity, and infectious, upbeat energy. My agent, Victoria Sanders, is one of the funniest people I've ever met (her e-mails are legendary), and she's wicked smart. V, thanks for making my dreams come true.

I don't think I'll ever be able to adequately express my gratitude to the author Jennifer Weiner for her unprecedented support, which still takes my breath away—but she told me she doesn't need to be thanked. All she wants is for me to pass along kindnesses to other authors. Yup, she really is that incredible.

Super publicist Marcy Engelman took an interest in my first book and decided to spread the word about it in a very big way—despite the fact that I once sent her a gift that broke en route. Luckily, she has a sense of humor as well as a giant heart and I'm proud to be her newest client. My thanks also to the lovely Dana Gidney Fetaya.

My dad, John Pekkanen, is still my first reader, a first-rate editor, and an even better father. My mother, Lynn, single-handedly sells my books to all of her neighbors as well as to random strangers at Barnes & Noble. And my brother Robert and his wife, Saadia, generously gave suggestions to help shape my first draft. My brother Ben and his wife, Tammi Hogan, created an incredible trailer for my first book (um, guys? This might not be the right time to ask, but I may need help with another one soon). And my sister-in-law, Carolyn Reynolds Mandell, astutely critiqued my early draft, as did the author Amy Yurk Hatvany and my friends Rachel Baker, Anita Cheng, and Janet Mednick.

My agent's literary director, Benee Knauer, as always, made this a much better book with her spot-on editorial suggestions and thoughtful, encouraging notes. And my thanks to Chris Kepner in Victoria Sanders's office.

Several books were invaluable as I researched opera, including Renée Fleming's wonderful autobiography, *The Inner Voice*; *Opera Anecdotes* by Ethan Mordden; Arianna Huffington's *Maria Callas: The Woman Behind the Legend*; and *Opera for Dummies* by David Pogue and Scott Speck. The Kennedy Center also kindly welcomed me to a behind-the-scenes opera workshop.

And Mark Hillman patiently answered my questions about the finances of wealthy, made-up people.

My thanks to Chandler Crawford, international agent extraordinaire, and to my foreign publishers. My deep gratitude to everyone at Atria Books/Washington Square Press, including Judith Curr, Chris Lloreda, Rachel Bostic, Lisa Keim, Natalie White, Carole Schwindeller, Anna Dorfman, Yona Deshommes, Paul Olsewski, and the amazing sales team. And to Sarah Cantin, who is a pure pleasure to work with.

My publicists Jessica Purcell and Crystal Patriarche worked magic on *The Opposite of Me,* and I'm so lucky to have them both on my side and ready for round two. My deep thanks also to Susan Coll and Steve Hull of *Bethesda Magazine* for their continued support (and you guys really know how to throw a party!). And to Lindsay Maines, who started a trend with her brilliant idea for "Spike Day."

Thanks again to the bloggers, who keep spreading the love of books around, and to the readers who have friended me on Facebook, found me on Twitter, and sent me notes through my website. I love chatting with you.

All of my love, as always, to my four boys—my husband, Glenn, and our sons, Jackson, Will, and Dylan.

Skipping
a
Beat

Sarah Pekkanen

A Readers Club Guide

INTRODUCTION

What would you do if your husband suddenly wanted to rewrite the rules of your relationship?

Julia and Michael met as high school students in their small, poverty-stricken West Virginia town. Both products of difficult childhoods—Julia's father is a compulsive gambler and Michael's mother abandoned his family when he was a young boy—they find a sense of safety and mutual understanding in each other. Shortly after graduation they flee West Virginia to start afresh.

Now thirtysomethings, they are living a rarefied life in their multimillion-dollar Washington, D.C., home. From the outside it all looks perfect—Julia has become a highly sought-after party planner, while Michael has launched a wildly successful flavored water company worth $70 million.

But one day Michael stands up at the head of the table in his company's boardroom—then silently crashes to the floor. More than four minutes later, a portable defibrillator manages to jump-start his heart. Yet what happened to Michael during those lost minutes forever changes him. Money is meaningless to him now—and he wants to give it all away to charity. A prenuptial agreement that Julia insisted upon back when Michael's company was still struggling means she has no claim to his fortune, and now she must decide: Should she walk away from the man she once adored, but who truthfully became a stranger to her long before his near-death experience—or should she give in to her husband's pleas for a second chance and a promise of a poorer but happier life?

QUESTIONS AND TOPICS FOR DISCUSSION

1. When a teenaged Julie asks Mike where he sits in class, he responds, "I'm right behind you, Julie. I always have been" (p. 20). Does this statement remain accurate for their entire relationship?

2. Why is Julia so reluctant to hear about Michael's near-death experience?

3. "I had no doubt Michael would be successful, but as much as I loved him, as much as I wanted to, I couldn't bring myself to gamble on him" (p. 70). Why does Julia feel this way? Why does she insist on a prenuptial agreement?

4. When Michael leaves Julia a card telling her that he loves her, she crumples it in her hand and thinks, "I wanted to hurt him. He was ruining everything" (p. 86). Considering how unhappy she is in their marriage, what exactly is Michael ruining?

5. How did her parents' relationship affect the one she shares with Michael? Does Julia trust anyone?

6. Michael is often described as jittery. Why does he seem to never stay still for very long?

7. Michael senses that he doesn't have much time left. Does Julia believe him? Why does she have nightmares that she is losing him?

8. Throughout the novel, Julia frequently mentions her favorite operas. Why are they so important to her?

9. What significance do you see in Noah's restaurant riddle (pp. 153–54)?

10. Michael frequently laments that success changed him for the worse, from taking risks with the exploding glass bottles to the "Let's see you bastards ignore me now" (p. 204) checks for his family to Scott's lawsuit and the many other examples of hush money. Do you agree that money changed him? Was he always a good man, or did power truly corrupt him?

11. What do you think the future holds for Isabelle and Beth? Will they stay in touch?

12. "'I never went with you to visit your mother.' This was what Michael and I had been heading toward ever since he'd fallen to that conference room floor, I realized" (p. 237). Why is it so important for both of them to visit Julia's mother?

13. Why does Julia confess her affair to Michael? Why had they never discussed Michael's assumed affair?

14. What does giving her jewelry to Michael symbolize? Does this decision mean that Julia wants to stay married?

15. At the novel's end, why does Julia return to her father's house? Does she forgive him?

16. Discuss how things could have been different if Michael had never collapsed in the conference room. Would he still be married to Julia?

ENHANCE YOUR BOOK CLUB

1. Did Noah's riddle stump you? Challenge your fellow book club members with your favorite head-scratchers and see who can solve the most!

2. At one point Julia contemplates the fate of Scarlett O'Hara, saying she's protected herself so she'll never have to make a dress out of drapes. Discuss which other famous literary characters Julia reminds you of, if any.

3. Michael feels confident that he only has a short time left. Discuss among yourselves what you would do if you knew you only had a few weeks left to live.

4. Julia is an opera enthusiast who frequently draws parallels between her own life and *La Bohème, Arabella,* and others. While discussing *Skipping a Beat,* play some of her favorite arias to discover why they're so important to Julia.

5. Author Sarah Pekkanen has a significant online presence. Visit her website (http://www.sarahpekkanen.com) to read her bio, find out about upcoming events, and more. You can also follow her on Twitter (@sarahpekkanen) and Facebook.

A CONVERSATION WITH SARAH PEKKANEN

***Skipping a Beat* has such a unique premise. What inspired the idea?**

For me, ideas take shape gradually. I knew I wanted to write about a married couple forced to reexamine their relationship after the husband's near-death experience, but other pieces of the book—like Noah's character, the specifics of Michael's company, and Julia's love of opera—didn't snap into place immediately. I think gearing up to write a book is like cooking soup on the back burner of your stove. Soup, like writing, works best if you swirl in a few ingredients and let it simmer for a long time (I'm sort of making this up, because I'm a terrible cook, but I'm pretty sure that's how they do it on the Food Network). It's actually more productive for me to open myself up to ideas by reading lots of newspapers and books, chatting with people, and daydreaming. Then I let my subconscious sort through ideas while I do things like grocery shop, do laundry, and walk the dog before sitting down to write.

As the novel unfolds and the reader discovers more of Julia and Michael's backstory, their perspective on the couple's marriage might change. Why did you decide to structure *Skipping a Beat* in this manner? How did you decide when to reveal certain aspects of Julia and Michael's relationship?

As *Skipping a Beat* opens, Julia and Michael are thrust into a crisis, and it's unclear whether their marriage will survive. In order to move forward, they also need to look back at the decisions and moments, both big and small, that shaped their relationship. So I wove in scenes from their past to show how complicated their life together has become, and to reveal why Julia feels so conflicted. But there are two sides to every story—

so even though everything is unfolding from Julia's point of view, it's not necessarily the complete picture. She, like the readers, discovers how much more there is to the story of her marriage.

When Julia is recalling her favorite parties, she remembers the affinity she felt for a woman who said, "How can I be eighty years old when I'm still a girl?" (p. 164). Of course you're a safe distance from eighty, but do you ever relate to her statement of still being a little girl?

Absolutely! I do feel young at heart and hope I always will. I saw a quote on one of those refrigerator magnets recently that said something like, "How old would you be if you didn't know your age?" My age would probably be nine or ten.

If you believed you only had three weeks to live, how would you spend your remaining time?

I didn't have to think about this one for longer than a second—the answer is, with my family. I'd take photographs and film some moments, but mostly it would be cuddling and talking and storing up as much love as possible.

You used to work as a journalist covering Capitol Hill. Do you have a favorite story from that era of your life?

Probably the most memorable moment would be the time an elderly senator's thumb and index finger made contact with my rear end as I got out of an elevator and he got into it. I've since learned I'm not the only one he pinched, but I laughed it off. He was a frail old guy, and if I'd exhaled vigorously, I could've blown him over.

I'm proudest of my yearlong investigation into the tangled, highly illegal activities of a U.S. congresswoman from Detroit. I uncovered evidence that she set up a college scholarship fund for poor kids from her district, then used the donated money to go shopping. Not only did she get voted out of office, the Justice Department, House Ethics Committee, and Federal Election Commission launched simultaneous investigations as well.

I'm so lucky that I get to dust off my old reporting skills as a fiction writer. For example, for *Skipping a Beat,* I interviewed the founder of the Honest Tea company to learn how my main character could invent a successful beverage company from scratch. Of course, as the head of my fictional company, Michael did some underhanded things—which is not at all the case for the very reputable Honest Tea company. Those scenes were purely imaginary, but I loved learning about the origins of the company and weaving realistic details into my book.

How much of your own personality do you imbue in your heroines? Do you also celebrate your successes with chocolates and margaritas?

I've heard that a writer's "voice" is similar to her personality, and for me, that's true. I love to laugh, so I try to inject humor into my novels, but I'm also sentimental. I cry easily, and sometimes I laugh so hard that I cry (causing my husband great confusion and the desire to go do something simple and manly, usually involving power tools).

And no celebration would be complete without margaritas and chocolate! Even minor triumphs—like successfully navigating the pickup line at my kids' school every day, or writing a line of dialogue—should be rewarded with chocolate. Lots of chocolate.

Did you learn something about your own marriage while writing *Skipping a Beat*?

I tend to take on the emotions of the scenes I'm writing, so I learned I had to be careful not to snap at my husband when Julia was annoyed with Michael! I think marriages are so fascinating; no one really knows what goes on inside of them except for the two people involved. It seems like many marriages contain mini-marriages—times when the relationship goes through a high, then a low, emotional cycle. My own father says it best: When asked how long he and my mother have been married, he often replies, "Forty-five wonderful years. And three not-so-good ones. And two really bad ones." They're about to celebrate their fiftieth wedding anniversary, and they've never been happier.

Julia notes that "Sometimes following the path that looked the safest was what led to the most hurt" (p. 284). Do you feel the same way?

Sure; if you don't follow your heart, for example, but only do what others expect of you, that's a powerful recipe for unhappiness. I think the things we regret most in life are the things we don't do—the challenges we shy away from. For me personally, writing a book was a huge gamble. I knew I could make a decent salary and have some success as a freelance writer, but I couldn't stop dreaming about writing a novel, even though there was no guarantee it would ever be published.

On your website you list "writers [you] love," such as Jennifer Weiner, Lisa Tucker, Emily Griffin, Jodi Picoult, and Marian Keyes. What have you learned from these women?

So much! Especially Jennifer's books. After I read them for pleasure, I go through them again to marvel at how she puts together scenes and develops characters. My husband once asked me if it took away from my reading enjoyment when I scrutinized books I love to uncover plotting secrets and the author's use of elements like tension and character development. I said it actually increased my enjoyment—it's like being an art history major and going to the Louvre. You just look at things differently.

Have you ever met someone who claims to have had a near-death experience? Did it change them? How? What do you imagine happens to someone during that time?

Yes, my maternal grandmother. During a near-death experience, she said she traveled through a tunnel, then was greeted by a sister who had died years earlier. My grandmother said the experience was wonderful, and not at all scary (and, incidentally, my grandmother, who was quite vain, said one of the best parts was how young and beautiful she felt). I wish my grandmother were still alive so I could ask her more about the experience. She told my mother about it right after it happened, and I've never forgotten it. I find it so comforting.

What message about marriage do you hope readers will take away from *Skipping a Beat*?

I hope it doesn't sound sappy, but the message is that love is the most important thing in this world. At a time when there are so many competing demands for our attention, and so many external stressors in life, it's easy to lose sight of that.